ALEXANDER JABLOKOV

A TOM DOHERTY ASSOCIATES BOOK | NEW YORK

BRAIN THIEF

A Tor Book
Published by Tom Doherty Associates, LLC
175 Fifth Avenue
New York, NY 10010

www.tor-forge.com

Tor® is a registered trademark of Tom Doherty Associates, LLC.

ISBN 978-0-7653-6172-1

First Edition: January 2010
First Mass Market Edition: November 2012

Printed in the United States of America

0 9 8 7 6 5 4 3 2 1

Praise for *BRAIN THIEF*

"Just great, full of crisp, hilarious dialogue, bizarre and vivid characters, and the farcical adventures of a narrator whose gift for trenchant observation cannot hide a melancholy and romantic soul. It is a madcap science fiction mystery, whose elements seem simultaneously random and controlled, and whose aspirations rise beyond nature to the stars. Reading it, I begin to understand one of the things that has been wrong with the last decade of my life—not enough Alexander Jablokov!"

—Paul Park, author of *The Hidden World*

"Serial-killer murder mystery, artificial-intelligence bildungsroman, a celebration of Americana diner shtick—Jablokov's return to science fiction after a decade-long absence is all of these and more. . . . A fun read with plenty of unexpected turns and a genuinely surprising ending."

—*Publishers Weekly*

"Alex Jablokov is one of the most interesting and inventive science fiction writers in existence. Miss this book at your peril!"

—Michael Swanwick, author of *The Dragons of Babel*

"A style of humor that rarely emerges in science fiction; a hip, sarcastic mix of personal observations mixed with pop-culture and historical references . . . *Brain Thief* is that rare combination of humor and SF that strikes all the best chords at once."

—*SF Site*

"Alexander Jablokov is a little nuts, and that's a good thing. He's a wonderfully funny and diabolically inventive writer."

—Kit Reed, author of *Enclave* and *Thinner Than Thou*

"With an array of quirky characters and a tornado of a plot that doesn't stop twisting until the last page, here is *the* science fiction page-turner of 2009. Imagine the mordant humor of a Kurt Vonnegut illuminating the future-shocked landscape of a William Gibson and you'll get a sense of the pleasures of *Brain Thief*. At once hilarious and scary, this is the Alexander Jablokov novel we have been waiting for!"

—James Patrick Kelly,
Hugo and Nebula award winner

"Alarmingly intelligent, wickedly deadpan, and weird as rollerblading lobsters, Alexander Jablokov's *Brain Thief* channels Charles Stross through *8 Heads in a Duffel Bag*. Giant AI bugs, serial-killer fashion, and laid-off personality engineers are no problem for Jablokov's part-time detective, who belongs in the action-hero pantheon right between Harold and Kumar. The best Jablokov book yet!"

—Sarah Smith,
author of *Chasing Shakespeares*

"*Brain Thief* is a solid caper novel, and reliably entertaining; it reads a bit like a soberer northeastern Carl Hiaasen. . . . I hope this signals that Jablokov really is back in the field, and that it will be a lot fewer than twelve years before we see another new novel from him."

*—The Antick Musings
of G.B.H. Hornswoggler, Gent.*

To my daughter Faith,
Who has waited quite a long time

ACKNOWLEDGMENTS

Thanks to the subset of the Cambridge Science Fiction Writers Workshop who sat down with me to hammer this out: James Cambias, Brett Cox, James Patrick Kelly, Steve Popkes, and Sarah Smith.

Thanks also to David Hartwell, who took more than the usual amount of time with this, to Martha Millard for her patience, to Stacy Hague-Hill for keeping things on track, and to Ellen Asher for doing her best to fix what still did not work smoothly.

BRAIN THIEF

1

For Bernal, the message in the cowboy boot finally confirmed that something was wrong.

Muriel liked to make her communications to her single employee works of art. The one standing on the windowsill at the end of the hall was an elaborately decorated cowboy boot, complete with spur. In it were three foil-wrapped chocolates, bittersweet, and a 3×5 index card on which was written, in Muriel's slanted handwriting, "Bernal. What I learned today changes *everything*. Head over to Ungaro's lab if you crave an explanation."

Of course he craved an explanation. Muriel was supposed to be at the opening of an exhibit of Renaissance silver at the Cheriton Art Gallery that night, not hanging around the lab of her pet AI researcher.

Impromptu visits to Muriel-funded research programs were what Bernal got paid for. He'd just gotten back from one, a road trip to South Dakota to deal with some bad feelings about the mammoth project, with a few side visits on the way. Bernal rubbed his eyes. It had been a long day's drive from the campground at Seneca Lake, and he'd been looking forward to a hot shower and quick sleep in a back bedroom, with business left for the next day.

But something had seemed off as soon as he had made it into the house, a quality of deliberate silence. He'd run up the curving staircase to the sconce-lit hallway upstairs and said hello to the tailor's dummy in the military dress jacket that guarded the low bureau with the turned wood bowl on it. A glance into Muriel's bedroom had increased his unease.

Clothing lay piled against a radiator. An old wooden soft-drink box, smelling of damp cellar, had been dumped out, and the toys that had once been stored in it, things like stuffed tigers with green eyes and long-obsolete video games, lay scattered across the dark-red Oriental carpet at the foot of the bed. A doll's head had rolled under a highboy. It stared demurely at Bernal from beneath long lashes, one eye half closed.

Found objects, like a wooden shoe form, the numerals 6½ bold black on its side, and a row of glass eyeballs of various colors, rested on top of door moldings, safe above the mess. Her bedside lamp was an Art Deco Atlas nobly holding up a frosted glass circle with a 40-watt bulb behind it. What looked like the contents of her jewelry box had been poured over his patinaed bronze feet.

The yellow silk-upholstered daybed was piled with shoe boxes. Dozens of them. He knew that Muriel loved shoes, but this was ridiculous. The entire top layer was new purchases from some store called DEEP. A receipt showed that they had been purchased just that afternoon, and the figure made Bernal's male eyes bug out.

He'd worked for Muriel for two years now, and he knew how to judge her mood from the disorder in her private space. This was worse than he'd ever seen it. Something was definitely up with her.

A suit bag, unzipped and empty, lay on the bed.

He'd made fun of her for that bag. It usually contained what he called her ninja outfit: fitted black microfiber and Kevlar, which she always insisted would come in handy some day if she had to commit a crime. Muriel was somewhere beyond sixty but fit enough to carry the suit off. Accessorized by some usually over-the-top diamonds, the thing actually looked like a real outfit. He understood that she sometimes wore it to the gym. But not to a gallery opening.

Hanging by the mirror was the gown she'd been prepared to wear, a bronze knee-length. If she'd decided to switch outfits, she'd done it recently.

When he saw the cowboy boot on the windowsill, he figured he'd have his answer. But all he got were more questions. He ran his fingers through his hair as he reread the card, wondering what she was up to.

A door slam downstairs made Bernal jump. Just as he was turning from the window to head down there, a flicker of motion outside caught his eye. He pressed his forehead against the glass and peered through the tree branches to the ground.

A figure in a pink nightgown ran across the lawn, heading toward the garage.

He recognized Muriel.

2

Bernal ran down the stairs and along the hallway toward the kitchen. This hallway was dark, and he didn't take the time to turn on the light. The rear door was right—

He tripped over something heavy, windmilled arms, and landed with a crash amid outdoor boots and umbrellas. The pain was shocking. He'd smashed the side of his head and his upper body. He rolled and pushed himself up, favoring his right side. He felt up the wall and found the light switch.

The light revealed what he had tripped over: a large flowered bag, something he would have thought was much too old-ladyish for Muriel. It was lying right outside the closed hall closet door. Muriel was messy, but she kept her messes private. It was unlike her to leave things like that out in the more visible parts of the house.

The back door hung open. A cool breeze blew in.

He ran out through it and up the rear driveway.

Muriel's Audi was inside the dark garage with its door open and keys dangling in the ignition. Its dome light lit up rusty shelves packed with oil cans and cleaning rags.

He stopped himself from throwing himself into the car, peering behind the seats, under the seats, in the trunk. She wasn't there. She'd abandoned the car, even though she'd clearly been heading for it.

The key was turned, but nothing glowed on the dashboard. The thing was dead.

He swung himself back out of the garage and stopped there. He let the night wash over him. Stop, he told himself. Let it come. A few houses down some teenager played music, nothing but the thumping bass notes making it out. The air had that sweetish smell of long-frozen things rotting at last, making way for new life. Cool breeze shouldered past him on its endless errand. Glowing cirrus revealed the otherwise invisible moon. Dry leaves crackled, and a branch snapped.

Down the yard, by the fence. Where the hell was Muriel heading?

It didn't matter. That was a blocked corner. Her yard was a worse mess than her bedroom, overgrown and savage, hidden behind stockade fences so it did not affront the neighborhood. She probably had forgotten what was back there.

Bernal was still sucking breath. He could shout or run but not both.

He ran.

But there was no one there. Had he imagined it?

No. There were dark streaks in the gray of the decaying leaves covering the beds. Bernal pushed past the sharp points of gigantic rhododendrons, right up to the smooth boards of the fence. Muriel was pretty old, but maybe, in her panic, she had managed to climb . . . he pushed, and found a loose board. How long had she been planning this? He flipped it up and squeezed under.

He found himself in the opposite of Muriel's overgrown yard: an expanse of trimmed lawn and mulched flower beds glowing with daffodils. A Tudor mansion loomed overhead.

Muriel disappeared around the corner of the house, her robe pale in the darkness. He sprinted across the grass after her.

Tires shrieked on pavement. Bernal came around the corner to catch a glimpse of a car, a Mercedes sedan by the looks of it. The left taillight had a piece of orange tape across a crack. It fishtailed onto the street and vanished. If there was a stop sign or something at the end of the block, maybe he would be able to catch up with her when she . . . no, that was ridiculous. She was gone

In the stunning quiet, Bernal heard the breeze blow a branch against a window with a faint click.

"Hey!" A man ran off the porch and stood next to Bernal. "My car! I didn't even . . ." He put down a cast-iron borzoi and felt at his pockets. "He took my keys!" He looked up at the house. "How the hell am I supposed to get in?"

"No one's home?"

"Nah, they're all down in Hilton Head. Coming back tomorrow." He checked his watch. "Today, I guess. Do you know who the hell took my car?"

He was being remarkably calm about it, Bernal thought. He was a kind of young-old guy, with graying hair but a slim build. He wore white running shoes, gray wool pants, and a sweatshirt from a music school with a picture of a harpsichord on it. The man picked the metal dog back up and cradled it in his arms.

"Friend of mine," Bernal said. He decided not to identify Muriel as this guy's neighbor. No need to cause trouble before he knew what was going on.

The guy eyed him. "Not a fugitive from, ah, justice, I hope."

"She was just in a hurry."

To Bernal's surprise, the guy laughed. "I've been there. But it looks to me like you and your friend got my car stolen. Can you help me get it back?"

"I'd love to. What was the license number?" Bernal let his mind clear. After a moment, he saw a couple of letters, DA. That memory hadn't had time to get associated with anything, but it had to belong to the car.

"Come on. You got a phone?"

"Only in my car."

"I really need to use it. This is really annoying."

The two of them walked down the street. Damn it, Bernal thought. He had to get rid of this guy and figure out what Muriel was up to.

His Dodge Ram came into view. The beat-up old red van with the scratch on its side wasn't a sexy ride, but it carried his gear without attracting attention. He unlocked the door.

Then what he had seen finally came clear to him. When Muriel had stolen the man's car, he had run *down* the stairs, as if interrupted while opening the door. But his keys had been in the car, motor running. And he had come down with a cast-iron dog. He'd carried it so naturally it had seemed like an accessory.

He'd stolen it. Bernal was suddenly sure. This guy had broken into the house, stolen some stuff, the dog among it, and been finishing up, ready to load the car, when Muriel took off with it.

"Look," Bernal said, trying to be reasonable. "I don't care what the hell you're up to out here—"

"Step away from the car."

"What?"

The guy was all of a sudden sweating and desperate. "I need to go. I need to get out of here. Give me your keys and there's nothing else that has to happen."

"Look, I'd like—"

Bernal never saw the swing of the iron dog, but pain flared in the side of his head.

3

Something slapped his side and he regained consciousness. He lay on his back on someone's front lawn, staring up at a sky that showed the first hints of morning. He felt around himself in the grass and found what had hit him: a *Cheriton Telegraph-Examiner* in a clear plastic bag. People still read paper newspapers out here. By the time he managed to sit up, the delivery car was gone.

He steeled himself for a moment and prodded above his ear with his fingertips. Not much blood, and that had dried. It felt like a surface wound, with no damage to the underlying bone. It could have been worse.

A timer tripped and the sprinklers came on.

He made it back into the house and up to the bathroom before he threw up. His head, which had not felt too bad when he woke up, now swelled and pulsed.

He felt light, almost weightless. He turned the water

in the sink to its hottest, and then scrubbed himself. The bathroom was beautifully tiled, decorated with leaping dolphins. There was a row of giant candles on the windowsill above the tub, a couple, melted deeply enough, with votives frugally inserted.

He met his own bloodshot brown eyes in the mirror. He hadn't shaved the previous day, but his beard tended to be so fine that it didn't really matter.

He was alive. Once again, he was alive.

Blood had gotten on the collar of his teal windbreaker. The damn thing was new, a gift from his mother. He shrugged it off, tried to clean it, but quickly gave up. He found his bag and pulled out his old bomber jacket, this one from a girlfriend, and put that on instead. He looked longingly at the shower he had been heading toward so many hours before, but that would have to wait.

What had Muriel said in her note? "Head over to Ungaro's lab if you crave an explanation."

He'd have to . . . damn it. His van. That lunatic with the iron borzoi had stolen it. He walked to the front of the house, still dabbing his wet hair with a towel, to look out at the street.

The red Dodge Ram stood exactly where he had left it.

He walked around it slowly. Had he really missed it on his way back to Muriel's house?

He didn't think so. He thought the space had been empty, but he couldn't be sure. The unimpeachable redness and vanness in front of him right now polluted his knowledge of himself.

He had a spare key in his wallet, but the driver's door wasn't even locked. And his keys hung in the ignition. He swung himself up into the seat.

Sitting in the passenger seat next to him, neatly belted in, was a cast-iron borzoi doorstop, with a yellow Post-it sticking up from its tail. On it was one word, "Sorry," in dark cursive. It did not look like a man's handwriting.

Real borzois rarely look intelligent, but this one gave him a look of sly complicity. Bernal supposed a paint chip had been knocked off by the impact with his head.

Bernal had started going to South Dakota after the citizens of Evanston burned Muriel in effigy.

He and Muriel had watched the video of the proceedings in her living room. He'd gotten it from a station in Billings, and it was much higher resolution than the tiny one available online. People gathered along a stretch of highway and hoisted a manikin dressed in a ball gown on a cherry picker. They doused it with the gasoline/ethanol mixture that helped support the local economy, and set fire to it. The clothing burned quickly, but the smooth plastic didn't catch, finally leaving a naked manikin dangling on its gibbet, black streaks of melted eyelashes on its face, plastic hair smoldering. First one shoe fell off, then the other. Eventually, the crowd got back in their cars and drove home. The cherry picker swung and deposited Muriel's effigy in the back of a pickup.

"Someone went through the trouble to make it recognizably me." Muriel scanned back and went through the scene frame by frame. "That's a Balenciaga ball gown, vintage, maybe twenty-five years old. They must have a hell of a consignment shop in Evanston. I'd definitely wear it, given the right occasion. But, Jesus, not with those shoes. I mean, they aren't bad shoes, can't focus close enough to be sure, but they look like Charles Davids. Decent for an afternoon get-together, maybe a trip to the mall, but not for evening wear. And don't get me started on those Wal-Mart hose. . . ."

She crossed her legs with an expensive whisper and pouted.

"They really don't like my mammoth idea."

"Nope. If possible, they like it even less than having their lands turned over to bison in that Buffalo Commons proposal a few years back."

"Bison." Muriel snorted. "Those ruminants-come-lately? Please. Some of the most boring mammals ever evolved. Mammoths or nothing."

Muriel had been financing a program to use bootleg mammoth DNA from a defunct South Korean lab, implanted into African elephant ova, to recreate mammoths and release them on the depopulated Great Plains. She'd expected some local resistance but not an actual riot.

So Bernal had repeatedly visited the small towns along the strips of asphalt to work things out. Bernal was naturally better at ideas and things than at people, but he had learned a few simple heuristics from Muriel—mirroring people's postures, flattering them, doing them small favors so that they felt obliged to you—and found that they worked for him. Muriel had originally hired him for logistics and operations, but had found that he was good at getting people to understand and agree to her grandiose plans. Over the past year he'd spent a lot of time shivering on bleachers above floodlit high school football fields, packing in hot dishes in church basements, hunting prairie dogs on the rez with angry young Oglala Sioux, handing down tools while politically significant people ranted at him from under pickup trucks with transmission problems.

But the place was emptying out, and no one could really deny that. A vast region in the center of the country had dropped below the six-people-per-square-mile standard that the 19th century had defined as "frontier." And a frontier required tenacity, imagination, and a willingness to take risks, or so Bernal portrayed it. He reconstructed Muriel's vision as he talked with people. African elephants were under extreme environmental pressure on their native continent, but their genes might run free on the northern plains of North America. He worked out pricing schemes to give them water, migration routes that would silhouette them against the sky for compelling images, roles for American Indians, whites, and more recent Hispanic and Orthodox Jewish immigrants as hunters, herders, trainers, and nomads. Every time a light went on in someone's eyes, or two seemingly unrelated incentives came into alignment, Bernal felt joy. He was a man with a job suited to talents he hadn't known he possessed.

But Muriel had known. She had hired him almost out of his hospital bed and given him a new life.

Muriel Inglis had made her money the old-fashioned way: she divorced it. Actually, that was unfair, Bernal thought. She'd divorced two, but the last husband, Tommy, had died of a heart attack on the golf course before their divorce actually became final. There was a plaque to him in the clubhouse.

At any rate, in her late fifties, Muriel had found herself with an astounding amount of money and some odd ideas of how best to spend it. She already had an Italianate mansion in the nice section of the town she had grown up in, her daughter was grown and out of the house, and she'd made her requisite donations to the art museum and local artistic hip-hop troupe. Some women might just have bought another house or gotten a lot of cosmetic work done.

Instead, Muriel funded lunatic projects that would have been unable to get money any other way: urban reforestations and wild animal reintroductions in depopulating rust belt cities, negative sculptures carved into the bedrock surrounding defunct ICBM silos, the reintroduction of nomadic cultures to the Maghreb, and intelligent planetary probes, like the one Madeline Ungaro was working on right here in Cheriton.

Because of Bernal's history, Muriel had kept him largely away from Ungaro and her AI-based exploration vehicle. At first, that had been fine with him. It had the same aura of dramatic uselessness as her other projects, but seemed much more specialized and constrained. It was the only one that couldn't be easily put on a tourist brochure. Bernal didn't do much more with Ungaro than manage financing disbursements, pay the lease on the lab, and make sure all the paperwork was in order. But recently, as he realized that he had created an entirely new life for himself, the interests of his old one seemed to reassert themselves, and he began to wonder if there really was a functional AI growing in a warehouse on the outskirts of Cheriton.

Now that Muriel had asked to meet him there, he wondered what Muriel hadn't been telling him about that particular project.

4

Bernal pounded on the featureless metal door, hearing the thump sound through Ungaro's lab. He'd already given up on the doorbell. A red LED blinked in the black rectangle of a card reader next to the loading dock door. Muriel might have had the card to open it, but Bernal had no idea where he'd look for it.

The marked parking spot in front was empty. He didn't see any sign of the Mercedes Muriel had stolen, either.

Ungaro's lab was at the end of a brick warehouse converted to light industrial and inventory uses, divided into units, each with a loading dock and an office door. It included a blacksmith and an office-supply distributor. Bernal walked across the parking lot, looking around for a concealed place Muriel might have put her car the previous night.

The rear end of a newer office building poked out of the scrub woods. Where there were office buildings, there were parking lots. He trotted down a rough track between adolescent trees, hopped a mucky stream, and stepped over the crisp asphalt rim of the other parking lot.

At this hour of the morning, there were few cars in the lot. Again, no Mercedes. But a police car had pulled up next to a Dumpster and was taking a report from a young guy who stared sadly at a dent in his car door, not looking up.

"Why were you parked here?" the cop asked.

"What? Look at this!"

"I see it, sir. This isn't a residential lot."

"I told you. There was a party. I live over at the McClintock Apartments. Some bozo, last night, was having this humongous party. Filled the parking lot. And some of the grass too. I got home, couldn't find a spot. So I parked here."

"It's marked 'no overnight parking.'"

"I know. Jeez, I know."

The cop looked over at the Dumpster. "Looks like something hit it. Pretty hard. Shoved it right over into your car."

"Yeah. So what are you going to say?"

"Say? I'm not giving you a ticket."

"Thanks."

"But you had a fender bender with a Dumpster. I'll just write that up. No vehicle, no evidence. This'll be between you and your insurance company."

"I've talked to them before."

"Good. You know the drill, then."

The world looked full of troubles this morning. Bernal was about to head back to Muriel's, to reconsider and regroup, when he looked past the dented Dumpster and noticed something.

From this angle, he got a view of the back of the warehouse. Whoever had been responsible for the adaptive reuse of the old warehouse had bermed and stabilized the building's rear. The berm was planted with decent sod. A few of the tenants had fenced their back areas for additional storage, but Ungaro, at the end, had not.

A black angled line led up through the grass to the rear of Ungaro's lab. Something had torn the grass out in a wide strip, exposing earth.

He looked down. A shopping cart lay on its side in the dark water. The stream curved along the warehouse's rear, where it managed to hold on to a bit of its old floodplain after everything else had been torn away. Opposite the warehouse, backyards pushed stockade fences against the willow trees. The patch of scrub woods, reeds, and weeds existed as a tiny wilderness behind the world that faced the roads.

Bernal slid down the slope. The mud was slippery and stank. Each stick and reed wore a garland of soggy grass, souvenir of recent spring floods. He stepped on the cart, which wobbled but didn't sink any further, and made it safely across the stream.

Something had come through here. And recently. Weeds had been pressed down, their broken leaves not yet wilted. Reeds had been torn away and lay in clumps in the slow-flowing water. The mud was too soft for footprints to remain clear, but it did look like they were deep and there were a lot of them, as if two or more people had hauled something heavy through here. Had whoever it was smashed into that Dumpster? He looked back. It lined up. That hadn't been caused by anyone carrying anything. It had been done by something heavy, a vehicle, moving pretty fast.

The rear door of Ungaro's lab, painted metal over thick wood, was scored with bright new scratches. It hung open, revealing darkness beyond.

Bernal pushed it open and stepped in. "Madeline? Madeline Ungaro?" Then, more quietly, "Muriel?"

A combination padlock meant for the door hung on a wall hook. Bernal's guess was that the door was normally locked. But last night it had not been.

Light streamed in through windows overhead, illuminating high fiberboard shelves loaded with motors and joints. Junction boxes hung from the shelves, strapped-up masses of PVC conduit dangling like drying laundry. A couple of chunks of crumpled gold foil, something that might once have held and protected some piece of delicate equipment, lay on a shelf. Each shelf was neatly labeled: "Proprioceptive joint indicator." "Visual/Tactile signal mixer." "40 & 60 watt bulbs." A bucket, a mop, and other cleaning equipment lay on the floor by the door, along with a shattered fluorescent tube and a transparent garbage bag filled with empty Diet Coke cans.

He looked carefully, so he perceived it, but he also took pictures, as backup. If it came down to a question of how many Coke cans had been in the bag this particular morning, he didn't want to rely on his unaided memory.

There were fresh scrapes along the battered and stained concrete floor, along with mud and weeds, still wet. He followed the trail past a folded-back accordion door into what looked like a vehicle maintenance and repair area.

A heavy rack against the brick wall held complex legs ending in wide pads, springy wheels, a part of a carapace, an aluminum chassis, a collection of oculars, antennae, and other sensing equipment.

What looked like a gigantic bug hung from a sling.

Crude welds marked its carapace, and its six legs didn't quite match. Spare legs hung askew, and a toolbox had been knocked to the floor, spewing nuts and bolts.

Ungaro was Muriel's private project, but Bernal still knew a bit about it, just from the invoices. A few years ago, a local start-up called Hess Tech had built a prototype planetary rover under a speculative NASA contract, supplemented by a grant from the state, which was trying to move some research business outside the Harvard/MIT zone near Boston. The rover, called Hesketh, was meant to explore earthlike planets on its own and had incorporated a lot of experimental technology along with its AI. Like anything that experimented with more than one thing at a time, it hadn't worked that well, and a new administration had not renewed the contract. The company had gone out of business, and the developers went their separate ways.

But one of them, Madeline Ungaro, had acquired the company's assets and settled some of its debts. With a further grant from Muriel, she had moved Hesketh, its various parts, and its support gear out here to this lab, and continued working on it.

Bernal looked at the mess of complex mechanical gear. Ungaro, as he understood it, was on the cognitive, not the mechanical side. She'd developed the intelligent processor that would guide the vehicle across rough terrain and, if possible, contact whatever life lived on that mysterious planet circling a distant star. More than once, he'd wanted to call her, just to chat things over. He'd been out of the field since Muriel had hired him, and he'd never managed the call.

This ugly thing had to be Hesketh itself, or, rather one of its bodies. The name applied specifically to the processing unit, which contained whatever identity a self-directing planetary explorer had. The thing was supposed to be flexible and easily modifiable.

This vehicle configuration was about six feet long and vaguely arthropod. One side of the carapace was open. A half dozen manipulator arms, very much like something you might see in an automated manufacturing facility, stood at the ready above the interior. Each arm was tipped with a different tool. They looked like they had stopped in the middle of something, but Bernal couldn't tell what they had been working on or what had stopped them. A constellation of glowing LEDs communicated a message about the state of Hesketh's universe that he could not interpret.

The entire setup mixed sophisticated with crude. A lube gun lay on the floor, with two rubber gloves on top of it. If Hesketh had to be lubed up like this, how would it ever have managed to move around alien planets? Back when Hess Tech was strutting its stuff, looking for venture capital, someone had probably been in charge of making sure Hesketh got greased before any serious VC demo. Keeping the undercarriage from squeaking and then seizing up while exploring some kind of jungle planet would have been a cost-plus improvement. Bernal knew how these things worked.

The leg pads were covered with mud. The trail had come up the back slope, through the unlocked door, and across the floor to here. Where had Hesketh come from, and why had there been no one here to receive it?

And where was its main processing unit? The bodies—the carapaces, wheels, legs, manipulators—were just the externals. Somewhere in here was the genuinely interesting thing, the intelligent processor that could direct the exploration of another world. That was the actual thing Muriel had been funding.

This carapace looked mostly hollow. It was either just a simple mechanical device, mostly motors and legs, or disassembly had proceeded for quite a while before Bernal had shown up. Was this sorry-looking thing really some kind of intelligent being?

Beyond the maintenance area was the loading dock, with a large garage door. Trash was piled up in the pull-in area: empty paint cans, the large cylinder of what looked like an automatic transmission, a big canister of oil. It didn't look like the dock got much use, but simply served as an additional storage area.

Just off the loading dock was a small office, with a desk on casters and an equipment cart made of red metal tubes and with large rubber wheels. It was loaded with gear: a couple of PCs, a large LCD screen that showed a scene of some lake in the North Woods, a laser printer, a power supply with glowing indicator lights, a rack of pressurized gas cylinders, a keyboard, and the joystick controller from a game console. One end of the cart was a crane. A shiny cylinder, about as wide as it was long, dangled from a cable at its end, with gas and power lines running into it. A cable ran from the cart to a locked high-amp plug in the wall.

Bernal pushed the cylinder. It was massive. His first poke barely moved it.

He looked at the gear on the cart and put his hand on the joystick. With a hum of a motor, the massive cylinder lowered. The other way, and it went up again.

The thing looked like a superconducting quantum interference device, a SQUID: a device for measuring incredibly small magnetic fields, consisting of two cryogenically cooled superconductors separated by an insulating layer. Electrons snuck through the gap via quantum effects, and their alibis revealed the details of subtle magnetic fields. They were used to read the internal states of computers and processors, among other things. These things had lots of uses in intelligence work, and much of their early development had been during the Cold War.

You didn't go through the trouble of maintaining a SQUID unless you had a good use for it. The gadget was touchy and the constant cooling expensive. It helped explain the size of the utility bills for Ungaro's lab. But why would Ungaro need to use quantum interference to analyze the outputs of a device she herself had put together? Why didn't Hesketh just have a USB port on its side, or something?

And the thing had a huge amount of cooling, with racks of nitrogen tanks. Even as he sat there, a massive compressor hummed up, cooling the nitrogen further. The maze of piping seemed to have access ports on it for more. It looked like enough cooling to run two or three of the big devices, but Bernal saw no sign of any other SQUID cylinders. There was nothing else in the lab that would have required any liquid nitrogen to operate, much less the huge quantities this thing could produce.

A counterweight lowered in the loading dock and the door rumbled up, letting in a flood of morning sunlight.

5

When Bernal stepped out, a Hummer stood backed into the loading area, its rear hatch open. It was shrinkwrapped with a forest scene. A doe drank from a clear stream while a bald eagle stared nobly off at the whip antenna. The wrap had wrinkled, and was starting to peel.

There was no one in the vehicle, but the double doors to the lab were still swinging. Bernal pushed through.

A large woman in a puffy red parka and jeans leaned over Hesketh's hanging carcass, peering into the open interior. She shook her head at something.

He waited to see what she would do next, but the swinging door must have made a sound behind him, because she turned and stepped back from him, so the space between them opened up. She looked him up and down quickly before speaking.

"Sorry. I didn't know anyone was here."

"Who are you?"

"Charis. Charis Fen." She had a wide face and a huge tangle of dark hair. Her eyes were pale brown, almost yellow, nearly the same shade as her skin. She had a gift for stillness, and stood and stared at him, feet spread wide. She wore a bulky sweater under the parka.

"What are you doing here?"

"I could ask you the same thing."

"You didn't."

Charis paused. "Right. I didn't. Where the hell is Muriel?"

"Muriel?" Bernal was startled. "She send you here?"

"You got it. You too? Whatever your name is. I guess I didn't ask that first either."

"My name is Bernal. I work for Muriel."

"That girl has employees? Who knew? What's that like?"

"It's fine. You still haven't told me what you're doing here."

"Well, if Muriel didn't inform you, I'm not sure it's my job to do it." Charis patted the leg she had been examining. "Were you here when this thing came home?"

"I haven't been here long at all." He had to regain control of the situation. "How did you get in here?"

"Key card."

"Did Madeline Ungaro give it to you?"

"Nah. Muriel. She's got some *issues* with this Ungaro gal, I'm guessing. You know anything about any problems Muriel might be having with her?"

"No."

"How long you been working for my friend Muriel, anyway?"

"Couple of years. Now what did she want you to—"

Charis stepped up to him and examined his face. "You know, it looks like you got smacked pretty good there."

Bernal put his hand up to where the doorstop had hit him. "It's nothing."

"Nothing? A subdural hematoma's nothing to screw around with." She pushed her fingers into his skull. She wasn't taller than him, but she seemed larger in every dimension that mattered.

"Ow!"

She wore a springlike scent. Strong. Lilac didn't suit her. "I'm no doctor, but it don't look too bad. More cosmetic. You got lucky."

Bernal pulled himself away from her. "Does Muriel know you're in here?"

"Just remember that every superball-headed PI in those old detective books ended up as a drooling vegetable in some Home for Old Flatfoots. A brain's not a basketball."

She was evading his questions, but that in itself was a kind of answer.

"You're here for some reason," Bernal said. "If you don't want to tell me what it is, I guess I can't force you. But I can ask you to leave."

"Really." Charis seemed amused. "You have control over Madeline Ungaro's lab? Does she know that?"

"I represent Madeline Ungaro's funding agency. We hold the lease. In her absence, I am in control of this space. I was about to seal it up. You're trespassing. Could you please leave?"

"Funding agency, my ass! Muriel funds this. You're just her gopher."

"If you don't leave, I'll have to call the police."

"You call that a solution?" She sounded outraged. "Interpersonal problem starts to get a bit hairy, you decide you don't need to bother yourself with conflict resolution, you call the cops? We . . . they can't be solving everything. Not and do their job, which is to guarantee your personal physical safety. Not your emotional well-being, for crissakes."

"You were a cop?" He thought about that for a second. "But you're not anymore."

"Don't you worry about my career path. That's my misfortune."

"That's too bad. For a second there I thought you were going to actually answer a question. Are you going?"

Charis took a long look around at all the rover parts. "I'm going. You have yourself a good time with this stuff."

"Oh, and one more thing. . . ."

"What?"

"I'll want your key card."

"You . . ." Charis thought about that one. "Why don't you recode the entry if you don't want me coming in?"

"I just want your card. You shouldn't have one."

She was back to being amused. "Because you don't have a clue as to where Madeline Ungaro is, and she doesn't even know you're in here. You have no idea of how to rekey the entry. And Muriel hasn't clued you in. You should bring that up with her at your next performance review. No way to get productivity out of your employees, keeping them in the dark like that." She handed him the card. "Good luck figuring out what the hell is going on here."

The Hummer's engine roared up. There was a loud clunk as something engaged. It lurched forward a few feet and then died. Charis ran the starter several times, but the vehicle refused to respond any further.

"Damn it!" She got out and stalked around it, looking as if she wanted to kick it. "Bought this thing from Greenpeace. Jesus! Thing's falling apart. Those whale-chasing nimrods didn't do even the most basic maintenance, but they sure enough took me for a ride. They're all about publicity, not mundane crap like changing the oil."

"It just stopped?" Bernal didn't believe her.

"Yes! What, you think I crapped out my engine on purpose?"

"I interrupted you, didn't I? Maybe you want to stick around. But I'm not letting you go back into Ungaro's lab."

"I have no interest in going back in, and I got nothing to accomplish. Muriel and her stupid-ass schemes. . . . Can't make up her mind, that girl. 'She's good, stay away, she's bad, get right over here.' Like I got nothing better to do than save her from her own messes. Like I don't have me a legitimate mission of my own."

"What is your mission?"

"Right now, my mission is to get the hell out of here. You think I'm faking it? Tell you what. You get the damn thing started for me. You think you could do that?"

Bernal was about to refuse. Then he realized something; a quick look around the front of her vehicle might tell him something about her, since she wasn't going to give up anything on her own.

The inside of the Hummer was decorated with decals of cute animals: baby seals, koala bears, even a crocodile with what looked like an ingratiating grin. There were some signs that Charis had tried to scrape them off, but they had resisted her efforts. There were a lot of papers, maps, and magazines piled on the passenger seat. The cup holder held a new-looking stainless steel travel mug with a logo made out of an intersecting S and P. A photograph of a skinny man with glasses standing in front of an open door and gesturing into it with a grin was attached above the gear shift. He looked South Asian.

"Well?" Charis said outside.

He made as much noise with the keys as he could, rattled the gearshift. "No, you're right, nothing."

The top map on the passenger seat showed a couple of twisting roads crossed by three parallel lines made up of straight segments that changed direction every time they were interrupted by a row of Xs. Wind directions? The plan for some game? Her big leather purse was on the floor. And there was probably a mess of stuff in the glove compartment.

"Yes." She was on her phone. "Shepard Road, toward Dana. Thanks." She put her head in the window. "No luck, right?"

"No."

"Good thing I paid my Triple-A bill this year."

Bernal refused to say anything that would make it seem like a normal conversation. He just got out of the car.

"Let me give you a piece of advice, friend." Charis sat down on the front steps, leaned back, and spread her legs. Her thighs were thick in her jeans. Drying mud flaked off her leather boots. She looked completely relaxed. "I've known Muriel Inglis for a while. Smart gal. But not what you'd call trustworthy. Am I right? Oh, you trust her fine, because you need to, she's your bread and butter, but I'm an independent. So, when she asks me to take a look-see into Madeline Ungaro, and I find Ungaro gone, and you wandering around, I got to wonder what she's up to. Maybe you shouldn't trust her quite so much. What did she tell you about Ms. Ungaro, anyway?"

"Like I said, we're her funding source."

"Yeah, yeah. Muriel keeps you on a short chain, does she? You look at what she puts in front of your nose, and nowhere else, am I right?"

Bernal felt himself flush. He prided himself on his wide-ranging curiosity, so he felt like defending himself.

"I don't remember seeing any disbursements to you, though," he said instead.

"Oh, I'm a volunteer. A noble fighter for lost causes. Working pro bono. Muriel knew she could rely on that. That's what pisses me off. Taking advantage of my dedication. I'd closed the file, and then—wow, that was quick."

A tow truck had pulled into the parking lot. It was a big one, used for heavy vehicles, and said it was from IGNACIO'S DEVICES & DESIRES.

The driver's door opened. She was a small woman, not much over five feet, and skinny into the bargain, but looked taut in her blue coverall. She slipped as she stepped out, and almost fell.

Bernal was close enough to jump forward and steady her.

She sucked in a startled breath, as if he was a statue that had suddenly revealed itself to be alive. Under her shoe-polish-black hair, her small nose, fine mouth, and pale eyes seemed to be notes scribbled to indicate future feature placement rather than features themselves. More prominent features were a scar on her forehead and what seemed like a depression in her skull.

"What . . ." She looked around vaguely.

"Are you okay?" Bernal now noticed the bruises that stood out on her pale skin, one on her cheek, another on the side of her neck. A fresh gash sliced across her jaw, held together with butterfly adhesive bandages intended for some other type of cut. She looked like she had had a much rougher night than he had. The name PATRICIA was embroidered over her right breast.

Her weight sprang off him, and she jumped to the ground. Newly energized, she moved lightly to look into the open loading dock and then back at the two of them.

"What happened here?" Her voice was quiet.

"Damn thing won't start," Charis said. "I need to get it out of here, now."

The woman, Patricia, walked around the Hummer. She knelt and glanced underneath. "What seems to be the problem?"

"Started up fine, then died."

"Okay. I'll haul it over to the yard. Someone there can look at it."

"No. I need it back at my office."

"It won't take more than a few minutes. You'll be on your way in no time."

"Sorry. I don't want it anywhere but back at my place."

"I have to tell you. Ten dollars per mile extra if we don't go to Ignacio's."

"That's fine. I'll cover it." Charis glared at Bernal as if the whole thing was his fault. "I actually get some jobs that pay the bills." Patricia hesitated, as if wanting to argue again, then pulled out chains.

Another tow truck, this one from Frank's Tow, rolled off the road. "Hey!" The driver leaned out of his window. "What you doing here?"

Patricia didn't even acknowledge his presence, but attached the chains.

"I got a call. A Triple-A call. From here."

"I've got it under control." She pulled her truck back and raised the Hummer's front. Then she stepped out and checked the chains. She never looked at the other driver.

"How much extra can you guys get, anyway? For God's sake, we all got to make a living. Right? That's all."

"Talk to Ignacio, if you want," she said. "I don't make these decisions."

"Ignacio . . ." The other tow-truck driver shook his head in disgust. "Sure. Sure thing. I love talking to that guy. This ain't going to end well, miss. You know that, right?"

"I know that neither of us is earning anything if we stand around arguing."

He didn't say anything else, but backed with a screech and took off.

"A long time since I've been fought over."

Charis hopped into the tow truck's cab, moving surprisingly easily for a big woman. "Good luck, Bernal. If you're smart you'll forget all about Muriel and her stupid projects. That's sure my plan. I doubt we'll be seeing each other again."

He raised a hand to Charis and Patricia as they drove off, but neither of them looked back.

6

Bernal had an innate sense of privacy. He'd never snooped in his sister's diary growing up, despite the fact that she left it neatly centered on her desk, and his worst girlfriend hadn't even bothered to come up with a strong password to hide all the meticulously kept records, written and photographic, of her cheating on him. She knew he would never try to break into her account, no matter how suspicious he became. He'd found it all when he cleaned up the hard drive before getting rid of the thing, over a year later, long after he broke up with her because he couldn't stand her. So, even if he'd had a better chance, he might not have dug into Charis's purse. That might have been regarded as a weakness, a refusal to stoop down to pick up information lying out in the open, but he was just as glad he'd never read Marcy's erotic messages to her economics professor, her boss at the copy shop, or her downstairs neighbor, the lawyer, while it was all going on. He didn't read much of it then either, but let it vanish along with the other files on the hard drive as he destroyed it.

But as far as Madeline Ungaro was concerned, he thought he had more reason to pry. Muriel had headed over here, saying something significant was up. Chances were that Muriel had picked Madeline up in the stolen Mercedes last night and gone elsewhere. But that was just a guess. In any event, there had to be something here that would give him a clue as to where he should look next. It still made him uncomfortable.

Behind the office with the SQUID, past a tiny modular bathroom, was Ungaro's private living area. A ridged sleeping pad, rolled and tied with multicolored nylon webbing, a deflated air pillow, and a folding sling chair were all the furniture. Folded sweaters, slacks, and shirts, sensible but high-quality, were stacked on metal shelving next to canned goods and ramen packets. There were three pairs of shoes on the bottom shelf: white sneakers, sensible black pumps, and loafers. A gap between sneakers and pumps marked where whatever shoes Ungaro was wearing now had been. Given the person and the arrangement, Bernal guessed hiking boots or maybe trail runners.

A total of four pairs of footwear? Bernal thought of Muriel's hundreds of shoes, each stranger looking than the next. It seemed odd that these two would have gotten along.

The kitchen was a stainless-steel sink and two burners with a propane tank. A copper-bottomed Revereware saucepan stood upside down on the grooved drainboard. It was completely dry.

The one piece of visible luxury was a lacquer case with ornate handles that looked like a China-trade antique. The case was locked. He pulled out the multitool on his keychain, opened the tiny pliers, and delicately manipulated the keyhole. In a moment, he had it open. He looked closely to make sure he hadn't scratched anything. Inside was a bundle of high-end cosmetics and other grooming equipment. He found a silver-framed hand mirror that showed a slight bloom in the backing, and a hairbrush that looked like it was really made of tortoiseshell. It was worn, the bristles well used, but there wasn't a single hair in it.

In the bottom drawer was a piece of Belgian extra bittersweet chocolate, 80 percent, one-third finished and carefully wrapped back up in its foil. Bernal looked for bite marks, but each piece had been snapped off neatly by hand. He thought about that chocolate. It looked rationed. She'd been so precise about her fractions that she hadn't even finished a row, leaving two squares sticking out, despite the fact that that made it harder to rewrap.

There were other gaps on the shelves, he saw now: next to an old tent, next to a headlamp, a few other places among her impressive collection of camping gear. He glanced to see if something had been shoved back and saw a couple of framed photographs. One showed a group of smiling people in white lab coats sitting around a table in front of some vending machines. The other showed another group of people, this one on a mountain trail, all with expensive-looking boots, aluminum trekking poles, and internal frame backpacks. The only person in common between the two groups was a beautiful woman with chin-length blond hair. In neither photograph did she look directly at the camera, and in both she was with the group and not of it, giving the impression of having been Photoshopped in later. Madeline Ungaro. His guess was that each member of both of those groups had received the same photo as a souvenir. From the dust on them, Bernal wondered if Ungaro had even remembered that she had them. They had been stuffed behind whatever had been here on the shelf.

Something lay on the floor by the shelf. Bernal knelt and tugged it out.

It was the pink sash from Muriel's nightgown. Wherever else she had gone the previous night, she had definitely come here.

A horn beeped outside.

A Fleurs du Mall delivery van had pulled up next to his red Ram. A slender black man in a white uniform stood, one foot in the open front door, looking at a tablet PC. "You Bernal Haydon-Rumi?"

"I am."

"Finally! I don't usually deliver to vehicles, but I had to make an exception. . . . Wait a minute."

He climbed into the van and came out with a huge bouquet. "Get this in water as soon as possible. We've done our best—ball-peened the lilac, charred the monkshood stems—but there's a lot of stuff in here that requires contradictory care—"

The mass of flowers was almost intimidating. Lilac, tulips, Peruvian lilies, Bernal recognized those, but there were metallic, spiky blue ones, and ones with hoods, and a variety of fleshy orchids. The thick scent was halfway between funeral home and unmade bed.

"People used to say to drop half an aspirin in the water," the delivery man said. "Doesn't really work, but for this stuff, a Prozac would be more appropriate." He handled the bouquet carefully. "The greens are acanthus. These are the leaves on Corinthian columns. Not many places carry it, mostly because no one wants the damn fleshy things. That's why Muriel uses us."

"Muriel Inglis sent this?"

The delivery man checked his tablet. "One of our best customers. And most demanding. She's real specific about what she wants." He shook his head. "Between us, I think she should let us do the arranging, but often she has some . . . notion. And, by the way, she hasn't paid for this."

Bernal peeled off a couple of bills, tipping him generously in his happiness at getting a message from Muriel.

But wait. "When did you get the instructions to deliver?" It could have been before Bernal even came to Cheriton.

"Some time this morning . . . yep. Six thirty. They got it done quick for her."

So, quite a while after he had seen Muriel run off. She was okay. Nothing bad had happened to her. The sense of relief was overwhelming.

The van drove off. Bernal opened his van's rear and wedged the flowers into a space against the wall. He pulled off the card.

On it was a late-evening time, a GPS location, and a note: "A crew called Enigmatic Ascent will be here. Tell them you are a local. They don't know me directly. I will be along a bit later, and all will be explained." It wasn't signed, but it didn't need to be.

His happiness faded. Muriel was alive, but she was still running around, making him miserable without good reason. She'd hired him because he was smart and because he knew how to figure things out. Maybe she'd been sorry for him too, but that had to have faded as he proved his value. In fact, lately he'd gotten the sense that she was getting a little competitive with him. This was a sign of it.

So he'd be damned if he was going to show up at that rendezvous to be spoon-fed some information.

She'd learned something the previous day. It had been significant enough for her to blow off her gallery opening and decide to go out and play DAR ninja. She had come here, scooped up Madeline Inglis, and vanished into thin air. What had she learned?

When he saw her that night, he would know. He felt the pleasure of an unsolved puzzle. He would find out what she had learned and be able to explain to her why she should have waited for him.

Boxes of shoes were piled up on the daybed in her bedroom. Shoes she had bought that day. He remembered the receipt.

Given Muriel, it made sense that he would start with shoes.

7

"There's a spiritual dimension to your feet." The clerk reverently pulled a huge shoe out of a box. "Standard sizes don't speak to it."

"I like my shoes to fit." Bernal felt like an old fogy.

"Of course, of course! You want to get at least within screaming distance of those physical specs, sure. But, think about it, the lines of *qi*, the pressure points, the chakras, everything that focuses through those poor stressed metatarsals. Your feet are the most specialized part of your anatomy, did you know that? An evolutionary kludge, something we came up with on the fly when God flicked us out of the trees for getting too good at picking apples. We're stuck with these smushed-up hack jobs, fallen arches, bunions, and all. Believe me, you don't find many creationists working in shoe stores. So, of necessity, post-somatic evolution happens through *these*." The iridescent niobium shoes dangling from his finger by their transparent laces did indeed look like some piece of orbital gear. The human race had lost space. All it had left were the shoes. "That's why we here at DEEP leave the size for last. I mean, I can give you the length of every tendon in your foot down to the millimeter, and it still won't let me grok the fullness of your needs."

He slipped the shoe onto Bernal's foot. It hung there loosely. He had to curl his toes to keep it from falling off.

"See what I'm saying?"

"Uh, I'm beginning to. Should I walk around in it?"

"Oh, no, no, no. No. Not yet. That's the problem, isn't it? People look at a foot as something to slap against the ground, and that's it. But they're knots of spiritual energy. Too much pressure against Mother Earth's face, and they get karmic overload. And when that happens, everything else gets constipated. Kind of a chain reaction. Your liver gets hard, you start seeing yellow. Foot reflexology evolved to take care of those issues, but it's better to hit the problem up front, with shoes, don't you think? Just sit for a minute, let the energies reflect inside the shoe, and you'll see what I mean. Here, here's the other one. Balance the pair."

A pale girl slouched past with acromegalic basketball shoes hanging from her thin ankles. Along with the shoes, she carried a bowling bag stained with red.

"Feeling it?" The clerk was back, with a stack of boxes.

Bernal recognized the bag. The head of the third victim of Cheriton's own serial killer had turned up in a bag just like that one, in the locker room at Memory Lanes, a local alley. Now they did photorealistic knockoffs of it in Indonesia. Bernal watched that element of fashion go by again. He understood that the victim's sister had sued to recover some of the earnings from sales of the bag.

The receipt on the pile of shoes in Muriel's bedroom had been from this store.

"Yesterday, I think this woman came into your store." Bernal flashed a photograph of Muriel. "Did you see her in here?"

The clerk smiled at the photograph. "Muriel? Let me think. . . ."

"You know her?"

"Sure. She's, like, a bit out of our demographic, you know? But the girl knows shoes. I think we're part of her regular cycle. Sometimes it's us, sometimes it's a Manolo Blahnik, sometimes it's a high top Chuck Taylor. I'm okay with that. What's up with her?"

"I'm checking up on something for her. She's away, some kind of business, didn't really tell me, left me some kind of vague instructions I can't really understand. Wants me to talk to someone she met yesterday . . . so I was down here at the mall and thought I'd see if I could figure it out. If I can't, she's just going to have to wait."

"Yeah, she always has that oblique way. Wants you to guess. It's worked for her for a long time. Why should she change?"

Add shoe salesmen to the list of people we have no secrets from. "Okay, so she came in yesterday. Do you know where she went after she left?"

The clerk shrugged. "Don't know. She did have a lot of shoes, though. More than usual. *Way* more. And those things aren't light. They're Gaian anchor points, you know? To dimple the space-time matrix, you need some mass."

"Or velocity." Bernal had taken physics.

The clerk goggled at him. "Too close to C, and that sizing you think is so important becomes pretty irrelevant, you with me?"

Bernal felt like he'd just lost his money to a pool shark.

"Okay. Any idea of where she had been before coming here? Any bags from other stores, anything like that?"

"Not that I can remember." He sighed. "She *was* in an odd mood, now that you mention it. Not herself . . . no, that's not right. Too much herself, maybe."

"Too much?"

"White sugar, distilled alcohol . . . shoes. Needs are signals. But supernormal needs . . . system's not built to handle it. I never saw Muriel as one of those who wanted to . . . want things too much."

This was delicate. The clerk was getting at something, but Bernal wasn't sure what it was. Drugs?

"It might have gotten her in trouble," Bernal said. "What did she do?"

The clerk glanced around as if embarrassed. "People under the influence support more of our business than you might think. Binge purchasing. But you didn't hear it from me."

"Of course not."

"You ever hear of 'tooning'?"

"Something about it. . . . Personality building?"

"You can spell that T-U-N-E or T-O-O-N, however you like. Never picked Muriel for the type, actually. She always seemed herself, you know what I mean. But then, well, it can happen to anyone. More when you get older, if you'll excuse me. You get up one day, and you don't know yourself. Things that you like don't seem so fun, things you hate are just . . . boring. You don't care. Not anyone's fault. It's a brain chemistry thing. Too much blow can leave you that way; some other street stuff. Screws with the dopamine. Why should Muriel be immune? And I'll bet she tinkered with the neurochemistry in her younger days, too. . . ."

It annoyed Bernal that the clerk, not more than ten years younger than he was, was treating him like some veteran of forgotten wars.

"You think Muriel had gotten 'tooned'? There somewhere around here to do that?"

"Um, sure, yeah. Like I said—"

"Just a name. I won't connect it with you."

"Spillvagen. Norbert Spillvagen. Spill's got a business

therapy cover: motivation, posture and dress, transcend your carpal tunnel syndrome without surgery, that kind of thing, but, really, he's a hack. He sucks at all that stuff. Not bad at the 'tooning' stuff, but I got the names of some better practitioners, you ever think of polishing up a few engrams."

"You know where to find him?"

"Easy enough. He leaves his card here. Maybe that's how Muriel found him in the first place. We toss them out when we clean the desk, but one might still be back there. Stop by on your way out and ask."

"Thanks."

"So, you doing the shoes?"

"Frankly, they're making me lightheaded. Too much *qi* in my sinuses, maybe." Bernal pulled his feet out, and the shoes fell to the carpet like reentering spacecraft. "You wouldn't happen to have something in an easy-wear sandal, would you? Size it for thick socks."

"Let me check." The clerk sauntered off in a way that led Bernal to understand he wouldn't be back.

Bernal looked around for his own shoes and spotted them in a mesh basket extravagantly grounded by gold-and-silver cables in transparent insulation. A young woman with bone bumps on her cheekbones pulled them out for him. She also found him a bent business card that said NORBERT SPILLVAGEN, PERSONALITY ENHANCEMENT.

"A lot of negative energy pools in this kind of shoes," she said. Bernal noticed she wore latex gloves.

He rubbed his socks on the carpet. As he reached for the shoes he brushed against her. A tiny spark hit her shoulder. She jumped back with a gasp.

"Better check the leads on that mana drainage box," he said. "I think it's getting full."

8

The lawn sloped and was bumpy to boot, but the two kids had set up an idiosyncratic arrangement of croquet hoops and were attempting to play. The older child, a girl with straight blond hair and a matching posture, tapped her ball. It wobbled and came to rest against a hoop's edge.

The boy, with curly dark hair but the same look of placid intensity as his sister, swung his mallet as if playing polo, and sent his ball crashing off into the untrimmed shrubbery by a neighbor's garage. They both stared after it, saying nothing. After a few moments, the ball came back out from under a hanging rhododendron branch, rolling down the slope. It stopped against the wrong side of a goal stake.

"I think you're supposed to come hit me now," the boy said.

"No." The girl reached into a bag lying on the grass. "I play another one."

"But you have to hit me."

"Not if I don't want to."

The boy pouted. "Then I'll put myself somewhere where you *have* to hit me."

"That's up to you."

She stroked the new ball gently and this time made it through the first hoop. Afterward, however, the ball took a dogleg through a pothole and ended up far to the left.

"Excuse me." Bernal paused by a particularly bright orange pickup truck in the driveway. "Is—"

"Dad's in the garage." The boy didn't even look at him, being intent on setting up another long-distance shot.

The girl shaded her eyes against the morning sun and examined Bernal. She was reluctantly pretty, just at the point where the smooth course of her life was about to be disrupted by adolescence. "Be careful. He's in the middle of something."

"He's always in the middle of something," the boy said.

"Thanks."

"Muriel Inglis." Norbert Spillvagen was a pudgy man with thinning hair. He wore a short-sleeved dress shirt and a too-wide tie with gondoliers on it, and looked more like a radar antenna engineer than a therapist. Maybe he had a clientele who found the look of precise and obsolete knowledge comforting. "Maybe. I have a lot of clients. But what about you?" He eyed Bernal. "What do you feel you have lost? Aside from a fight, I mean."

Bernal put fingertips to his bruise. "Just an accident. Do people come to you because they feel they have lost something?"

Spillvagen hooked a wheeled desk chair with his foot and pushed it over to Bernal. "Sure. We collect a bunch of stuff—knowledge, ideas, passions, hopes, fears—then end up losing it all as we go along. And we never seem to pick up anything else. It's a sad state of affairs."

"Yes," Bernal said. "Yes, it is."

Spillvagen's garage office, with its heavy metal desk, its Shop-Vac, and its filing cabinets, looked like the sort of place a retired man was sent by his wife to work on his "projects." Star charts and astronomical photographs hung on the walls. A bulge-bellied telescope stood on a tripod with complicated motors to control its orientation.

A menu with looping cowboy motifs—a lasso, a cowboy boot, a branding iron with a spaceship on it—from a restaurant named Near Earth Orbit stood precariously on top of the stacks of paper that covered the desktop.

Spillvagen examined Bernal sympathetically. "We live our lives. We do what we do. Everything moves smoothly. Then . . . we don't even know how, but we lose ourselves. It's easy to do. And we don't feel fully alive, somehow. Those we know seem like poorly acted characters in a second-rate movie. Even the items around us seem like props rather than things we own. Does that sound familiar to you?"

A little more than was comfortable. "I guess."

"Sometimes the people around you seem two-dimensional, poorly realized. That's when you recognize that those wooden characters some people complain about in movies and books are totally realistic. Most people we know, in fact, are flat: an interest or two, a couple of catch phrases, and a defining desk decoration."

"That's a cynical attitude," Bernal said. "What kind of people come to you for help?"

"All kinds. We've all been dunked in the universal solvent of modern civilization. In a tribe, your evolutionary adapted role, your sense of self is always reinforced. Sometimes oppressively so. People remember who you were and expect you to fulfill the role you have. Modern society is the opposite. Everything is calculated to abrade your sense of self and then offer you items of various sorts to restore it."

"So is that what Muriel Inglis came here for? For 'tooning'?"

Spillvagen winced. "I know how you're spelling that, just by the way you say it. I started with 'tuning,' like what you used to do to a car, so I'll pretend that's what you said."

"Maybe there's a good reason for it. I hear that Muriel came out of here with her personality artificially distorted."

"I warn everyone that the procedure's experimental."

"For a lot of people," Bernal said, "'experimental' just means 'so potent that *they* don't want you to know about it.'"

"I should have talked to you before building my practice. But, experimental it is. So, sometimes your gain and saturation end up off. It's a known risk. A dislike of heights leads to a panic attack on a stepladder. A liking for bicycling leads to saddle sores, a pointless upgrade to Dura-Ace shifters, a Tour de France marathon with a stack of DVDs, an unnatural fascination with Eddy Merckx. What do you claim happened to Muriel?"

"She was impulsive and would confront people if she thought they weren't being straight with her. She liked communication that was more mysterious than direct. In the last few weeks, she's been completely off the scale on everything. I'm worried about her."

"Muriel didn't come here because she was worried her personality was getting vague. Because she'd heard how good I was, down at the shoe store. And you're not here because you think her personality isn't vague enough. She kept slipping in questions, like they were about the treatment, but were really about my old job."

"I don't think Muriel cared much about your old job." Bernal knew better than to chase after it. Spillvagen was being a prima donna and would just clam up in a self-satisfied way if he did.

"That what she told you?" Spillvagen's hurt look confirmed that Bernal had picked the right approach.

"No. She just never mentioned it."

"I used to work for a cryobank. Long Voyage. A couple of hundred frozen bodies and heads, waiting for resurrection. A decent-enough enterprise, fully bonded and insured, the works. That's where I invented my methods of personality enhancement. People were preparing to get themselves frozen for a long journey to the future. It's a mission no one has the training for. It's hard to keep yourself conscious and alive for that. The brain isn't just a gadget. Well, maybe it is just a gadget, but we've put our personalities on top of the gadget's functions. It's not very secure. You don't want to wake up five hundred years from now only to have to start again from scratch because your personality did not survive the trip."

"I'm sure that idea was comforting to your customers."

Spillvagen scowled. "I did have problems with my employers. I was a counselor. I prepared people for their future lives. You have to recognize, you could emerge in an economy without money. Or a world without genders. Without sex at all. People might not even be human beings. You might be homeless, or a food source, or . . . who knows? You might find yourself fighting invading Mongol hordes. . . ."

"I'm beginning to see why your supervisors might have been concerned."

"Listen, it's all something you need to pay attention to. It's not like a ride at Disneyland. I used to believe in the future. I did. I preached that gospel." Spillvagen looked haggard, even a little deranged. "I had the faith. There are solutions. There are ways of taking care of those ancient spiritual problems, ways that are within our grasp. You can still find what I wrote, floating around the Internet: 'If you want to live forever, why die first?' I was a transhumanist, a propagandist for the future. I *believed* in it."

"And now?"

"And now I sit in my garage and try to find people's personalities for them." Before Bernal could say anything else, there was a knock at the door, and a woman with frosted hair, wearing a clingy denim dress, rolled in a cart with a coffee urn and some bagels on it.

Norbert sighed. "Bernal, Melissa, the spousal unit."

"Hi," she said. "You're not here for a treatment."

"Melissa!"

"Oh, don't fool around, Norbie. I can tell." She touched Bernal's shoulder. "Do me a favor: get him involved in something. All he does now is sit around here chewing over old stuff about Long Voyage. Oh, Norbie, speaking of that, I think she's been around again."

"Who?" Spillvagen said.

"Who else? That crazy lady with the uncle in the cryobank. What's her name?"

"Yolanda."

"Yes, her. She's been walking around through the foxgloves. Clay knocked a ball over there. He and Honor saw her footprints. She wore heels! Here they're just coming up, and she's torn them up."

"I'll bet it was Ripper."

"They say it wasn't. They say he's been tied up."

"Those people will say anything, Melissa. Their son has pet weasels, for God's sake. And I think I've seen a snake. Here they have a German shepherd the size of a buffalo, and raccoons still knock their garbage over.

Morons. Dog owning is the new smoking. We're about to realize it."

Melissa grinned at Bernal. She had uneven teeth and was cute, the way you always wanted your neighbor's wife to be. "The Batchelors do have a nice party every summer."

She had the sparkle of a habitual flirt. He had to smile back. Bernal was slender and intense and occasionally befuddled. He had smooth skin, clean nails, hair that got unruly when he was thinking too hard, and smelled gently spicy. Women liked most of what he had to offer and looked forward to fixing the rest. He wasn't always sure what to do about that. Sometimes he was distracted and missed his chance. And sometimes he fell hard in love, revealed his puppy-dog devotion too clearly, and failed to provide the uncertainty any relationship needed to grow. Any of his, anyway.

"It's just an attempt to make us feel guilty for complaining about their stupid animals," Spillvagen said. "They *are* smarter than most people with annoying habits, I'll give them that. Most people hide out when they have a barking dog or a sadistic child, get all sullen, threaten you, pee on your leg. These guys put on a Fourth of July spread and invite the neighborhood. Plenty of beer. So everyone feels guilty about confronting them."

"That woman is a menace, Norbert. I'm worried about the children."

Spillvagen rubbed his forehead. "I know. I'll take care of her."

"But I'm interrupting," Melissa said. "I'll leave you gentlemen to your discussion."

"I'm here about a friend of mine," Bernal said. "Muriel Inglis. Have you met her?"

"Oh, Muriel." Melissa gave her husband a frosty look. "She was here just yesterday, wasn't she? She seems like a very nice lady." She pushed the cart out, clipping the edge of the doorway on her way.

Spillvagen had moved into the crowded depths of the garage, where old appliances and other yard-sale-ready items crowded gray metal shelves, and pulled out a framed astronomical print that showed a cluster of bright blue-white stars in a swirl of pink dust. He leaned it up.

Bernal joined him. "What is that, the Pleiades?"

"Nah. Pretty similar bunch, though. That's actually a cluster called NGC 2264, associated with the Cone Nebula, in Monoceros, the Unicorn. Can't see it with the naked eye. Can't find the constellation either. Kind of a low-rent district next to Orion. Don't know who came up with it."

"You take the picture yourself?"

"Yeah. Dumb hobby now, right? You got the Hubble up there, giving us cosmic beaver shots, and I'm on a ladder trying to get a glimpse of panty through a sorority window."

"Sure."

Spillvagen sighed. "Yolanda MacParland. We had some trouble at Long Voyage. Yolanda's uncle is a client, and she's convinced that there's something wrong, that something happened to him. Your friend Muriel was a little on that. I think . . ." He glanced at Bernal, then returned his attention to his astronomical photograph. "Don't take Melissa too seriously. It's weird. Muriel is way older, I mean, you wouldn't think there would be anything to worry about, but Melissa took her as a kind of challenge. How to hold yourself together, you know."

"It doesn't look like Melissa has any trouble holding herself together," Bernal said.

Spillvagen gave him an appraising glance. "I'll let her know you think so. I guess she'd need to hear that sometimes. It would get things off Muriel, that's for sure."

Spillvagen enjoyed Melissa's jealousy of Muriel, but it looked like he was jealous of her too.

On the shelf next to Bernal was something that looked like an igloo made of crumpled gold foil, and a tray of plastic ice cubes. He pulled one out. The cube had a tiny human form in it, lying flat, as if asleep. Something fun for the Long Voyage New Year's party. Nothing you'd really want to show potential clients. Maybe he was only thinking of the gold thing as an igloo because of the fake ice cubes, because it seemed like he'd seen something like it before.

"I kind of got left holding the bag," Spillvagen said. "That's why I'm now in business for myself. Long Voyage did have security problems, all kinds of stuff, but nothing to do with me. But I was kind of up front, dealing with intake, all that, so . . . But now, it's just Yolanda. She won't let things go. You should go talk to her."

"Why?"

"She . . . Muriel. Your friend Muriel said Yolanda knew more than she was telling about what happened at Long Voyage. Talking to Yolanda was what put Muriel onto me in the first place. Yolanda knows something your friend was really interested in. That's great. But that Yolanda . . . I'm trying to hold things together here, and it's nothing but an endless campaign of harassment. I'm getting too old for this, Bernal. I really am."

9

"We know you slept with him, you little slut!"

The voice came around the side of the house.

"Why don't you read your own subtitle? It's right across your chest. You can read, can't you?"

A TV audience hooted.

"Oh, yeah, that's what you'd like to think, you pathetic wannabe studmuffin."

It was a woman's voice, husky and irritated. No one had responded to the doorbell, so Bernal walked around the silver Lexus GS in the driveway and past the garage, pushing his way through overgrown hostas.

A woman in a yellow bikini lay on a lounge chair on a patio. Despite her pose, there was no pool in evidence. She was protected from the cool spring air by a kerosene burner hissing overhead. A television stood on a round glass table, the extension cord snaking along the flagstones and into the house. An excited host was yelling at someone that she had to get her life together, while the studio audience stomped feet and applauded. A laptop, a bulky older model with duct tape holding on a loose cover panel, lay on the flagstones.

The woman looked up at Bernal through her sunglasses, then raised her remote and muted the show.

"Excuse me," Bernal said. "Do you know Norbert Spillvagen?"

Instead of answering, she turned and picked up a cocktail shaker from the rolling bar next to her chair. She reached underneath, pulled out a cocktail glass, and poured something into it. She handed it to Bernal. She was in her mid-forties, maybe older. Her skin had lost some of its elasticity, and veins showed on her pale legs. But she wore maroon toenail polish and had some clear muscles in her shoulders. Her bobbed hair was the pale zoo-polar-bear yellow of a porn star. She tilted her sunglasses up to look at him. Her blue eyes were expertly outlined with eyeliner, her pursed lips outlined in a pencil darker than her not-too-vivid lipstick.

Bernal took a sip: slightly watery sour-apple martini. He gazed up at the sun. It was moving into late afternoon, so maybe this wasn't as decadent as it looked.

"Come sit next to Momma." She patted a spot on her recliner. There was a stack of white resin chairs on the other side of the table, so he had a choice of wrestling rudely with the stack or perching ridiculously on top of it. He sat down next to her knee. She tilted it away, but he still felt it, as if it radiated like the heater overhead. "Spill complain about me? Are you here to administer some discipline?"

"I just talked to Norbert Spillvagen."

"And he complained. Stalking. Harassment. He's such a whiner. Spiritual types like him often are, you ever notice that?"

"I'm not so interested in Spillvagen himself. But he said you had been talking with Muriel Inglis. In fact, that you had sent Muriel to him. It's Muriel I want to talk about."

"I'm sorry, but I don't know any Muriel."

Bernal described Muriel Inglis to her and showed her a picture on his phone, the only one he had of her, taken at some charity event as she listened earnestly to someone accepting an award, a china coffee cup at her elbow.

Looking at it, Yolanda shook her head slowly. "No. Might be someone I'd like to know, but . . . I've never seen her before."

Bernal was stunned. "But . . . Norbert said Muriel had gotten some information from you."

Yolanda laughed. "Oh, oh. You're so cute when you look betrayed. What, you thought Spill cared about your little mission or whatever? He's a little snake. The one good thing about him is that he doesn't really know what he's doing. He sent you to harass me, because he's scared of me. But, no offense, you're not really the heavy type."

"None taken." Bernal couldn't have said why that perfectly reasonable observation nettled him.

"Though those bruises on your face do make you look a little scary."

"You don't have to flatter me. You've really never seen her?"

"Cross my heart and hope to die. So now you go back to him and tell him you scared the hell out of me and I will never bother him ever again, no matter how he ruined my life."

"What did he do to you?"

"Don't get me started." Yolanda leaned over and poured the last of the green apple martini. But Bernal found himself looking at the bumps of her spine as it curved. She brushed her hair back and smiled slightly as she poured.

"No, I'm curious." He had to think about what to do

next. He'd been more than half hoping that Yolanda would tell him exactly where Muriel was.

"My uncle died a couple of years ago. Uncle Solly. I always liked Uncle Solly. When I was little, I used to go play with all that space stuff he had in his house. Telescopes, star charts, little Revell models of spaceships. All that stopped once I hit puberty, of course, and got to find that stuff kind of boring. Poor Uncle Solly. I ignored him for quite a while. I got interested in other things.

"Solly didn't have kids. His wife, my aunt Helga, died quite a few years before him. I never really knew her. Solly had worked hard his whole life. Nice house, nothing too big. But when he died, it turned out he had a lot of money stashed away. And aside from a branch of the family that moved to Colorado, I was it as far as relatives was concerned.

"There wasn't really a funeral, just a kind of ceremony at Long Voyage, that cryobank over toward Prescott, where that charlatan Spillvagen worked. I guess it shouldn't have surprised me that Solly wanted to get himself frozen. Just his kind of thing. His little statement that they read at the ceremony said that he wanted to live to see human beings on other planets. A lot of stuff like that. Very inspiring. But it was a little room, hot, and he had a lot of people read stuff, and someone even played a video of the first man landing on the Moon. Don't you think that flag on a stick was kind of silly? I mean, if you don't have wind, think of something else. You should be able to. Those space types tend to be unimaginative.

"Okay, fine. He'd set up his accounts in a variant of a dynasty trust called a 'personal revival trust.' Seems to be legal, though it hasn't been tested in court. Dynasty trusts let you leave stuff to remote descendants. A personal revival trust lets you leave it to yourself, when you're revived. And, of course, there's rental. On the facility. There's a fund for that too, otherwise there's a chance they'd just dump you at some point, when you couldn't pay to keep the liquid nitrogen cold or something. And that's the way things stood, for a couple of years. I'd go visit Uncle Solly, now and again, just to see how he was getting on."

Bernal thought two things. One was that she had done a fair amount of research on the structure of her uncle's trust. And two, that there was no way she had ever struggled over to Long Voyage to visit her frozen uncle.

"Then, things went kablooie."

"What do you mean?"

"Of course, if Uncle Solly had picked a classier cryobank, one housed in a black glass pyramid or something, none of this would have happened. 'And we pass the savings on to you!' just wasn't the most comforting marketing positioning for a cryobank, even though it actually makes sense. Somebody has to pay for keeping that damn black glass pyramid clean. That stuff really shows marks.

"Long Voyage was in an abandoned mall along with a lot of other low-rent places. Well, something went wrong, and there was a fire. It was a pretty serious fire, and there were all sorts of power failures, the works. And their security was down for who knows how long."

"Do you think your uncle was . . . defrosted?" he said.

"Of course I do! Why else would they stonewall that way? They screwed up, let the nitrogen boil off. It's just horrible, thinking of Uncle Solly ending that way. Is that murder, do you think?"

"Defrosting someone who could potentially be revived? In some kind of potential way, maybe."

"Well, I think someone should pay."

There really wasn't anything for Bernal here. He

thought Yolanda was right about why Spillvagen had sent him. He'd just wanted to yank Yolanda's chain.

He started to get up. "Well, I won't take up any more of your time. . . ."

"Wait, wait. Hand me that computer." She flipped open the laptop and, after a few clicks, opened a photo. She held it on her lap, forcing him to lean over her to look at the picture. It showed solemn people sitting in folding chairs, with some pictures of rockets taking off on easel stands behind them. Bernal pretended to examine it as if it was important.

"That's the funeral," she said. "Uncle Solly's. See all his friends." She shook her head, and there were tears in her eyes. "Even that lady from that other company, the space probe place, she came by. Nice of her. One space nut honoring another."

He should have seen it right away. A blond head popped out of the group of faces. Here, too, her vaguely distracted expression made her look like she wasn't a part of what was going on around her.

"This one?" He pointed to Madeline Ungaro.

"Yes. That's the one. She wasn't invited, but who was going to keep her out? It's not like you had to show ID or anything."

"I'm glad you remembered this."

"I lose a lot of stuff, nowadays. You're lucky my days are empty enough that it was worth my remembering."

For a moment, she looked bleak. Bernal admired her romantic melancholy, her knees, and her use of the gerund.

10

The road went around a field, past an old farmhouse, over a slight rise, and down into a patch of woods. Ahead, the trees opened out on a power line right-of-way. One arm out, one akimbo, pylons carried their delicate triple skein of high-voltage power off toward Boston. A track down the slope marked where mountain bikers and trail runners found their entertainment.

Bernal pulled the van into a spot under an overgrown hedge, at the location Muriel had specified in her note, and waited. He was a bit early. He'd grabbed some Indian takeout and settled himself into Ungaro's lab. He had decided to make that his base of operations here in Cheriton. His plants in Boston would just have to rely on his downstairs neighbor's services for a few more days. If anything happened, he figured, it would happen here.

After about ten minutes, headlights played across him. He sat still, waiting for the car to pass. Instead, the car cut in ahead of him and parked a dozen yards or so farther up.

The Plymouth Voyager had its parking lights on, organic ambient music with instruments from a dozen tribal cultures playing soothingly. Scorch marks had been painted on the side, as if it had recently endured reentry.

Bernal walked up to them. "Glad you guys could make it tonight. My name's Bernal. I'm a local."

Two long-haired men in microfiber windbreakers peered around the back of the van. They had already set up cameras and netlinks, and one had optic cable looped over his shoulder. Brightly colored fast-food wrappers, souvenirs of their road trip, drifted out onto the gravel as they yanked out more equipment. One of them knelt and shoveled everything back into the car.

"Hey." The driver, a girl with a square jaw but surprisingly beautiful lips, swung open her door. "My name's Oleana. These guys are Len and Magnusen." The two men nodded, but didn't say anything. "Len's from Baraboo. I'm from LaCrosse. Magnusen here's a bit of a ringer: New Ulm, Minnesota." Magnusen nodded again, embarrassed. "Hesketh is supposed to be along pretty soon. That your understanding too?"

Hesketh? "Pretty much."

On the back of Oleana's windbreaker was a blue-green alien planet with the words ENIGMATIC ASCENT around it. She wore a scent that was more floral than seemed right for her.

And that was that. They settled down to wait.

Magnusen sat hunched over a laptop. In response to a question from Bernal, he said, "Hesketh has a predicted route. Sometimes we get that, sometimes we don't. But aren't you guys the source of the data?"

Bernal had to think fast. "Not my side of it. I do

support work. The main source is supposed to be along pretty soon. You can meet her."

Magnusen smiled. "I'd like to, finally. We've been all over the country, chasing rumors and sightings. Around here's the first real stuff we've found. The device has stuck to pretty much the same route for the past couple of runs, so our first guess is that it will again."

"I wish they'd just stop testing the thing and move on to the next phase," Len said. "It's ready to go. We all feel it. Ready to take on the stars. We're getting kind of worried that it will be stuck here on Earth, just like us, for the rest of its existence."

"We've been all over," Oleana said. "We all saved our pennies one year and went to Tyuratam, watched a launch. The Russians still have the largest launch vehicles. Shakes you right through. Everyone's got to run to the bathroom right after. Out in the middle of Kazakhstan. Miserable, miserable. But we found fans there, right, Len? Guy named Yuri had hitched all the way from Kiev to watch a Proton booster. Just a comm satellite for a Japanese company. And Yuri was a young guy. Didn't even remember the Soviet Union. And there he was, standing in the scrub grass, watching the flames come out of the concrete base, because he wanted to reassure himself that maybe it was possible to get the hell off this dustball after all."

"They're selling off all those boosters." Len was mournful. "Even the experimental stuff. Those little high-thrust things. Different countries use them for ICBMs, force projection, that kind of thing. And not just countries. Private consortia of all sorts."

"Private's better anyway." Magnusen snorted Red Man, neatly folded the top of the bag and put it in his boot. "Hey, remember that Ariane launch we got to see in French Guiana?"

Bernal had to endure a number of stories of difficulties surmounted in pursuit of watching routine rocket launches. These guys were fanatics. Nuts.

Len kept peeking out of the window.

"See anyone?" Magnusen asked.

"Not tonight. But, God, it gets crowded out here sometimes. . . ."

"Other teams searching for Hesketh?" Bernal said.

"Nah. But other fans of other things."

"Like what?"

Len made a face. "You got a serial killer out here, I hear."

"Yeah. The Bowler."

"Some of his fans wander around. We've run across a couple of them."

"Weird people," Oleana said with distaste. "Looking for bodies. Looking for someone who might well behead them. We stay away from them. As far as I'm concerned, they're as dangerous as what they're looking for."

"Some people are sex tourists," Bernal said. "Some people are suffering tourists."

Len shook his head. "Whatever happened to taking a novel to the beach?"

Bernal looked at him. "You tell me."

"Touché. I don't do that much anymore. Sand gets in my keyboard, and suntan lotion stains the screen. But these guys . . . they wear titanium dickeys."

"They do not." Magnusen was disgusted.

"They do! They may be crazy, but they're not . . . well, they're crazy."

"Where would you buy a titanium dickey? Russia? I think you—hey! I just got a completely new observer message. Says Hesketh isn't on this track at all."

"What?" Len tried to yank the laptop away. Magnusen held it in an iron grip. "Who's the message from?"

"Not sure. It's the same signal I got last night, when it completely left track and looked like it was mating with the abandoned car over by the Black River. Got right on top of it—and after that, we lost it for good."

"I can't believe you're developing your own sources out here," Len said. "Who the hell is it?"

"Could be Hesketh itself, for all I know. Its information was good last night."

"Let's go!" Oleana was clearly the decisive one of the group. The other two could have argued this out all night.

"Don't you see?" Len snapped the tripod legs shut, fumbled with a lens cap. "It's making a break for it. Someone's trying to kill it, and it's trying to get away. We knew this day would come. Didn't we, Oleana? We knew it."

He threw equipment into the back of the van.

"What the hell are you doing?" Magnusen shrieked. "Some of that shit's rented!"

Len slowed down and snapped shock cords over the equipment. "If we can get into contact with the rover—"

Oleana chimed in. "Render appropriate assistance—"

"Gold," Magnusen said. "Pure, undiluted gold."

Len was breathless. "Then we find a surplus launch vehicle. . . ."

"I saw an old Japanese one on auction last week," Magnusen said.

"Rent a launch site in Brazil or Congo. . . ."

"Plenty of slots, nowadays. . . ."

"Achieve the Enigmatic Ascent!" they shouted together.

Oleana hit the accelerator and they tore down the unevenly patched asphalt of the road.

They passed someone walking up the road in the opposite direction, toward the power lines. They were past before Bernal realized who it was.

He had to get out of this car and after her. He used the first stratagem that came to mind.

"Oh, God," Bernal said. "I feel sick."

"Don't lose lunch on the optics!" Magnusen couldn't believe what he was hearing.

"Rented," Len said. "They have his credit card! The damn thing's almost maxed out as it is. He just isn't careful with his money. . . ."

"Never mind my finances, Len."

"Please . . ." Bernal whimpered.

"Do you really need that gym membership? You never go. And what's up with the almond butter? What's wrong with peanut?"

"Oh, for heaven's—" Oleana slammed to a halt.

Bernal pulled open the side door and stumbled out.

"Hey, you okay, man?" Magnusen leaned out after him.

"Go." Bernal stood bent over, holding his stomach. He hoped he wasn't overdoing it. "Go ahead. You can't let me hold you back."

"You sure?"

"For God's sake, Magnusen." Oleana was furious. "Stop being nice, and get back in the car. We'll come back and pick you up later, mister."

"Yeah," Len said. "I'll have pictures for you to look at. With this lens . . ."

"Len! Stop gabbing!"

In a moment, their taillights had disappeared around the corner.

11

Who Bernal had spotted on the road was Charis Fen, walking with a heavy, relaxed pace, like a householder carrying the trash to the curb.

He straightened up and trotted up the quiet street lined with small split-levels on lots that had returned to woods. He hadn't been paying attention to the drive, but they couldn't have gone far from the rendezvous point. And he couldn't remember Oleana making any turns.

Bernal was surprised at how angry he was. Charis clearly thought he was an idiot.

She'd told him she'd decided to move on to a more promising project, and advised Bernal to do the same. Move along, nothing to see here. Hesketh's just a collection of spare parts. He'd bought it.

But here she was, heading for where the Wisconsin gang had said Hesketh was due to take its run.

He was breathing hard when the metal struts of the power pylons were finally silhouetted against the sky ahead of him. Of course. The map Charis had in her front seat, the parallel lines with the Xs. It had been a map of this powerline. She'd been planning this all along. He paused, listening. Nothing.

Presumably Charis had linked herself in as a local info source to the Enigmatic Ascent team. And she had just sent them a completely false piece of information that had them charging off in pursuit of a wild goose, while she came here and took care of Hesketh in peace.

Bernal found the mountain-bike path, ran up it, and then sat down in the dry grass. He'd probably have to sit here by himself for the rest of the night, but crashing around looking for her wasn't going to get him anywhere. He forced himself to be calm. The air was still. Bernal didn't hear a lot of bug action this time of spring, though there was a twittering of frogs down in the drainage ditch that ran past where he had originally parked. He consciously relaxed his muscles.

For a few minutes, nothing. Then—was that a rustle in the high grass? Bernal raised himself up.

Someone was walking toward him. Bernal tried to change his angle so that whoever it was would be silhouetted against the sky. But he couldn't manage it. But wait . . . was someone *crawling*? He couldn't stand it. He finally stood up.

A crackling and a snapping of twigs, and a dark carapace appeared in the weeds. It struggled along on its six legs, each of which felt carefully at the surface before committing its weight, and carried specialized manipulator limbs folded along its back. Four feet long, three wide, the body's basic hexagonal shape was obscured by the various crude functional additions that marked Hesketh as a classic garage product.

As he gaped at it, the rover jumped into the air, tucked all of its legs, and rolled back down the hill.

"Goddammit!" Charis half-rose from the depression that had concealed her. She held what looked like a toy gun: a stubby black thing with a parabolic antenna on the end. A curly cable led from that to a backpack. "What the hell are you doing here?"

"I—"

"Jesus!"

The gigantic insectoid figure hung in the air. Hesketh had jumped. Without aiming, Charis fired. Instead of a bang, all Bernal heard was a loud sizzle, not much different from the sound of the power lines. Then Charis's shoulder hit him, and he hit the ground.

The impact had taken him in the solar plexus, and for a long few moments he thought he'd never breathe again. He lay on his back, looking at the stars. Was that really Hesketh's goal, somewhere out there, crawling across the rocks of some distant planet circling one of those . . . something unclenched, and he was able to draw in a thin stream of clear, cool air.

Charis stood over him, looking down at something on her gun. "Come on, baby. Come *on*! Cheap-ass capacitors!"

Hesketh rolled on the grass and then was moving again. But even from where Bernal lay, he could see that something had happened to the legs on one side. They shook, as if the machine had just developed Parkinson's. Instead of attacking again, it scuttled up the hill, away from them.

Bernal pushed himself up to a sitting position.

"What is that thing?" he asked.

"This?" Charis waved her stubby weapon. "A piece of crap. Those guys in supply think they're so smart. Then they short me on the capacitors. 'Plenty of speed,' they said. 'No need for more weight.' Ha!"

"That's a herf gun, isn't it?"

"You could call it that. I call it—"

"A piece of crap," Bernal finished. "If you—"

"There you go, baby!" Charis charged up the hill after Hesketh.

"HERF" stood for high-energy radio frequency. It was like a focused electromagnetic pulse and could fry complex electronics with minimal physical damage to anything else. Bernal had heard that they could be made with easily available materials, but this was the first time he'd ever heard of one actually being used. Charis's backpack presumably carried the capacitors that held the massive charge the device required to be effective. The high-energy radio waves generated by the parabolic antenna set up currents in printed circuitry and destroyed it. It was the perfect weapon to use against an uppity planetary probe.

Bernal got to his feet and followed. He hadn't responded fast enough. He'd already let her damage Hesketh. He couldn't let her destroy it. This was probably why Muriel had wanted him here in the first place, and he was falling down on the job.

They crested a hill. The right of way roller coastered down from there. Charis walked down the mountain-bike path, scanning fences to the right and left, looking for a break. A plane heading for Logan flickered above the power lines. A few moments later, its distant roar filtered into the silence.

He ran after her. "Stop!"

"What?"

She had half turned to look at him, when Hesketh jumped again, from behind a hummock. She tried to aim properly, but set off her herf gun too early. Hesketh shuddered away, its still-functional legs churning through the grass. She clipped her herf gun to her power pack and pulled out something else.

Bernal didn't know what else to do, so he tried to tackle her.

It was like hitting a foam-covered concrete post. She

didn't go down, but she did drop the beer-can sized device she had been pointing at Hesketh. She lowered her shoulder, slid under him, and was out of his grasp.

"Damn it!" she said. "Just let me do my job."

"No. I can't let you do it."

He threw himself at her again, but this time, forewarned, she dodged, and he didn't even manage to get a grip on her.

"This isn't a good idea, bucko," she said. "I don't have time for it."

"You have to make time." He thought about trying to punch her but realized that his chances of landing anything were slim. What was he supposed to do with her?

"No, I don't." This time she charged at him. She caught him just as he crested a hillock. He found himself propelled down a steep slope, lost his footing, and fell headlong. But that was it. She didn't knock him out with a rock or anything.

She searched in the grass for whatever it was she had dropped, and then her footsteps receded into the darkness.

He scrambled to his feet. He ran up the slope after her and crested the hill again. The trail dropped steeply at first, a fun drop for anyone mountain biking, then bottomed out in a swale before rising again in a series of bumps.

Well, at least he was faster than she was. He could see her blocky shape struggling up the opposite slope, not too far ahead of him. He didn't see Hesketh, but the thing was too low to be spotted easily. From Charis's intentness, it must have been just ahead of her.

By the time he caught up to her again, the air was tearing in his lungs.

"Jesus, can't you just give it up?" She turned to face him. "I need to check the thing out. Relax."

"I . . . won't . . . relax."

"I'm sorry. Here's a bit of mandatory vacation." She raised the beer can.

Bernal heard a loud *thwang*, like a giant rubber band. Something grabbed his legs and threw him backward. He fell on his back and tried to get up, but something held his legs in a firm grip. He felt at them. Rubbery cords had wrapped around them, pinioning them. When he struggled, the cords grew tighter.

He forced himself to relax and really analyze what held him. The cords were elastic, but not sticky. At least, they didn't stick to his pants, though they did seem to stick to each other. He swung his legs around so that he had some chance to see what the arrangement was.

They were mutually sticky through something like Velcro. He could feel how the ends of the cords penetrated each other. He was held by a dense network.

He managed to slip his hand into his pocket and pull out his multitool. If he had to cut every cord, he would be here all night. But networks often had points of maximum vulnerability. He plucked the cords to get a sense of the tension, cut one, then another. Already the net was looser, but he had to be careful not to try to escape too quickly, which could cause it to twist and tighten up again. He thought carefully and cut a third.

Ah. He wriggled out of it and was finally able to stand with his legs free. Then, moving deliberately, he set off after Charis and Hesketh.

12

The right-of-way crossed a road. Bernal saw Charis's Hummer parked a few yards away, but it was dark.

Scratches on the asphalt ran across the road and back into the grass. The damaged Hesketh was still going strong.

Bernal moved more quickly. Beyond the road, the right-of-way swept wide to the left, where it met a high chain-link fence. Tracking Hesketh was easier than it might have been, because the right-of-way was hemmed by back fences and other barriers on both sides, and because Hesketh made an astonishing amount of noise pulling its body along on its remaining functioning legs.

He almost went past it, but some noise beyond the fence redirected his attention.

Something had ripped a hole in the fence, partially screened by dried weeds. Some of the weeds were freshly broken.

He pushed his way through.

The giant shapes of tire shredders bulked in the darkness and the air smelled of burned rubber. Dishwashers and clothes driers stood in crushed rows. Two bulldozers stood in mid task, construction waste for recycling piled up in front of their blades. Above them rose a tire hill, with a subpeak of giant truck tires, and a sinuous wave of car tires.

Charis carried another of her blocky, cheesy-looking weapons. She should hire a decent props department, Bernal thought. She'd climbed partway up the slope and was now looking downward, almost at Bernal.

Below her, Hesketh climbed tenaciously up the slope of tires, its legs spread wide. Two of the legs on the left side were dead and dragged uselessly, while one on the right jerked spastically. It was a wonder it was going anywhere.

Charis bent over, heaved, and toppled tires down on top of Hesketh, yelling something Bernal couldn't hear. It slid a few feet back, then spread its legs out farther and climbed more deliberately. Charis chucked a couple more tires, but they bounced harmlessly off its carapace and off a projection on its back.

It was an antenna. The thing had a high-frequency antenna on its back.

Why was it still heading toward her, instead of fleeing?

"Charis!" he yelled up.

He thought back to their fight. She probably could have taken him out at any time, much more effectively than the guy with the cast-iron doggie doorstop had. But, at every point, she'd only used as much force as she needed to.

"Give me a minute." Her voice was surprisingly calm. "Then we can have a talk."

She shouldered her weapon and fired. It seemed to be some kind of crowd-control hoser and fired padded pellets. They were meant to stun unarmed rioters. And it had the desired effect, knocking Hesketh completely off its legs and rolling it down the hill. She charged down after it.

He was finally close enough to get a look at Hesketh. It looked really slapped together, with bubblegum welds that would have shamed a first-year shop student. Nothing about this operation was as high class as he would have liked.

She knelt over Hesketh and looked up at him. "You okay? I mean, I had to—"

"Charis," he said urgently. "That thing is radio-controlled. I'll bet it has no more processing in it than a remote-controlled airplane. It's nothing but a decoy."

"Then why the hell would it be—" She glanced down at it, then ran.

She'd almost gotten out of range when the thing exploded.

He felt the compression wave of the explosion. He stumbled backward, hands in front of his face.

But he was still there. He hadn't been knocked into blackness. But, for a moment, he remembered what had happened to him, and huddled, curled up, hoping to protect himself.

"Where are you injured?" Charis's big hand on his shoulder, her wide face shoved into his.

"I'm . . ." He took a breath. "I'm fine. Just . . . I had something happen once. Still cracks, here and there. Give me a minute, I'll be okay."

Blue flames licked up from where Hesketh, or whatever, had been. Its pieces lay all around the crater it had blown in the pile of tires. Bernal choked on the smell of burning rubber.

He looked up at Charis. "How are you?"

"Alive. Thanks to you. But not much better than that." He now saw that half her face was black, and there was a bloody tear in her leg.

"Bandages?" he said.

"In the car. But don't worry about that now. Get the extinguisher. Under the steering column."

"Let me help you down—"

"*Now*. Tire fires are nightmares. *Move*."

Bernal found the red extinguisher easily enough. The climb seemed much harder this time. Every third step, his foot sank into a tire. Loose lengths of radial belt tore at his pants.

The stench was incredible.

By the time he got back up the hill, Charis had torn a length of cloth from her shirt and tied off her bleeding calf. Her fingers moved with quick expertise; she knew field first aid.

Bernal sprayed foam on the stinking rubber.

"So, what the hell was this thing?" Charis held a length of the device's leg. "Packed with half a pound of Semtex, I'd estimate. Not a crowd shredder, but nothing to pick your nose with either."

"Some kind of decoy, not Hesketh at all." Once burning, the rubber decided it liked it that way. The fire retreated only reluctantly. The extinguisher was meant to suppress an engine fire. Its capacity was limited. "Just a little remote-control crawler. No processing in it at all."

Charis shook her head, then winced. "I've been skunked. All the way through. There's no Hesketh. There's nothing. Muriel asked me—"

"What?"

"Muriel Inglis. You remember her. Your boss. She

asked us to look into what Ungaro was up to. Said she'd lost control, that things were going bad and she needed our help. . . ."

"Whose help?"

"Social Protection. We provide . . . technical security services, you might say."

"Who might say? Not me."

"Argue with me, but keep working that fire. You've almost got it under control. Look. Muriel's taken off and I don't know what the hell she's up to. I do know that she's taken off with a spare herf gun of mine that I would like to have back. I should have just called it all off this morning when I saw no Hesketh in that lab and got roughed up by Muriel's attack dog employee."

It took Bernal an instant to realize that she was talking about him. "What do you say Muriel asked you to do?"

"She asked me to grab Hesketh when I could, so that she could examine it. She didn't think Missy Madeline Ungaro was reporting adequately. Muriel had funded the thing, so I guess I was some kind of high-tech repo man. Muriel's got a talent for getting people to do what she wants. Right? So, tell me, why are you here? I had information from before, from my surveillance, on where Hesketh was going to be. What brought you out?"

Muriel, Bernal didn't say. A message from Muriel. He didn't have any interest in sharing that information with Charis. He'd have to find Muriel and talk with her first. He kicked a big truck tire onto some fugitive blue flames and got a last dribble out of the extinguisher.

"Just a hunch," he said.

If Charis hadn't shown up, he would have waited for Hesketh and then met the detonation himself. He was sure there was a good explanation, but one thing he'd have to ask Muriel was why she had sent him a message that had almost gotten him killed.

13

Something glowed above the trees. As Bernal drove, it grew and turned into the toe of a cowboy boot, brightly spotlit.

The boot was at the end of the kicked-up leg of a cowgirl straddling a rocket. She was thirty feet high, a masterpiece of fiberglass craftsmanship. She wore two sheriff's badges, one on each thrusting breast, and nebulae decorated her short denim skirt. The rocket she rode was a nondescript thing of creased metal. Beneath her feet lay a diner, like the box her high-heeled ostrich-hide boots had come in.

Near Earth Orbit. Bernal was burnt, stinging from cuts, and his ears still rang from the detonation. What he wanted more than anything was to get back to Ungaro's lab and get to bed. But something about the cowboy motif snagged his thoughts. He slowed and pulled into the gravel parking lot. Vast fields spread out around the diner and barren hills. Whether toxic waste, ancient

Indian curses, or lack of easy highway access, something had prevented any kind of development nearby.

The cowboy boot. Muriel had sent him his message about Madeline Ungaro's lab in a cowboy boot. But that seemed overly subtle, even for her.

Wait. A Near Earth Orbit menu had been propped up against the wall in Norbert Spillvagen's garage office. And with that as an additional piece of information, the orange pickup he'd seen in Spillvagen's driveway suddenly emerged out of the murky parking lot into Bernal's consciousness. Once he saw it, it seemed obvious, like he should have spotted it from the road. It had extra chrome detailing on it, which made Bernal think Spillvagen must have bought it used. That didn't seem like Spillvagen's style at all.

Bernal felt an unexpected surge of anger. Spillvagen. What the hell was he up to? Bernal was searching for something really important. Spillvagen had deliberately lied to him, for reasons of his own, and sent him on a ridiculous detour to talk to Yolanda.

Bernal didn't usually let anger guide his actions, but being tossed around by Charis and then almost blown up had put him in a bad mood. Plus, he realized he was hungry. Might as well take care of all his current needs in one place. He pulled into the parking lot. The cowgirl above now faced away, staring off into the depths of space.

He went in to confront Spillvagen.

"May I join you?" Without waiting for an answer, Bernal slid into the booth opposite Spillvagen.

Spillvagen still wore his short-sleeved dress shirt and tie, but he'd eaten a donut with powdered sugar some time during the day, and the gondoliers now poled through a snow-covered Venice. He looked around, as if hoping for some escape. Then he shook his head. "Sure. Why not?"

"You sent me to harass Yolanda," Bernal said. "You didn't actually think she had anything at all to do with what I was interested in. You just wanted her to think that you had a lot of agents doing your bidding. Put the pressure on."

"Well . . ." Spillvagen said. "That's not strictly true. I was wondering . . . oh, Jesus, I'm sorry. But if you knew how deep her loony campaign has put me in the shit. . . ."

"Your goal should be to not get in any deeper." Bernal picked up a menu. "There are a few things I want to know."

"You want to know something? Stay away from the paella." The waiter was tall and mournful. BOB was embroidered on his bowling shirt in elaborate script that matched the menu. "I think it has squid in it. Those things evolved too long ago to be edible."

"Just a burger, Bob."

"How's the salmon?" Bernal asked.

"You ever smell one of those fish farms? Makes a beef lot seem like a resort spa. And enough PCBs and mercury to yellow your eyeballs."

"Maybe a burger." Bernal closed up his menu.

"Excellent choice." What Bob scribbled on his pad, however, seemed much more complex than their actual order. "The real question is, of course, was 9/11 Pearl Harbor, or was it the Reichstag fire? Or to put it another way, did we simply *allow* a real enemy to attack us, or did we have to *create* one? Now, don't get me wrong. I think Roosevelt did what he absolutely had to do to preserve Western civilization, however he set it up. He had to get an isolationist, xenophobic, racist, mob-ruled, Hollywood-addled nation to do its duty. Think of the challenge he had! They thought they could pull the Atlantic and Pacific oceans over their heads and go to sleep.

Greatest Generation, my ass. The last generation for whom lynching was considered an evening's light entertainment. And the whining! An overdue stock correction and they all fell on their backs and lay there for a decade with their legs in the air like stunned beetles. So FDR really had to let that bunch of losers get kicked in the ass to wake them up.

"But at least the Japanese had a country willing to mix it up, death-obsessed frat house toga party though it was." He shook his head. "What about our so-called opponents now? We finally had to go out and squat right in the middle of their territory, stick our ass in their faces, and still . . . nothing. It really does look like our enemy was a stage creation, like the burning of the Reichstag or the killing of Kirov. Maybe we should just see about dealing with our cultural gangrene on our own, but I'm betting we'll just see ever more complex manufactured disasters. Watch for an asteroid on an orbit intersecting with Earth next. That'll give us all something fun to work with. I'll see about getting these on the griddle."

They watched him march gravely into the kitchen.

"Hey, Bernal," Spillvagen said. "If anything, you look worse than you did this morning. You look like you've actually been catching flak with that jacket. When's the last time anyone actually used it for that? And that aftershave . . . very manly."

At this hour, there was no one else in the diner to smell the burnt rubber stench. He hadn't thought about it, but now Bernal fingered the cuts in his leather jacket. It had had its day. He'd have to hang it up as a souvenir.

"So," Bernal said. "Whatever happened to poor old Uncle Solly's head?"

"What, are you on first-name terms with him now?"

"Your friend Yolanda and I had quite the little chat."

"Yolanda's a psycho! She's claiming something happened, just to screw some money out of the cryobank."

"So, did it?"

"Did it what?"

"Did something happen to the head?"

"No! I mean, nothing permanent. Nothing you'd call actionable."

"I can see why Yolanda's so pissed off at you."

"Why?"

"No one likes being stonewalled when they know there's real information to be had."

"Okay," Spillvagen said. "We had a bad concatenation of events. A real failure cascade. First, an electrical fire. There was some kind of flammable insulation packed in the party wall. Old stuff, from when they built the mall. Burned out the wall. Tripped breakers and dumped our power. I mean, all of it. Hit the redundant systems, it was dark, the emergency doors didn't work, smoke alarms, nothing. Weirdest damn thing you ever saw Halon came on, though, and put the fire out. Fire never got anywhere near the dewars. But we got emergency power supplies in, hooked everything up. Cleared out what was near the wall. Not a dewar went above spec on temperature. We got the graphs, everything. Yolanda makes it seem like a really big deal."

"Yolanda had a picture. Of someone at Solomon MacParland's funeral. It was—"

Spillvagen sighed. "Of course. That was what your friend was after. I should just have given it to you."

"Muriel?"

"Yeah. She was all up on me about this company, Hess Tech, and this Madeline Ungaro woman. There was a lot of business flotsam in that mall. The stores had all closed, the owners had debt service, needed paying tenants, and weren't too picky about who it was. Lucky there wasn't,

I don't know, a lead smelter in there, or a biohazard facility. You never know what's inside an old mall."

The food had arrived. Bernal put ketchup on his fries. They were a little limp, but, hey, the place had beer, and he'd made out worse in the past.

"Like a cut-rate cryobank."

"Nothing cut-rate about it." Spillvagen took the top bun off his burger, shook his head at what he found there, and replaced it. "Shouldn't do that. Should just accept the cowgirl as my personal savior and stop asking uncomfortable questions, like 'Is the food edible?' Look, I've had my differences with the Long Voyage administration, but I have to give them this: their gear really was state of the art. Like the field kit. People with contracts don't die only when it's convenient. Our unit took care of that. Someone gets hit by a car, is bleeding to death out in the hills, the unit could be out there, sitting by him, waiting for the moment of death. As soon as the EMTs admit they're useless, the guy is sincerely dead, the field kit goes to work. The field kit pumps cryoprotectant right into the carotids, dropping the temperature slowly but steadily, bringing the body down to cryogenic temperature. I've heard of teams having to stop by the liquor store to buy out their supply of ice, trying to get the body cooled before the inevitable process of decay. Long Voyage had it down to a science. The best way to cool is from inside. Believe me, that fast perfusion really can cool you. Meanwhile, under pressure, cryoprotectants are penetrating the cells, preventing that nasty crystal formation. If it's a neurosuspension, just the head with no body, it takes only a few seconds. Think of that! And the unit would maintain the body, the head, whatever, at cryogenic temperature for as long as you needed to get it back to the bank. So, don't give me 'cut rate.' "

"What did you tell Muriel about Hess Tech?" Bernal said.

"What I've already told you. I had no idea what they did, and I'm not sure I even saw Ungaro around. Okay, we did think about expanding into their space when they left, but the issues after the fire cut into our new business. And, you know, retention isn't really our problem. It's getting new customers. . . ."

Something caught Bernal's attention, out of the corner of his eye. He glanced around, trying to figure out what it was.

"They were right next door?"

"Yes. But that's about it. Muriel was on my case about it, but I didn't really notice them much. What's up with that? What did this Madeline Ungaro do to Muriel?"

Bernal caught a swing of bobbed black hair, and a slender figure dressed in a blue coverall carried a toolkit across the end of the hallway leading past the kitchen to the bathrooms. He recognized it.

It was Patricia, the pretty, dark-haired tow-truck driver who had picked up Charis's Hummer that morning.

"Did Muriel say Ungaro had done something to her?" Bernal said.

"No, nothing like that. But it was really an important issue for her." Spillvagen looked apprehensive. "Muriel turned me on to this restaurant. Left that menu one day by accident, I checked it out, decided I liked it. What else? That's what I got. Honest. I don't really notice much, tell you the truth. Melissa's always on me for that. Tells me to pay attention. I do my best. If I think of something else, I'll let you know."

Bernal realized that the other man was frightened. Of him. Yolanda had made fun of him, but Spillvagen was genuinely intimidated. Bernal fought down a brief feeling of satisfaction and almost apologized.

But that, of course, would have been a mistake. As Muriel had once said, human relationships were reciprocal, although what was being traded was not always obvious. Suddenly backing down here wouldn't make Spillvagen like him, but it would justify Spillvagen in keeping things from him. And he was in no way persuaded that Spillvagen had given him the whole story, though that last bit about Muriel having the Near Earth Orbit menu was interesting. It wasn't her usual kind of place.

"You do that." Bernal stood up, not offering to pay his share of the bill. "I hope you manage to keep Yolanda out of your bushes."

The hallway was empty now, and Bernal pushed the bar on the rear access door and went out into the dark parking lot. There wasn't much traffic out on the road.

A panel truck stood parked against the cinder-block wall that screened the trash from view, its rear doors open and an assemblage of gear spread out on the ground behind it. A dim figure was extending a ladder to the roof. Bernal looked up. The cowgirl blazed bright above, the rocket shining between her thighs, her gaze fixed upward at something no one else could see because they just weren't big enough. Those below could only wonder at her glory.

"Patricia?" Bernal walked up to her. She looked at him. Her pale eyes were made for display in the dark. Washed out in sun, they seemed to glow in the cowgirl's reflected light.

"Who are you?" She wasn't worried. A tow-truck driver knew how to take care of herself.

"You towed a car this morning. Remember? Out on Collins."

She returned her attention to the ladder, leveling its feet and locking it to the roof edge. "I tow a lot of cars."

"It was a Hummer. You wanted to tow it to your yard, and she wouldn't let you. I just . . . I have a few questions about it. You don't have to stop what you're doing."

Despite her slight build, she was clearly strong; she smoothly lowered a set of gas canisters in a rack without making a sound. She wheeled them up to the ladder's base.

Just as he thought she would climb up without responding again, she tilted her head and looked at him solemnly. "You look like you've had a rough time. Kind of like me."

"Someone hit me." He didn't see any reason to go into the details.

"Here. You can help me." She opened the truck's cab, got out a small vinyl bag that looked like it had once held skin products, and handed it to him. "While you do, we can talk about a towed Hummer, if you want." She pulled her shirt away from her neck, revealing a long, shallow cut.

He unzipped the bag. It was full of adhesive bandages, antiseptic, antibiotic, and some concealer and foundation suitable for pale skin: the complete kit for the fashionable victim.

"I don't even know why I got that call," she said. "Come on, it will only take a second. I got to stay on it, or I'll get an infection." Patricia was skinny and birdy, with a thin collar bone and a slender neck, a type Bernal was attracted to. He put a gob of antibiotic on his finger and rubbed it across the cut that ran down toward her breast. Either she had a high metabolism, or there already was infection, because her skin felt hot under his fingertip.

"Thanks. Big help. She had me haul her out to Cooper Road, no repairs. Shouldn't complain. Paid me in cash, off the record."

"Where on Cooper Road?"

"Thirty-seven. Used to be Hemmett Oil. We ended up with some of their pumps at Ignacio's yard. Refurbished them and sold them off to Slovakia."

"She talk about what she was doing there?"

"You were with her. Don't you know?"

"I don't."

"Well, she talked about a lot of stuff. Spring training. Some show at Foxwoods. Did I think it had been a dry spring. That kind of stuff."

"Nothing else?"

"That's enough. Now it's time for me to help you." She touched his jaw with just enough pressure to get him to turn it. Her fingers felt warm too. She sprayed some stinging antibiotic on his fresh cuts.

"Something happened to you," she said. "I don't mean whatever tore you up. That's nothing. You got some damage."

It had been two years. Bernal himself had trouble seeing the traces. He thought he'd healed well. "Something blew up in my face. I mean, a few years ago, not just today."

"You have a real problem with that? Things blowing up?"

"Didn't use to."

"Oh, Jesus, he's here. What's he doing here? Why won't he just let me get my work done?" She stared at the black SUV that had just turned into the lot. "Look." She was suddenly urgent. "Do me a favor. Take this up. Will you? I'm kind of doing Bob a favor here, and Ignaz doesn't know about it." She picked up something that might have been an old reel of film, but unbalanced and weirdly heavy. "Haul this up to the roof, stick it somewhere."

"Sure," Bernal said.

"Careful with it. It's kind of delicate. And . . ."

"Yes?"

"It would really help me if you came out, in a bit, and mentioned the AC. That I'm working on the air conditioning, bringing in the Freon. Could you do that?"

"Um, sure."

She turned to go. "Wait a second," he said.

She stopped but did not look back at him. Her slim form was silhouetted by the harsh blue headlights of the SUV.

"Will you be okay?"

"I'll be fine."

She squared her shoulders, waited a second, and then stepped out into the parking lot.

14

Bernal almost dropped the thing twice on the way up. But he finally made it over the lip and onto the tar-and-gravel roof. It was surprisingly crowded up there, with heavy air-conditioning units, grease traps, and power supplies for the cowgirl's lights. There was a line of other gear, strapped under a tarp. Bernal set the new piece at the end of it.

He looked out at the parking lot and caught sight of Norbert Spillvagen driving away. He'd had enough, Bernal thought, and grinned as a silver Lexus GS peeled out of the parking lot after the orange pickup, clipping bushes as it took the corner too sharply, and accelerated down the road. Spillvagen had clearly underestimated both Yolanda's persistence and her skill as a tail.

"Pat really helps us out."

Bernal jumped at the voice, then saw the glow of a cigarette end. Bob had come up to the roof for his break.

"Yeah?"

"Regulations. Trying to drive us out of business. Big

business interests, after the diner. Any environmental regulation is easier for a big conglomerate with a million locations to comply with than a small, independent business. Always that way, and it's not accidental. Environmentalists are cat's-paws of the big guys. And they hate diners. You know that? They just got a thing about people being comfortable. Want us hoeing rows of rutabagas in the hot sun." He took another puff. "Pat helps me out, gives me those classic CFCs. Illegal cooljuice. And I let her store crap up here. Like that." He waved his cigarette at the tarp.

"Like what?"

"Ah, I don't care. Stuff she steals from her boss, I guess. We got an arrangement, her and me. I save some bucks by not upgrading to new compounds that supposedly spare the ozone layer, like anyone believes that, and she gets to transship product. Makes the world go round, right?"

"Is that what the problem is about?" Bernal paused at the lip. The parking lot was dim below. He could see a big male figure standing over Patricia's slumped, dispirited shape. The spark he'd seen in her for a few minutes there was gone.

"Could be."

Bernal now saw how far from the edge Bob was sitting. He was willing to accept whatever services Patricia provided for him but was not going to go a step farther.

Bernal had a moment of contempt for himself, wondering if he would have wanted to do the same thing, if he hadn't already agreed to go help Patricia.

Before he could think more about it, he turned and climbed back down the ladder.

Ignacio wasn't that big a guy, but his body was a tensed spring. He paced back and forth. His curly hair was trimmed perfectly around a blocky head. "I notice stuff like that, Patty girl. Answer me!"

"I just . . ." Patricia spoke so quietly you could barely hear her.

"What? You just what?"

"Never mind."

"No, really. I'm curious. I'd like to know why you took off with the maintenance truck in the middle of the goddam night to come out to this miserable place. What are you moving, Patty? What are you up to?"

"I'm not up to anything."

"Oh." Ignacio must have been working on his "obviously fake" laugh for it to sound so implausible. "You're smarter than that. You're real smart. I'm starting to see how things really fit together—"

"Excuse me," Bernal said.

The hair on the back of Ignacio's head twitched. He turned. "You!"

"Me?"

"Right. Who the hell are you?"

"Is there a problem?"

"That's not a name. 'Is there a problem' is not a name."

"Listen."

"Are you telling me to listen? To what? What am I listening to here?"

"Me."

"What?"

"You're listening to me." Bernal knew better than to try to sound ominous. That just wasn't in him. So he tried for matter of fact. As long as he kept a terrified quaver out of his voice, he should be all right. "You've interrupted my dinner."

"I'm sure sorry about that. Now that things are cleared up, you should probably get back in. We don't want your food to get cold."

"Very thoughtful."

Bernal didn't move.

"I said, you should—"

"She's here working on the air conditioning."

"And what the hell would you know about that, Mr. Sophisticated Diner?"

"I know when an HVAC crew comes in and starts clanking tanks of Freon. Kind of a pain, tell you the truth. I'm not complaining, but I know what's going on."

Ignacio stared at him for a long moment. His face was smooth and olive colored. He was handsome, actually, the kind of guy women seemed to accept bad treatment from. He wore a black suit jacket, which Bernal pretended to himself he could identify as Armani, and a white shirt that looked similarly expensive.

"You know HVAC. Everyone knows my own shit better than I do. That's just wild."

"The surplus," Patricia said, a bit louder this time. "They want to buy it here."

"Our registered illegal toxics?" In a split second, Ignacio had gone from swollen with rage to coolly professional. Bernal didn't relax. He could just as easily switch back. "The ones we got set up to ship?"

"Yes."

Ignacio stalked, stiff-legged, over to the tanks, pulled a small flashlight out of his jacket, and peered down at their tags. He whistled. "Wow. This was going to cost . . ." He tilted his head up. "How much were you paying for this stuff?"

There was no sound from the roof.

"You, up there! I'm talking to you. How much is Ms. Foote here charging you?"

The seconds stretched, and Bob finally poked his head over the edge of the roof. "Five hundred a tank."

"Five—" Ignacio was clearly startled, but recovered quickly. "You're getting a deal, my friend. A boner fide deal."

He looked at Patricia. "Were you going to tell me about this?"

"I wanted to see if it would fly first. They have some compressor repair work, too. Got to redo the paperwork, update the F numbers, all that, but it comes out pretty clean."

"Good. That's real good. If I see it juicing the bottom line, I might overlook a few things, right? And, for heaven's sake, can't you use the electromagnets to attach them to the undercarriage, like you're supposed to? Don't want to be caught with shit like that."

"You're right. Thank you."

Ignacio grinned, suddenly relaxed, moving fluidly, his hands hanging loose at his sides. "Matter of fact, there's a little reward in it for you right now, you hurry your ass back to the yard. You up?"

"I'm up."

"Let's make that trailer swing, girl. See you there." He turned to Bernal and gave him a wink. "Got to keep the staff happy. It's a full-time job."

Bernal watched Patricia's taillights as she left the parking lot, followed a moment later by Ignacio's.

"You want some more fries?" Bob was at his shoulder. "I got a lot left over. They're on the house."

"Some other time, thanks."

15

Bernal checked the address again, but it was right. Social Protection's northeastern regional headquarters really was in a cinder-block building in an industrial area on the east side of Cheriton. The access road was entirely generations of temporary hot patches, with no trace of the original roadway, and most of the other buildings were either shuttered or housed startups trying to get in touch with the area's last economic heyday, which had been some time in the 1950s.

Charis, dressed in painter's pants and a worn jean jacket, poured concrete into a hole in the ground. Below her, a toppled chain-link fence straggled down a slope to a drainage ditch. Charis had already levered out the old concrete anchors. Poles and a new coil of fencing lay next to her Hummer. It was still early, but she had clearly been busy for some time.

"What the hell are you doing here?" she said, as he got out of his van.

"What about, 'Hey, good morning'? We went through

shared danger last night. Isn't that supposed to be a bonding experience?"

"I've got nothing for you, Bernal." She didn't sound angry with him, just tired. "We've both been skunked, according to our own fashions, and we should just cut our losses. We're no good for each other."

"I need to talk to you. I have to find Muriel."

She said something he didn't hear.

"What?"

"I said, you're pretty sure she wants to be found!"

"Of course, I'm . . . what are you getting at?"

"I'm getting at a missing AI researcher, a missing funder, and a remote-controlled decoy that almost killed us both."

They must have looked pretty funny, he thought: a skinny vaguely Asian guy facing off against a gigantic vaguely Afro/Hispanic/West Asian woman, both with poorly kept hair. He was still suspicious of her motives, but she knew things that could be useful to him.

"I can help you true that, if you let me." He got out of his car. "I worked for my uncle's yard company a few summers. We did a lot of fences. What happened, by the way?"

"What happened? The usual shit happened. I'm a terrorist, you ever hear that? A lunatic who wants to drag humanity back to the Stone Age. Aside from the stupid-ass e-mails I get every day, people key my car, mail me dog shit, fun stuff like that. And, last night, in addition to trying to blow me up, someone came in here and knocked over my fence. The landlord will be on the rampage if I don't get it fixed."

Bernal looked down at the fallen fence. Something had hit the center pole, bending it almost double, and then pulled the rest of the fence right off its supports. A Bobcat lay on its side in the drainage ditch. Looked like someone had gotten it started and used it as a battering ram.

She didn't say anything else, but she didn't stop him from helping her, either. She was strong, stronger than he was, but she had a casual attitude toward fenceposts. They had to do more than look straight—they had to be straight. The previous fence had not been the best quality, so perhaps her standards had been encouraged to slip. He measured carefully. Maybe the next fence could hold back a rampaging Bobcat.

"At one time I worked in cognitive research," Bernal said. "And I have to admit, I've never heard of Social Protection."

"Yeah, we've had some positioning problems. You know, your messaging goes too far one way, you're a homicidal terrorist, the other, just an ineffective viewer-with-alarm. We hired a marketing consultant, she charged us a lot, designed a logo, wrote a few press releases no one picked up, and cashed her check."

"I searched for your name." All he'd had to go on was the logo on her travel map, but he'd finally found it.

"I hope that was informative."

"Informative. Sure. I found some kind of retro ska band, a homelessness advocacy organization, a dance club, a homemade deodorant, some kind of pyramid scheme where you sell home-security equipment to homeowners, a designer condom, and a dog-walking service. The dog-walking service had by far the best-designed Web site, by the way. Some nice Flash animations about proper leash technique."

"We neglected to trademark our name. Those lawyers have been fired."

"When I tried to tie Social Protection down to artificial intelligence, it didn't help. First of all, a lot of the same sites showed up. I guess modern home-security apparatus has a substantial AI component, homeless people benefit by communicating with AIs, the band has a song called 'Artie's Fishing Intelligence.' "

"Maybe we should fire our search engine optimization guys too."

"Charis," he said, "I don't have any reason to like or trust you. But I need to figure some things out."

She wiped her wide forehead with a bandanna. "Let's get some food. You may be a weenie, but you've earned it."

"Gee, thanks."

The office space was as bleak as the exterior: a couple of gray partitions that looked like they came from an Air Force base circa 1960, metal desks and heavy filing cabinets ditto, a Ridgid Tool calendar from three years before, showing a woman in a yellow bikini posing with a pipe wrench, and a wall sign that said SOCIAL PROTECTION: DELAYING THE SINGULARITY SINCE 2005. Coffee rings patterned the top of the minifridge in the food area. She tossed two frozen burritos into the microwave.

"You don't have to tell me that the office could use a little sprucing up. In movies your basic organizational HQ has gleaming $200 per-square-foot office space, with Herman Miller furniture and a carpet that requires weekly cleaning, not a toxic-oil-soaked square of asphalt with a cinder-block shed on it. What can I say? The donations aren't exactly rolling in."

There was no sign that anyone else used the office, though there were three desks, two of which had fast-food containers in their wastebaskets.

"I looked you up, too." Charis shook crumbs off a paper plate and dropped Bernal's burrito on it. "That was hard luck, getting blown up like that. Since it's exactly that kind of thing that gives us a bad name, I'd like to hear your story."

"What's earned you a story?"

"Tell it to me, and I'll tell you exactly why I'm so pissed off at this entire Hesketh deal. Then, having established why this is all a crock of shit, we'll go our separate ways and never see each other again. There should be a couple of packets of hot sauce in the basket there . . . careful, that's duck sauce, or some damn thing. And old too. Toss it."

"Two years ago I went to get the mail for my office. I was doing PhD work, data analysis. A project about cardiac outcomes that was getting canceled for public relations reasons, and I was searching around for another topic. There were a bunch of packages there: books, manuscripts, all kinds of things. There was . . . I don't know . . . a leak, something. A pipe, I think. There had been some kind of exhibit in the front hall, promoting something or other. Diversity, ecological awareness, open enrollment for health plans. I don't remember, but someone had shoved all the big mail over into a corner, right under the drip from the pipe. The addresses were all smeared. I hauled the stuff in."

Charis just sat next to him and listened.

"I was expecting a book on fake Minoan relics. Pulling a signal out of noise is . . . was . . . part of what I did. I'd read that many things we think of as coming from ancient Crete were actually forgeries made to reassure ourselves that Arthur Evans's Knossos was the real deal. Edwardian design with bare breasts, clearly the best of all worlds. I was eager to see how archeologists distinguished the signal from the noise. So I didn't look at the label carefully and opened the package. I clearly had my own problems with signal and noise. It detonated. Semtex."

"My God." She looked at him. "It's amazing. I think whatever happened to you yesterday did worse damage. I mean, before that decoy exploded."

"Cast-iron doggie doorstop. Another story. But, yeah. I came out of it pretty well. Good plastic surgery. I get headaches sometimes. All my fingers work."

"If it had been Caspar Nordhoff, everyone's favorite anti-AI activist, there would have been a manuscript. That was his MO. Back in the day, sitting in his asphalt shack, he could churn out ten thousand words a day on that Smith Corona upright, with the ribbon he managed to buy in a thrift store in North Platte. They found all that stuff in his fawlty in the Sand Hills. He has to write by hand now, fountain pen on copy paper. When they let him have it. But it wasn't Nordhoff."

"Why are you so sure of that?"

"As it happens, Nordhoff contacted Social Protection. Wanted to work together."

"Why didn't you?"

"Are you crazy? Because he sure was. We're a real organization, Bernal, not a bunch of nutcases. Nordhoff was nothing but bad news. After that, we kept an eye on him. I know every case, every attempt, how much he spent on postage, how many cans of Indian pudding he had on the shelves when he got arrested."

"How many?"

"Thirteen. He got them delivered from Massachusetts. He was from Ohio, but I guess he picked up the taste for classic New England cuisine while he was at MIT. The stupid stuff's easy enough to make, cornmeal, molasses, heat it up in a saucepan, that's about it, but he was too busy setting the world straight to cook." She paused. "So who had it in for you?"

One of Caspar Nordhoff's characteristics had been that he never attacked anyone famous. No Minskys, no Moravecs. His reading of cognitive science research had been deep and extensive, and he had proved an astute and perceptive critic of the field. He never tried to murder anyone who wasn't a genuine contributor to the intellectual dialogue. He picked, unerringly, only those researchers whose colleagues were in awe of them, brilliant men and women who would someday transform the field but were not yet widely known. Most of his victims had been young, although one had been a former Fidelity fund manager who turned his mathematical skills to the human mind after his retirement.

"No one had it in for me," Bernal said. "At that time, if your research had anything to do with cognition or AIs, searching through your mail for suspicious packages had become like looking for a letter from the MacArthur Foundation. One of the guys on the second floor was looking for tenure. Things were tight, the market real competitive."

She thought about that. "He faked an explosive device in his mail as evidence to his tenure committee that he was a credible scholar?"

"Yeah, well, if you're not an academic, maybe that doesn't make much sense. He didn't fake anything. It was a real bomb. He was going to pick it up, then call the bomb squad and have a professional defuse the thing, but he got delayed on the way down by a graduate student with a question, something like that. He had no idea that a leak would smear the label and that I'd pick it up and assume it was for me . . . and did I really think it was the Minoan book, or did I suspect that the Résumé Bomber had read my stuff and decided to pick me? I don't know now. The guy did some jail time and now teaches high school science."

After Nordhoff's capture at a gas station in northwestern Nebraska, the survivors had published an anthology of their work. A miscellaneous collection of learned essays by various people to honor an eminent colleague on a special anniversary, such as retirement, was called a festschrift, and *Thoughts on Thoughts, After* could have been regarded as a bizarre festschrift in honor of Caspar Nordhoff, who, of course, denounced it from his prison cell, extending its run on the *New York Times* bestseller list. Bernal had been invited, as kind of a collateral victim, to contribute. He had refused.

He'd quit without finishing his degree, even though his school offered to grant it to him almost automatically, and had drifted around, unable to settle on anything, until Muriel Inglis, having read an old article of his and then learned of what had happened to him, called him and, out of the blue, offered him a job.

"Let me ask you this question," Charis said. "What the hell were you doing out there last night, anyway? How did you find where Hesketh was supposed to be running?"

"I thought it was your turn to explain something to me."

"It is. This will help. If I understand it."

"Muriel often sends me messages that take a little effort to figure out," Bernal said. "At first, I thought she was kind of making fun of me, giving me more hoops to jump through. But as time went by, I realized that she used it not when she was sure of what she wanted to say, but when she wasn't. Or, rather, when what she wanted to say wasn't just a discrete piece of information. If it involved a mood, or some allusion, or some piece of contradiction. Plus, it was fun for her."

"Oh, like this?" Charis pulled a sheet of paper off an old beige fax machine. The top part was an ad for a sales training seminar: WANT TO IMPROVE YOUR SALES PRODUCTIVITY 330%? After a few lines of promotional text, the letters wavered. Below some completely garbled letters was an irregular line, as if someone had torn off a piece of paper, glued it over some other content, and then faxed the result.

The bottom of the sheet was part of a note in Muriel's

handwriting. The fragment started in the middle of a sentence.

"—got most of Hesketh's parts from Ignacio's D&D. Must tell Bernal. The connection isn't clear, but someone there should know a little more about—"

And that was where it ended.

"On my machine this morning. Came in while we were chasing that damn booby trap around the countryside." She folded it in half and handed it to him. "Seems like this is for you. What message did you get before this?"

"Yesterday morning. The one that took me to the power line."

"Ah. So she brought you there."

"Are you suggesting that she wanted to set me up? Kill me?"

Charis spread her hands. "I'm just suggesting that someone asked you to put your head into what proved to be the mouth of a hungry lion. If it's any consolation, I was there for pretty much the same reason. Muriel had given me Hesketh's proposed test paths for the month, so I knew where it was supposed to be. I can't claim any specific targeting on that one, though. I could have been anywhere along the path, and on any night. And Hesketh did not always follow its prescribed path. . . .

"I'd checked into Hess Tech and its doings a couple of years back, since it was a scrappy start-up with a hell of a design for a planetary exploration vehicle. It was just a vehicle with some elementary route-finding algorithms, the ability to right itself, stuff like that. Pretty sophisticated, really, not technology to sneeze at, but nothing that implied the redundancy of humanity, or anything like that. We shelved it. These AI researchers will break your heart, if you let them.

"Then, a few weeks ago, Muriel called me."

"She called you?" Bernal couldn't believe it.

"Hey, don't take it personally. She needed special

servicing. And deniability. I mean, she sends you sniffing around and you get spotted, could be a big problem with Missy Ungaro. Me—I'm just a loose cannon."

"Maybe." Bernal had thought of himself as ultimately useful to Muriel. As someone who could take care of everything. He managed lunatic animal breeders in plans for urban ecologies and dropped incentives at just the right spots to get feuding subterranean artists digging tunnels off ICBM silos to compete rather than trying to arrange for cave-ins at each others' works. Muriel saw the potentials in the situation, and he realized them. He'd never had so much fun. But it now seemed that there was something she did not think he should handle.

Or even know about.

"Let me ask you something," Charis said. "You've got your eyes on the bottom line, right? How much stuff did Ms. Ungaro buy? How much circuitry, how many processors?"

"None that I've been able to find," Bernal said. "All she drew was a lot of power, and some mechanical stuff, for the body. I haven't found anything that looks like high-end AI gear. Not since Muriel has been funding her, anyway." He'd checked the numbers that morning before coming over.

"That's what I suspected."

"Why?"

"Because the damn thing wasn't an AI at all. I mean, it seemed kind of smart, running around there, but that's just another step, not the end product. It was just a fancy gadget. Muriel had some reason to get me on Ungaro, and it wasn't because Hesketh had suddenly transcended its mechanical nature. I got set up. Maybe you did too. Here."

She reached into a drawer and pulled out a high school yearbook with colorful pictures of student groups at various angles on the cover. It said Cheriton High School on it. She opened it to a marked page and spun it around for Bernal to look at. The double-page spread showed the rectangles of smiling senior photos.

"What—?"

"Just look. You'll find it. You ever wonder why Madeline Ungaro ended up in Cheriton, Massachusetts, working on a low-budget planetary probe program? What the hell she's after?"

With that clue, subliminal though it was, Bernal found it. Two thirds of the way down the right-hand page, in the middle, was the gently smiling photograph of a beautiful blond girl named Madeline Cantor. There was no doubt that it was a photograph of a young Madeline Ungaro. He looked up at the grim Charis.

"Okay. Now that you have her pegged, back in her previous incarnation, you can make sense of this."

She pulled out a clipped newspaper article with the heavy gothic masthead of the *Cheriton Telegraph-Examiner*, a decade and a half old.

Local Boy Dies in Climbing Accident

Paul Inglis, 17, son of Tommy and Muriel Inglis of Walnut Street, Cheriton, died yesterday in a fall in the Shawangunk Mountains of New York. Apparently, he was attempting a dangerous pitch in the Skytop area. A succession of cold nights and warm days resulted in some unexpected fracturing in the rock face, causing a large piece of rock to peel off, taking Paul Inglis with it. According to local climbers, Inglis had followed his partner beyond his level of ability.

Inglis's climbing partner, Madeline Cantor, also 17, was unable to revive him after his fall. She ran to get help, but by the time an emergency team reached him, it was too late. He was pronounced dead at Kingston Hospital at 6 PM.

The funeral service will be held at the Inglis home, 217 Walnut Street, on Thursday. . . .

"And now she and Muriel are both gone." Charis spoke with a kind of glum satisfaction. "I feel like a fool for getting anywhere near this personal revenge crap."

"What? Just because Ungaro was involved in the death of her son a long time ago? This all seems pretty elaborate."

"Believe me, people around here remember what happened," Charis said. "He followed Madeline where even she shouldn't have been going, and she was a much better climber than he was. Experienced enough to think about the rock, too. But that girl liked taking risks. Muriel thought she was testing him, seeing how far he'd go. All the way, as it turned out. Muriel always blamed the girl. No one thought that was fair, but they understood."

Muriel had never said anything, never mentioned that the AI researcher she was funding had once been involved in the death of her son. And now Muriel and Madeline were both missing. What else had Muriel been keeping from him?

"I don't know about you, but I don't like being gamed," Charis said. "Muriel tried to game me. I don't think there is any AI. She just wanted to harass this woman, Ungaro, Cantor, whatever. Madeline. Maybe worse than just harass."

"But if Ungaro had no AI, then what's she been doing here for the past two years?" he said.

"Who knows? And I suppose there's someone who cares, but it sure as hell isn't me. Not anymore."

"Come on," Bernal said. "You did the work. I know you did. No reason for it to go to waste."

"Everything goes to waste, eventually." Charis sighed. "Oh, okay. Jesus. The girl did create herself an interesting life, looks like. Dropping someone down the side of a mountain was just a start. Somehow she slid right over and ended up at Caltech. Kept to herself there, did her work, moved on to graduate work, started her own research project, part privately funded. Cognitive algorithms having to do with movement, maneuver, orientation. Did animal work. Chimps, seems like. Hard to get the records, because at one point some radical animal-rights types broke into her lab and, seemingly by accident, started a fire that destroyed the whole thing. I never found a casualty list for the animals, and all that has to be registered. She was working on chimps, what I've found says so, and those animal-rights terrorists clearly thought she had animals, but there's no sign any of them were killed in the fire. And it was a big one.

"All her work was destroyed, whatever she was working on. So she quit. She gave up her research position and went to sit in a redwood tree in Northern California."

"What?" Bernal said. "Why?"

Charis shrugged. "Someone was trying to cut it down. A lot of board feet in one of those things. Activists got all excited, decided to take a stand on the trees. Madeline was tough. She sat up there for over a year. Weather's not like around here, but that still must have taken some 'nads. Quite a poster child for the movement. Bulldozers and lumberjacks sat there, she sat there. Even people in the movement found her odd, but she was useful because she didn't seem to need to talk to anyone. Perfectly happy just sitting a hundred feet up in a tree, thinking about stuff. And she was damn good at evading the extractors the lumber company hired to get her out. One of those guys fell out of the tree while chasing her, broke his leg. Maybe that hit too close to home. Not too long after that, she climbed down and walked away. She didn't tell any of her movement associates that she was leaving her post. So by the end of the day, the tree was down, and that particular environmental skirmish was over."

"Where did she go after that?" Bernal said.

"Here."

"She came home to Cheriton?"

"Yep. Doesn't seem like the kind of girl to do that, does she? This one dedicates herself to something until, for one reason or another, she doesn't, and steps smoothly away, moving on to something else. Returning to something seems out of character. Well, we're all still allowed to act out of character, aren't we? Her mother died about that time, so maybe she came back for the funeral and stayed. But I think she came back to see someone else."

"Muriel," Bernal said.

"Was there a weepy scene of reconciliation? Stranger things have happened . . . actually, no, they haven't. I've met Muriel, I think I understand Madeline. That particular scene never happened. But Muriel did help Madeline find a job at Hess Tech. And when Hess Tech went under, spotted her some funding to keep working on Hesketh. Then got worried about what Madeline was actually working on, and called me. And I found out it was all bullshit. Because Muriel never did get over losing her boy, and probably wanted Madeline around to give her a hard time. So, now you know it all. Help any?"

Bernal thought about it. "What was Madeline working on in California before she got burned out?"

"Like I said, no idea. Didn't get that far. I did have a contact, a guy I found who was one of the terrorists, from a group called the Bald Chimps, if you can believe that—"

"Charis, there's more to it than we see. This isn't some kind of delayed revenge for a climbing accident. Muriel set Madeline Ungaro up with a lab and then began to realize that there was more going on. That's why she called you. I want to know what Muriel figured out.

This guy you were talking to, your Bald Chimp, any way I could get in contact with him?"

Charis stared at him in disgust, big cheeks puffed out. "Tell you what. As my last act before closing the book on this case, I'll let him know you're interested. If George feels like talking, he'll call you. Or you can go visit him."

"Where is he?"

"Prison. Facility in southern Illinois. Seems Ungaro's lab wasn't the last place he hit, and he ran into more trouble. This whole thing is full of charming types, isn't it? I'm glad to get out."

"Don't you care what might have happened to Ungaro, then?" Bernal said. "Or Muriel for that matter?"

"No. I'm done. I've turned the case over to you, my friend. Go to Ignacio's junkyard, talk to my prison buddy, whatever. I ask only one favor."

"What?"

"Don't keep me updated on the case. Thanks for the help on the fence, and good luck."

16

Inside the office of Ignacio's Devices and Desires, two men, one middle-aged, one young, but both with the look of calm satisfaction car guys always seemed to have, briskly processed customers from behind a counter laminated with old repair manuals. They produced, in short order, a cam shaft for a bushy-haired Latino in creased trousers and a NASCAR T-shirt who rejected offers of help, put the thing over his shoulder, and walked deliberately out; a power-steering pump for two large-chested black guys in golf shirts; and an air-conditioning compressor for a tensely fit middle-aged white woman in a red dress, who asked about its provenance, maintenance record, and efficiency before finally accepting it. Bernal admired her calves as she walked out.

Bernal went up to the desk. The young guy was alone, the older one having vanished through the door into the yard.

"I need to talk to Patricia," Bernal said.

"We handle car parts here." He was tattooed with a mixture of slashing monochromatic tribal patterns and delicately shaded, almost Pre-Raphaelite images of knights and damsels. "Other stuff too, by special appointment. Cyclotrons. Whatever."

"I just want to—"

"Look." His gray eyes were intense. "You guys come in. All the time you come in. Try to fix her. Help her out. I think some of us might have tried it, too. But she's not interested in your help."

The older guy slid back behind the desk. He looked back and forth from Bernal to the young guy. "What's up?"

"This gentleman is worried about Pat."

"I just want to ask her a question!"

The older guy blew out his cheeks. "We don't want trouble. We got a business to run."

Bernal had an inspiration. "It's about a cooling problem. If you know what I mean."

The two men exchanged a glance. "Not that Freon shit again." The young guy was irritated. He pulled out a hand-rolled cigarette and put it behind his ear. "I'm tired of it." He walked out.

"It's just that Pat and the boss have an arrangement." The older guy pulled out some brochures advertising a car show and made a show of fanning them out on the counter. "To others, it seems to be broken. But it works for them."

"I'm not interfering with anything. I just want to talk to her."

The guy paused, glanced behind him at a door, then shrugged. "If anyone asks, you snuck in through the automatic gate when a delivery came through."

A man wearing a cashmere sweater with a hole in the elbow came up to the desk.

"Um, my car's pulling to the left. It's a Honda. Accord, '04."

"Okay." The counter guy was noncommittal.

"It's when I put on the brakes. Sometimes it's pretty sharp. My wife's worried about it."

"Your wife's smart."

The man pulled out a piece of paper with a long drug name logo in purple across the top, and a penned list of parts. "I know what parts I need."

"Take it to the shop. I can recommend a couple of good ones. Buddies of mine. Won't gouge you too bad. And you won't get killed next week. Good deal."

The doctor's manhood had been challenged. "I've already got it up on floor jacks."

The counter guy sighed. "Be a few minutes." He took the list and disappeared through the door, leaving it half open. Late afternoon sun spilled through.

The doctor sat down on a recycled bucket seat with Smurf decals on the back, pulled out a Chilton's, and opened to a grease-stained page. He stared intently at a photograph of a disassembled brake.

Bernal waited a few moments, then went around the counter and through the door.

He found Patricia in a narrow area surrounded by stainless steel medical refrigerators plastered with biohazard warning signs and yellowing doctor/patient cartoons, many of them featuring large-breasted nurses. The politically incorrect cartoons showed the age of these refrigerators. And the age of the dangerous but still-marketable chlorofluorocarbons inside them.

"Thanks for helping me out last night." Patricia Foote stacked compressors on something that looked like a golf cart. She clicked something with her toe and the golf cart whizzed off, without driver or other guidance.

Bernal thought he could see where guide wires had been buried in the ground.

"You're welcome. I hope it worked out." He thought about Ignacio's coming back here to have sex with his abused employee.

"Oh, it worked out fine."

"I have a question for you."

"What?"

"Yesterday, when you towed that Hummer—"

"Haven't you already asked me about that?"

Bernal was startled by her sharpness. "I wasn't going to ask you about that. I just wanted to know, do you guys deliver stuff there?"

"Nah."

"Oh."

"That lady there, Ungaro. She comes here to pick up. Come on, I'll show you."

He followed her out of the dead end with the medical refrigerators and past a rack of massive pumps, the hex nuts that held their flanges the size of walnuts. The yard was amazingly trim and well-organized. Parts lay on racks, bar codes stenciled on their sides. They passed the dismantling area. Bent, torn, and flame-blackened cars, the gouges of their final accidents still shiny, snuggled against each other with the easy familiarity of the damned. Several had already been eviscerated. Another driverless golf cart scooted by, this one holding a box full of electrical cables.

Patricia sucked a breath through her nose, and Bernal realized that she was crying. "Why? Why all this shit? It's stressful. I got a spot, you know? A good spot. I'm *good* at this shit. Learned it from a boyfriend, in high school. Not . . . I wasn't in high school anymore. Should have been, I guess. But after the accident and everything . . . well, no one expected much of me after that, and I don't guess they got it. Merrick knew cars and shit. Really knew 'em, but he wasn't one of these guys like around here, it wasn't like he ran carnival rides in the summer and scared kids. You know?"

"I think so."

"He, like, knew what things were like, underneath, inside. Why they did the things they did. Not people. No. People were, what did he call them? Dark boxes?"

"Black boxes?"

"Yes. Right!" And in her pleasure at his getting the right answer, a smile almost made it to her face. Almost, but it glanced off some invisible obstruction and sank again. "Like your head is shut in a black box, and it can't see nothing or hear nothing when you try to think about how people work. I know that. I know that feeling now. I learned how to do all that stuff. Fix cars and computers and lawnmowers and shit. Couldn't do anything at school, but I had the way for that. So I don't . . . I don't want to lose this place, you know? There's a lot of shit, sure, but what place in the world doesn't have a lot of shit? It's all a matter of how you handle it. How you take it on."

She led him to a back area, where random gear lay piled on pallets.

"Your friend Muriel came around asking about the woman in that lab where I met you. Ungaro. Her company's always been a good customer here. Picked up a lot of interesting stuff. Merrick would have loved that stuff she needs."

"'Would have'?"

"Merrick's dead."

"How?"

"Merrick pulled some leaf springs off an old truck. Those things are whippy. He made . . . I don't know why, it wasn't like for a history project or anything, he usually didn't care about stuff like that . . . a crossbow. Big-ass thing. His parents never seemed to care much, but his mom did say that it made it hard to park the car in the garage. She was always worried about scratching the paint. But they didn't ask what the thing was for."

"What did he use for arrows?"

She gave him an appraising look, and he wondered if his choice to be practical rather than sympathetic had been the right one. "Those green fence posts, the kind you string square mesh on. They have flanges, like rockets. Merrick, he . . . they said suicide. Screwup, is what I think. He cocked the thing, just to see, you know, what tension you need. He went to readjust something at the piece of plywood he used as a target, and some bunch of crap fell down, set the crossbow off. His parents always packed the garage with shit, you know? Magazine, cans—anyway, something dropped. The fence post went . . . right through him. I ran away from home the next day. Maybe they still think I had something to do with it, I don't know. I had other things to worry about."

She gestured at a shelf. "Take a look at it. This is Ungaro's stuff. She's late getting it. Maybe you'll learn something. I'll be right back."

He watched her swing off. Whatever had happened between her and Ignacio the previous night had increased the confidence of her movement. He didn't want to think about what that might have been. His own sexual needs were pretty much straight down the middle. He wasn't embarrassed about that. But sometimes what other people did for pleasure still startled him.

The shelf was loaded with tiny metal nozzles. The tubing that had once connected them lay neatly coiled next to them. At the end of the shelf was a pair of large compressors. From what Bernal could tell, all hooked up, they would have pushed air through the tubes and out of the nozzles. Something from a Jacuzzi? It seemed excessive, though they might have been for a very large one. The compressors were marked Aker Finnyard.

Madeline Ungaro hadn't picked this stuff up. That was interesting, but didn't really add much to what he already knew.

"Well, well, well, if it isn't Mr. Independent Testimony."

Bernal turned to find Ignacio behind him, staring at him with gray-green eyes.

"I came to see if Patricia was all right," Bernal said.

"Okay. And is she?"

"I don't know."

"You don't know. What would it take for you to know?"

"I don't—"

"Maybe a few hours with her bare skin and a magnifying glass? Would you like a chance at that, eh?"

"What's this stuff for?" Bernal pointed at the nozzles and compressors.

"Eh?" Ignacio seemed taken aback by the change of topic. "Looks like icebreaker hull stuff . . . hey. Hey. You planning on buying them? No. No, because they're already under consignment. Never mind what they are."

Some icebreakers used bubbles to break ice adhesion on their hulls. It looked like Ungaro had been planning some extensions to Hesketh's body plans. "So, you maintain client confidentiality?"

"Sure do. People got their business and like to deal with those as don't blab about it. You got any questions I might feel like answering?"

"You ever see a woman named Muriel Inglis around here?"

"I don't do much direct customer work. I leave that up to my employees. But there are some kinds of stuff I like handling myself." He stepped a few inches closer.

"Older woman. Nice dresser." Bernal inclined his head at Ungaro's icebreaker gear, not wanting to set things off by moving too much. He was terrified of the other man, but he would be damned if he'd show it. He'd never been able to dominate other men physically, though he could give a good account of himself if absolutely necessary.

"More poking around!" Ignacio was outraged. "I know just who you mean. She sauntered in, just like you, and—"

"Ignaz—" Patricia had returned.

"Don't call me that!" He closed his eyes. "I hate it when you call me that."

She thrust out her chin. "I'll call you what I want."

"*What?*"

"Bernal's here to help me. To get away from your shit. So I can call you what I want, Ignaz."

"Come here." Ignacio's voice was now quiet.

"No . . . I . . ."

"Come here."

Bernal wanted to yell at her to run but wasn't sure that was quite the right thing to do, and she stepped forward before he could think of what would be better.

Without any windup, Ignacio slapped her. He was standing right next to Bernal, and the rest of his body barely moved. The sound of the slap was loud among the shelves. Her head jerked, but she didn't put a hand up to her reddening cheek. Instead, she just looked at Ignacio. Just him, past Bernal, as if Bernal was not even there.

Before Bernal could move, Ignacio had shoved him back against the shelves. His arm was like iron.

"Go back to work, Patricia." Ignacio spoke gently. "I got some things to do. We can talk this over a bit later."

Patricia turned and walked away.

Bernal stared after her, unable to suppress a feeling of betrayal.

"Not a great idea," Bernal said.

"Don't talk to me about my ideas. You broke into a dangerous industrial area. I mean, you could end up in a car that gets picked up by the magnet, dropped in the compactor. And wearing a nicer jacket than when you gave me shit last night. A real pity."

Bernal tugged at his leather collar. "Jesus. Don't you think they'd investigate you? Shut this place down? And don't ask what it would do to your insurance rates." Bernal tried to play it light. But he knew that people could kill you, even when it didn't make any sense whatsoever.

"Yeah. The human body is such an annoyingly *physical* thing, isn't it? Just another form of toxic waste, really. And you're right about those premiums. Eat you alive. Come on. Let me . . . escort you out."

They walked through the narrow aisles between the car parts.

A cell phone played the first few bars of *The Flying Dutchman*. Ignacio stopped near a stack of wheel rims and pulled it out. He put it between his ear and his shoulder. With his other hand, he pulled out a savage-looking serrated knife and pressed it against Bernal's throat.

"Yeah?" As he talked, Ignacio looked off down the wide aisle.

"Those things have decent magnets on them." He was all business. "But, I don't know, that mercury . . . Look, you know as well as I do that they use security as a way of getting out of taking care of their waste. Look at that crap from Area 51. If they *did* have aliens there, they'd have died from the PCBs and the heavy metals." He laughed. "And it's these bastards from Liverwurstmore . . . I mean, they'll try to sell you a coffee maker and tell you it's an industrial annealer. Am I right, or am I right? So you got to be careful . . . look, tell you what. I'll take four of them for, oh, two thousand each, and check them out. Take 'em apart, run some tests. We'll spread the risk. Sound good?"

His voice was completely calm, as if Bernal had never

been. Bernal shifted his weight. The knife pressed firmly against his throat. He could feel the tips of the serrations pushing through his skin. He barely breathed.

"So, let me know." Ignacio folded his phone and calmly put it back in his pocket.

Jesus, Bernal thought. This guy could kill me. And he had no idea why. Ignacio was jumpy and paranoid about something. Bernal didn't think it was just car parts. God only knew what Bernal had been near, there at Ungaro's stuff.

A golf cart like the one Patricia had been loading things into zipped down the aisle. It slewed sideways suddenly and ran into the bottom of a stack of wheel rims. They toppled over, and Ignacio dodged out of their way, releasing Bernal in the process. The wheel rims hit the concrete in a succession of rings, bounced, and rolled off in all directions.

Bernal took the opportunity and ran. He dodged around struts that stuck out of the shelves at irregular intervals. Behind him he heard footsteps, then a crash and a shout.

He took a chance and turned to look.

Ignacio had struck his head against a strut. Blood poured out between his fingers, and he sank to his knees. "Oh my God. . . . Patricia! Where are you?"

Patricia came up to him and, heedless of the blood, put her arms around him. Neither of them paid the slightest attention to Bernal.

Someone stood next to him. It was the young guy with tattoos. He shook his head at Bernal.

"Don't ruin the payoff," he said. "Things only get really bad around here when you ruin the payoff."

Bernal followed him out of the yard, not daring to glance back again.

Bernal glanced in his rearview mirror as he pulled out of the parking lot, and slammed on the brakes.

A bunny in a bonnet dangled right in his field of view. He pulled off into a rougher parking area, down below the yard, maneuvering carefully between two concrete blocks with rusty tangles of rebar sticking above them like failed comb-overs.

It wasn't a threat. The thing hadn't been hung there to scare him.

He instantly recognized a message from Muriel. He yanked the rabbit off the pink ribbon that suspended it from the roof and examined it. There was nothing in the basket of Easter eggs, or under the bonnet, or printed on the linings of its long ears.

How the hell had she gotten the thing into his car? She'd known he would be at the yard, of course—she had sent him there. So she had sent some minion, or just hired some high school kid adept at breaking into cars.

She really was pushing it.

He turned the bunny over again and this time saw the button on its back. He pushed it.

Vaguely, through static, he could hear the tinkle of "Here Comes Peter Cottontail." Then it cut off, and there was silence.

"Bernal." The fidelity wasn't good enough to recognize a voice, but it had to be Muriel. ". . . sorry . . . been out of contact . . . no chance . . ." Then it got clearer. "Talk to Jord. He's a drug dealer in Creek Hollow. He's worried about the Easter Bunny . . . someone dumping drugs in abandoned places . . . as bait . . ." More static. ". . . information . . . say you talked to me . . . pay attention . . ." Then clearer again. "I'll try to find another way to talk to you. This will be blocked soon. And Charis . . ." The static sounded like a waterfall. ". . . trust her. . . ."

And that was it. Peter Cottontail finished up.

He listened to the message a couple more times.

Jord the drug dealer, and the Easter Bunny. Was this just another attempt to get him killed?

Ignacio's Devices & Desires loomed above him like a fortress with walls of rust-streaked corrugated metal. Chunks of concrete littered the steep hillside. New supports had been poured here and there to keep the fence from losing its grip and tumbling down the slope. This last winter had dug a particularly deep gully. Bernal followed it up with his eyes. Water had eroded the earth under the yard's asphalt, and, unsupported, it had collapsed.

The gap looked at least a couple of feet high.

Well, that was just great, but there was certainly no way he was going in there again. Let those people do to each other whatever they wanted to do.

He had an appointment with a drug dealer.

17

The identical three-story buildings of Creek Hollow stretched along the road in clusters of three and four. Hooded teenagers in doorways watched Bernal's car as he drove past. A woman pushed a stroller with one malfunctioning wheel up the hill, plastic shopping bags from Food World dangling from the handles.

"Hey," he said to a couple of teenagers, one black, one white. "Where's Jord?"

They didn't say anything, their faces impassive in their hoods.

"He's, like, a friend of a friend. Um, Muriel Inglis said to talk to him."

Finally, still not saying anything, one of them jerked a thumb to the left, toward a courtyard.

"That's really a question, isn't it?" Jord was thin, light-skinned, and looked barely out of high school. He wore a red shirt, open to expose a hairless chest. "Really a question. The Easter Bunny. But, now, I got one for you."

"Okay." Bernal couldn't quite believe he was here, talking to this guy. It was bold and scary, but he was doing it because it made sense to do it.

He'd have to feel impressed with himself later.

"How you hear? Why are you interested in who's dumping drugs around? I know you guys, I see you. Not your thing. I see you, I be moving you along, you're nothing but a tourist. No offense."

"No, of course not. A friend of mine, a woman named Muriel Inglis. She asked me to check up on this for her."

"Well, hell, aren't you a nice friend, though."

The secret to Jord's success was obviously the fact that he could make any phrase sound pleasant and ominous at the same time. There was no way to tell what was going on behind his smooth face.

"I don't have any interest in interfering with your operations."

Jord laughed. "I don't think you'd be interfering for long. Not scared of that. I've run into Muriel. Smart lady. And balls. I seen her poking in boilers in abandoned buildings and shit. The Easter Bunny. Well, and look at that." He turned to look at something across the parking lot. "Hey. Hey! Spak! Come over here, will you? The gentleman's got an important question he needs answered."

It would have been impossible to load any more black garbage bags into the shopping cart. They were piled so high that even a sharp turn would have sent them cascading. A few had ripped, and clothes poked out of the holes. A heavy black man trotted along behind it. It was impossible to tell how old he might have been. He moved with buttock-wiggling vigor but did not make much progress across the cracked asphalt of the parking lot.

For a moment, it looked as if he wasn't going to react, but finally, he shifted direction and drifted toward them.

The shopping cart was from Caldor's, a discount chain that had vanished some years before. It was amazing that he'd kept it functional all that time. Jord winced as it seemed to be about to run into the fender of his perfectly polished Lexus, but Spak had more control than it looked and stopped a foot or so short.

"Tell him, Spak. Tell him what you've found for me. The man has, like, an interest in my business. How it works and shit."

Spak wore sunglasses with one lens missing and brightly colored medical scrubs.

"They got . . ." He was out of breath. He yanked at the neckline of his scrubs. "Someone dumped a whole bunch of these. Found 'em the other night where I was sleeping. We could all wear them."

Jord grinned at Bernal. "Not my kind of fashion statement, Spak. Tell us about the Easter Bunny."

"I don't know nothing about no Easter Bunny." Spak didn't want to look at Bernal. "I don't want to do it anymore, Jord. Don't wanna do it."

"Why not, Spak?" Jord sounded perfectly reasonable. "Doesn't the extra money keep you in clothes?"

"Don't need more clothes. Got plenty of clothes. People throw the most amazing shit out. Like . . . look at this—"

"I don't want to look at any frickin' underwear you pulled out of some landfill, Spak."

Spak finally looked at Jord. He adjusted his glasses, as if having one sunglass lens gave him the proper stereoptic view. "People now shoving . . . *machines*, strange shit, out there. Still *working*. Can hear 'em hum, you put your head right up to 'em."

"That what you see while you're looking for the drugs? You still see it once you find what you need?"

Spak looked stubborn. "I know what I seen."

Jord turned to Bernal. "Since he's being kind of shy . . . The Easter Bunny. That's what the street folks call him, her, whatever, anyway. Someone floats around and, get this, *gives* drugs. Gives 'em out! In, like, a little scavenger hunt thing. Hides the drugs places. Packet of H. A few pills in a baggie. Even weed. All over the place. Well, not in your normal kind of place. Old buildings, like I saw your friend checking out. Abandoned cars. In culverts. Spots people like my bud Spak like to hang out."

"Hate culverts," Spak said. "They flood."

"Smart." Jord was getting bored. "Real smart."

"Bad for business?" Bernal guessed. "Too much free product floating around."

"Nah. Not so much. Demand is, like, big. A few free samples don't put a dent in it. But, my question is: who's moving in? I think that's my explanation. I mean, some stores, you know, they give stuff away free to get people to come, buy other stuff. You ever hear of that?"

"Sure. Free samples. Loss leaders."

"Loss leaders? Nice. I got some free skin cream the other day. Kind of greasy, though. You use skin cream?"

"I've been known to."

"What?" Jord eyed him with what Bernal was startled to see was a new respect. "What do you use?"

"Skin So Soft."

"Skin So Soft. You like it?"

"It seems to do the job."

"I'll have to try it. Particularly in the winter. But I don't like that greasy shit. Even though it was free. Got it in the mail, in a little bag. You ever get those? In the mail?"

"Sure."

"I hate all that crap I get in the mail."

"How long has this been going on?"

"Long time, I think. Maybe a year. Someone moving in, they're taking their sweet time about it. But I keep an eye on it. Through people like my man Spak here. He's been keeping an eye out for me. But it sounds like he's finding all kinds of useless shit instead."

"I been *looking*," Spak muttered. "I ain't going down the Black River no more. Don't need those gadgets. Don't need no frosted bowling balls."

Jord sighed, having gotten bored. Bernal wasn't sure the question of the Easter Bunny had any real interest for him to begin with. It was more a professional concern, something he knew he should keep an eye on.

"Get going, Spak. Have a nice day."

Bernal and Jord watched Spak trot away across the parking lot.

"Twitches his butt like a cheerleader," Jord said. "What's up with that, d'you think?"

18

Bernal sat on a rolled sleeping pad and checked images. He'd taken another set of pictures and was now comparing what things had looked like the first day he came into Ungaro's lab with the way they looked now. If anything had been moved, if Ungaro had snuck back in while he was out or asleep, it would stand out as different.

Madeline had disappeared from the scene before, sliding neatly out from under Paul's death, the destruction of her lab. But he couldn't imagine her just leaving her creation like this.

She had to still be around somewhere.

His phone rang.

"Hey. Charis Fen said you were interested in the Bald Chimps." The speaker introduced himself as George. He had once been an animal-rights activist but in prison had joined a group called the Sons of Klaatu, some kind of white-supremacist organization. "We got set up. I'll bet you hear that a lot. I hear it, too. Don't hear much else, actually. But true, here. We all got set up. We all got ourselves tempted. Without temptation we'd be happy frickin' campers, singing 'Kumbaya' and making 'smores over the campfire. Right?"

"My chocolate never melted," Bernal said.

"What?" The connection was sharp. Despite being locked in a cell in southern Illinois, George sounded like he was breathing in Bernal's ear. "What did you say?"

"The chocolate." Bernal held the phone a little away from his head. "For the 'smores. Never melted. The marshmallow . . . I don't know. Not enough heat. Heat content. I forget the physics. . . ."

"Huh. I never had trouble. Next time you try it? Just warm the chocolate over a hot Girl Scout beforehand." George laughed wetly. "Always worked for me."

Bernal resisted the urge to dab his ear with a tissue. "You were an animal rights activist?"

"Hey. I paid the price for it, too. Try to save animals from torture, and they throw you in prison. Hell of a situation, eh? It's a brutal world out there. Why do you ask?"

"It's just that you don't . . ."

"Yeah?"

"Sound like one."

"Like some faggy crunchy cute-animals-with-big-eyes type guy? That what you mean?"

"Well . . . yes."

"It's a real genuine moral issue, buddy. Our responsibility to those we torture, kill, and eat. Not some kind of joke. It just tends to attract a bad element. That kind of whiny douche bag element you were just kind of mentioning. So, sure, you get the lames. People with multiple chemical sensitivity. Phobias. Scary weight problems. You run into people allergic to cats who own five, get shots every week, put pictures of them on their Christmas cards, and never put a sock on any of their heads, even at a party. Even for the pleasure of guests. Even though there's not a decent cat in the world that doesn't see being abused that way as a sign of true affection. So, I was kind of put off at first, as you would expect. It all happened, though. The mission happened. Following your morals can end you up with all sorts of sketchy types, you see what I'm saying."

"So what was Madeline Ungaro working on in that lab? What were you trying to destroy?"

"Nothing funnier than a cat with a sock on its head. Ever see one back up trying to get the damn thing off?"

"Sure."

"Okay, okay, so it's evidence of the fundamental evil of the human spirit and how we should really be extinct so that all the other beasts can start living it up again, laying eggs in our rotting foreheads, whatever. I've heard all that. I'm sorry about it, real sorry, but it still makes me bust a gut. Particularly after a couple of beers. They'll back up all the way around the room. Dumbasses."

"I'll have to give it a try," Bernal said.

"Hell, you called to talk about something serious, right? Not some kind of regular fun thing I may never get to do again in my life. Okay. Let's get ourselves serious. You ever wonder what happened to the aboriginal inhabitants of this continent? And I mean the originals, the Solutreans who came across from Europe in skin rafts, lived in peace with the megafauna, and then went down along with every mammoth, ground sloth, and short-faced bear when those damn Asians came strutting across the Bering Bridge with their fancy Clovis points. You ever spare a moment to think about their fate?"

Bernal considered connecting George with the South Dakota mammoth project, but realized that that wouldn't be doing anyone any favors. "Was this your motivation for setting a fire in Madeline Ungaro's lab? Pleistocene megafaunal extinctions?"

"It's all related, buddy, it's all related. Peace-loving, animal-loving Europeans are our honored ancestors. Might look weird at first, not like what your prejudices want you to believe, everyone's on 'colonialism,' 'genocide,' 'slavery,' all that crap, but it fits. I won't say all the Bald Chimps bought into that line, though. There was a diversity of opinions. But, actually, you know, I don't got much time. Lights out is pretty soon, and they can get kind of rough with infractions."

"I'll try to move it along," Bernal said.

"One of the guys learned what she was doing in that lab. Experimenting on chimps. On their brains. That makes for good PR, you know, chimps with skulls sawed open, that kind of weird stuff. Scientists."

"Chimps," Bernal said. "What were the experiments? What was going on?"

"Who knows, really?" George sounded disgusted. "We were going to go in, grab a bunch of stuff, take pictures of the chimps, all that, have a press conference, present the evidence, really get some mileage. But we had some cowboys on the team. They were going to show exactly how much stuff like that disgusted them, so when we got in there, they set a fire. You know, some old files, binders, crap like that, a squirt of lighter fluid, and *foof*, you got a little fire. I was yelling at them, they were crazy, that sets the alarms off, so that's what you do last, if you feel like it. Dead last.

"I think that place was kind of unregulated, if you see what I'm saying. Corners being cut, inspections not being done. Anyway, the alarms didn't go off. And the fire spread like hell. I mean, isn't everything supposed to be flame retardant these days? This kinda crap only happens in movies. But the place went up fast.

"But that's fine, because there wasn't anything there, nothing like what we were looking for. No cages, no food, no live-animal gear. Believe me, there's a lot of it.

You got to keep those things alive in order to experiment on them. All there was was a whole lot of stuff that seemed to be cooled with liquid nitrogen."

"What?" Bernal said. "You recognized that?"

"You still think that because I care about animals I must be kind of a moron."

"No," Bernal said. "I don't think that at all."

"Well, don't think it, because it's not true. Yeah. Cooling equipment, big humping bunches of it. A line of coolers. And stuff hooked up, you know, wheeled carts, manipulator arms. Robotics stuff, not like you'd expect to find in a place like that at all. And here's the thing . . ."

Bernal waited.

"I was looking around, trying to figure out where the hell those supposed chimps were, when something touched me on the back of the head. Well, that scared the crap out of me, as you might imagine. I might have jumped. Screamed, even. Don't know. It happens. No sense in pretending it don't. And, okay, that might be what panicked the guys. Everyone was already on edge, you know, and they might have jumped the gun on the fire because of that. That's pretty much what they claimed afterwards, anyway.

"It was one of those damn arms. It kind of stroked the back of my head. I felt like there was something there. Something watching me. Something real, something that understood things. Maybe that's me 'claiming afterwards,' just like those morons with the lighter fluid. How do I know? I only got this brain, and I'm like inside it, so it's not like I can go back and run the tape. I'm stuck with the rumors behind the news. Anyway, that's when things got out of control and we had to bail.

"We got nothing. And I mean nothing. There weren't even any chimps there, or at least none that I saw. Just a bunch of stuff. Turned out all the records were there, everything, even the backup disks, the whole works.

After it was all over, she'd lost every bit of research, and no one had a damn idea of what she had been working on. Weird, huh? It must have depressed the hell out of her, because she left right after that. Sat up a tree, I hear. A victim of out-of-control animal-rights activists, was the story. There's always a story. We got pulled in, questioned, the works, they weren't nice to us, not a bit, but there was no proof. Everything. Everything was destroyed. They had to let us walk.

"We didn't get along too well after that, us Bald Chimps. Chimps are aggressive too, you know. Don't think they aren't. Kill each other over a nice piece of jungle. So I broke off, moved back to the Midwest, joined a group over at the University of Illinois. Champaign. And that last little mission . . . well, let's just say, I've had a lot of time to think things over in this here five-to-ten aftermath. There's a lot to think about."

At the risk of having the lights go out and never hearing the end of it, Bernal waited. George would tell on his own, or he wouldn't tell at all. All Bernal could do was listen and hope.

"I did grab something when I ran." George's voice was almost inaudible.

"What?"

"Oh, shit, wait." Bernal heard George yell, "Just a second, for God's sake. I'm learning . . . I'm learning how my old man really died. What? Yeah, I'll tell you. I'll tell you first." His voice got closer. "Sorry. Narrative, you know. That's our main medium of exchange, made up or not. How my dad died is actually kind of interesting in itself. . . ." He paused. "Dog heads. Soviet. I mean old stuff, you'd think it would be something we'd know about by this time. On a VHS videotape. All jerky and out of focus, like the worst home movies you've ever seen. And no sound, like they didn't manage to figure out how to work a mic.

"Now, people pretty much know that somebody over there used to chop the heads off of dogs and keep them alive, all hooked up to tubes and stuff. But this was about something else, something after that. It had big tanks of some kind of liquid with mist spilling off of them. And down inside you'd see . . . the heads, the dog heads, only with wires coming out, not tubes. Then the scene cut, and you saw some kind of vehicle with tracks. Ugly, welded piece of crap, lousy gas mileage, probably broke down once an hour. It didn't have a crew. It tore around this field, made turns, maneuvered past obstacles, all without anyone on it. Now, maybe it was radio controlled, like a model car or something. But I think it was that cylinder you could see on some kind of framework above the engine. The one with the mist coming off it."

"You think it was a frozen dog head, or something."

"Look, I don't know what I think. But, yeah, maybe these guys figured that instead of messing with a bunch of complex electronics they'd have to buy from us anyway, they'd just take something that was already pretty good at maneuvering across unmarked terrain, chop its head off, and stick that nice little hardware/software combo onto some Soviet crapwagon as a guidance system. If things had turned out different, we might have been facing God knows what across a battlefield somewhere."

More voices, someone yelling.

"Hey, look," George said. "Gotta go."

"Thanks for talking to me," Bernal said. "The tape . . ."

"Hell. My brother. Frank. Frankie. He wanted to . . . well, he did a video of himself and this girl having sex. It goes on for a long time, and you can't really see anything, but he taped the damn sex scene across my Soviet cyborg stuff. Nothing left. Just a girl with jiggly boobs bouncing up and down on what looks like a half-inflated sea monster beach toy but is, God help me, my little brother. He pops up a couple of times to take a swig of beer, and if you know him, you can recognize him."

"That's too bad," Bernal said.

"Yeah. She keeps yanking up on her boobs, like that will make them ride higher or something. Nothing you really want to look at. I'm glad he found someone, though. Everyone should have someone. Right?"

"Right."

"You think about that stuff, in here." George sniffed. "A lot."

"I understand," Bernal said.

"No, you don't, buddy. No way you could."

19

"You think what?" Charis stood carefully clear of everything in Ungaro's lab and stared at Bernal. Away from any object to give her scale, she might have been a vast statue, miles away.

"I think Hesketh exists."

"I knew that. I knew you were crazy. I just didn't . . . come on, just say it. I don't know why I'm asking, it's really too early in the morning to have my head explode."

"I appreciate you're coming over on such short—"

"Just say it!"

She was close to being angry, and Bernal could already tell that he did not want Charis Fen angry. He didn't believe in what she was doing, he didn't even trust her, but he realized he needed her. No one else could help him now. Once she got angry at him, all bets would be off.

"Hesketh exists, as a real, independent entity. It's really an AI, of a sort. But the reason you couldn't find any trace that Ungaro had ever acquired any processing gear sufficient to develop anything like an AI was because she didn't. She didn't base her AI on the usual hardware. . . ." Charis half turned to leave, and Bernal hurried on. "Her work in California involved chimps. Chimp brains. She had information from some Russian experiments on preserved brains, dog brains . . . I think she extended that knowledge. I think she learned to use the actual existing circuitry of a human brain in order to run her own cognitive software.

"I think she got the raw material for Hesketh from a cryobank called Long Voyage." He gave Charis a quick rundown: the co-location of Hess Tech and Long Voyage, the fire, the power failure, Spillvagen, the accusation that heads had been moved.

Yolanda. He remembered her chasing after Spillvagen that night at Near Earth Orbit. He hoped she wouldn't exact some dangerous kind of revenge on the pudgy Spillvagen. She looked like she could be vicious, if she had to be.

Then Bernal held his breath. Charis stared at him. She wore an embroidered shirt that shifted her apparent ethnicity in a Hispanic direction without actually getting there.

"What are you offering me, Bernal? The ultimate propaganda tool? 'Here are your AIs: they're made out of human brains!' Hell, I could work the rest of my life and not come up with better PR than that. With this in my pocket, I could bus some good citizens down to Home Depot to pick up some manure forks and tiki torches and have them storm the MIT Media Lab, looking to lynch Marvin Minsky. Rope. I'd have to make sure they picked up a decent length of line. Not that anyone knows how to tie a knot anymore."

"I don't—"

"I'm serious about what I believe." To Bernal's surprise, she wasn't raging. Instead she sounded close to tears. "I didn't choose my position lightly. I don't expect you to sympathize with it, but I want you to understand it. I didn't just decide that AIs were icky, or unnatural, or might lose me my job. I didn't just consult my inherent sense of pollution or propriety. I thought about it. And after I thought about it, I decided that what we had essentially done was turn over serious societal decisions to a group of people who believe themselves to be smarter than they actually are, and we did it without any consideration of the consequences. And, sure, I did it because I got tired of those little shits shoving their damn Singularity up my ass every time I turned around and telling me that I better enjoy it because that was what I was going to be getting for the rest of my miserable, irrelevant, transcendent, incredibly connected life. So I figured, when the grandly intellectual and the truly petty coincide so neatly, I would be a fool to resist. Hence my career with Social Protection.

"But don't try to take advantage of my urges, or game me. Icky, gross, disgusting—those don't ring my activist chimes. They're there. Those parts of our mind are always there. But I resist them, because those signals are really something like phantom limb pain. And now you come and . . . what made you think I would fall for this?"

"The fact that there is a very good possibility that that is exactly what happened." Bernal spoke carefully, because he knew he would have only one chance, and was grateful that Charis was the kind of person who could ask that last question and then stay to hear the answer. He told her the story of the Bald Chimps, the burning of Ungaro's lab, and the Soviet dog experiments. He told about the location of Hess Tech, the cryobank fire, and the possible disappearance of some frozen heads, followed by the departure of Hess Tech and its transfer here. He pulled out the piece of gold foil that had been lying on the back shelf, the foil that matched the foil sphere in Spillvagen's office: part of the head-protection system of the cryobank.

She held it in her hand. "Okay. I'll buy some of that. But it's no picnic, maintaining cryogenic temperatures. Nothing for an amateur."

He showed her Ungaro's SQUID, the thing he had been wondering about. "This thing generates something like four times the cooling needed just for this sensor here. I couldn't figure it out. I've signed off on the power bills for this place and always wondered what the hell was going on. . . . Now, this may all be a combination of coincidences, misinterpretations, and lies. But how much do you need in order to want to learn more?"

"What's the next thing you want to learn?" Charis asked, and Bernal knew he was in.

He was careful not to sigh with relief. "I want to see if I can figure out what Hesketh was up to on the night Muriel disappeared."

"So," Bernal said. "You were out watching Hesketh that night."

"At Muriel's request. Handy for her, right? Having a devoted activist on tap for when your AI project goes rogue on you? Nice and deniable. I was a chump."

"But you went."

"Yes, smartass, I went. She was . . . Muriel was scared. I could hear it in her voice. She said she was thinking that maybe she shouldn't have chased me off, that if she'd let me keep nosing around I might have spotted some of the stuff she'd only lately discovered. I asked her what she'd discovered. She said she didn't want to prejudice me, and would I please take a look at Hesketh and tell her if I thought it was actually intelligent. She sent me a series of maps, Hesketh's planned test runs for the month.

Muneer was off in California the whole week, trying to sell those equipment casings his company makes, and there wasn't anything good on TV, so I went. And damn if I didn't figure she'd screwed me over good. Hesketh didn't show up. I mean, I sat out there in some bushes, and nothing whatsoever happened. I mean nothing. I'm good at stakeouts, have an ability to sit motionless for hours. No one saw me, I was undetectable, the thing never showed up.

"Come morning, I unkinked myself to come on over here to see what the hell was going on."

"To find me." Bernal remembered the mud on her boots.

"Yeah. An open lab, a bunch of tossed-around crap, and a smarty-pants green-eyeshade type who got all snotty and talked lease arrangements."

"I'm not an accountant," Bernal said.

"Sure, fine. You're not an accountant. Nothing to be ashamed of. Honest work."

Bernal thought about what she had just told him. "Muriel sent you more than one route map?"

"Yep. You got it. So, that next night, I have no idea why, I decided to go out and check the route again."

"And take control of Hesketh?" Bernal said. "Wasn't that a little more than Muriel had asked you to do?"

"Look, Bernal." To his surprise, she looked nervous, even a little embarrassed. "I sit in my office there, you've seen it, waiting for something to come up. These guys, assholes every one of them, they keep promising . . . stuff. Things going on. Great advances. Constantly increasing speed, infinite power, all knowledge and cognition sliding down into an expanding Singularity that will suck everything up and remake the universe. And what do I actually get? The ability to learn the uninformed opinions of everyone in the world through round-cornered communications devices my fat fingers are too big to use.

"So, when I learned that there might be some kind of real thing out there, something significant, I got . . . excited. I teach myself not to, and I always end up fooling myself again. That's why I got so pissed off when you called me this morning. Because you were pulling me back into it. Feeding my addiction.

"Plus, Muriel was gone. She'd told me stuff wasn't going well, and there was Ungaro's office, looking like it had been tossed by some search-and-snatch team, and she was out of the picture, and there was no sign of the stupid gadget. So, yeah, I got a bit out of hand and tried to do a little catch-and-release on the space bug when I saw it. With results that you saw."

"Show me," Bernal said.

"What?"

"The map. The map of Hesketh's route on Sunday night, the first time you were supposed to try to assess it. Do you have it?"

Without another word, Charis pulled out a thumb drive and walked over to Madeline Ungaro's computer. A few clicks, and an image of a map replaced the lake view on the screen. Bernal could see a few roads, a river, some scribbled streets marking built-up areas. A red line squiggled in a rough circle around the map. Spots along it were marked with symbols: triangles, circles, dots, each marked with one to five exclamation points.

She fiddled and called up an overlay menu. When she put road names up, he recognized what he was looking at: the land just west of Cheriton, a landscape of hills, abandoned farms, new subdivisions, industrial zones, and old mills perched on sloping layers of rock. It was a forgotten part of Massachusetts, belonging neither to the greater Boston metropolitan area nor to the more tourist-friendly hills west of the Connecticut River, which culminated in the Berkshires.

The red line of Hesketh's planned test route squiggled

its way across the landscape. It was a loop that stayed away from roads as much as possible, running along an abandoned railroad right-of-way that had not yet been turned into a rail trail, through what had once been a lumberyard, along the one shore of Shining Lake that was too unstable, as yet, for housing construction, through a gravel pit, and along a power line right-of-way. Then past some sewage settling ponds, through a state wildlife management area, some conservation land, over Double Hill, into another gravel pit, through the extensive grounds of the regional high school, along the wall of a development, along the rocky bed of Middle Brook, up a gas pipeline right-of-way, past the Department of Correction Pre-Release Center, past a highway rest stop, then actually along a road so that it could dodge through an underpass under Route 2, then back to the railway right-of-way.

"Where does this path start?" Bernal said.

"Want a clue?" Charis moved the focus in on a road that led to one of the gravel pits. "A pickup truck registered to Madeline Ungaro is, right now, standing in the woods just off this road. It has not been marked as abandoned yet, and it's not in anyone's way, but someone at the department is keeping an eye on it. My old department may have a lot of problems, but they're right up on vehicle abandonments. It's an environmental issue, I hear."

"So she drove out there and released Hesketh for its run," Bernal said. "Just as planned."

For a moment, he imagined Ungaro sitting alone in her truck, at night, wondering where her device had gone. She heard a noise, like someone coming up, but couldn't see anything. Someone who had reason to hate her had set a trap for her, a trap that had finally sprung. . . .

That was ridiculous. Muriel had not spent all this time setting up Madeline's murder.

But where were they both?

"But it did not come back," Charis said. "Somewhere along the way here, it deviated. Who the hell knows where it went after that."

"I think we know where it went."

"Where?"

"It came back here. Let me show you." Bernal led her through the lab to the rear door. He undid the new lock he had installed and threw it open. The black trail torn at an angle up the grassy berm was still clearly visible. "And that is the way that it came. If we track back, we have a good chance of figuring out where it deviated from its route, and why."

20

There were a few weeds underneath the scrub oaks, but mostly bare earth. A washing machine, two sofas, and the battered cylinder of a hot-water heater lay at the bottom of the slope, no doubt tossed from the road above. Old clothes had burst from black garbage bags and were strewn across the ground, including some colorful hospital scrubs. The Black River flowed a short distance away. On its other side were thicker woods and the bulk of Mt. Marty.

Hesketh's backtrail had led, finally, here. Bernal couldn't have done it on his own, but Charis had been able to spot scrapes, depressions in lawns, broken branches on rhododendrons, and kept them moving.

And a car, an old Peugeot, with a boxy roof. The once-red paint had long ago chalked into dusty pink and cracked like drying mud. A fast-growing sapling had pushed in the driver's side door. The windows were gone, the upholstery split. Some kids had plastered brightly colored "Doom of Humanity" stickers all over the inside.

Stylized images of the animals that were to witness the human race's extinction grinned at him.

"That was its planned route." Charis pointed. "Middle Brook is just up that way. But instead of turning to head up the gas pipe right-of-way, toward where I was waiting for it, like it was supposed to, it must have turned back to the lab. What, was it homesick? Tired of being made to run pointless loops in the middle of the night by someone who didn't seem to have any bigger ambitions for it? Ungaro must have been sitting in her truck, waiting for it, getting increasingly pissed off. But pleased, I suppose, if she thought about it. Slacking off is an undeniable sign of intelligence. It's only the non-self-aware devices that uncomplainingly do everything you tell them to. What, Bernal?"

He was staring at the Peugeot, remembering something the Enigmatic Ascent folks had said to him. "Hesketh . . . those guys, the ones I was with the other night. They've been tracking Hesketh too. They were out and about that night."

"Damn crowded out here," Charis grunted. "I had no idea."

"They saw it leave its prescribed route, come down to the river and . . . do something to a car. This one, I think."

"'Do something'? That's pretty coy, Bernal."

"Okay, they said it looked like it was mating with it. Got all up on top of it, and for a while. Then it took off, and they followed and lost it. We've just been over the route." Both he and Charis were muddy to the knees. "The ground was even wetter that night, and Hesketh outpaced them in the underbrush."

"This car, eh? Well, let's see what made it so interesting." She popped the trunk with the screwdriver on a multitool. The lid creaked up painfully.

Someone had taken the spare, unless Peugeots usually

kept it somewhere else. Something had creased and bent the trunk, and it sloped downward. Anything you would have wanted to keep in there would inevitably have slid somewhere into the depths of the car. "The Easter Bunny . . ."

"Where did you hear about that?" Charis said sharply.

"Why, have you heard of it?"

"Never mind. I'm interested in how *you* heard about it."

He wasn't ready to tell her that Muriel was communicating with him through stuffed animals. That seemed to undercut the credibility of the information. "Muriel talked with this guy Jord a few days before she disappeared. He was willing to talk with me, too."

Charis shook her head. "Muriel. Everyone gets seduced by her. Yeah, I've heard the stories. And remember that Jord is not necessarily reliable. He has his own goals. But I don't see anything in here. Not now."

But there was another connection. . . . He looked at the scattered clothes. The bags hadn't just burst when they were thrown down here. Someone had methodically gone through the clothing. The guy with the shopping cart, Spak. He'd scored himself some nice hospital scrubs. The ones remaining hadn't passed muster somehow. Spak had been here too.

Charis walked around and did the same to the hood. The engine was all there, though its hoses sagged and its belts dangled shreds. "You know, I'd like to figure out the cause of death. The car's, I mean. Why it's been abandoned. What the final, irrevocable failure was. Unclear here. Can't figure it out." The window washing fluid reservoir was empty. She yanked at the rear of the engine compartment. Nothing behind the firewall.

She checked under the seats. Cubes of shattered glass covered the rear seat. After a moment's hesitation, she popped off the rear side panel. The panel was stuck on its clips and came off in rough chunks. Behind it were nothing but a couple of electrical wires bundled with cable ties, and a dangling electric window motor.

She got a good grip on the next panel and pulled. It popped right off its rusty clips. Something tumbled out onto the seat.

"Jesus!" Bernal said.

She looked at it. "Friend of yours?"

"Funny. How long do you suppose it's been here?"

Sharp teeth stuck out from between the dried lips of the mummified cat. All that was left was fur stretched over bones. They both stood and looked at it as if it were going to tell them something else.

"Who the hell put it in there?" Bernal asked.

She shrugged. "Somebody. Teenagers. Who knows? Just a joke. This isn't what Hesketh was after, is it?"

"I don't think so."

She sighed, then got on her back and slid herself underneath the car. Pretty soon all he could see was her boots.

"What do you see?" he asked.

"Can you find a stick, maybe three feet long?"

"A—sure."

"As straight as possible."

A moment later, he had one. "Careful. It's muddy on one end."

"That's okay. Go over to the other side of the car."

He did so and was startled to see a flap open on the fender, a big one, maybe eight inches square. It had been hidden by what he had taken to be checked paint. Charis stopped pushing with the stick, and it clicked shut again.

She climbed back out from under the car. He helped her brush dirt from her back.

"What's under there?" he said.

"Nothing."

"Okay, so—"

"But it looks like there used to be something. Not sure, but . . . there are some scratches and a couple of places that look like an attachment was removed. Mud smeared in there to hide it—and that's what attracted my attention. Attempts to conceal often end up revealing."

"Does that flap connect up—"

"You know it does, right up against it."

"Where Hesketh must have . . . done whatever it did."

Bernal looked up at Mt. Marty, a big pile of rocks left by the glaciers that made the Black River detour around it. The river grumbled in annoyance at the obstacle. The ground around it was still damp from its recent floods.

"This was all that same night," Charis said. "Muriel gone, Ungaro gone, Hesketh gone . . . whatever we mean by 'Hesketh.' I'm not liking this. Come on, Bernal. Do you have any idea of where Muriel is?"

"No. She's sent me a couple of messages, the way she always has, but . . ."

"We have to find her," Charis said. "There's no excuse for this kind of game playing."

"She might be in trouble," Bernal said. "That might be the only way she can get a message out."

"All the more reason to find her."

"The guy with the Mercedes," Bernal said. "The one who hit me."

"Clocked you with the canine?"

"Please, Charis. I know you're rough and tough, but it really isn't funny."

"You're right, of course. Sorry. You think you can find the Connoisseur?"

"Who?"

"Oh, you're not familiar with the Connecticut Valley's own cat burglar? I don't know who called him the Connoisseur first, but that's the name everyone uses. He does something like one or two break-ins a month, ranging from roughly Williamstown in the west to Pepperell in the east. And up into southern Vermont and New Hampshire. A lot of different jurisdictions, and his rate is low, so he doesn't come up big on any one chief's radar screen. He likes older houses. He might just like them, or they might tend to have loose windows and rotted sills.

"He likes American work, mostly early stuff. Not European so much, though he does sometimes take off with some Central European Art Nouveau or Biedermeier. Once he found a whole Art Nouveau collection, some guy in Templeton. He left a Horta sideboard in a carport, all he ended up taking was a couple of Hungarian pieces, Zsolnay. And, no, I don't know this stuff. I just look it up.

"He takes good care of his stuff. Sometimes he finds out that a piece is too big and heavy to be handled safely by one guy. So he leaves it. Sometimes there's padding still attached when someone finds it. A few times there have been packing peanuts, but what can anyone tell from packing peanuts?

"What's more of interest to you is that he always steals cars to use. Never uses one more than once. And often returns them where he got them. Sometimes the car owner doesn't even know. Once someone got back from vacation and found a single silver button under the backseat. Turned out to come from a haul of Revolutionary-era stuff, up in Portsmouth. Once someone found a scrape on their door that hadn't been there before they left on vacation. The paint matched that found on a chunk of granite near a farmhouse in South Hadley where an eighteenth-century vanity had vanished. The driveway had a tricky dogleg. Our Connoisseur might have good taste, but he's not so hot on the driving.

"A few people have seen him. They didn't know who he was at the time. They only realized later, when they found something missing. Young-looking guy, though probably older than he looks. Slender, kind of formal-seeming. Caucasian. Probably sandy hair. Sometimes a beard, sometimes not, could be a fake."

"That's him."

"And you want to find him. Well, Bernal, your police work has been pretty good so far. Let's see what you can do with a random assortment of Mercedes. Hell, maybe you can help Cheriton PD make the collar. I've heard that the Connoisseur has been seen in the Walnut Street hood a couple of times. Maybe what he learned that night is keeping him around. That's not like him."

21

By his third Mercedes, Bernal was already running into trouble.

"The bastard," the woman, Serena, said. "Can you believe that bastard?"

"No," Bernal said. "I can't."

"I mean, after all those years . . . I supported him. Through truck-driver school, through computer-repair school, through art school . . ."

"Art school?"

Serena was a thin woman with tight jeans, cowboy boots, and fluffed blond hair, and looked like a young woman dressed like an older woman trying to look young. Yolanda could have taught her a few things, Bernal thought.

"Petey could always draw Binky," she said. "From the matchbook cover. Pretty good. I got that fawn head somewhere. He drew it on the back of a miniature golf scorecard with that little pencil they give you. He cheated: kicked his ball through that windmill. But the fawn looks real nice. That was for my birthday, the second one we had together."

"Is the car in the garage?"

"Oh, the damn car. So, here I am, supporting him, and what does he do? Goes down to Foxwoods, bets it all on 18 black, which is my birthday, November 18th, and wins fifty thousand dollars. My birthday. And never lets me know."

She viciously punched the keypad and the garage door opened. A black Mercedes stood there, crammed in among gardening tools, old tires, and neat bundles of newspapers. Getting it in and out without knocking anything over would have taken some skill.

The taillight was fine. This wasn't the car Muriel had escaped in.

"So he buys this thing and brings it home, like it's nothing, like he picked it up along with a bottle of Colt down at the packie. I ask him where he got it, and he's like, 'what?' And I'm, 'where'd you get the money for the car, didn't you borrow money against the truck?' And he's like, 'you can get a deal on these things if you know where to look.' Bastard never used a coupon in his life, even when he could get two-for-one on the Quilted Northern, he used TP like a girl, like a troop of Girl Scouts, we were *always* out, and he's talking deals."

"But you think he's been here, driving this car?" For a new vehicle, it was fairly dinged up, as if someone had been using it in speed trials on gravel roads.

"Look, I can tell when he's been in here. He moves stuff around. Can't help himself. Always done it. You'd think he'd sneak in, steal money out of my bedside table, beer from the fridge, whatever, and get the hell out, but he has to sort my magazines, or pull dead leaves from the dieffenbachia."

The doors weren't locked. Bernal examined the interior. Where the radio and CD player should have been there was nothing but a hole with wires sticking out. And someone had even pried the steering wheel open and taken off with the airbag.

"How long ago did he leave?" Bernal asked.

"He didn't leave. I kicked his ass out."

"Good for you. When was that?"

"Two months, eight days ago. On the anniversary of our second date. The first one he'd come on gangbusters, taken me to some Italian place with white tablecloths. They had great tiramisu, let me tell you that. Second date he took me to Bernard's. You know Bernard's?"

"Can't say I do."

"Some guy threw up on my shoes. Buddy of his, in fact. Nice ones, Ferragamos, I got them at DSW marked down, a steal. Never wore them again, that alligator hide really holds the smell. I love a 'No Gang Emblems' sign, don't you? It's the mark of a real class place."

Feeling uncomfortable with her confession, and looking for something to do, Bernal popped the hood. For a moment he thought it was just the shadows from the overhead light, but then there was no doubt: most of the pieces were missing. Alternator, starter motor—the fuel injectors had been yanked out. All that was left was the engine block and the heavier mechanical parts. It didn't look like this car had gone anywhere recently.

Serena took a glance, wailed, and collapsed on a bag of Scotts Turf Builder. "Oh my God! Is there anything left?"

The front right wheel, invisible unless you clambered over the gigantic rider mower and peered over, was gone too, the car propped up on a jack. Mercedes wheels fetched a nice price. The guy had eaten the thing away from the inside, and Serena had never realized. It was only the shell that was left. The shell, three wheels, and the leather seats. He had no doubt that those were going next.

"How the hell did he get in here?"

"Doesn't he know the combination?"

"I changed it!"

"To 1118?"

Serena looked flabbergasted. "How did you know?"

"Just a lucky guess."

She grabbed Bernal's arm, sharp nails digging in. "Help me with this, will you please? What am I supposed to do now? I have a dealer coming over to look at the car in a couple of days. The thing is worth—"

"All you'll get from a dealer is some more room in your garage." Bernal felt tired. The cars he'd looked at so far had shown him absolutely nothing, while this one had showed him entirely too much. "If you're lucky, he'll tow it for free. I'm sorry."

He glanced back as he got into his car. Serena was still sitting on the fertilizer, staring at the shell of the Mercedes. All Bernal could do for her was hope that there were no particularly valuable plumbing fixtures or structural members in her house.

22

"Should I be worried?" The guy named Alistair scratched his thinning hair. "I mean, I drove the thing home. Anthrax? Explosives?"

"Nah, nothing like that," Bernal said. They trudged up the long driveway. "How long were you gone?"

"A week. Eight days, actually, Monday to Tuesday the next week. San Francisco, Tucson, and, God help me, Omaha. I left the car at the Enfield station, took the train to North Station, then the T to Logan. I like taking the train. I don't have to fight the traffic. It's really pretty easy."

It sounded like he was trying make sure Bernal didn't think he was lame for taking public transportation.

"Anything different about the car when you got back?"

"No! I mean, I didn't notice anything." Alistair sounded genuinely panicked. "But . . . okay, I don't know if this is a clue or anything, but . . ."

"Yes?"

"I'd been expecting to pay sixteen bucks for the time I was parked. They charged me only two. . . ."

"You thought it was just good luck?"

"I get reimbursed . . . what the hell? What's up with my car?"

"Don't worry. We just know a guy who take joy rides in nice cars that are left somewhere for an extended period. We're trying to build a case. That's all."

"Sure." The garage door hummed up. "Um, car's unlocked."

Bernal stopped. "What the hell is that smell?"

"Ah? Oh, my wife . . . Rue makes calamari when I'm on the road. I don't like it. She doesn't eat the tentacles, though. I don't know why that's her sticking point, but it is. So—jeez, it does stink. Trash pickup is tomorrow."

"How does she cook it?" Bernal said.

"The calamari? I hate the stuff. I don't know."

"She home?"

"No. No, she's not home. She's . . . well, to tell the truth, we've been having a bit of trouble lately. Communications . . . issues. Nothing we can't handle. We've gone through worse things before."

Hence the week-old squid in the trash, Bernal thought. Poor Alistair.

"Go ahead, take a look. There it is."

"I see it." And it was the right one, this time. He could see the strip of tape across the taillight. Until this moment, he'd been fearing he imagined it and would be searching for the rest of his life for something that wasn't there.

"What happened to the taillight?" he said.

Alistair looked at it. "Rue backed into our mailbox. Just before I left. Now that I'm home, I can get it fixed."

"That's a good idea."

Bernal tried to figure out the course of events. Only one really made sense right now. Alistair drove his Mercedes to Enfield and parked it in the lot, then took the train into Boston. The Connoisseur boosted it from the lot. Then Muriel stole the car from the Connoisseur and . . . drove it back to the Enfield lot? That seemed to explain the ticket issue. Pretty smooth, actually. Maybe she hopped the train into Boston, just as Alistair had. If Bernal hadn't come along looking, no one would even have noticed that the car had ever been missing.

Muriel was much more evaporative than he had given her credit for. Now she was sending him messages from wherever she was, guiding him without really being clear.

Alistair stopped outside. The guy wasn't going to go into his own garage. That was fine with Bernal.

Not that there was anything for him to worry about. It was a nice car. Leather upholstery, walnut burl trim, individually heated seats . . . and it was as clean and neat as if it had just been driven off the showroom floor. There were a hell of a lot of stickers on the windshield. Alistair and his wife had joined a lot of local organizations, looked like: Historical Society, Arboretum, Nature Conservancy. . . . Alistair was as fastidious as the Connoisseur. Every crime left a trace, but somehow it would have been easier if a loose piece of birds-eye maple veneer had peeled off a dresser.

Bernal went around to the back and opened the trunk.

For an instant he thought that he'd found some inadequate lubrication. But that creak was Alistair groaning. Then he was throwing up into the bushes by the side of the garage.

It was a decent-sized trunk. The corpse, a woman, dressed in black microfiber, was curled up on its side with plenty of room to spare.

Of course, it wasn't quite the challenge it could have been, since the body had no head.

23

Morning light seeped in through the high windows. Bernal could feel the pad hard under his sleeping bag. He could hear his own breath whistling through his nose. He could move his eyes and examine the struts and hanging lights high above.

What he couldn't do was move anything else.

Something pushed down on his chest. The pressure was strong but soft, like a big hand . . . or something sitting on him. Something with a huge ass. He couldn't see what it was. All he could see were the sharp details of the struts that made up his sky. He found himself tracing them out, as if there was some solution to his life in the way they distributed the weight of the roof.

Was this a heart attack? He was young, he'd never even had his cholesterol checked, and now . . . Maybe it was a stroke. The pressure grew stronger, and his panic grew with it.

"Hesketh?" He tried to say it, but nothing came out

of his mouth. His breath kept going, but he couldn't control it.

He would lie here forever, he knew, with his thoughts running around the inside of his immobile skull like crazed lab rats. And something would sit there and watch him. He sensed a presence, an observant intelligence, out there in the half-darkness of the lab. It had been there all along, it had never left, and now that he was alone in there, it had him to itself.

It could do what it wanted.

Something tapped at the door.

The pressure vanished. He tried to unzip his sleeping bag, but the zipper stuck, and he writhed on the floor, finally pulling himself out on the end. He rolled to his feet.

He took a couple of slow breaths. His heart wasn't even beating fast. He felt fine. He felt better than fine: he felt alive.

The tap again, louder this time.

He pulled on his pants and buzzed the front door.

Charis's huge shape filled the doorway, black against the wet morning glow. She wore something that was almost a dashiki. That was quite a claim, but she came close to carrying it off. Her dark hair had frizzed in the moist air. Strands draggled down on her shoulders, as if she had tried to get it to behave and then had given up.

She paused there.

"Come . . ." He cleared his throat. "Come on in."

Without a sound, she slid to the side and vanished into the shadows of the loading dock.

What the hell?

"Charis?"

What had she seen? He turned slowly around. There was nothing in the shadows. Hesketh's limbs hung in a still row. Tools lay on their racks.

While he waited for her to reappear, he pulled an electric shaver out of his overnight bag and ran it over his chin. Despite the fineness of his beard, it labored, reaching the end of its charge.

"What the hell was that?" Charis had made her way completely around the perimeter of Ungaro's lab without making a sound and now stood in the doorway to the office. "That the way you normally greet people at the door? You sounded like a hostage situation. All fake normal like."

"Sorry. I didn't mean to sound like that. I've been faking normal all my life. I thought I'd gotten pretty good at it. I had a bad dream. Sleep paralysis."

"What the hell is that?" Charis brushed big hands over even bigger upper arms. She could have had a position as Strongest Woman in the World in some traveling show in an era before steroids changed the ideal of what a really strong person looked like. "This gal Ungaro was a neatnik, but only about stuff that touched her own body. Typical."

"Your body normally disconnects its motor neurons during REM sleep, otherwise you'd be breaking windows and humping your pillow as you dreamed." Bernal rubbed his chin and realized he'd missed a spot, but this time the shaver refused to even start. "Under stress, they don't reengage when you wake up. 'The hag,' it's called. The old hag. Sits on your chest. I'd never had that happen. Incredibly real." He paused. "Did you think there was really something back there?"

"I wasn't going to assume anything. I leave that kind of thing up to smart people who already know all the answers. Do you have any coffee around here?"

"You want me to make coffee? Is that a way of calming me down?"

"No. It's a way of getting coffee. I love my husband, but Muneer's coffee sucks. You'd think it would be scientific or something, and right up his alley, but he always makes it too weak. And I didn't have time to stop at a Dunkin' on the way over."

Bernal had gotten used to Ungaro's tiny cooking area. He set up her complicated camping coffee maker.

"I pulled all the strings I could, but they still wouldn't let me see you yesterday." Charis pulled over the desk chair and sank her weight down on it, legs splayed. "How are you?"

"Fine. You know, Charis, I thought it was Ungaro in the trunk. That Muriel had, I don't know, hunted down and killed her. Then, I realized . . . Who killed her, Charis? Who would murder Muriel?"

The Cheriton police had questioned him from soon after his discovery of Muriel's body until late in the evening. "I mean, they wanted information, and they were all excited because they thought it was the Bowler, and didn't want me to know they were excited, because, after all, it was my friend who was dead, and I had seen her headless body in the trunk of a car. . . ."

Charis had a wide face, suitable for expressing emotion across a stage and into the last row of the second balcony. Up close like this, it was almost too much. Her hoop earrings swung and caught what little light there was. She put a hand the size of a catcher's mitt on his shoulder and pushed him to sit down.

"Did they offer you any help? Support?"

He shrugged. "The usual. Grief counselors, stress counselors. Nothing that would really help me." He packed some ground coffee into the coffee gadget and poured water. He clicked the spark on the cookstove, and the burner came to life with a heavy hiss.

"What would help you?"

"Understanding a few things would help me. They think the Bowler killed Muriel. That night. I saw her run off. She came here, then left, either with Madeline Ungaro or without, and then died."

Charis caught it immediately. "You know she came here?"

Bernal reached into his shirt and pulled out a pink sash. It was soft, with satin on one side. He held it out to her, but she didn't take it. "She had a pink nightgown on when I saw her. Over that ridiculous black Kevlar ninja outfit. She was over sixty, Charis. She shouldn't have had anything like that in her wardrobe. I found this sash here, in Ungaro's lab. She made it at least this far that night."

"Let's not get ahead of ourselves. Let's put things in some order."

"Okay. Makes sense. I've heard of the Bowler, of course. They were sure it was him, but they were pretending they still had their minds open to other possibilities. They asked about drug connections, her grief over her son's long-ago death, all sorts of stuff, but their hearts weren't in it at all. They knew it was the Bowler. The other possibilities were just ritual, so that they could pretend to themselves to be open-minded. I want information from you, Charis, so I can understand what they're after."

"What? About the Bowler?"

"Yes. I want your facts and your interpretations of those facts. I want to know how you see it."

"First, pour coffee."

A fountain of brown liquid spilled over into the serving flask. The gadget was too complicated but seemed to do the job. And it was light, presumably the point.

She held out her Social Protection travel mug and he filled it.

"In the past two and a half years, there have been four murders in the Black River Valley that involved beheading." Charis spoke carefully. "That's out of a total of fifteen murders, sixteen if you count one that got listed as accidental, but looked like a woman offing her abusing husband. The victims were Damon Fry, Warren St Amant,

Christopher Gambino, and Aurora Lipsius. And now, they think, Muriel Inglis."

"But you don't?"

"My opinions are complicated. Like I said, let's try to keep it a bit organized. Now, with a serial killer, 'first victim' is something you only know later, maybe much later. So, Damon Fry and Warren St Amant were known murders, and their heads were indeed cut off, but they weren't tied together until the murder of Christopher Gambino."

"Whose head ended up in a bloodstained bag at a bowling alley."

"Right. That kind of focused people's attention, as well as getting a lot of media coverage. But Gambino actually came out as Victim #3. There was a look back over the previous couple of years for common traits, and Damon Fry came up as the earliest in time. A manager at a marketing consulting company, forty-three, divorced father of two, man with a nasty whore habit, Caucasian. Liked to go down on South Main, pick up some drugs, and pick up a prostitute. He never used drugs himself—they were for his woman of that night. He was known for being . . . a bit rough. Kind of a pudgy guy, not in the greatest shape, but he could get violent. I think the drugs were really for that, so that it was easier for him, dealing with someone whacked out. And, despite his rep, girls would go with him, because of the drugs.

"Then, two years ago on the night of January 18th, someone killed him. Bruises and cuts on his body: someone had decided to fight back, and fight back hard. No one ever figured out who he had been with that night. Area got rousted, everybody questioned, most of the girls had some story about Damon and his habits, but no one would say she was with him that particular evening. Cause of death was blunt force trauma that might even have been accidental. Near as anyone could tell, he was backing up, tripped over something, and hit his head on a concrete block. They later found the block, and the corner seemed to match the depression in his skull.

"That, of course, took a while to figure out, because when his body was pulled out of the Connecticut River, down around Sunderland, it didn't have a head. It had been in the water two, three days. Someone saw it swirling around with a bunch of floating cans and milk bottles, downstream of a sewer outfall, coated with ice.

"Head had been removed by a high-quality carbon steel Chinese-style culinary cleaver. And I can say all those words that fast because that's all anyone ever described the murder weapon as, a 'high-quality carbon steel Chinese-style culinary cleaver,' like it was all one word. That's what the ME made of the scratches on the top remaining vertebrae, guess he was a bit of a cook, and everyone kind of glommed on to it. Bad practice, since one or another feature might be wrong, and accepting them all as necessary can cause you to miss stuff, like something only medium quality, or a heavy chopping knife instead of a cleaver.

"Now, whenever a reporter writes about a killer chopping a body up, he'll always emphasize the 'surgical exactness' of the cutting. Same way any woman involved is a hottie and any kid an honors student. Well, in this case, the cuts didn't show much surgical ability. Or even culinary. 'Rushed chopping' was the order of that night. Took the killer a while to find the gap between the vertebrae, and the neck got pretty well turned into hamburger in the process."

"You guys did eventually find the head," Bernal said.

"Yeah, we did. About two weeks later. It was dangling in a culvert, in a sling made of orange safety mesh. Nothing weird had been done to it, except that it had been kept in a freezer, and it was in pretty good shape. Aside from freezer burn. But it didn't tell us anything.

Theory was, the killer, we guessed a woman at that point, panicked and cut the head off to conceal the body's identity. That didn't work, but no one could figure out who the killer was, so whoever it was finally dumped the head.

"Searching for Fry's head had been a bit of a local hobby for a while, but other than that, it was a fairly normal case. Six months or so goes by. South Main had another regular, guy by the name of Warren St Amant, black guy, looked to be in his fifties, maybe older, but, later, when his body was identified, everyone found out he was thirty-six. Rough life. Rough death.

"He'd moved up here from New York, bus, the way people do. We got some good benefits up here, people say the town's on the bathroom wall down at Port Authority. I've never gone down to check. Warren was a drug addict, with a preference for sedatives of various sorts. Oxycontin was his favorite, but he would do almost anything that depresses your central nervous system. Codeine. Heroin. He wasn't fussy, Warren. He helped out with the girls, picked up some extra money from the pimps, did favors, people kind of liked him, he got by.

"One day he told some people he knew that he was going to make a big score. As in a big pile of product, somewhere. He was kind of vague as to what it was, and various people had different opinions: case of oxy that someone had stolen from the CVS warehouse, some H condoms a mule had crapped out in a stall in an interstate rest stop, not noticing because one had burst, and he was hallucinating and dying. Even a shoebox full of Quaaludes. Remember 'ludes?"

"No."

"Ah, kids these days. No contact with the self-screwing habits of their ancestors. Sad. With that particular variant, some guy was getting promoted to CEO and found a shoebox full of his old crap, hash pipes, 'ludes, a rolled-up hundred dollar bill white with old cocaine, who knows, and dumped it in a garbage can. I guess street folks can't be expected to know much about vetting procedures at Fortune 500 companies, but they had a whole story going.

"Anyway, old Warren was heading for it. Knew where it was. People agreed on that. He went off and disappeared. No one thought much about him, until, a few days later, there was a huge flock of crows on the median of the Mass Pike, down near Springfield, tearing at something. Road crew got out there and found Warren's head, or what was left of it.

"The body turned up the next day, inside an old boiler in an abandoned apartment building. His head had been chopped off with a guillotine of some sort, spring-loaded was the guess. And he'd died right there, right in the rusty boiler, lying on a bunch of trash, and bled out without being moved. There was no sign of any drugs.

"This time the slice was much neater. It was starting to look like some kind of weird drug-related thing, though no one could come up with a good motive. I suppose if Warren was right, if he'd actually found something valuable, someone else might have killed him for it. But there was no reason to try to conceal his identity, or any of the possible explanations for Damon Fry. And it looked . . . neat, kind of planned, even. Like someone set him up."

"The Easter Bunny," Bernal said. "Right?"

"I forgot about your little chat with our friend Jord. Maybe. Warren might have been looking for drugs, but not in there. He had been sedated and put in there by someone else. A transfusion from him would have knocked out a bull. He wasn't even conscious when he died."

"Oh," Bernal said.

"Don't worry. More support for that particular theory coming right up, with the next victim. But first, there was a gap. Almost a year. Damon dies in January, Warren in

June. Then a whole year where everyone's heads stayed on their shoulders, and we figured whatever conflict there had been in the local drug world had kind of run its course.

"Then Christopher Gambino's head turned up in a bloody bowling bag at Memory Lanes. His body was found a day or so later, dumped in a patch of woods just over the border in New Hampshire. He'd been beheaded by a single swing of a sword. Some long blade anyway, with a bit of a curve to it. The ME went crazy with that one too, and it turned into an antique Samurai sword. He talked crystal structure, folded metal, all sorts of crap.

"Gambino was, no surprise, tied into drugs too. Just as a consumer. He was a smart guy, a professional, electronics and software when he could focus, and he had a whole spiel about souping up inadequate neurotransmitters, leveling the brain with hallucinogens. Saw himself as a kind of home garage mechanic, pimping his mind. Sometimes it seems that the only point to getting smarter is to have better explanations for why you're doing something stupid. He could hold a job, and was good, when he'd leveled out. And here's a piece of info for you: he did a bit of work for Hess Tech."

"What? Did he work on Hesketh?"

"No way of telling. All we really have are some 1099s from the company—which, I don't have to remind you, went bankrupt. But he had skills that would have made sense. He might have worked on some of those stepper motors up there." She waved her arm at Hesketh's dangling limbs.

"And Hess Tech was right next to Long Voyage." Bernal found himself excited. "This was the connection. That was what put Muriel onto the Bowler in the first place. Gambino. She'd been trying to figure out what Ungaro was really up to and started checking out that connection." He looked at Charis who stared back at him impassively. "What, you think it's just coincidence or something?"

She wiggled her coffee cup until he refilled it. "No, I think they're pretty clearly connected, just that the chain of causation runs opposite to what you want."

"'Chain of causation'?"

"What, I don't have a graduate degree, so I can't talk fancy?"

"I don't have a graduate degree," he said quietly.

She briefly put her big hand over his. "I'm sorry, honey. Someday you'll get over it. But I can still say 'chain of causation' if I feel like it. The connection is *Muriel*. Now you're making me do what I said I wouldn't do, which is wander off a clear presentation of the facts—"

"All right," he said. "All right. Park it. Put Gambino's connection to Hess Tech, and to Muriel, aside, and we'll get back to it."

"You won't forget?" she said.

"I won't forget."

"Gambino worked around, took his drugs, lived pretty clean aside from that. Had friends, though none of them knew where he lived, which was in an apartment over west. Old woodframes over there, mill housing, plastic factory housing, shoe factory housing. None of that's there anymore, but the buildings still are, so the rent's cheap. He had a little room there. Just a room, nothing much in it when we looked. He didn't talk to anyone, he didn't have a blog, he didn't leave a diary, and he didn't have a psychiatrist or confessor or spiritual leader he would spill his guts to. So no one knows what the hell he was up to or where he was when this happened. Blood spatter must have been something to see. No other damage to his body at all, so that was the one and only act of violence committed against him. No drugs in his blood that you wouldn't expect. Meaning he had enough in there to knock any regular person out, but it probably just made him bubbly and attentive.

"That bowling bag thing made everybody go crazy for a while. Very popular image. And attention really got hot when Aurora Lipsius was murdered only two weeks later. She was a prostitute, from Gardner. Thirty-three years old, been in the business a long time, didn't know any other. A couple of kids found her rear end sticking out of the trunk of an abandoned car over on Farthingale Road. Beheaded. Tight skirt, fishnets, high heels—her ass was in the newspaper, on TV. Everywhere. I'd been a cop for a while. It still disgusted me. Murdered prostitutes are just a decorative item now. Like cherubs used to be in old paintings. They don't really have to have anything to do with the story.

"Her father left home before she was born. Mom raised her and her siblings alone . . . well, not alone, of course. Succession of boyfriends, even one more husband, looks like. Two of the kids had one dad, one another. To be frank, I don't remember which group Aurora fell into. Now, it's not like we investigated her whole spiritual biography. She made it through the junior year at Gardner High. Started having sex for drugs pretty early on. Suspended once her freshman year for dealing coke in the gym locker room. Typical story? Not really, but I see things like that often enough. It was the drugs, really, on top of everything else. She loved them, it seems. Could never get enough. I'm not sure this knowledge of her biography helped in any way, but I thought I owed it to her. For most people, the way they die has nothing to do with the way they lived. It's not a natural consequence. It's not something to be expected. People say that, afterward, but almost always, if that person had not been in the wrong place at the wrong time, they could have gone on living a whole lot longer.

"Anyway, Farthingale's a common place for abandoned cars. People often torch the things, just to get something out of having their vehicle die on them. The thing's usually traded hands a few times unofficially, lacks registration, and it's not worth trying to stick someone with disposal fees. People trade drugs in the ones that don't serve as bonfires, low-end pros work some of the ones with better upholstery in the back, so we do our best to keep them cleaned up. The car Lipsius died in had been there two or three days. Since it was directly involved in a murder, they did considerably more work tracing it. Not easy. Vehicle identification numbers had been burned off, even ones no one knows are there. And a fair number of the parts had been switched with other cars. Some of them were even from other model years. There was some doubt whether the car would actually have run, in the configuration that we found it. Near as we could tell, the chassis, at least, was from a car that had been stolen in Yakima, Washington, a few months before. How it got to a side road near Cheriton, Massachusetts, no one has ever figured out.

"Her death obviously occurred right there. Blood spatter. All pretty clear. She hadn't been taken there and dumped. She had half-climbed into the goddam trunk. Why? Had someone forced her? Gunpoint? Who knows? What it really looks like is, she went looking for something and, instead, found something that took her head clean off. From the scratches on the vertebrae and the impact effect, the guess was something like a spring-loaded guillotine, similar to the one that had taken out Warren St Amant. Then, without the weight of her head, she slid back, until she was halfway out of the trunk again, feet resting on the ground."

"So the guillotine wasn't in the car when you found it."

"No. Someone, whoever, came and took the head and

the spring-loaded guillotine. We found it, later, or at least the spring part of it, in a stack of fence hardware at Home Depot. The blade never turned up. The soil under the car was soaked with her blood."

"Did they ever find her head?"

"Nope. But here's where we talk—"

"About the Easter Bunny. Someone who hides drugs in concealed locations. Jord was furious, saw it as some kind of unfair competition."

"It's a reasonable explanation: the Bowler, or whoever, puts drugs into hidden locations, suggests that people look for them, and then kills them when they find them."

"You don't believe it?" Bernal said. "It explains why anyone's giving out free drugs in the first place and why at least St Amant and Lipsius ended up where they did."

"Oh, no, I don't think it's a bad explanation at all. Fits into a nice progression, if you throw Gambino out as someone who just ended up in the wrong place at the wrong time: Damon Fry as the accidental first case, Warren St Amant as a kind of test of the concept, and Aurora Lipsius as the first successful use of an automatic death device of some sort. Everything's getting automated now, can't get any living being to answer the phone when you call to complain, so, sure."

Bernal picked up on her subtext. "Gambino doesn't fit, though the drug connection is certainly there. You think Muriel doesn't fit either."

She sighed. "Part of my fight. Oh, it's not like my suspicions that there was more than one person who ended up under the label 'The Bowler' was what made me leave the force. But it was part of it. Just the groupthink, the way people settle on an idea and hold on to it, no matter what. You detected it yourself. Cops decide someone's guilty. Prosecutors sign on. They pressure the lab techs to make sure that the evidence supports that theory.

Witnesses are coached, consciously or unconsciously, all the way from identification to court testimony. There's a story, and nothing that doesn't fit makes it in. Any attempt to put checks in, to try to make sure that you've looked at all the possibilities, is regarded as . . . treason. Not just not going along, not just being a pain in the ass, but as genuinely being an enemy of everything that is good and true. And cops, as we all know, are good and true. My last year there was hell. And that was one year too long. I had other dominant paradigms to subvert, so I left. There were still years left before I would be able to pull a decent pension, the reason most folks hang in there. So I decided to go for the big bucks in AI surveillance."

"All right. Let me subvert your paradigm," Bernal said.

"Lay it on me, brother."

"You think that Muriel was investigating Hess Tech, found a connection to the Long Voyage cryobank, and came up with a crazy theory about Madeline Ungaro stealing heads as a way of jumpstarting her project. When Christopher Gambino, for his own personal reasons, went out to buy drugs and got himself killed by the Bowler, she tied that into her thinking and started researching the Bowler. But the Bowler had nothing to do with Hess Tech, with Madeline Ungaro, or with Hesketh. She linked everything backwards into one theory, but they were really only linked through Gambino, and he was just coincidental. Right?"

"Close enough."

"But there's another connection. We're sitting in it. Just yesterday, we backtracked Hesketh from here, all the way down to the Black River, to a car that had had something taken out of it. . . ." Now that he said it out loud, none of that seemed particularly persuasive. "Did the police check the scene?"

"They will," Charis said. "I'll be surprised if they find anything. It was pretty clean. No blood, no hair, nothing visible. But they may find the connection. Muriel might have died there that night, tying it right back to Hesketh and Madeline Ungaro. But you're thinking something more, aren't you? I mean, the connection isn't just that Ungaro, Muriel, Hesketh, and the Bowler were all there at the same time, right? That's just some kind of weird-ass jamboree. So tell Auntie Charis what insane theory you're operating under."

"Muriel is communicating with me. It looks like her usual signs-and-symbols stuff. But it's gotten way beyond that. She sent me the flowers that took me to watch Hesketh. Then, the next morning, she sent a fax to your machine, the one you gave to me. Neither of those things is so weird. But then she somehow got a musical Easter Bunny into my car, with a voice message from her. All of that happened after she was beheaded. I had taken it as evidence that she was alive. Until I found her dead. But, somehow, she is not dead. Somewhere, she is conscious, and trying to communicate."

There, he'd said it.

Charis's ponderous shape looked carved out of a particularly smooth, honey-colored wood. Rings, bracelets, earrings glittered in the dim light from the clerestory windows.

"Muriel got her head cut off," she said. "Just as with Aurora Lipsius, we have not found her head, just her body. You think that head is—what?—frozen and incorporated into Hesketh somehow."

"Hesketh is made out of brains stolen from Long Voyage—"

"But that's not enough for you." She was almost yelling now. "Frozen brains turned into a homicidal AI, lumbering around Cheriton at night seeking brainssss . . . that's not enough to ring your bell. Muriel is still conscious, somehow, inside this . . . thing. She thinks, she wills, and she tries to communicate with you, using coded messages the way she always has. Do I have that about right?"

"I know her," Bernal said. "I know what she would know, how she would do things. What can I say? I have a sense of her personality still there. This isn't just denial, Charis. This isn't just a refusal to acknowledge her death, anything like that. This is something I see, out there."

"I know why you think she's alive. But our brains don't always work so well. We think we can detect a liar, we think we know the truth. But we don't. This contact with Muriel, it persuaded you that she's alive?"

"Yes."

"You want her to be alive. But she's *not alive*. You, of all people, should understand that. Someone out there . . . or something . . . knows what you want to be true. Psychopaths are often uniquely attuned to the needs and wants of other human beings. They don't share those needs and wants. Theirs are simpler and more elemental. So they can perceive our weaknesses much better than we can and exploit them."

And that, Bernal realized, was as clear a vision of how an artificial intelligence was going to perceive us as anyone was likely to come up with.

"There's someone out there that's killing people. Can't you understand that? It's not some kind of intellectual puzzle, something to entertain your brain with. Whoever that is lured Muriel Inglis out to a place where she could be killed. Muriel was an intelligent person. So are you. If someone as intelligent as Muriel can be tricked and killed, so can you."

"Okay. How about this. I'll aim at something else. I won't look directly for Hesketh."

"Hoo-boy, that sounds promising. What are you going to look for?"

"Whatever was in that Peugeot and was removed. Does that make sense to you?"

"It makes me think you're still secretly looking for Muriel. That she was . . . inside the thing. Something."

"Charis. Please. Someone saw the device, still active, on. Inside that car."

"What? Who?"

"A shopping-cart guy named Spak."

She snorted. "Spak. Hangs his many hats in a group home over on Aldrin Place. That'll be instructive for you, to see if you can come up with a comprehensible message coming from him."

"Don't make fun," Bernal said.

"Bernal. Those messages came to you for a reason. You think it's Muriel communicating. It's more likely to get you to do something."

"I know that," he said. "I know. I'll let you know what I'm doing."

"Okay. What are you doing?"

"Going to Muriel's funeral. It's tomorrow."

"That's quick."

"Muriel's daughter has already shown up. Seems to be an efficient sort, has things all worked out. I got an e-mail invitation today, along with an apology for not having something more formal. And she's put up a little memorial Web site for her mother. It looks pretty good, really. Some nice photographs of her. She was quite beautiful when . . . she . . . was young."

"So which is it, Bernal. Dead or alive?"

Bernal blinked at her. "I'm going to find that out."

24

Somcone had chosen a nice medley of music for Muriel's funeral, from Carole King to Cole Porter. Not exactly funereal, but certainly elegiac. Bernal found that he had trouble breathing.

"Were you friends with her?" The large woman in the nice suit eyed Bernal. She looked familiar, but he was sure they'd never met.

"We worked together. Are you related?" Bernal wondered at his own trouble in talking. By now he should have gotten used to the idea that Muriel was dead.

"My mother."

"You must be, ah . . ."

"Jennifer. I'm not surprised she never mentioned me."

He found himself shaking a firm, dry hand. He examined her. She had inherited little of her mother's good looks. Bernal felt like a traitor to his generation to even think it. But Jennifer Inglis was not an attractive woman. Muriel's elegant nose had ended up just a bit lumpy, her defined chin too wide, her clean complexion nowhere to be seen. Jennifer was bulky, even under the expensive suit, and her movements were graceless and abrupt.

She noticed him looking at her and turned away to flick at a loose strand of her thin hair.

"Why not surprised?" Bernal said.

She sighed audibly. "This is no place to work through my *issues*. I pay people for that. But you're not some son of somebody, are you? So tell me: what was it with you?"

"With me?"

"I mean . . . she was old enough to be your mother. Your grandmother, for God's sake. What was it with all of you?" The last sentence came out in a harsh whisper.

"We were business colleagues." He really didn't want to deal with this. With her pain. With his. "I earned a salary. Spent a lot of time in missile silos in South Dakota, that kind of thing."

"I'm sorry. I'm sorry." She clutched his upper arm for a moment in a painful grip, then sat down on a black folding chair. Muriel's memorial service was being held in a glassed-in space whose official name was the Memory Center, but which more than one employee had already been fired for calling the Mallsoleum. The air conditioning was cranked too high.

Far off, across the flat green lawn, automatic sprinklers shot parabolas of water into the sunlight. A procession of cars snaked along a cemetery road, and the sprinklers, all at once, shut off. For an instant the water continued, still leaping, ignoring the fact that it had lost its source, but then all of it came to ground.

"She . . . we . . . it was never the same after Paul died." Jennifer spoke quietly and quickly, not looking at him. "She tell you about Paul? No? Well, then I don't feel so bad. Oh, don't think badly of me, worried about myself at my mother's funeral. She was my mother, and she cared for me. That was why she wanted me to draw a clean line with my mascara, and dress to minimize how hippy I am, and eat . . . the . . . right . . . things." She pulled out a handkerchief and dabbed at mascara that, if it had been drawn cleanly, had long been smeared. "Paul was my younger brother. Great kid, Paul. One of those guys everybody likes. Including me, and I didn't really want to, because he was Mom's favorite. You have brothers or sisters, um . . . ?"

"Bernal. Yes. A sister. She lives in Maine. Portland."

"Your folks—"

"Her. They liked my sister better." He thought he was saying it just to calm Jennifer down, align himself with her, and was surprised to discover that it was true. Though his mother still sounded pleased when he called. Really, she did.

"Okay, then. So you know."

"What happened to Paul?"

"What happens to anyone? He died. Excuse me." She bit her lip, then got up and went across the room to a group of well-dressed older people. Because of what had happened to Muriel, there was no question of an open-casket funeral. In fact, there was no casket at all. Attention was focused, instead, on a small collection of personal items of Muriel's: a small leather notebook, a dark-blue coffee cup, a well-worn gardening knee pad, a porcelain doll's head, and, of course, shoes. A row of elegant shoes stood beneath the table, a black ribbon around each. For all her never-to-be-resolved hostility, Jennifer clearly knew her mother. Jennifer hugged a couple of the people who milled, uncertain, in front of what could easily have looked like a random mess pulled from a closet, directed them into a line of chairs, and returned to Bernal.

"It's only going to get worse. Mom knew everyone, just everyone. Those guys are, like, fund-raisers, museum board people, Friends of the Arboretum. Paul was killed rock climbing. He was seventeen. He had a daredevil of a girlfriend. Not the kind of person Paul usually hung around with. He was . . . he looked like Mom, I mean, no wonder the girls liked him, but he was really a conservative person, more like Dad. Dad sold cars. But Madeline—"

"Madeline Cantor."

She looked at him, both curious and annoyed. "Oh, so you're up on the whole story, are you? My mom convince you that stuff that happened twenty years ago is still interesting?"

"No. I know her as Madeline Ungaro. A completely different connection."

"Completely different?"

"I'm hoping to figure that out."

That relaxed her a bit. "Yes. Madeline Cantor. She—oh, shoot, it's the supper club people. I'll be right back."

She talked to two couples with elegantly frosted hair, the men in expensive-looking suits, the women in somber dresses. There were several distinct groups of people in the room. Muriel had clearly gotten around. Two older men put down a pot with an orchid in it and leaned a card against it: care instructions. Bernal looked at Jennifer, who smiled and spoke to the supper club people. He pictured her piling all the flowers somewhere, afterward, and forgetting about them. She looked like a practical woman. Practical people did not care for orchids.

There was a woman with bright red, curly hair, about Muriel's age. She wore a star-covered dress with a matching cloak and carried a crocheted handbag.

She talked earnestly to Jennifer, head cocked to one side, a glowing look on her face. Jennifer looked like she would rather have been discussing cough syrup flavors with an alcoholic street person, but managed to settle her features into a look of attention. The woman tugged at her sleeve. She had the solution. You could see it. Not the real solution, because there was no real solution. The spiritual solution. She shrugged her cloak, pure Madame La Zonga, and explained the way to Jennifer.

After Jennifer managed to peel her off, the woman wandered over to the display of personal items. In addition to the careful arrangement that Jennifer had put together, there was an area of personal donations, things people had brought that Muriel had given them or that had a strong personal association. She swirled her cloak like a toreador and yanked at something in her pocket. It seemed to be stuck, and she struggled with it, finally having to lean her weight on the table to pull it out: a figurine made of seashells, from some Florida vacation.

Despite the solemnity of the occasion, everyone's eyes had been glued to her mighty struggle. She smiled apologetically to the crowd and placed the figurine gently in the middle of a scattering of postcards from various locations around the globe.

There was just one thing. Bernal hadn't actually seen it, but he had the distinct sense that, while she was leaning and distracting attention with one hand, she had managed to scoop something up from the memory table with the other and drop it into her big bag.

He was trying to figure out what it might have been when Jennifer came back.

"Oh, God. Naomi." Jennifer plopped down.

"Friend of your mother's?"

"Best bud, really. Since high school, I think. Naomi Wilkerson. Pity she's so crazy. Talks to the dead. I'll be hearing a lot from her, you can be sure. And you know, I don't think she was raised Gypsy."

In between other interruptions, Jennifer Inglis told the story of Paul Inglis and Madeline Ungaro.

Madeline Ungaro had always had some flash, with ash

blond hair pulled back tight and dark brown eyes under heavy lids. A reading of *The Tale of Two Cities* or something had given her an obsession with tumbrels and guillotines, and for some time in late high school she wore a red ribbon around her neck, as fatalistic yet fashionable aristos had during the Terror. No one had understood it, but it became a bit of a fashion with other girls, who chose to change the ribbon's color, accessorize it, or wear it around an arm or other body part. Mortified, Madeline had stopped wearing her ribbon and stopped talking to anyone else who wore one. She couldn't bear people who didn't get the point.

Muriel hated Madeline as soon as she learned about her. Paul was closemouthed, even sullen, quite unlike him, which frightened her, so she turned her interrogation skills on Jennifer. She even softened to Jennifer's smeary and appalling goth style, reducing her criticisms, suggestions, and purchases of what Jennifer called "Barbiewear" to the point that, for a while, Jennifer even felt safe coming home. But Jennifer really knew little enough, and nothing that was important to what later happened.

What was interesting was that Paul and Madeline had met over a nerdy interest: space travel. The glory days of the space program were gone by then, and interest in free-market solutions had not yet come. A vague group had come together around the time the *Challenger* exploded. They, like kids across the country, had been hauled in front of TV screens to watch the schoolteacher Christa McAuliffe take a flight that seemed only slightly more interesting than a routine flight to Europe, only to find themselves watching the endlessly repeated sight of the detonation and the two plumes of smoke in the sky.

But there was one huge difference between them. Madeline was a risk taker. Paul, in his essential self, was not. That neurological difference, rooted somewhere in the adenosine system of the brain, was not as obvious as some of the more commonly worried-over differences between members of a couple, like age, race, or religion, but was a fundamental split that Madeline might have recognized but Paul certainly did not. He persuaded himself that it was a matter of choice, of will and focus, and followed, and even tried to lead her in her exploits.

Madeline was also an athlete, something Paul never really was. She played lacrosse. She swam. And she climbed. Rock climbing wasn't the popular thing it was to become. That was almost geeky, too. She'd go down to the Quincy quarries south of Boston, all sorts of places, looking for rock. And Paul would go with her. From what Jennifer understood, he'd gotten pretty good at it, at the end. But never as good as she was.

So, one weekend, senior year, they went on a big trip. The Shawangunks, in eastern New York. Famous for their rock. It was spring. Ice still lurked in the shadows and cracks of the rock and still expanded during the cold night. Madeline had been leading a difficult pitch, more difficult than either of them should have been doing. It was Paul's turn to climb, and Madeline was holding the rope and looking down at him when some shift of weight or final giving way of support led a head-sized rock to slide down the cliff and knock Paul loose. He had also been overconfident with his protection. His last chock stone was ten feet below him and not placed to withstand much force. By the time Paul had fallen twenty feet, he had generated enough force to pull the next, well-placed one loose as well. And rocks came after him. He might still have been alive, half buried, for a few minutes, but by the time Madeline had gotten to him, he was dead.

No one was sure, there was no accusation that could be made, but it seemed like she left him there for a while, maybe hours, maybe most of a day, before she reported it. She might have panicked. There were signs of some violent chest compression, an attempt to restart his breathing. All postmortem: he was dead when she hauled him out. But no one could know what she had done after she realized he was dead, or how long it had really taken her to decide to move.

The worst part was Paul's funeral. Madeline had come in some dark mourning of her own devising and looked stunning, quite outshining Muriel. Jennifer, whose already bleak dress did not require many changes to be suitable for the occasion, uncharitably thought that it was that losing competition that had really created the hatred that Muriel felt for the rest of her life: "'And the way she dressed as the Bride of Death was really the last straw! It was all a game to her, a theatrical game.' That's what Mom said, like that was what really mattered."

"Maybe," Bernal said. "But, you know, sometimes it's easier to hold on to a petty emotion than a grand one. It doesn't mean that the petty emotion is the underlying driving force. It just speaks to our inability to hold on to anything large."

"Oh my God!" Jennifer was suddenly enraged. "You're not going to defend her to me, are you? What did you know about her? She gets to take care of you, pretend Paul's still around, and you don't know anything about it. I come back here, I never wanted to come back, not ever, and the house is . . . things are missing, stuff's been sold, stolen, I don't know, everything's left in a dismal mess . . . and she's not even here to tell me what happened."

With calm dignity she got up and stalked off. And in that moment of disdainful dismissal, Bernal did see her mother in her, still alive and embodied somewhere in this world.

25

"Hello?" Bernal shouted in through the open front door of the big vinyl-sided house that Spak sometimes identified as home.

"Back here," a voice called. "Back in the kitchen."

Arnie turned out to be the boss of the place. He wore a too-tight pink oxford shirt with a couple of missing buttons and had long, lank hair. He stirred stew in a huge pot on the stove. Two men at the kitchen table paused, white Chinese-restaurant spoons held at identical angles above their bowls, then dabbed their lips with napkins and left.

"Hey, bowls in . . . oh. Okay. Feed the bunnies, can you, Nourse?" He called after them. "I'll put these in the 'wave when it's safe for you to come back in." He shook his head. "Don't get many visitors. Not used to it." Arnie himself seemed nervous, throwing glances at him when he thought Bernal wasn't looking, the rest of the time focusing intently on the spicing of his stew.

"Spak gives this as his address," Bernal said.

"It's . . . well, it's not an official center, if you know what I mean. You know, all that licensing and stuff. I used to run real residential facilities, oh, years ago. I . . . yeah, well, we do get money. Grant money. It's kind of experimental, what we're after here. We got all sorts of sustainable gear in back, you want to see. Rabbit hutches, pigeon coops, an aquaculture pond. Tilapia. It's a converted hot tub, works pretty good. That's funded by some folks in New Hampshire."

"I'm not concerned about your licensing," Bernal said. "I'm looking for Spak. I hear he lives here."

"Yeah." Arnie was reluctant. "Most of the time. He in trouble?"

"No trouble. Just a few questions. He saw something I want to learn more about."

"All of a sudden people are interested in Spak."

"Really?"

"Well, someone gave him a hat. Schiaparelli. Red velvet, feather, veil. Big old jewel on the front."

"Schiaparelli? You recognize things like that?"

Arnie chuckled. "You know Spak, you know old clothes. He digs around, makes some real finds. Loves every decade, every style. His only hobby."

"So who gave him the hat? And in return for what?"

"You'll have to ask him that."

The living room was stuffed with armchairs and sofas. Crumpled baby wipes made a dune behind a big camelback couch. Someone must have swiped a case or two from the back of a truck at a drugstore, and now the inhabitants fastidiously used them to clean their hands and wipe surfaces, and then tossed them in the corner. A loud snoring came from under the heap of old jackets on the couch. It reeked of unwashed skin.

Arnie looked around the living room and sighed, seeing it through someone else's eyes. "Please be kind to him. These guys seem like they've been hit with everything there is to be hit with, but sometimes it's surprising how much there is left to break. Now, excuse me, I got people to feed."

Spak was wearing even more clothes than he had been the last time Bernal had seen him, having thrown a silk dressing gown on over his flowered surgical scrubs. He was bent over, fiddling with a black garbage bag filled to bursting. He then swung around and squatted behind it. He still wore the sunglasses with one lens.

"Hi, Spak. Remember me?" Bernal squatted down next to him.

Spak glanced up at Bernal, then huddled in on himself and looked away.

"You saw me when I was talking to Jord."

"Nah. Maybe. Don't remember."

"Come on. You were peddling . . . scrubs. Surgical scrubs."

"Got some. Got some, you want. Don't remember then, though. Too long ago."

"How long ago?" Bernal was eager to trap him, as if that would make any difference.

"Whenever it was."

Bernal realized that he should have planned a fallback position before even coming in here. If Spak continued to pretend to never have seen Bernal before, what was he supposed to do? Hit him?

"You said you saw something, in a car down by the Black River."

"Ain't never been there."

"Where?"

"Anywhere!" Spak's anguished shout was loud enough for a few heads to poke in through the doorway, to vanish again quickly.

"Spak." Bernal was earnest. "This is important. People's . . . lives are at stake. It's about finding a killer. Someone took something from that car. You told someone about what you saw, and they took it."

"I didn't tell nobody nothing about nothing."

Bernal caught a glimpse of dark-red velvet inside the bag.

"So," he said. "I hear you got a new hat. A beautiful hat. Who gave it to you?"

Spak looked betrayed. "Who tell you that?"

"Never mind who told me. It's all over. Everyone knows. Where did you get it?"

"Found it. I find everything."

"Sure. And where is it now?"

"Lost it."

"Now, Spak. I've heard all about you. You take care of your clothes. Lose a classic like that? Not you, Spak."

"Some kids. Beat me up. Took it." Spak moaned. "Back still hurts. Got to keep sitting here until it doesn't."

"Come on. Kids beat you up to steal classic 1930s evening wear? This is important. Tell me the truth." He reached into the bag, trying not to think about what else was in there, and pulled out a turban-like red felt hat with a costume-jewelry medallion and a battered peacock feather dangling from it.

"Mine!" Spak grabbed for it.

Bernal held it away. "What, Spak, those punks feel all guilty and give it back?"

"It was something else they took. Made a mistake."

"The only mistake you're making is not coming clean. You talked to somebody else about what you saw. And they told you to shut up about it. Tell me, Spak. Who was it? Who did you tell?"

Spak hunched his head into his chest. "Can't. Promised."

"A promise sealed with a hat?"

"Nice hat."

"Fabulous hat, Spak. Much too nice to shove into a bag because you want to avoid telling me the truth."

Spak sat with his face in his hands. He wore at least a dozen rings on his pudgy fingers. Most were battered costume jewelry, but a couple had the gleam of true quality. A cracked fire opal was held in its setting by a wad of pink chewing gum.

"Prelate and Vervain," another voice said. "Why don't you want to tell this nice man about your dealings with those babes?"

Spak whimpered.

The pile of jackets on the couch shook and cascaded to the floor. A bearded face appeared, and Bernal realized it had been a few minutes since he had heard the snore.

"Let me introduce myself. Name's Walligan. And the Walligans, sure as shooting, have ears." He grinned, revealing gaps in his teeth. "That's my main source of entertainment, these days."

"Who are Prelate and Vervain?" Bernal asked.

Walligan narrowed his eyes suspiciously. "You gotta know who they are. Big time operators, both of them. Run this part of the state. What line of business you in, anyway?"

"I'm an . . . investigator," Bernal said.

"Really? A PI? Too much *truth* out there already, without you digging up more. You ever think about leaving some things the hell alone?"

"I have things I want to find out. Do you know anything about them?"

"A dark being wanders the streets and fields, but that's like a theological issue to you, you don't care about Death and its manifestations. You care only about those poor schlubs who are persuaded to act in its name." Walligan paused. "I was talking about something. . . ."

"Prelate and Vervain."

"No . . . no, that wasn't it."

"Yes it was." Bernal reined in his impatience.

"Maybe it was, now you mention it." Walligan bared his teeth. "They're real babes, eh, Spak? Prelate and Vervain. I think in a news story it would say 'not their real names,' like you'd ever think they were. Recycling's what they're into. Big industrial equipment, mostly, but they do anything. Got a nice eBay slot, trade across the country. And Spak's, like, a spotter for them. Once they got him a nice set of men's formal shoes, what do you call them, opera pumps. Nice, soft leather, he's probably got them in one of those bags, if you want to look."

"Spak," Bernal said softly. "Do you remember now?"

"They curious," Spak sobbed, broken by Walligan's revelation. "Heard, right when I got back from finding it."

"Why were they so interested?" Bernal said.

"Those girls." Walligan shook his head. His bare feet were decorated with toenails of impressive size. "They're into everything. Someone's always on the lookout for something, and they cash in."

"And what were they looking for?" Bernal said.

"A machine," Spak wailed. "Hidden in a car, somewhere deep. A cold machine for keeping heads."

"Heads?" Bernal said.

"They don't want the heads. They want the machine. Just a clue. Who wants another head?"

"I could use one," Walligan confided. "Just as a spare."

Bernal found Arnie out back, where he was probing a sore on the side of a flopping fish from the hot-tub aquaculture tank.

The back of the house was a nightmare of poorly maintained sustainable experiments. A solarium with loose panes held racks of sprouting plants. They looked vigorous, but they were surrounded by the decayed remnants of previous attempts. Besides . . . Bernal looked up at the sky. It looked like the solarium had been built on the north side of the house, never a good idea in the Massachusetts climate. An old gray-water recovery unit with dangling filters made of nylon stockings stood next to a high-end rotating composter that smelled of rotting meat.

Arnie dropped the fish into one of a row of fish tanks. Then, squinting at the instructions on a large plastic bottle, he added a teaspoon of some kind of medication to the murky water.

He shook his head. "Some of the money comes from some kind of a commune in New Hampshire. They used to bike down here sometimes to check on the results of their funding. Nice guys. Older. Round glasses, big calves. All their land is worth huge amounts of money now, and people seem to love their . . . hammocks, whatever it is they've been making for the past thirty years, and they're all rich and kind of guilty about it. But they don't come around anymore. I think they've gotten more interested in a cohousing thing for young families up in Portsmouth. But we still get the checks, and I do my best." He looked mournfully at the fish, which was still alive, but seemed to be gasping for oxygen in the small tank. "You ever try to scale and gut a tilapia for dinner?" He sighed. "You know what? It's not even, like, a useful skill, fish gutting. These guys need to sustain their lives, not the environment. Couple of them now know how to make tofu. That might still go somewhere."

"Does Spak have anywhere else to go?" Bernal said.

"If he did, do you suppose he'd flop here?"

"I'm just . . . he helped me out just now. I don't think it's likely to come back on him. But I don't want anything to happen to him because of me."

Arnie stared at him. At first Bernal thought he'd just gone blank, but then realized he was thinking. "I got a friend over in Leominster who could take him for a couple of days, if . . ."

Bernal shoved some money in Arnie's hand. "You're doing good work. Now . . . two women," Bernal said. "Walligan called them Vervain and Prelate. They been in here?"

"They help out here. Last year they brought me a new blower for the furnace and installed it. We couldn't have made it through the winter without it."

"Where do they get their stuff?"

Arnie looked at him bleakly. "We do what we need to get by. For some people that's really easy. For some of us, it isn't."

"Look, stuff fell off the back of the truck, that's fine with me. I just need to talk to them."

"Do they want to talk to you?"

"I doubt that very much."

Arnie looked at him with surprise. "Well. It's important?"

Bernal nodded.

"Okay. Just don't tell them the lead came from here."

"I won't."

"I mean, the refrigerator compressor's started to make a clicking noise. . . ." Arnie paused. "They work out of an appliance repair place over in Greenwich."

"They have real names?"

"You bring hunger, despair, and a desire to survive here. You don't need a real name."

26

It was ridiculous. "Prelate." "Vervain." There had been a time when you had to earn your underground moniker. Now people who replaced the heating elements in toaster ovens had them.

The Ziggy Sigma dispatcher had told Bernal that the two women were working a job out on Scobee Road. It was an older house, big, with a gigantic addition that turned the original house into a hand puppet. Someone had parked the white Ziggy Sigma repair van at an insolent angle in the wide driveway. Bernal was about to pass it on the way to the front door, and then stopped. He glanced up and down the street. Nothing like the midmorning quiet of a bedroom community with high employment.

He grabbed a handle and opened the van's rear.

Racks held boxed parts. Transparent drawers were packed with O-rings, clamps, hoses, and mesh filters. Electronic testing equipment trailed alligator clips and power cords. Silvery quilted pads were folded and stacked on the foot of a handcart. And something lay on the floor under a grease-streaked tarp secured by straps. Wet leaves covered the floor.

Bernal thumbed the tension clamps, slid the straps off, and started to pull back the tarp.

The back door banged open, sending in a blinding flare of light.

It was a black woman with her hair under a sanitary cap with the Ziggy Sigma logo on it.

"Who the hell are you?"

Inside the house, a white woman with a turban sat at the kitchen table, watching a tiny TV and fiddling with the innards of a leaf blower. Someone on the show won something, and tinny gongs and munchkin cheers came from the speakers.

"My name's Bernal Haydon-Rumi. Which of you is Prelate?"

"I am Prelate." She had some kind of Eastern European accent. "This is private home. Get out."

"Worse than it sounds." Vervain put her foot on the massive compressor she'd pulled out of the multidoored refrigerator that made up a wall of the kitchen and rocked it back and forth. "He was in the truck."

"Bullshit!" Prelate yelled. "Total bullshit."

"I just need some information about that item you salvaged," Bernal said.

"Got wrong chicks," Prelate sneered. "We do repairs. All new replacement parts, guaranteed. Skip your Better Business Bureau bullshit, please."

"That thing you got out of that abandoned car down by the Black River? Murder evidence."

"What you mean, 'murder evidence'?" Prelate said.

"Don't listen to him, honey," Vervain said. "He's just blowing smoke."

"The Bowler," Bernal said. "Ever hear of him?"

"Bullshit!" Prelate said.

"Like my friend here said, we don't handle salvage." Vervain sounded calm, almost friendly. "So you got yourself some serious misinformation. I'd talk to that person. Tell him to get more accurate."

"Heads," Bernal said. "You find any heads in that thing?"

He struck a nerve. "No bullshit heads! You watch too much TV! No Bowler heads." Prelate set her long screw driver down.

"Muriel Inglis was murdered at the location where you got that thing." He was guessing, but he suspected that that was what Charis's follow-up investigation would show. Every line of activity seemed to knot up there, on the muddy bank of the Black, two nights ago.

"Bull . . ." Prelate couldn't get it out this time. The two women looked at each other. "Freezing asshole! Frickin'—"

"Shut up," Vervain said. "Just . . . shut up."

"Can't afford more trouble, you know that!" Prelate was suddenly close to hysteria. "This . . . did you know? What it was?"

Vervain turned back to Bernal. "Look, mister, what you after?"

"If he tell you and not tell me, what can I do?"

Bernal and Vervain both ignored the increasingly hysterical Prelate. "Me? I'm trying to find something out. But this . . . whatever it is. That's right in the middle of it. That car, the one you took it out of, there was a murder there."

Vervain shook her head. "Look, let me show you something."

She turned back to her refrigerator. She squatted down and slung the massive compressor easily. Bernal had to step back to avoid getting hit. She gave him a slight smile, radar-dish earrings swinging, and rested it on a red hand truck. She pulled out a bandanna and mopped her sweat-free face with it.

"I'll have to call," Bernal said. "I don't think you understand the ramifications of this."

But there was no signal on his cell phone.

"They got some shielding," Vervain said. "Like their privacy. Funny folks, the people who live in this house. They're not back for five weeks. They're in Africa, doing a safari. Asked me where they should go. Like I got some kind of native knowledge. In my blood, right? The homeland. I told them, stick to the Roger Williams Zoo, down in Providence. Nice place. Ever been there? I take my nieces. But it had to be Africa."

She was being informative, telling him exactly what he needed to know, but he wasn't really listening, trying to figure out how he could call Charis and still keep an eye on these two . . . where was Prelate? She was no longer at the kitchen table. Had she managed to—

As Prelate grabbed his arms from behind, Vervain gagged him with the bandanna.

It took a matter of seconds for them to haul him down a set of stairs and past a basement laundry area. They threw him down. Prelate clinked something that sounded like metal and glass. Vervain knelt on the small of his back and removed the gag. Then she stepped back, and a heavy door clicked shut.

For a moment, he lay stunned in the darkness.

Then he rolled and threw himself at the door. It was padded, so he didn't hurt himself much, but it didn't even make a sound.

He stopped, held his breath, listened. The silence was absolute. He couldn't imagine that Prelate and Vervain were still working upstairs, but if they had been, he wouldn't have heard them.

The darkness was just as absolute. He couldn't even get a sense of how large the space was. The air was definitely cold, but not meat-locker cold.

Bernal put out his arms and stepped forward, slowly, slowly. The floor was level concrete, so he could slide his feet. There. A wall, concrete as well. And the door was . . . this way? Yes. The padding was leather, or some close synthetic, with what he presumed were ornamental nail heads, diamond-shaped.

He could think of one reason to have a sealed cool room in your basement. He reached to his right and was rewarded with the rattle of glass against wood. Bottles, ranks and ranks of them. This was a wine cellar.

He thought quickly. Even with a locked and secure door, the place probably had an emergency exit lever as an elementary safety precaution. Starting in the center of the door, he searched to the left, up and down, and back the other way.

And here it was, a simple rod with a textured rubber handle. Bernal let out a sigh of relief and pulled. He felt the latch lift up.

Then something snapped, and the lever dangled loose.

For a moment, Bernal couldn't believe it, and worked the lever up and down. It still swung on its pivot, but was no longer connected to anything.

So he lay down on the floor. It was cool and smooth, a high-quality pour. Its hardness was the only thing that kept the place from being a sensory deprivation chamber. Did people still use those? There used to be quite a fashion for them, people floating in body-warm buoyancy-neutral pools, cut off from every sensory input. It was a kind of test of existence: if the universe disappeared, did you go too? If you didn't, what did you do for entertainment?

He found his thoughts running on their hamster wheels. The way Monique had laughed at him in fifth grade, when he decided that a *Star Wars* vest with pictures of Han Solo and Luke Skywalker on it would be elegant wear for the first day of school. Those damn cardiac action potentials. A package with a book about Minoan statuary that blew up in his face. All the ridiculous pieces of this puzzle of Muriel, Madeline Ungaro, and Hesketh.

There had be something he could do. They'd screwed with the safety release, but they hadn't had much time to do it. Maybe he could figure out how to get it to work.

Something clinked and rolled against his foot as he stood. He knelt, picked it up.

A wine bottle, open. About half of it had spilled out on the floor. Damn it. This was perfect. Not only had they locked him in down here, but now they'd made him look like a snooty drunk, only satisfied by a Grand Cru. He put the bottle against the wall and stepped around the puddle.

He had to see if there was something, anything, in this dark space that could help him. Starting at the top of the rack to the right of the door, he felt carefully, bottle by bottle, building a map in his mind. That was something he could do: carefully delineate the limits of his prison.

Each wall was covered, six feet up, maybe a thousand bottles per wall. That seemed excessive, somehow. But, hell, Bernal had plenty of frequent buyer cards from bookstores, and he never actually used them, waiting for that one big score, that *Phaidon Atlas of Contemporary World Architecture* that would get him the heftiest discount. So people waited to enjoy themselves at the perfect time. There was a lot of potential pleasure down here, energy like a boulder balanced on a cliff. Happiness research indicated that people overestimated pleasure both in prospect and in retrospect, but that in the single moving bead of the present moment, joy was always at a moderate level. Perhaps the cumulative anticipation in this cellar would, in aggregate, bring more pleasure than drinking it ever would.

He found useful things. A corkscrew dangling from a string meant that he could enjoy a bottle without smashing the neck against something and potentially slicing up his cheeks in the dark. A dust cloth, probably used to clean off the most valuable labels, could serve as a pillow, if he stayed here until the owners got back from Africa. And there, at the end of the last row, his hand encountered the rubbery grip of a flashlight.

As happens even in the best of households, someone had neglected to update the batteries, so its light was a dim yellow and wouldn't last long. He brought it over to the door and squinted at what he could now see of the handle mechanism. He pulled the handle. He could see that it didn't engage anything, but nothing seemed to be broken. He relaxed, trying to understand purpose, function, and the current mismatch between the two. And, ah . . . there. A linkage was missing. A cotter pin, or something, between the arm and the rest of the mechanism. They'd yanked it out or broken it.

He turned the flashlight off to spare the battery. There was only one way for this thing to work. The lever arm went down, the short end went up, yanking up a latch with a hook. Simple, something that had been around for centuries, no matter whether there was a keypad on the other side, with a code that engaged an electromagnetic lock. Lifting the latch overrode it. An emergency override had to work under all circumstances. But the lever now slid past the hook without engaging it. The impossible-to-anticipate situation: sabotage.

Without even turning on the flashlight, he walked over

and grabbed the corkscrew. Yes. It was a hollow spiral of metal, the kind that minimized the risk of splitting the cork. It took him a couple of minutes to untie the length of twine it was hanging from.

He had the theory. The corkscrew would certainly slide into the hole left by the vanished cotter pin. If he could just get it in there. . . .

There was a sound on the other side of the door. They'd returned to finish the job. Of course. They'd just been holding him here, out of the way, while they finished up whatever else they were doing, and they had now returned to tie up their one remaining loose end.

He stepped back. His only weapon was the corkscrew. Knowing he looked like a feeble idiot, he stuck its point out between his knuckles.

The door swung open.

"Jesus, Bernal." Yolanda's blond head was silhouetted by a single dim hall light. She sniffed the air. "I hope you saved some for me."

27

Yolanda knelt and dabbed at the puddle of spilled wine with a paper towel. She wore a toreador jacket and tight pants. Her pale blond hair was heavily processed into a lion's mane.

"This isn't going to do it." She took a long pull on the open bottle, which proved to be a Saint-Estèphe, though neither Yolanda nor Bernal proved able to determine whether it was a good year. "Go upstairs, will you, hon? Grab a couple of rolls from under the sink. And get me some . . . let me think. Cheese crackers, something like that. I need something to go with these jammy notes here."

"Cheese crackers?" He thought a moment. "How did you get in?"

"The security door has a code. Not a fancy one, but not one you're likely to guess quick. But they didn't think they'd remember it, so they wrote it on a piece of paper and put it under the cake of scented soap in the basement, over there past the Neptune washer and dryer. No one ever comes down here, so they figured that was safe enough. They got seven bathrooms in this place. I counted."

"No, I meant the house."

"I know this 'hood, Bernal. Used to have friends here, before I had all my unfortunate financial reverses, all that stuff that Uncle Solly could make good, if those idiots at Long Voyage would just see they were beaten. I do still come down here sometimes, drive around, see my old haunts. That beat-up red van of yours sticks out like a sore thumb. Around here, they have a big truck with a magnet to go along the curb and pick up crap like that. Must not be running today. So I stopped to see what you were up to. You know, Bernal, you really don't know what the hell you're doing. Nothing personal. I'm just saying."

"Bad luck. It was just plain bad luck. Could happen to anyone."

"Oh, sure. Any of us could end up getting locked in the basement by the appliance people. Get me those paper towels. And don't forget the cheese crackers or whatever else you can scare up." Yolanda winked and took another swig of wine.

"Um, are they—"

"Those scary women? They're long gone. Go on up, say hi to the folks. Nice crowd."

A handful of people sat around the giant coffee table in the living room. They nodded at Bernal, as if they knew him, but not well, and returned their attention to the TV. A woman on a talk show had just revealed that she'd been a cocaine mule on her honeymoon, while her husband sobbed and yanked at his long hair next to her and the audience hooted. Most of the people at the table looked like recent Hispanic immigrants, with a few other ethnicities thrown in. Four men, three women. Food littered the coffee table: chalupas, samosas, tomatillo salsa.

No cheese crackers.

It looked like most of the cleaning crews in this part of town took their break in the same place, the house of people known to be on an extended African vacation.

Bernal saw a row of plastic buckets with rubber gloves neatly hanging on their rims, a giant vacuum cleaner one step away from being a rider just beyond. Someone had vacuumed the thick pile carpeting into mathematically precise rows. The dishes on the coffee table were all disposable, and the table itself had been wrapped in a plastic sheet. When they were done with lunch, they would just pull up the sheet and throw the whole thing away, with not a sign being left.

Bernal went into the kitchen. The refrigerator was back in its place, humming gently. Two gardeners sat at the counter playing cards and drinking coffee out of delicate china cups. A plasma screen TV above the counter showed a jai alai game. The one with the do-rag yelled at someone on his phone—probably his bookie. The other one shook his head at the excessive enthusiasm and cut the cards. Bernal noted how he palmed a card and slid it onto the top of the deck. Bernal tried to smile at him in a conspiratorial way, but received a stony look in reply.

He opened a couple of cabinets, found a roll of paper towels and a box of Cheez-Its, and went back into the basement.

28

They crept past the corner of a garage. Bernal almost knocked over a garbage can but grabbed it just in time.

"Careful!" Yolanda slipped easily through a gap between two chain-link fences: neighbors who had not managed to cooperate. "Those people over there have some kind of vicious dog. It leaves gigantic turds. Though I hear some people get fake ones to throw around, to scare anyone who might want to break in. Come on, step on one, see if it's real. Put my mind at rest."

"Don't be so grumpy with me, Yolanda. I had no idea those crackers would be stale."

"Grumpy? I'll show you grumpy. I'll sic a vacuum cleaner salesman on you."

"Harsh."

"You don't know the half of it."

She sashayed ahead of him. She shook the Saint-Estèphe bottle over her tongue, getting whatever drops remained, then pitched it over a fence into a neighboring yard. They both listened, but it hit nothing but soft grass and was absorbed into the spring night.

"Where the hell are we going?" They were somewhere near Spillvagen's house, but she'd approached the neighborhood from an unfamiliar direction, and he wasn't sure how close they were.

"Surveillance. It's a hell of a job, but somebody's got to do it. Somebody who wants to make her dear uncle's death in some way meaningful, anyway."

They stopped by a large oak tree.

"These things look dangerous, but it's a fake." Yolanda climbed the tree's trunk. "Safety regulations, don't you know."

And, in fact, as he followed, Bernal saw that she was right. The steps looked like small boards nailed into the trunk in the traditional build-your-own-treehouse style, but were really a complete set in some weather-resistant composite, held up by two rubber-coated support bars sunk into the bark.

At the top was a treehouse, also composite made to look like mismatched plywood sections. All it lacked was a deliberately casual sign that said NO GIRLZ.

Yolanda collapsed on the floor, gasping for breath. "That's it for my nightly workout. Should stick to yoga, like the rest of the girls. Or maybe just acupuncture."

Bernal peeped through the window and found himself looking at Spillvagen's house. He caught sight of Honor stalking off to submit a formal complaint to her mother, while Clay danced apelike behind her, pirouetting and waving his arms.

"Here." Yolanda handed him a pair of binoculars. "This makes it way easier. You can pretty much read the shopping lists on the refrigerator with these babies. The Spillvagens buy a lot of crap. Not good for the kids."

"What the hell are you doing?" Bernal said. "Where are we?"

"Surveillance, sweet thing. Surveillance. Don't get no evidence without surveillance. And this is the hideout of the younger Ash Willingham. He's getting a bit old for this place. Even easy girls don't necessarily want to have sex in a kid's treehouse; you have to be a bit older to find that kind of thing interesting. But he still comes up here. And thank God, 'cause I don't have to haul my own molecules up here." She pried up a section of flooring. "Clever boy, our Ash. Take a look."

Bernal did. There was nothing under the flooring, just the bottom layer of the treehouse.

"Loose floorboards are one of those things parents do check. Think they're real secret squirrels if they do. They were bad in high school, think they know the score. But Ash . . . Ash is my man." She reached way underneath, feeling with her fingers. "The frame's metal. Steel. I mean, this poor tree. . . . Ash got himself a few of those really strong magnets . . . like *strong*. I like 'em."

"Neodymium-iron-boron," Bernal said. "You can get them online."

Magnets. When Ignacio had been yelling at Patricia behind Near Earth Orbit the night Bernal helped her lug the Freon up to the diner roof, Ignacio had asked her why she hadn't attached the tanks under her truck with electromagnets. Why had that popped into his mind now? He jiggled the moment, shook it, turned it upside down, but nothing came out of it.

"Oh, what can't you get online?" She grunted and tugged. Something finally came loose, and she pulled out a plastic box. The magnets were tiny dots on either end, glued onto the box. "Satisfaction. That's what you can't get online. He clicks this thing up under the support. Real smart. To find it you'd really have to look for it."

"How'd you find it?"

"I really looked for it. Believe me, I know my teens. Still inside their heads. So I knew it was there. Great time of life, you gotta hang on to it." Inside the box was a bag of marijuana, a small pipe smelling of burnt resin, and a few packs of rolling papers. "Hey, wow, this really takes me back. . . ."

"I can't believe you steal this poor kid's dope," Bernal said.

"Yeah, poor frickin' kid. Drives a new Mustang Shelby GT that takes a Saudi oil field to power and probably gets blow jobs in the hot tub from members of the school gymnastics team *and* from his dad's accountant." She already had the papers out and was nimbly rolling a joint. She crimped the ends between sharp red fingernails.

"Accountant? I must be missing out on the latest sexual fantasies."

"Sit up here, you wouldn't believe what you see," Yolanda said darkly.

"What do you see?"

Her face was illuminated for an instant by the lighter. "Want a toke?"

"It's been a long time . . ." Despite his better judgment Bernal inhaled a little. He held in his breath and felt swirling move from his lungs into the rest of his body. Magnets. There were a lot of different things that could hang on to things with magnets. "Spillvagen. You're still watching him. Find anything out?"

Yolanda wriggled closer to Bernal, reached over, and delicately took the joint out of his mouth. She smiled at him. Her eyes looked big in the darkness. "I've found out that for a retired cryobank therapist, he's a busy man. He's like a whole kicked-over ant nest, all on his own. Your fault, I think, Bernal."

"My fault?"

"Here. One more." She put the joint up to Bernal's mouth. He hadn't wanted any more, but he pulled the smoke in. "Can't let our friend Ash get suspicious, so enough for you." Her fingertips pressed gently against his lips as she took the joint away. "Our buddy Spillvagen's gotten all active lately. I've been putting in some miles just keeping after him, and that's expensive. Not even tax deductible, I think, even if I get that dough out of the trust. It's a real change. He usually just sits in that damn garage of his, beating off to Internet porn. Isn't that what men mostly do nowadays? I mean, those trendy ergonomic office chairs are just set up for that. I'm surprised they don't come with a tissue dispenser in the arm."

"So what has he been doing?" Yolanda's observations were too close for comfort. As was she. He could feel her body heat as her hip pressed against him. "Since I talked to him."

"Who?"

"Spillvagen!"

She giggled. "Don't be so impatient."

"Things are going on," Bernal said. "I'm . . . worried. There's a lot still I don't understand, and I'm trying to."

"Don't." She slid her cool fingertips across his forehead. "Don't wrinkle up so much. You look much better when you're just looking thoughtful rather than worried. You've got a nice thoughtful look."

"Okay. I'll try not to worry. Swear."

"'No worries.' Isn't that what the Aussies say? That's about all I know about Australians. Are there really Australians? Sometimes I think they're just made up for movies and ads."

She smelled surprisingly clean and floral, a note too pure for her jungle-cat persona. He sensed that she was matching him breath for breath. That was a technique he used. It was unfair to use it back at him. He felt his heart beating. He felt everything, the jittering in the big muscles of his thighs, a tingling in his shoulders, a stirring along his spine. It had been a while.

He had to figure out what she was talking about, before things went too far. "Spillvagen. What is he doing? What has he done?"

"You tell me something first." Her breath was warm on his ear. "What went down, there at good old Long Voyage?"

"I don't—"

"Oh, I'm sure he told you, finally. He wouldn't tell me, but he told you. They had a fire. A breach of, like, *containment*, right?"

"They had problems, he said. Yeah, sure, security wasn't as tight as it might have been."

"They lost him, didn't they? Uncle Solly. They didn't just, I don't know, defrost him or give him freezer burn or something. They out-and-out lost him."

"How do you suppose they lost him?" he said.

"Oh, Bernal." She pouted. "I think you must have some idea. You've been thinking about it, haven't you? And I'll bet when you think about something, you figure it out."

To get her to leave him alone, he kissed her. He felt her smile against his lips. As he pushed forward, she pulled back, just enough to keep him going. Her knee slid past his hip. His heart was pounding so hard he felt like throwing up.

"Oh, ow, just a second. . . ."

She turned and knelt, her body sharply curved beneath him. She snapped Ash's stash closed and put it back into place underneath the steel support rail. The clank was surprisingly loud. Permanent magnets, even NdFeB, that were strong enough to hold something really heavy would be too strong to easily detach. For something heavier, you would use an electromagnet, preferably superconducting. . . .

Yolanda turned back. She was a genius. His hand had ended up between her breasts, cloth over silk over lace, and the front snap, easy, pressed against his fingers.

"Oh, I . . ."

Even as he fumbled with her bra, he sensed her attention directed elsewhere. Headlights streaked the rafters, and a pickup backed into Spillvagen's driveway. The garage door rumbled up. The vehicle backed a bit farther and stopped.

She pressed the binoculars to her eyes. She was quite a picture, pursed red lips under black tubes, blond hair fluffed out above.

Spillvagen got out of his pickup. Bernal didn't need magnification to recognize his squared-off pudgy shape. He seemed agitated. He glanced up at his house, where his family waited for him, then hurried into his garage. In the next few minutes he carried out a line of gym lockers, some hi-fi speakers almost as tall as he was, and half a dozen cardboard boxes that looked like they had been carried the last three times the Spillvagen family had moved, and never opened. With a cracking of branches, he shoved everything into the hedge that protected the neighbors from having to see a yawning pajama-clad Norbert walk out to his office in the morning, and backed his pickup in. The garage door, complaining louder now about being awoken from its ancient slumber, rumbled down . . . and bounced off the front bumper. It started to retract but stopped before getting all the way back up.

It whined mournfully. A dog barked in the next yard. Great, Bernal thought. Now that stupid German shepherd was out and whipped into a frenzy.

"What the hell does he have back there?" Yolanda laughed. "A case of Girl Scout Thin Mints? Or Girl Scouts? God, look at him! He's desperate."

Spillvagen had run out to stare in disbelief at his bumper. He pushed against it with his foot as if trying to compress his pickup, kicked it, then ran back in.

He bumped his head on the lowered garage door. He

grabbed his forehead and bent over to go in, too frantic and demoralized to even swear. The truck pulled forward enough to push its windshield against the edge of the door, then clunked into reverse and slammed backwards into the garage. Something big and loaded with breakable items fell against the back wall with a crash. Bernal remembered the vast warren of shelves, boxes, and old gear back there.

Spillvagen waddled back out of the garage, remembering to duck this time. He jumped up, grabbed on to the garage door handle, and dangled there, feet flailing.

Yolanda was laughing so hard she couldn't even sit up. She'd dropped the binoculars and was pounding her head on the windowsill. Spillvagen seemed to hear something and even in his anxiety to get the garage door back down again, glanced around.

She put her hands over her mouth and curled up, but Bernal could still see her back heaving.

The garage door suddenly gave up the unequal contest and rolled down. Spillvagen jumped aside just in time.

"Oh . . ." Yolanda tried to get a breath. "Oh my God." Yolanda slumped against the back wall and looked at Bernal. Her eyes glimmered with tears. She had never been more attractive than in that moment. "That was just what the doctor ordered."

Bernal glanced back out the window. Spillvagen had come out of the garage carrying something like a small barrel. Moving carefully, he waddled into the yard and set it down.

It was his reflector telescope. With shaking fingers, he punched some sequence of coordinates into the computerized equatorial mount. He hadn't brought a chair, so he kneeled by it like a man by a sick child's crib. He put his eye to the eyepiece. The universe waited for his reaction.

Spillvagen's shoulders relaxed. For a moment, he pulled

his eye away and rested his forehead against the telescope's belly. Then he put his eye back to the eyepiece and looked up in perfect silence at the stars.

"Now, where were we?" Yolanda said.

Bernal wouldn't just be touching her, much as he wanted to. He'd be allowing himself to be recruited and attached to her mission. He couldn't allow his body to make that kind of decision for him.

"I'll have to take a rain check," Bernal said.

"Really." Yolanda wasn't surprised at all.

"Look, I'm sorry, but—"

She pressed her finger hard against his lips. He could feel both the sharpness of her fingernail and the softness of her finger. It was almost enough to excite him again.

"Nothing less erotic than an apology," she said. "You can get things dry cleaned, repaired, replaced. Just don't apologize."

"I'm . . . okay, okay."

"Goodnight, Bernal."

"So, um . . . Keep an eye on Spillvagen. Call me if he goes anywhere . . . odd."

"Odd." Yolanda leaned back against the wall, closed her eyes. "That loser's not doing anything odd. All of you guys are really boring. Might as well be frozen already."

29

"Everything operates in that zone between determinism and randomness," Bob the waiter said. "That's what makes analyzing conspiracies so difficult. Some of the unfortunate events that actually occurred and made our world what it is really were the result of a predetermined plan, worked out at board meetings with catered lunches and matching leather-bound briefing books, and then stitched together by gritty-eyed techs in some cube farm using project management software to generate Gannt charts. Others just happened. The best conspiracies are actually reactive, springboarding off real events, incorporating them into their comprehensive worldview. When you look at them later, it's tempting to think that each one of those events had to have been planned. Screws you up something awful. Particularly when you expect the seriousness of the consequences of the event to somehow relate to how contingent it was. You already know what I'm getting to here."

"How's the lamb today?" Charis regarded Bob with

her pale brown eyes. Today she wore an official-looking dark blazer, which accentuated her shoulders.

"As far as I am aware, we are the only restaurant that still serves mutton. If you're nostalgic for the cooking of English boarding schools . . ."

"Not Kennedy again," Bernal said.

"But of course. I measure conspiracy theory plausibility in Oswalds. Not a high standard, in case you're wondering."

"The pasta primavera?" Charis persisted.

"Canned vegetables have more vitamins than fresh, I've read. I'm sure it's nutritious."

"Burgers," Bernal said. "Two?"

Charis stared at him. She'd been unwilling to come here, but Bernal had insisted. "Sure. Well done."

"Always a good choice." Bob collected their menus. "Kennedy! Bastard had one foot in the grave, one foot on a banana peel as it was. Addison's disease, osteoporosis, he was doped up with cortisone, painkillers, relaxants, stimulants . . . incredible. You know what killed him, in the end?"

"A bullet," Bernal said.

"Uh . . . exactly! A 6.5 × 52mm slug from a Mannlicher-Carcano. Oswald's first shot hit him in the neck. Serious wound, but possibly not fatal. Normal guy would have slumped down into the seat, out of sight, off to the hospital, maybe recovered. But Kennedy had a back brace that kept him upright. Second shot blew the front of his head off. You ever hear one of those spittle-spraying conspiracy buffs work that into one of their miracles of Balanchine-level assassination choreography? No! And why? Because if they did work that back brace in as a functional element, like the course of the car, the view lines from the knoll, all the rest, they'd come right up against the inevitable knowledge that Kennedy was incredibly easy to kill. They've set up a locked-room mystery in a house with no doors. An aide always followed him around with a black bag full of medicine from JFK's Dr. Feelgood, Max Jacobson. A modification in any of his drugs might have killed him in a way that was wholly deniable. The treatment regimen was such a secret that any investigation of the death would have been perfunctory and the results always ambiguous. An overdose! What could be more likely? It was the fact that he actually stayed alive so long that was the real conspiracy." He paused. "Two burgers, you said?"

"Yes." Charis was clearly holding on to her patience.

"Coming right up." Bob sauntered back to the kitchen.

"You like the food here?" Charis said.

"Ah, no. It sucks, actually. I come here for the atmosphere."

"So what do you think this thing was?" Charis got down to business. "And what reason do you have to think that it was in that Peugeot we looked at?"

Bernal had told her what he had discovered the day before, leaving out his encounter with Yolanda in Ash's treehouse, which did not seem relevant.

"I think it was a . . . headtaker. Something that severs human heads and then keeps them in cold storage until such time as Hesketh can find a use for them."

"And you think your buddy Spak saw it? The night Muriel died? With her head in it?"

"I do."

"But you didn't actually get to see it yourself. Under the tarp."

"No. I was interrupted by Vervain. But, Charis, I'm sure—"

"Bernal. I believe you. I talked to some of the higher-ups at Long Voyage. Not easy. They're a bit on edge, as you might imagine. They revealed something to me. Some months ago, they lost a piece of equipment. Something pretty expensive, I guess. It was something they used when someone died away from a medical facility—"

"The field kit!" Bernal said. "Spillvagen told me about that."

"I'll bet he did."

"What does that mean?"

"It means that they suspect he's the one who took off with it. It vanished just around the time he quit and set up his own business. But they don't have proof or even any vague evidence. But I bet they've got these gals out looking for it. They're really desperate to have the thing back. It's a product differentiator for them. 'Our heads are fresher.' "

"Maybe," Bernal said. "But that doesn't explain what it was doing, attached as part of a headtaker, under a car by the Black River."

"Because it wasn't any kind of 'headtaker,' Bernal. Spillvagen was just moving that field kit around, keeping it hidden. He couldn't take the risk someone would just break into his garage."

He looked at her. "You don't believe in it anymore. In Hesketh."

"You make it sound like I've stopped believing in Santa Claus. Get serious, Bernal. We have a killer, a real live killer. One person, maybe more than one, but a regular old psycho who happens to have connections to Long Voyage, to Hess Tech, all through this case. Those of us who want to believe in hidden truths are amazingly easy to bamboozle."

"What do the other people in your office think?"

"Who?"

"In Social Protection. Have you reported this up, national headquarters or whatever, or have you been keeping it private because you didn't really believe in it?"

She sighed. "Speaking of Santa Claus . . ."

None of this was really a surprise. "No SP?"

"Well . . . no. It doesn't exist. When I was asked to leave the force, I didn't know what else to do. You'd think there would be plenty of badass technology-specific activist organizations out there, but that's just a media thing. There ain't none. Everyone who is interested in artificial intelligence pretty much agrees on everything. They're all standing around their backyards waiting for the magic nozzle of the Singularity to suck them up. Pussies. All there is is pussies." She shook her head. "So I juiced up my own organization. Not too hard. Got a book on HTML, bought a few domain names, got a designer to whack me up some templates, went to town. Looks pretty real, right?"

Bernal had gone from passionate opposition to grudging collaboration, all with an organization that did not really exist. It left him with an odd sense of emptiness. He never would have thought he'd miss Social Protection.

"So, what, you think you're going to go out and trap the Bowler on your own and get back at all those guys on the force who never believed in you?"

She looked as if he'd slapped her.

"I'm going to do what I need to do, mister. Someone killed Muriel. Someone tried like hell to kill you and me. Madeline Ungaro vanished the night Muriel died and has never been seen since. This is no kind of shit for you to be anywhere near."

"Because I'm crazy and believe in real AIs."

"Because killers are dangerous people, Bernal. And you've never seen a killer without a remote in your hand. All you can do is get in the way. And maybe get killed."

She was furious with him. And she had good reason to be. Why was he perceptive enough to know what motivated someone without being perceptive enough to shut up about it?

"I'm sorry, Charis. I didn't mean . . . I understand why you need to do this. I'll stay out of your way."

"It's really not that interesting, Bernal." She tried to be light, but he could see she was still pissed. "Just the usual. Just a killer."

"Yeah," he said. "I know. I should just move along."

He got into his car, even though there was nowhere he wanted to go. The cast-iron borzoi still sat in its seat, the Post-it sticking up at a jaunty angle on its tail. "Sorry," the note said.

Well, hell, we're all sorry about something.

The Mercedes had been driven by the Connoisseur, whoever he was. Muriel had run out and taken it. Pure coincidence, right? Blind luck.

But now, according to Charis, the Connoisseur had been seen several times in Muriel's neighborhood. And Jennifer said things, specific things, had been taken from her house.

That looked like a little more than coincidence. What if Muriel had been working with this guy to begin with?

He looked back at NEO. Charis had already stumped out to her Hummer and driven away. Off to catch a killer, a game Bernal couldn't play.

He yanked the Post-it off. Then he looked at it. The "Sorry" was scrawled in pencil. But . . .

He tilted it. The note had come from a pad. And was that the faint impress of the previous note on it?

He fumbled in his glove box and found the pencil stub that had probably been used for the note. He examined it, but the Connoisseur hadn't left tooth marks in it, or anything else of forensic interest.

Working gently, barely touching the paper, he left a thin layer of graphite on the sheet. Everything got a tiny bit darker, but the slightly impressed letters stayed light. Pretty soon he could read them.

"Dr. Kerakian. 2:30 Thursday, April 14."

That was still two days away. A quick online search revealed one Dr. Kerakian in the Cheriton area: a gynecologist. Bernal thought about this for a moment. He'd been clocked by a man, not a woman. This was annoyingly disconfirming. Coincidence again?

He dialed the number.

"Dr. Kerakian's office," a woman's voice answered.

"Hi." Bernal adopted what he hoped was a light tenor that could be interpreted as either sex. He could only hope that the person who had made the appointment was not personally known to the receptionist. "I have an appointment? Um, on Thursday? At 2:30?"

"And your name?"

Bernal froze and almost hung up at that point. Instead, he turned, pulled the phone away from his ear, and yelled, "Please stop that, Sam. Please don't make me take it away. What? No, lunch will be in a few minutes. Just let me—"

"Here it is, Ms. Rennie," the receptionist said. "Do you need to change it?"

"No," Bernal said. "I don't think so. But I wanted to be sure. . . . Did I leave the lake number?" He'd flipped to a display of vacation homes at Lake Winnipesaukee. He rattled off the contact number for one of them.

"No." The receptionist read back a different number, which he scribbled down.

"Oh. We're back from the lake, and I didn't want . . ."

"Will there be anything else?" The receptionist made it clear that absolute clarity in backup contact information was not her highest priority. Bernal could hear a child crying in the waiting room, and someone was asking an increasingly urgent question.

"No. Thank you. I'll see you on Thursday."

With a last name and number, it didn't take him long to fill things in. Maura Rennie, 37, single, 2561 Old Enfield Road, East Cheriton. Parents deceased. One sibling, a brother, John Rennie, 34.

John Rennie. Was that him? The long-sought Connoisseur?

He almost called Charis. But, no. She'd just read him a lecture. And despite what Charis had told him, all that entirely reasonable, sensible, and smart stuff, he was going to try to find Muriel. She had had some kind of arrangement with the Connoisseur, one that seemed to still be in operation. That was a route to find her.

He thought the Connoisseur, very probably named John Rennie, might be able to get answers. Plus, he had to admit, it would be kind of nice to chat with the guy who had smacked him with the borzoi.

John had no address. Only Maura did.

"Please go away." The woman was fuzzed behind the screen door.

"I need to see John. John Rennie. He here?"

"I don't . . . he's not . . . oh, hell. You . . ." She stared more intently at him. "He's not."

"I have something for him. Something he left with me."

"Don't give it to me. I don't have any interest in his stuff."

"He tends to have a lot of nice stuff, John."

"Sure, nice stuff. Bastard knows enough to have invented *Antiques Roadshow.* But that's not the way his mind works. Dumbass from birth, and believe me, I've been there all the way along." She crossed her arms and leaned against the side of the door, still not opening the screen. She wore a long-sleeved man's shirt over a T-shirt and had curly red hair, too wild to be cared for easily. Crossing her arms brought her breasts into prominence. "Plus, you're not here to return anything."

"No. I just want to see if he's working with someone I know. Someone who's missing. Someone I need to find."

"John never works with anyone. If you knew him, you'd know that. Please go."

"Look." Bernal was desperate. "Terrible things are happening. People are dead. And a friend of mine . . . it's too complicated. But your . . . John Rennie could really help me out by answering a few questions. I mean, he hit me." He pointed to the bruises on the side of his face. "Knocked me out and stole my car and left me on a lawn overnight."

"He . . . what car? What model is your car?"

"Dodge Ram. Red. Nothing sexy, but it gets me and my stuff where I need to go."

"And he hit you with a cast-iron doggie doorstop, right? A borzoi."

"Um, yeah. How did you know that?"

She grabbed two giant handfuls of her hair and pulled. "Never mind how I know that." She flipped the hook off the screen door and walked back into the kitchen. Bernal pushed it open, then caught it so it wouldn't bang.

"My name's Bernal," he said. "I'm not a cop."

"Maura. Like I couldn't tell that. Only reason I'm talking to you."

"You," he said. "You wrote the note. The apology."

"Look. I had no idea he'd, like, left you somewhere. He didn't tell me that. He just had me pick him up at the mall parking lot. He was going to leave your car there, let you find it later. Jesus, I still can't believe John hit you. He's not like that, you have to believe me. Crazy. But just not that way."

Bernal remembered the man's obvious terror. He'd been caught and had done what he needed to do to escape. "Fine. But I still need to talk to him."

"To hit him?"

Bernal considered his reply. "Maybe."

"Turn him over to the cops?"

"Not unless . . . no. I wasn't actually thinking of that. He has information. He knows things I need to know. I think. He might have been hired by a friend of mine. I mean, I'm not sure. I just need to . . ."

"Look, ah, Bernal." She sat down at the kitchen table. "Maybe John's not the only one who's so stuck he's doing stuff he sucks at. Um. Look, I can't just sit here with you, and I don't smoke anymore." She swung around in her chair, opened the refrigerator, and pulled out two cans of Heineken. "This okay?"

Bernal popped the top, took a swig. "Perfect." And it was.

The table was small. But she'd put a tablecloth on it and a vase with a spray of miniature pink carnations. Real ones—Bernal had felt at the petals, assuming they were plastic, and now hoped she wouldn't see the torn one. It was facing him. Chances were good she wouldn't notice it until he left.

"Maybe John has been working with someone," she said. "Not like him. But . . . is that who you're after? Who he's working with?"

"In a way." Bernal wasn't about to say that he was looking for the technologically retained ghost of a dead person, so he had to figure out what he could say. "My friend's . . . hiding out. Hanging low. She hasn't committed any crimes but . . . there are people after her. I think she's hired your brother to steal her some of her own stuff. She lives in a big house on Walnut Street and can't get back to it."

"Must be nice," Maura said. "To have stuff you want to keep. You don't know where your friend is."

"No. I don't."

"Reason for that? Maybe she doesn't want to talk to you. Wants to make a clean break."

Just what he needed: Maura sticking up for Muriel's

privacy. "Please. She's in real trouble." He stopped himself from saying "you have to believe me," because he'd never believe anyone who would say that.

"Hmm. I'm not sure what that lady's up to, that's for sure. Warned John about her. But he never listens to me."

Bernal drank his beer, carefully silent. Damn. He was almost done, and he wanted another one, and he wasn't about to ask her.

"First, the hair." Maura curled some of her thick, dark red hair around her finger. There was a glint of silver in it, which she scowled at. "This is real, my real color. Not a great color, really, and I'm going to have to give up on it, before it gives up on me. But . . . people go for red, because it's obvious, and it looks easy. It's not easy at all. Takes a while to learn to carry it off. Like learning a foreign language. You put the red on when you're an adult, and you'll always have an accent. So that was the first thing I thought when I saw her. Bright, flaming, curly red, not even remotely convincing. Big Gypsy earrings, the whole flouncing, fabricky thing. Some girls get old, they think Gypsy's the way to go. And, sure, the chance to wear a couple of pounds of kohl and Morticia lipstick lets you cover up a lot of hard-winter potholes."

Bernal was stunned. "Naomi Wilkerson." Had he been chasing after a complete side issue? Charis would have said he never did anything else. He remembered Naomi stealing something from the table at Muriel's funeral. Muriel's oldest friend. Had she just taken advantage of her knowledge of Muriel and what Muriel owned to loot the house after her friend's death? Jesus. He felt the air come out of him. He'd talk to her. But the chances that she would be able to tell him anything useful had suddenly grown much less.

Maura looked down at her own hand. It was big and rough, but she kept the nails nice. She had deep lines on either side of her mouth. Her life had not been easy or happy. But she worked with it.

"You know her, then."

"I've met her."

"I never asked about his work, never. Didn't want to know, and believed him every single goddam time he told me he'd given it up. I promised Mom I'd look after him, even though he's older than me. She knew. Hell, one time getting trapped in a culvert section at a construction site where he was building a 'secret hideout,' and you knew this kid was trouble. And I inherited the trouble when Mom died. She had some heart thing, I never did figure out exactly what, and she went when we were just on our way out of high school. Not a lot of money for college, which is how I ended up working office supplies at the SuperMax. Not a bad job, really, but not what I had originally planned."

Bernal shifted around. The chair he was sitting on wasn't particularly comfortable. Maura sprawled on hers like an empress being fed grapes by a slave, her thighs tight in her faded jeans, but his had all sorts of odd bumps in its back. He looked down, to see lion-clawed feet. Nothing like you'd expect from a kitchen chair.

Unless it was a chair in the kitchen of an antiques thief known as the Connoisseur. "What's this doing in here?" he asked.

"It's a chair, bro. Your ass is in it. Otherwise you'd be on the floor. Want another beer?"

"You bet."

She hesitated. "You prefer bottles? Or 'on draft'? I got draft in cans, that's it."

"Never mind the socioeconomic status indicators," Bernal said. "Just give me the goddam beer."

He'd gotten her to grin. It felt good. They clanked cans and drank simultaneously.

"I'll bet you don't usually store his stuff for him." Bernal was sure the chair was from Muriel's house. And, what's more, that he'd seen it: it had been the chair at the desk in her bedroom.

She sighed. "No. Damn thing was in my car. And my car was in the shop. John always has problems with cars. He drives like an old lady. An old lady who's trying to bulk up and has 'roid rages. So he'd picked this chair up, using my car, bashed the thing into a wall somewhere, and took it in for body work, hoping to get it fixed before I noticed. Like I wasn't going to notice that my car was gone. And I know Frankie, I do most of the arrangements for repair, and I went to school with his brother Dan. He let me pick it up, no charge. I can pull out a damn door dent and do the repaint, no need to pay those ridiculous body shop charges. John was never smart with a buck.

"It's weird, about him. He hid a lot. Cops chased him around at night. He had a rule, one that worked for him. Don't look at them. Sounds like a little kid, huh? But it's not that 'you can't see me if I can't see you' thing at all. He'd hide. But . . . he explained this to me once . . . I don't know why. I think it's got to do with the way we see things. Faces are something that we always see, even if they are not really there. So a face, with eyes, gets seen, even if nothing else does. It's an unconscious thing. So he wouldn't look. Once he was hiding in the bushes, and a cop even stepped on him. He thought that was it, but he didn't move, and the cop, if he felt him, figured it was something else, and moved on. So he got to rely on it. Maybe he's bashed up my car before, and I didn't notice. Could be." She jerked her head and listened.

"I don't want to get you in trouble," Bernal said.

"Ha. He's the one who's in trouble. You sure you don't want to do something to him?"

Bernal got up. "I just want to talk to him. There's something I'm after."

"Finding your friend."

"Um, yeah. And . . . can I call you?"

"What?"

"After I clear this up. Can I give you a call?"

For a second, he thought she wasn't going to answer. "Sure. You have the number, I guess. And most of the time I work over at the SuperMax on Scott, if you feel the yen for some jelly bean pens or something. Just one thing."

"What?"

"You look like you're right in the middle of something. Right?"

"Well, yes."

"Not a good time to add stuff to your plate. I don't want to get lost in the shuffle. So call me when . . ."

"Right. That makes sense. When I'm done."

It was silly, how good it made him feel. He picked up the chair and stepped out on the porch to talk to John Rennie, the Connoisseur.

31

Rennie hopped back from the open hatch of the Geo Metro when he saw Bernal come down the steps. "What the hell—"

"It's been a bit of work," Bernal said. "You're a hard man to find. Though I bet you thought it was impossible. Remember me?"

"I . . ." Rennie looked exactly as he had when Bernal had seen him the night Muriel disappeared, slender, with the neatly trimmed gray hair that made his age hard to judge. His sweatshirt was from Jacob's Pillow and showed stylized dancers leaping through space. "You're . . . the guy . . ."

"The guy you hit in the face with a hunk of iron? Yeah, that's me."

It had been kind of an intellectual puzzle, finding the Connoisseur. He was a guy who might have information about what Muriel had been up to and what had happened to her. But now that Rennie was in front of him, Bernal was furious.

"I . . . I'm sorry." Rennie shifted his weight in his impeccably white sneakers and looked everywhere but directly at Bernal.

"You're sorry?" Bernal found himself yelling. "That's it? That's what you have to say? I was just standing there. . . . What the hell do you know about the judicious use of force? You could have killed me, you moron."

"No, really, I'm sorry." Rennie's eyes, to Bernal's dismay, were full of tears. He blinked, then shut his eyes deliberately a couple of times. "I just didn't . . . I didn't know what to do. I was . . . your friend stole my car; I had a plan, and the car was gone, and I had to get out of there, right then. I brought your car back. Didn't I? I brought it back."

"Did you check me out? See if I was okay?"

"You were gone! On the lawn, there. I did look. You were gone, and the sprinklers were on. Everything was quiet, and you'd gone on your way, or someone had picked you up. No cops around, no ambulance, no one out, nothing. I left your car."

Bernal thought about how the car had seemed to appear while he was in the house, washing up. He'd thought he just missed it on his way in but hadn't been sure.

"And that makes it all okay?"

"No. Not okay. But I did the best . . . you got my car stolen. You left me no choice."

Despite himself, Bernal had been cooling down, but this attempt to evade responsibility sparked him up again. "We all have choices. Don't we? You could have decided not to hit me with that stupid metal dog. You could have."

"Yes. I could have. I don't know what else to say."

For an instant, Bernal thought about just hitting him. He didn't really even know how to hit someone and knew he'd probably hurt himself in doing it, but it was the only thing that really made sense.

A hint of motion at the edge of his vision caught his attention. He looked up at the house. Had that curtain been up before? He sensed someone, far enough back in the room to be invisible.

Then he snapped back to Rennie. That was exactly what had caught him the last time, a moment of inattention, and Rennie had clocked him.

But Rennie stood right where he had been. Bernal set the chair down, and Rennie winced. "Please. The concrete . . . you'll scratch the legs." He reached into the open hatch and pulled out a blanket. He laid it on the sidewalk and placed the chair carefully on it.

Punching Rennie was no way to get Maura to like him, Bernal figured. If that was important. If that mattered.

"You didn't arrange with Muriel for her to take the car?"

"What? No! I was just minding my own business when someone ran up, hopped into my car, and took off with it."

"First of all," Bernal said. "It wasn't your car. It belonged to a guy named Alistair Smithson. And you weren't minding your own business, you were breaking into a house."

"Okay, fine." Rennie sighed. He too looked up at the window with the pulled-back curtain. Maura had kept Bernal from hitting Rennie. Maybe she was keeping Rennie from running away. "I knew I should have left the area when I saw you wandering around the side of Muriel's house."

"Muriel's . . . So you admit you knew her."

"I didn't know her. I've never seen her, except, I guess, when she took off with the Mercedes. But," he patted the chair, "I have been in her house since. Nice place, Italianate, 1870s, designed by Elbridge Boyden I think—he did a lot of stuff, Gothic, whatever, but I think it's his. I should look it up down at City Hall."

Now they were just two guys, standing on a sunny street, talking, feeling the spring breeze. Bernal wasn't sure he was quite comfortable with that but didn't know how he was supposed to change it. Just be glad Rennie was talking rather than running, he supposed.

"Wait," he said. "Back up. You saw me around the side of her house?" He'd never been there.

With one finger, Rennie caressed a spindle on the chair back. He glanced at Bernal and looked puzzled. "That wasn't you. It was someone else. Bigger, anyway. Wider."

"How long before you saw me?"

"An hour, maybe. Not more than that."

An hour before Bernal got to Muriel's house for some R & R, eyes gritty, off the road from western New York, someone had been prowling around Muriel's house. Someone big, someone wide. Someone who had finally succeeded in breaking in and threatening Muriel. Only Bernal had stumbled in and thrown off the plans, allowing Muriel to escape.

And as she had run, she had thought she was still being pursued by the same person, who had, instead, stayed somewhere inside the house.

Suddenly, Bernal knew who it had been.

When he had run into Ignacio Kuepner, sullen and wrathful proprietor of Ignacio's Devices & Desires, in the Near Earth Orbit parking lot, Ignacio had seemed, for a moment, to recognize him. Bernal had decided that that impression had been wrong, since they had never met. But then, during their confrontation at the yard, Ignacio had remarked that he was now wearing a leather jacket, rather than the windbreaker he had been wearing the last time they met.

But Bernal had been wearing that leather jacket at

NEO. He had worn the windbreaker the night he came to Muriel's.

He had taken it off because of the blood on it from getting smacked in the head by John Rennie.

Oddly, now, that reminder did not raise his anger at Rennie again. He had other things to think about. Ignacio had been there that night at Muriel's, hidden somewhere, but he had seen Bernal.

"Okay," Bernal said. "You didn't know Muriel, and it was just a coincidence that she stole your car. So why the hell are you now breaking into her house? Why do you have her desk chair, right from her bedroom?"

"Because you just gave it to me."

Rennie looked guileless and straightforward. Bernal had to remind himself that Rennie was anything but. He was a criminal with a long and successful record. He didn't get that from being stupid.

"You're working with Naomi Wilkerson," Bernal said. "What do you two want with Muriel's things?"

"Sounds like Maura's been chatting up a storm."

"Hey, your sister cares for you. Wants the best for you. You should give her a break once in a while."

Rennie raised palms. "Whoa. Back off. I just don't like people in my business. I think you can understand why I'd be nervous."

"So why are you working for her?"

"She made me."

"Made you?"

"Yeah. Blackmail."

"How did Naomi blackmail you?"

"By knowing things about me. By knowing who I was. By knowing that I had stolen a car that had ended up with a body in it. I would have tried to do something about it, but stealing a few pieces was all she wanted. No vig, nothing like that. Just a couple of pieces. I decided to take the chance."

"How did she find you?"

"I don't know. She came up to me in the grocery, and I was so off my game I forgot the food. Boy, was Maura mad. We had to order pizza again. She hates that. Says it's bad for her complexion. Like you can do anything about her complexion."

"Her complexion looks fine to me."

Rennie eyed him. "Okay."

"Can you help me put the chair in my van? I know you'll want to pack it up nicely."

"You know . . ." Rennie paused.

"Yes?"

"That would actually be a big help. This Naomi . . . nice folks, really. But a bit intense. All witchy and all. Kind of hard to deal with. It'd be fine for you to make this final delivery."

They picked up the chair together, even though it was not that heavy. Bernal thought that he'd have to find Maura a substitute chair for her kitchen table. Was that a good first date? A visit to Jordan's? Maybe it was.

32

"I didn't expect to see you." Naomi's bracelets jangled as she put her hands on her hips. "Is . . . John all right? Did you . . . ?"

"I didn't do anything to him." Bernal was startled, and almost pleased. Someone thought he looked dangerous! "Not that he wouldn't have deserved it. I just told him I could handle things from here on. Where do you want this?" He looked up the steps at her. He'd had to haul the chair several blocks from the only parking spot he'd been able to find.

She hesitated.

"Let me get this up there for you," Bernal said. "It's one of Muriel's best pieces. I'll be careful with it."

"I just wish he'd said goodbye." She held the door open for him.

He carried the chair after her as she clipped up the narrow stairs on short heels. Naomi lived in an old courtyard apartment building partway up a hill above Cheriton. The railings and lighting fixtures looked original. Light came from a skylight above the stairwell.

"Careful with that thing," she said over her shoulder. "Muriel always told me it was Biedermeier. John doesn't think so—but then, he doesn't care for Biedermeier, except for some unusual Russian stuff. He loves that birch veneer. John's an interesting man. I'm sorry you two didn't get along . . . oh, here we are."

She spoke as if the appearance of the door to her apartment was a surprise.

"Why?" he said. "Why have you been stealing all of Muriel's things?"

"All in its time. Bernal, right? Come in and have a seat—not in Muriel's chair, just set that down . . . thanks. Take the club chair there, it looks like your style. I'll be right back out."

Late afternoon sunlight came through the wide slats of the blinds. He'd expected somewhere crowded with tchochkes, peacock feathers, draped tapestries, but her apartment was serene and bright, with little on the walls. The chair she'd directed him to was leather, with a masculine feel. It was, in fact, his style, and so he picked the pale-green upholstered wing chair by the fireplace.

In a couple of minutes she was back out with a silver coffee service, complete with sugar bowl and tongs. She smiled to herself when she saw where he was sitting and set the tray down on a small table. She wasn't dressed for being home alone, he saw. She wore a skirt and jacket of some nubbly fabric, in lilac, and earrings in addition to the bracelets.

She'd been looking forward to John Rennie's visit.

"Mr. Haydon-Rumi, you strike me as black." She poured before asking whether he wanted coffee at all.

"Um, light, no sugar, actually."

"Oh, dear. Just a moment." Naomi bustled back into the kitchen.

She emerged a few moments later with a small carton of half-and-half. She took a quick glance at the expiration date, hesitated, then added some to his coffee. He sipped and nodded. He hated cream in his coffee, but he was going to be damned if he'd admit it.

It didn't help that the cream was going sour.

"I know why you're here," she said.

"I'm here to find out what you know. You've been stealing Muriel's most important possessions out of her house. I don't think you decided to do all that yourself. You even boosted something at the funeral."

"A porcelain doll's head. Sure. I needed it."

"You needed it? For what?"

"Bernal, can I ask you a question?"

"Sure."

"You think I'm not doing this on my own. And you're right. But whose directions do you think I'm following?"

The believer in messages from the afterlife was teasing him. Well, he could take it.

"If you're going to be difficult . . . Muriel." He found himself speaking louder than he planned. "Muriel Inglis."

"You think she's still alive," she said, with sudden fierceness. "She's *not*. Everyone thinks I don't take death seriously, because I think souls can communicate from the other side of it. Well, that's just not true. It's because I'm one of the few people who does take it seriously. Death is real, irreversible, and awful. Do you want some advice? Don't wait until you're dead to try to communicate. Do it now. You still have a chance. Not a great one, but a better one than you will have. If you think it's hard to get your point across now, and that no one really understands what you're about, just try it when you're dead."

"I'll keep that in mind."

"No, you won't," she snapped. "No one ever does. I

guess I shouldn't complain, it's how I make up the shortfall in my retirement funds . . . but think of what you want to say, who you want to say it to, and for God's sake *say* it."

"But you think Muriel has managed to . . . communicate with you?"

Naomi smiled. "Muriel. She always was clever, you know. Sly, you might even say. I didn't like her when I met her, but I grew to like her. Took a few months, actually. In high school. But we've been friends ever since."

"How did she manage to get you to steal her furniture?"

"I was coming back from the dry cleaners. Muriel was missing. I don't know if anyone else knew she was missing, but I did. She usually gave me a call during the week. We didn't talk about much, movies, what we'd been reading, whether we'd get out to the Arboretum this spring. When I called, she didn't call back. She always called right back. I tend to put my dry cleaning off until I have absolutely nothing left to wear, so I had a huge amount of stuff hanging in the car. I used to kind of throw it back there, but it would get all creased. Muriel read me a lecture about how to treat my clothes. She always knew the best way to deal with things.

"I'd been in such a hurry, and there had been so much, that they had given me a few things that weren't mine. Not typical for them. Nice place, Armstrong Street Cleaners. Laotian. But this time they messed up.

"I had all my windows open, the radio on. And I saw a blue dress in the rearview. It blew around in the wind, and it wasn't mine.

"It was Muriel's. I recognized it immediately. Muriel always dressed like a grown-up. Not like an old lady. Oh, okay, I see that look on your face. She wasn't old. I'm not either. You were about to point that out yourself, weren't you?"

Bernal hadn't been about to say anything, and felt embarrassed.

"So I recognized the dress. Dark blue, rayon, a classic. Fit her perfectly, and she still had a great figure. A pair of spectator pumps, the Dooney and Bourke bag, pearl earrings. No hat. Not even Muriel could pull *that* off anymore." Naomi sighed. "So I glanced in the mirror, and there it was, waving at me, from among my own clothes. Like it was trying to get my attention. 'Hey, Naomi, over here!' It was right then that I knew she was dead."

"Just . . ." Bernal cleared his throat. "From a dry-cleaning error?"

"Why, yes. That's how these signs come. Through life as we live it. As soon as I could safely do so, I pulled over to the side of the road to have myself a little cry. Easier said than done, with the traffic. Traffic engineers don't design grief turnouts." And she brushed at a tear. "Oh, dammit. When you get older, all sorts of valves get loose, or stuck, or whatever. And you know what? Your emotions go along with them. I cry now more, so I feel grief more. Hard to imagine what emotions you might feel without a body . . . but I have one, and it's giving me the raspberries right now. You'll have to excuse me."

She pulled out an embroidered handkerchief and wiped away her tears. That, at least, looked just as he would have expected.

"And then?" Bernal said. "How did she communicate with you after that?"

"Well, once I understood that she needed to communicate, that there was something she had left undone, I went to work. I knew that the most comfortable thing, the thing that was most likely to bring her out, was her own space, her own furniture, everything she'd had around her. So I got John to take a few pieces. I know I shouldn't have done it, Jennifer must be furious, I'll have to apologize."

"How did you get Rennie to do it?"

"I don't really need to reveal all my sources, do I? I knew who John Rennie was. A few people do. You can't run his type of business and not reveal yourself at least a bit. Never mind who told me or what they said. John asked me, and I didn't tell him either. I came up to him in the produce section of Whole Foods. He was poking at some vegetables. I came right up to him and said 'John Rennie, I need you to steal something for me.' You should have seen him! He didn't know whether to run or smack me with an eggplant. Then he pretended he had no idea what I was talking about. I mean, really. You can tell he's a behind-the-scenes kind of gentleman. Not quick with his words. When I mentioned Muriel Inglis, he just about came apart. I had to take the eggplant away from him before he put his fingers through it. I hadn't known that . . . that he had been there that night, the night she died. She died in a car he had stolen. Did you know that, Bernal?"

"I did."

She eyed him more closely. "So you understand. He had to help. He was unhappy, but he felt guilty or something, I don't know. He's a good man, really, despite his unfortunate habit. He loves beautiful things. And he just has so much fun stealing them."

"So, what else has Muriel told you? What else has she communicated to you?"

"Nothing."

"What?"

"I'm sorry to disappoint you, Bernal, but she has been silent. I do feel her presence, but, despite everything, despite all that I have arranged, there has been nothing from her. I really had thought . . . but we're not always right about these things, no matter how much we hope for them."

Bernal was overcome with the immensity of his own

disappointment. He'd thought that, in some way, John Rennie was working for Muriel. That assumption went all the way back to the fact that he'd left a car running for her to escape in.

But, of course, that had been coincidence. A coincidence, he saw now, that had eventually given Naomi a lever on Rennie and made him a tool in her own strange schemes. And Naomi no more thought Muriel was alive as a disembodied brain than anyone else. She thought Muriel was a ghost. It had absolutely nothing to do with what he was looking for.

What he was looking for could not be found: proof that whoever it was he had been communicating with was actually the uncorrupted mind of Muriel Inglis. So there it was. "Muriel" was a fictional construct invented by Hesketh to delude foolish human beings, or she was just a ghost, an expression of a human refusal to let go of the dead, or she was a trick being played on him by a serial killer called the Bowler.

He'd be damned if he'd just stop right here. Not after everything he'd been through. "Where is that chair supposed to go?"

"No need. I can handle it from here."

"I need to see what you're doing. I need to get as close to Muriel as I can. Can't you understand that?" He stopped himself from leaning forward and grabbing her hand. "I have to."

"People use that as an excuse all the time." Naomi was crisp. "It sounds like an explanation but doesn't mean anything."

"It means that if Muriel is in trouble, if she's not a ghost but something else, then I'm her only hope. It means that if you want to help your friend, the highest-expected-value thing you could do is let me see what you've set up for her."

"Just a moment." She got up and disappeared into the

kitchen. He heard the clink of a cup, but when she came out a few moments later, she had nothing in her hands.

"Go in, Bernal." Once Naomi decided something, she didn't look back. "Take the chair into the room. Maybe she'll talk to you after all. She loved you, you know."

"She . . ."

"Oh, really, she did. She was so sad for what had happened to you, and then happy as you got better and were such a pleasure to work with. She had a lot of plans for what the two of you were going to do together. It was wonderful just to listen to her. Of course, as you know, it always was."

"I do know. I miss her too." He carried the chair down the hall, and through the door at the end.

"Put it by the desk, under the window," Naomi called behind him. "I think that's the last bit. We'll see what happens."

33

The door clicked shut behind him.

Even in the dim light that made it through the thick window curtains he could see that the room was a mess. Clothing duned against a portable oil radiator, toys and other items were scattered across the floor.

He stepped carefully across and set the chair by the kidney-shaped desk. A dim shape on the nightstand, next to a bed piled with shoeboxes, seemed to be a light, the only one he could see. He fumbled along the cord, found the switch, and dim light came from a frosted-glass circle held up by a muscular Art Deco Atlas of dark metal.

He was in Muriel's bedroom, complete to the doll's head under the highboy, the one Naomi had stolen at the funeral. It winked knowingly at him, waiting for him to figure things out.

His legs were weak. He dropped his weight into the chair. Since he'd just brought it in, it was the only place in the room clear of crap. Muriel had always been a slob.

It even looked a bit like Muriel, half-lying there on the striped silk of the daybed. It was actually her blue dress, her shoes, and a few pieces of jewelry, which glinted in the dim light. Behind the daybed was some equipment he didn't recognize, an old printer or something. He didn't remember seeing that in Muriel's house.

There was the shoe form with the black 6½, and a row of glass eyeballs, this time on the windowsill.

And a coffee cup, Muriel's favorite china, stood next to the daybed. He could see the steam coming off it. Once she had made her decision, Naomi had poured Muriel a cup and brought it in here.

It took a surprising amount of effort to move, as if he were stuck there, as motionless and still as the rest of the room. Even the traffic sounds from outside were muffled.

This was Muriel's desk. Maybe that could actually be made to mean something. Bernal bent and pulled open a drawer. Crammed with papers, opened but unemptied envelopes, paperweights. Nothing else. Muriel had always hated him poking around in her papers. He figured it was because she was embarrassed by how much undealt-with crap she kept.

The warbling bleert of an old dial-up modem jerked Bernal out of his seat. It switched to its hiss as something on the other end connected.

Naomi had really made the Connoisseur lower his standards. Bernal could see a phone handset in carnal congress with a 300 baud Hayes modem, a DECWriter II printer with fanfold paper spilling from it, what looked like a convenience store surveillance camera, and a field-phone setup, with a Weber-grill-sized antenna held up by a folding aluminum lawn chair with dangling webbing.

The print head rattled its way across the classic green-and-white fanfold paper, paused and made an oddly hesitant noise, then hummed back, coming to a stop with a little bump. The tractor pulled the paper up a line.

STAY OUT OF MY DESK

Someone had had trouble finding a ribbon with enough ink left in it. The letters were pale and fuzzy. But he could read them.

SIT DOWN SO I CAN SEE YOU

He hesitated.

PLEASE

Charis would have told him to get the hell out of there, and she would have been right. It was stupid. He was alone in here with . . . something. That was no guarantee that it was anything like Muriel.

THEYRE TRYING TO REMOVE ME NO TIME

He stepped back to the chair and sat. The surveillance camera stared at him.

I CAN HEAR YOU
TELL ME WHAT YOU NEED TO KNOW
MOST IMPORTANT FIRST YOU KNOW THE DRILL

"Where are you?" he said. "What happened to you?"

I DONT KNOW WEIRD ALIVE SPILLVAGENS A LOON BUT TOONING SEEMS TO WORK MY MIND SURVIVED BEING

The typing stopped.

Even after a few moments, he'd starting thinking of that archaic pounding as having the tones of Muriel's voice, so the silence was piercing. He couldn't think of anything else to do, so he sat, barely able to breathe.

Someone had picked up on the other phone or something. He heard the mournful song of the audio code handshaking again, the hiss, and then she was back.

PAIN IN THE
ASS SORRY
PRETEND I EXIST PLEASE
IT WILL MAKE THINGS A WHOLE LOT EASIER

For an instant it really was as if she was there, lying back on the daybed, asking him for an explanation while he fumbled through his notes about ICBM silos or basalt obelisks being raised in a dry Nevada playa or whatever extravagantly arbitrary project had most recently captured her attention. In a minute she would ask him to—

COULD YOU REFILL MY COFFEE FOR ME

"Sure." He was already getting up.

ASK A QUESTION ILL ANSWER WHILE YOU REFRESH

"Ah . . ." He didn't know if it was his question that had made her vanish. She had been discussing how she had survived decapitation. Perhaps he should focus on more immediately practical topics. "Do you know where Hesketh is now and what its plans are?"

GOOD QUESTION
ASK NAOMI WHAT MADELINE DID AFTER PAULS
FUNERAL

He picked up the still-full cup and carried it carefully out of the room. If she wanted to pretend she had actually drunk it, he'd play along. He heard the rattle of the printer behind him.

Naomi moved about the kitchen, pushing things in and out of alignment, running a kitchen towel over a drain board as dry as that Nevada playa. She moved silently, and he realized she had taken off her jangling bracelets and put on soft slippers.

"She says she would like another cup of coffee," Bernal said.

"She must have been waiting for you," Naomi whispered. "That big stupid thing, it's been hooked up for a day but hasn't done a thing. She needed to talk to you. I had no idea. I'm sorry."

"No need. She told me to ask what happened to Madeline after Paul's funeral."

"Oh. Oh my. Give me that cup. I have some fresh here."

She emptied Muriel's cup into the sink and refilled it from a carafe, as if Muriel would notice that the coffee wasn't fresh.

"Madeline really was beautiful at the funeral. And seemed completely calm, as if she had come down from some higher place to comfort us in our affliction. I remember her walking out into the sun, not looking back.

"Her mother had had roof work done at their house, and it seems there was some flashing left over. When Madeline got home from the funeral, she took a file and sharpened that flashing to a razor edge. Then she took a bunch of spackle buckets, filled them with sand, and hung them from the garage door. She disabled the interlock that caused the door to go back up when it hit something and attached her little razor to the bottom of the door. Then she pushed the automatic garage door opener and lay face down on the driveway. The door came down and didn't stop. The heavy buckets pushed the sharp edge of the flashing against her neck.

"But her mother came home unexpectedly. She managed to get a car jack under the door and pry it up. Madeline was all bloody and cut up, but the flashing had not worked its way between her vertebrae. She was in the hospital for some time, but there didn't seem to be any permanent damage."

"She came back, all right," Bernal said. He took the cup. "How did Muriel get you to set up that room in there? Not just what you said, the dress."

"I got a note from her on a snow globe someone left on my front steps. It took me and Rennie to a bunch of old computer stuff someone had dumped into a drainage ditch. He hauled it out, complaining the whole time about thorns, mud, all sorts of stuff. But it was all good, wherever it came from, and we brought it here and hooked it up and it worked. But it took you to get her to communicate through it. It's always a fragile channel. No guarantees."

The Teletype was still printing when he returned to the bedroom. He set the coffee cup down next to the daybed and pulled off the dangling section of printout.

HESKETH PROCESSING IS HEADS FROM LONG VOYAGE YOU KNOW THIS
HUNTED MORE HEADS GOT ONE YOU KNOW THIS TOO
SOMEONE HAS BEEN HELPING IT A HUMAN ACOLYTE
HESKETH COMMUNICATES WITH ACOLYTE
I INTERFERE ADD COMMENTS AND COMMANDS ACOLYTE CANNOT DISTINGUISH
THATS HOW I CAN SEND MESSAGES AND AFFECT ACTIVITIES

THATS HOW I ORDERED THESE DEVICES TO BE PLACED HERE
HESKETH SEES ME AS AN ABERRANT MENTAL STATE AND WANTS TO ELIMINATE
MY PERCEPTION IS LIMITED
I DO NOT KNOW IDENTITY OF ACOLYTE
I DO NOT KNOW MY CURRENT LOCATION
HESKETHS PERCEPTIONS ARE SHUT DOWN AND WE ARE CONCEALED
HESKETH WANTS TO ESCAPE THE EARTH
I HAVE NO INTEREST IN GOING TO SPACE
I DONT BELIEVE ANYONE REALLY DOES
ARE YOU THERE

"I'm here." Bernal set the coffee down, making sure it made a clink that she could hear, and sat back down in the chair. "Do you think Madeline is the acolyte? Is she behind this?"

I WANTED TO TALK TO HER THAT NIGHT I THOUGHT SHE WAS GOING TO BECOME PART OF HESKETH VOLUNTARY INVOLUNTARY I DIDNT KNOW
BUT INSTEAD I ENDED UP IN HESKETH

"Did Madeline kill you?"

I DONT REMEMBER HOW IT HAPPENED
MEMORY WONT COME

That actually made sense, Bernal thought. The hippocampus took some time to consolidate short-term memory. He supposed getting beheaded and having your brain flash-frozen might disrupt the process.

DID I LIKE FLAN

"What?"

BEFORE DID I LIKE IT BEFORE WHEN I WAS

"I . . . I don't remember." He spoke quickly. It seemed important to keep her from admitting to herself that she was no longer alive. "Why?"

YOU NEVER PAY ENOUGH ATTENTION BERNAL
SOMETIMES I DISAPPEAR
I THINK ABOUT IT NOW EGG YOLKS CREAM VANILLA
I DISAPPEAR THINKING ABOUT IT
WHO WILL KNOW IF I DISAPPEAR
PAY ATTENTION SO I DONT DISAPPEAR
I THINK THE FLAN COMES FROM SOMEONE ELSE
SOMEONE ELSE IN

A long pause.

The door opened behind him, and Naomi stepped in. The room filled with the scent of perfume.

It was the scent Muriel had always worn. He'd never known the name of it, but it was subtle and distinct.

For an instant he really did almost see her, in that dress, those shoes, ready to reach for her coffee and take another sip before telling him what she wanted him to do next.

Naomi put the scent-soaked cloth away. "I'm sorry. I just wanted her to feel real. Is she still talking?"

"I don't know." He was annoyed at Naomi's presence but knew that was unfair. She had as much right to feel Muriel's presence as he did.

He'd seen her headless body stuffed into the trunk of a car, and here he was, wishing and believing she was still alive.

He knew what happened to people in stories who succeeded in getting that particular wish granted.

PAUL I

A pause.

BERNAL IM SORRY BERNAL

"There's no time," Bernal said gently. "We can talk about it later."

THANK YOU FOR EVERYTHING
BERNAL
I DO KNOW THE NEXT PLAN
PLAN IS TO REMOVE ME FROM HESKETH
I AM NOTHING BUT A PROBLEM FOR HESKETH

"How?" Bernal said. "Has Hesketh thought about how . . . ?"

PHYSICALLY
HESKETH WILL BE OPENED UP AND

Pause.

THERE HAVE BEEN DIFFICULTIES
I OWE MY SURVIVAL TO DIFFICULTIES
HOW TO KEEP HESKETH FUNCTIONING WHILE REMOVING ME
AN INTERESTING TECHNICAL PROBLEM
UMBRELLA

Bernal stared at the printer, wondering if she had finally vanished. Or perhaps images from another mind were infecting hers beyond repair. Eventually, he supposed, it was inevitable that she disappear. Hesketh would have its way with her in the end.

LOOK FOR THE UMBRELLA MY UMBRELLA I DISGUISED
THE HERF GUN NO ONE WILL RECOGNIZE IT
LOOK FOR IT AND YOU WILL FIND HESKETH
AND BE ABLE TO DESTROY IT
I DONT REMEMBER BUT KNOW I HAD IT WITH ME
THAT NIGHT
DESTROY US
DESTROY US ALL
PUT AN END TO IT

This time the pause stretched. One minute. Two. He found himself looking at his cell phone, watching the numbers change.

Three minutes.

ILL HAVE TO REACH YOU SOME OTHER

The phone rang in his hands.

He fumbled to answer it, almost dropping it. "Hello?"

"Bernal." It was Patricia. She was sobbing so hard that it took him a few minutes to even begin to figure out what she was talking about.

"I need . . . your help," Patricia said. "Ignaz has locked me in here. He's going to come back and then . . . I don't know what he's going to do."

"Where are you?"

"In the yard. Ignacio's yard. Is there any way for you to get in?"

"I think there is. I'll be right there."

Bernal grabbed the printout, folded it up, and put it in his pocket. Then, with a vague idea forming in his head, he knelt and picked up the sardonic doll's head under the highboy.

"Take it," Naomi said. "If you need it." She sat down where Bernal had been. "If anything happens with Muriel, anything at all, you call me. I'll be right here. If she communicates again, I will know it."

"I'll call," he said. "No matter what happens, bad or good. I'll call because you're the only person who could possibly understand what I'm talking about."

34

Bernal's hand slipped out from under him, and he almost bashed his chin against a chunk of concrete. He paused, sucked air, and then felt at what should have been a secure handhold. It was slick. Blood?

He was impressed by how black it looked in the light of the sky. But where was it coming from? He felt at the slab of concrete that he'd slipped on. Not blood. The slab was covered with oil. Looked like Ignacio's had a toxic-waste problem. If he lived through this, he'd have to report them to DEP. . . .

The gully he'd seen the other day proved a more difficult route up into the yard than it looked from below. Bernal pulled himself up past the shattered remains of a concrete pipe. Two concrete-and-gravel footings flanked the gully, half out of the ground. There was just enough room under the fence for Bernal to crawl through.

Ignacio stood at the edge of the hole, staring down at him.

Bernal gasped and jerked. Sharp wire ends jabbed his back.

Boots. Just a pair of yellow wellies with one broken loop, standing along the fence. The things wouldn't have fit a ten-year-old. Now he saw a bunch of other boots, from battered leather work boots to a pair of bright red thigh-high stilettos abandoned by some dominatrix, standing in a row along the fence next to some jacks, left at various heights when the cars they were intended to lift had been abandoned. No Ignacio. But the wellies stood firm, as if their former wearer had been assumed bodily into heaven.

The lot itself was silent. And dark. Bernal stood and blinked, willing his eyes to see better. He had brought an LED headlamp, but it was too risky to turn it on. The lamp's glow would be visible down in the parking lot and out on the highway. He could imagine some sleepless businessman on the red-eye from LA pressing his forehead against the window as they dropped toward Logan, seeing the light, and wondering "Hey, I wonder who that is, breaking into Ignacio's junkyard?" The sky glowed above, and that would have to be enough.

Racks of car parts bulked dark above him. As he walked, they slowly resolved themselves, developing edges of protruding bumpers and door panels, alternators with cables braided together like decorative garlands of onions, crankshafts, wheel rims. He started to orient himself and figure out how to move through the yard. Pretty soon he was striding quickly along.

He bumped his head painfully against a metal edge. LEDs in a chrome wheel cover blinked merrily, brought back to life by the impact, then went dark.

Following the instructions Patricia had choked out to him, he counted aisles and turns. There it was: Ignacio's mobile home. It rested on high cinder-block footings. Maybe the yard flooded in the spring. He'd welded some kind of decorations on the corners, and cables led up into the surrounding racks. The footings weren't that stable, then. Ignacio had seen the need for bracing. Staying here was probably the only way he felt he could maintain the security of his yard and his drug trade.

The door spilled light and Ignacio strode down the stairs and into the yard. Bernal crouched down behind what he recognized as Patricia's own tow rig. Ignacio did not see him. He got into his black SUV and drove off.

A light was on in the trailer. And he heard someone sobbing.

"Patricia?" Bernal said. "Is that you?"

A pause. "Who the hell is that?"

"Bernal."

"*Who?*"

He hadn't been expecting that. "Bernal Haydon-Rumi. You called me—"

"Go away."

"But you—"

"*Go away!*"

Bernal grabbed the door handle. The door was locked. He rattled it, but nothing gave. Damn it! What was she pulling?

"Patricia. You need help."

Now she didn't say anything.

He searched the area around the trailer but found nothing useful. He forced himself back into the dark alleyways and examined the shelving. He thought he heard sounds, things moving deep in the shelves. Rats? Just weight shifting? Or actual active machinery? He listened harder but now heard nothing.

There. A door. An old car door with chrome trim. He grabbed the chrome, pulled. The door looked beat, but the chrome hung on. Objects in movies were always so much more cooperative than they actually turned out to be in reality. He got his fingernails under the chrome and braced himself against the shelves. Finally it came loose, not all at once, but slowly and infuriatingly, refusing to give him any emotional satisfaction.

Bernal ran back to the trailer with his jimmy. This time it did work the way it was supposed to. He'd spent a few weeks at a boring job reorganizing phone information at a mail-order call center in Wichita and learning about lock picking from a series of animations an MIT student working for the summer had put together the previous year. He didn't really manage to pull much out of the call information, but he did learn about how to feel the binding in various types of locks.

The trailer door resisted for only a few seconds, then popped open.

35

Inside, the trailer was larger than he had expected. The living room was dominated by a sectional sofa at a finicky orientation thirty degrees off from the walls. A TV screen dominated one wall.

The walls were hung with landscapes. Watercolors, Bernal thought. He brought his nose up to one, a scene of a brook and a curved stone bridge. "Kucpner" it said. "Hopelessly sentimental," Bernal murmured to himself. Hitler had started out as a watercolorist, so he supposed he shouldn't have been surprised.

What looked like a samurai sword hung above a gas fireplace.

Salvage from abandoned cars was piled on the sofa. Golf clubs, with graphite shafts and titanium heads as complex as the heads of late-medieval maces. Garment bags spilling suits and shoes. Umbrellas. Wrapped presents with the bows still on them.

. . . Umbrellas. What had Muriel said? Look for an umbrella.

Was he truly insane for paying attention to what that DECWriter had told him?

"Bernal?" Patricia's voice was surprisingly tentative. "Are you there?"

"Yeah. Where are you?"

A moment's wonder at his inability to find her in a space so small. "Back here."

Black umbrellas, red umbrellas, umbrellas with Monet water lilies, and what looked like a hundred black travel umbrellas, many of them with bent and missing ribs. But there, next to a flowered bag, was one with an oddly thick handle. Bernal picked it up. Now that he'd seen it, it didn't look convincing as an umbrella. It was a small-charge herf gun. Muriel's gun, which she had disguised and told him to find.

How the hell had this gotten here? Sooner or later, all junk ended up at Ignacio's. It was clear that he just threw everything into various categories, and that this thing had not graduated from "umbrella" to "high-tech weapon" in Ignacio's classification scheme.

"Bernal?"

He scooped it up and headed through the well-equipped kitchen, with its racks of cleavers and Garland stove, for the rear of the trailer.

Patricia stood in the mobile home's small bathroom stitching up a cut in her forehead. The sink was spattered with blood. It streaked her high forehead and her hair. She pulled a thread through with a needle and winced. She scooped some white powder off the toilet tank and dabbed it around her cut, then did another stitch.

"Cocaine?" Bernal asked.

"Sure. Anesthetic. Local. Works pretty good."

"And a vasoconstrictor too," Bernal said.

"What?"

"Helps stop the bleeding."

"Yeah, well. That's always good, isn't it?"

"Where did Ignacio go?"

"Out. To get something, he said. Oh, Bernal, I'm so scared." She leaned against him then, and he put his arm around her. She was small. He could feel her bones.

It was hot in the bathroom. Not steamy. Just hot.

She shivered a little and turned a bit away. She scraped some of the cocaine off onto her thumbnail and held it up to him. Her eyes were downcast as she did so, like a geisha offering a client a cup of tea.

He refused hesitation, leaned forward, and snuffed it up with his nostril. An icicle traveled up his sinuses. He wasn't used to blow, it wasn't something he'd indulged in much. It was too physical a drug, too constricting, like being squeezed in a giant hand.

"Finish up, can you?" She handed him the needle and turned her face up to him. She really was small, not the dominating figure of Charis or the challenging one of Yolanda. Just a little girl. Even her teeth were so small that they looked like baby teeth that had never been pushed out.

He'd never done anything like this before. Her eye was just below the cut. It was an interesting puzzle, but he didn't want to blind her with the needle's point. She winced as it went in, and the stitch was uneven. The second one was straighter, and the third was the last.

"Thanks," she said. "All it takes is focus."

She scooped up another mound of cocaine. He did hesitate this time, but then inhaled that one as well. The effect was muted by his already sizzling nerves.

"I saw Ignacio drive away," Bernal said.

"Away? That's good. When he goes, he goes for a long time."

"Do you want to get out of here?"

"Yes," she said. "Yes, I do."

And then she was crying, her face pressed against Bernal's chest, her entire body shaking. He felt a tug on his shirt. Without really being conscious of it, he followed her lead, out of the bathroom and into the bedroom behind, Ignacio's bedroom, filled with a bed that left only a few inches to squeeze around it.

Patricia's touch was almost more than he could bear. He wasn't just a frozen brain. He did have a few seconds of understanding that he was doing something really stupid, and then she pulled him down into the stinking sheets.

36

Bernal and Patricia walked quickly down the dark aisles of the junkyard, feeling the time that had passed. But Bernal felt, in addition to fear, a thrill. He'd had sex with Patricia in Ignacio's bed. He'd just have to face the consequences.

She'd been silent since they had finished, dressed, and run out of the trailer, Bernal only just managing to remember to grab Muriel's herf gun. Patricia wore a long white jacket, oddly fashionable, that clung to her narrow waist. She looked beautiful and easily broken.

Finally, she spoke.

"He . . . you know, he recruited me here. Out of all the possibilities. And now . . . oh, I don't know how it happens, do you?"

"No, I don't."

"We can't go out the front," Patricia said. "He might be there."

"I have a way," Bernal said.

"It was really because of Fartface." She remembered

as they walked. "Poor Fartface . . . I guess we shouldn't have called him that. This was in Pleasant Valley. Residential facility. I kept running away from home. After Merrick died. You remember Merrick."

"Garage, crossbow."

"Yeah, him. Anyway, I kept ending up in different places, with . . . guys, mostly. They'd see me, I'd meet them. Mom and Dad were all upset about how I was acting. Blamed it on the accident, juiced the insurance payout, and got me put up."

He remembered her mentioning some kind of accident the first time they had talked, and she had described meeting the unfortunate Merrick.

"What accident?" Bernal said.

She shrugged. "Car. I wasn't wearing my belt, Mom bashed into the back of a truck that stopped for no reason on the highway. I hit my head on a pipe sticking out of the back of the truck. I was out for a while." She touched her forehead, and Bernal noted again the crescent-shaped scar and the cranial depression. Frontal lobe damage could be serious. She'd been lucky.

"Fartface had a home-meth-lab accident, ended up with a bunch of glass in his forehead and a bad attitude. I never learned his real name. He knew about network access, stuff like that. He had some sniffer software he brought in his iPod, did some keystroke logging. Didn't need it, these psych types are really lame, I mean, they hadn't changed the passwords for years, and they had them scribbled on stickies on their old monitors. We used our access for the usual shit. I sent naked pictures of myself to prisoners. They like that stuff, and those guys can help you out later. They'd write me back, call me, and we'd work things out.

"Then somebody else called me. Started sending me messages. Not, like, normal. Like from some kind of lockdown, kind of like mine. I didn't want other crazy people writing me. What good was that? But this person had a plan. This person wanted me out of Pleasant Valley so I could help with something important."

"Ignacio?"

She paused. "Yeah. Ignaz. He spotted something, I don't know, in me. The naked pictures, sure. But there are a lot of those. It was something else too. He said he needed me. Said he wanted me to get to Cheriton, however I could.

"So I straightened up and waited. They never have enough slots at those places, so they don't keep you if you're not a complete mess. So I acted right, and that was all I had to do. I was out in a month. Then, I made some money. The usual shit, hooking, selling drugs. Not so hard once you get the hang of it." She paused. "Does that bug you? What I used to do?"

"A little. Sure."

She rubbed his shoulder, which felt almost more intimate than what they had just done. "I followed a simple rule: Take the drugs, lose money. Sell the drugs, make money. Simple. Got a stake together, then hopped a bus to Cheriton.

"You know it worked out. The way it always works out. I got the job. I work in a junkyard. Good job. Right? And sometimes he's nice to me. Real nice. Sometimes not. That's really as good as I've ever gotten."

Out in the darkness, a whir. Patricia looked around.

"Do those golf carts move on their own?" Bernal said.

"There are some buried wires that they follow." She took his question seriously. "But they don't start by themselves. We should—"

The blow took her in the side of the head, and she fell to her knees.

"Patty," Ignacio said. "I'm really getting tired of everybody mixing into my business here. Just running a few drugs, but everyone acts as if—"

Bernal hit Ignacio in the chest with the top of his head. He didn't know much about hand-to-hand, but he knew he had to use as much momentum as possible and move as fast as he could. The impact was satisfyingly hard. They both went down.

Ignacio was big, but he was fast as well.

And he knew what he was doing. He shoved Bernal against a rack, twisted, and got hold of Bernal's wrist.

Bernal grunted and tried to struggle. But struggle just increased the pain. Ignacio shifted grips, and for an instant Bernal thought he was free. Then there was more pain, and his face was ground into the rack.

"This is it." Ignacio breathed like an enraged bull. "This is just it."

With the hand that was not holding Bernal, he searched him efficiently, removing his cell phone, his wallet, his multitool, his car keys.

"You should just leave her alone," Bernal said.

"You guys should leave my carts alone." Ignacio always spoke calmly. It was part of his threat. "I need them to keep my business working. Let me know how you got the damn things running, and maybe I'll be quick."

Then Bernal heard the sound of running footsteps. Something clanged. Ignacio fell off Bernal's back.

"Run!" Patricia screamed. "Run now!"

Bernal turned, holding his agonized wrist. He caught a glimpse of her as she disappeared down an aisle. Ignacio was on his hands and knees, blood streaming over his face. His one clear eye was focused on Bernal. Patricia had hit him with a suspension strut. He groped for it, found it, started pushing himself to his feet.

Bernal ran before he could get up.

The car parts on either side seemed to lean in toward him as the aisle narrowed. There was a cross passage just ahead—

A golf cart pulled out in front of him. Bernal slowed down, then leapt to clear the vehicle.

That instant's hesitation was fatal. He didn't jump quite high enough. His shins hit the cart. He spun over and smashed painfully to the ground.

Ignacio was out there somewhere, but he seemed to have decided to use his yard's transportation system to herd Bernal, so that he didn't have to strain himself chasing after him.

Because there was another damn cart. This one moved slowly toward him. It was surprising how menacing a golf cart could look.

As he backed away, it sped up.

"Bernal." Charis Fen's voice. Hollow-sounding, coming from . . . where? "Look out!"

It was just an instant too late. Bernal lost his footing and toppled into the concrete pit that had been waiting for him just behind his heels.

37

He and Charis lay together at the bottom of a concrete shaft about five feet square and ten or fifteen feet deep. The sky glowed dimly above.

For a moment. Then someone dragged a heavy metal plate across the concrete, then across the opening. The silence and darkness grew absolute.

"Great," Charis said. "Just great."

"What the hell are you doing here?"

"I was just trying to—"

"You knew something was up here!" Bernal spoke before thinking and only realized he was right when he heard his own words. "You think Hesketh is hidden somewhere in this yard."

"There is no Hesketh, you moron! I came here to save your stupid ass."

Bernal rolled to his feet. "Are you okay? I mean . . . thanks. Thank you. I landed on you."

"Believe me, I didn't plan it."

"But you think Ignacio has something to do with it. You were watching the yard."

"I saw you climbing under the fence . . . but when I came up to check it out, Ignacio got the drop on me. He was waiting out front. He knows something's up. He was ready."

Before Bernal could apologize for screwing things up, the metal plate over the hole's top was drawn away, showing the sky again.

They both looked up, but couldn't see anything.

"The drugs . . ." Bernal said. "The Easter Bunny. I think Muriel came here investigating. So he went to her house to threaten her. The night she disappeared. Ignacio was there. John Rennie saw him."

"And he finally finished the job."

"That may be the connection, but I'm not sure that—"

Something glanced off his shoulder, and he yelped. "What—" He felt around on the ground, and came up with a car mirror. "What the hell?"

A hum, and a loud scrape.

"Look out!" they both yelled, like it would help.

This time it was an entire car door. It fell between them, bounced off its corner, and landed resting on Bernal's toes. It was surprisingly heavy. He bent over, got his fingers under it, and pulled his toes out.

"Golf carts?" Charis stared up with puzzlement. "We're being attacked by golf carts?"

Of course. "Not golf carts," Bernal said. "Hesketh."

"Now don't start that again . . . Shit!" Crumbled concrete and dirt scattered down on them. Something big and dark appeared at mouth of the hole. "You back, me over here. Then . . . when I yell, you jump, boy. It's the bounce, the bounce'll kill us. You jump."

"Okay. Sure." Bernal bent his knees.

The black shape slipped down, and, for an instant,

looked like nothing at all, like the shadow of something far away. Then: "Now!"

They both jumped. The shape hit, teetered, then fell in Bernal's direction. Coming down, his knees hit it, and he fell forward across it. Charis caught him before his head hit the ground.

"I'm not going to ask if you're okay," she said. "But I can see you're alive."

"You've lowered your standards," he said.

"Hey, it's all about managing expectations. What the—"

The huge engine lay between them. It looked like a V-6.

Another moment, and a chrome wheel rim bounced off the engine, then spent quite a while rolling noisily around on its edge before settling down.

"More than one of those golf carts up there," Charis said. "You think Hesketh is controlling them. Couldn't it be anyone? Ignacio?"

"I would have thought it was Ignacio, but he asked me how we got them to run, like he had no idea."

Another movement, and a shower of nuts, bolts, and other connectors came down on them. One of them hit Bernal painfully in the head.

He pulled out the herf gun. "Well, didn't your personal ad say 'Enjoys walks in rains of car parts'?"

Charis stared. "Where the hell did you get that?"

"Found it. In Ignacio's trailer."

"That's Muriel's! She begged it from me the day before it all went down. And you still don't think Ignacio killed her?"

"I don't know what I think."

"Give me that thing."

Charis opened the umbrella. The thick ribs angled out, past the usual point, until it looked like it had been blown inside out in a high wind. The fabric flapped, clearly just camouflage.

They both peered up. Something heavy was getting dragged across the ground toward them.

"We've probably got one shot, if that," she said. "So we have to make it count."

She leaned back against the wall, braced her elbows against her chest, and pointed the parabolic antenna up. A dark shape appeared against the sky. Another engine, this one even larger, from an SUV or truck. When it hit, one or both of them would be crushed. There would be no way to escape.

It pushed forward, grinding against the pit's edge.

The herf gun buzzed. The engine tilted forward.

"Damn it!" Charis worked the trigger, but nothing else happened.

"Man," Bernal said. "Will you look at that?"

The engine had stopped. It leaned halfway down over the edge, but was no longer moving.

"That's just one cart." Charis said. "Another one of the damn things can be along in a minute. We've got to *move*. Come on, come on. Here, let me . . . thank God for this thing, anyway." She climbed up on the first engine that had fallen. "Up on my shoulders."

"Me? But shouldn't I be the one—"

"Look, boy, I outweigh you by forty pounds, and I'm way stronger than you. You going to worry about gender roles, or are you going to get moving? I'll brace myself, you climb me like a tree. You should be able to reach."

He pulled himself up on the engine and grabbed her shoulder. She was strong muscle under the fat. She bent her knees, so that he could step on one thigh and get himself up. He tried to be careful not to kick her in the face or pinch anything. Despite a couple of muffled grunts from her, he thought he'd done pretty well on that.

Bernal reached up and was able to grab the edge of the pit.

"Can you bounce me up?" he said down to Charis.

"Bounce you *up*?"

"Yes. Just a little, so I can get some grip on this. I don't . . . I don't have enough muscle to pull myself up, okay?"

"Don't get all defensive. You ready? On three. One . . . two . . . *three*."

He jumped up, but his shoulder hit the dangling engine, knocking him just enough to the side that he scrabbled and fell back. He froze, back on Charis's shoulders. The engine tilted and creaked. He thought he heard the cart's wheels drag across the ground. But finally, it settled and held.

"I'll have to make sure I slide right up against the wall when I do that," he said. Charis did not answer. "Okay?"

"Okay. You ready?"

"Yeah."

"One . . . two . . . *three*."

This time, by pushing his chest against the concrete, he made it up and got his elbows on the edge of the hole. He worked his way sideways to a corner, so that he had one elbow on one edge and the other on the one perpendicular. He was pressed right up against the precarious engine, but there was really no other way for him to get enough purchase.

"Okay," he said.

"You sure you're ready for this?"

"As ready as I'm going to get."

A moment of silence, and then she grabbed him by the waist and tried to pull him back into the hole. At least that's what it felt like she was doing. She grunted, switched grips, and grabbed his shoulder. Somehow, she braced herself against the opposite wall with her feet, and within a few seconds was hanging on with him.

"A couple more seconds," she said in his ear. "Just hang on."

He didn't have enough air in his lungs to answer her.

She jumped over, and ended up facing in, elbows on the edge. Then she pushed herself up and over.

Something grabbed his shirt. Bernal yelped. The engine fell past and hit the bottom of the pit with a crash. His shirt ripped, but he stayed up.

"Come on, man." He grabbed her hand and she yanked him out.

38

That golf cart had ended up in the pit, but the rest were moving. Bernal could hear them in the darkness.

"Have you seen Patricia?" Bernal said.

"Is she here too?"

"Yes. I hope I haven't made things worse for her. . . ." He suspected that that was an understatement. He couldn't even remember why he had done such an insanely dangerous thing. He'd made love to Ignacio's woman.

But he didn't even try not to feel good about it.

"God, I wish I had the charger." Charis waved the herf gun. A red LED glowed on the handle. "One shot, and capacitors are out."

"Did Muriel have the charger?"

"Sure. Big ass pile of batteries. I think she put them in a bag."

"A big flowered bag, like something an old lady would carry. I know where it is."

"Where?"

"Ignacio's trailer. I didn't know what it was. Even though I tripped over the damn thing the night she died." He remembered falling over it when he was chasing Muriel. She'd gotten it out for whatever confrontation she had planned with Hesketh, but had been forced to run when Ignacio showed up. She'd had to face Hesketh without the herf gun and had died.

And Ignacio, with an eye for interesting gadgets, had taken it along when he left.

Charis thought a moment. "It's not worth going back for. We just have to dodge Ignacio—"

The golf cart was so quiet that it was almost on them before they saw it. Charis, with nowhere else to go, dove forward and rolled across its top, to land heavily on the ground behind it.

"Bernal!"

"Whoa!" Bernal had jumped straight up and dangled from a bound batch of shock struts that was now tilting off its shelf. He let go and barely avoided getting creamed by it as it came down.

"I don't think we have a lot of choice," he said.

"Great," Charis said. "Ignacio's house it is."

The place was empty and silent. Neither Ignacio nor Patricia was in evidence. It was pretty much the way Bernal had left it.

As he headed for the closet, the floor tilted. Was he dizzy, hit worse than he thought? No. The floor was actually tilting.

Charis wrestled with the door, which had swung shut behind them. Outside, Bernal could hear a high whine, and suddenly, and much too late, put things together.

By the time Charis got the door open, they dangled in the air, twenty or thirty feet up. The cables at the mobile home's corners ran up to high-powered winches bolted into the racks. Together, they had just pulled the house up into the air.

"Well, we're good and stuck," Charis said, disgusted with herself—and with him? "Where's the charger?"

Bernal jumped on the couch, hoping it wasn't just a bag, something with a toothbrush and a change of underwear in it. There it was. He unsnapped the latches, and breathed a sigh of relief. Heavy batteries filled the interior. Everything in the modern world had become small and light, except the very heart of their power, which still had a Victorian mass.

Charis reached past him and pulled a recharge cradle out of the bag.

"Frickin' thing has terrible human factors." She pointed to where Muriel had taped a piece of paper in it with a picture of the umbrella herf and an emphatic arrow. "Bitch to snap your herf in the wrong way and then have a homicidal robot charge down on you while you wave the useless piece of crap at it. I hired a couple of guys who got kicked out of MIT for a near-fatal prank to build it for me. Smart guys, but clueless. We had a fight over the invoice, but I eventually paid it and ended up with this stupid thing. It does work, if you handle it just right."

She looked up at the gas fireplace as she waited for the herf to charge. The long samurai sword, in a lacquer scabbard, hung on a rack above the marble mantel hauled in from some demolition. She stepped toward it as if wanting to grab it by its sharkskin hilt, but then paused and looked toward the kitchen.

"This guy use cleavers, you notice?"

"Yeah. Nice, carbon steel, and he takes good care of them. Well, he takes good care of everything."

"Like he wants to take care of us."

An engine roared in the yard outside. A bright light flared through the front windows.

Charis ducked down, motioning Bernal to do the same. He dove behind a couch.

The truck's engine seemed to make the whole place shake.

"Come the hell out of there!" an amplified voice bellowed.

Charis listened carefully, as if to a secret message in the words, but did not respond.

"The front door!" Ignacio yelled through a buzzy speaker, competing with the noise of his own engine. "Come to the front door, and let's get this taken care of."

"We should—" Bernal stopped at a sharp hand gesture from Charis.

"There's an emergency rope ladder in there, near the front." Now Ignacio sounded reasonable, as if realizing that threats weren't going to get him what he wanted. "For when the motors screw up. I keep them up, but it happens. Just roll it out and come down. Just get the hell out of my yard, and we're okay, huh?"

Charis lay flat. For a moment, Bernal couldn't figure out what she was doing. Then he saw her work her feet over to the coiled rope ladder that lay by the door. It was attached to the door's sill by two bolts. She braced herself, then kicked the door open and kicked the ladder out after it.

The gunshot wasn't that loud, really. But the bullet tearing through the roof made the entire mobile home shake.

"Damn it." Charis scuttled back. "This tin is no protection at all."

It was as if Ignacio had overheard her and realized that there was no real need for luring anyone to the door. The lights moved until there was an upward glow all around the house, and now the rumbling engine was directly underneath. Shadows extended upward to the ceiling.

The bullet tore through the floor a couple of feet from him. The entire structure vibrated.

Bernal threw himself backward.

"Don't do that," Charis said. "He can't possibly know where you are. He can only shoot at random. Unless you make noise."

He realized she was right, so he didn't answer her.

From where he lay he could see that the herf LED was now a blinking yellow.

Another bullet tore through, this one at the opposite end of the room.

"There, see?" Charis said. "Once you get used to it, it's not so bad." She moved quickly around the mobile home, pulling open windows and screens. The cool night air blew in. "See if he's made a hole big enough for us to stick that herf through. I'd rather try that than lean out of a window."

Bernal rolled over to where the first bullet had come through. He pulled the rug aside. He couldn't judge caliber, but it seemed to have torn a fairly large hole. It glowed white from Ignacio's truck-mounted lights. The LED was now a placid green. He tore the herf out of its cradle and pushed the business end against the bullet hole.

It wasn't big enough. The end of the umbrella went in, but the rest of it, the necessary antenna, did not. Bernal pulled it back out. Was there anything around that would let him widen—

He didn't know whether Ignacio heard him moving around, saw the brief appearance of the umbrella, or just guessed that someone would decide that where the previous bullet went through would be the safest place.

But the next shot went through a few inches away from where the first one had.

It took Bernal a minute of severe shaking to even begin to move. Every muscle in his body seemed to move in a different rhythm.

But this hole was bigger, maybe shot at a different angle. The umbrella slid right through.

"This works!" he said.

"You do the honors. It doesn't really aim."

He clicked the latch, and it opened up. He pictured it, blossoming like an upside down black flower. He felt with his finger, found the trigger, and pressed it.

Instant darkness and silence. The engine and the lights had died. He was grateful for the insane technological complexity of modern vehicles, with microprocessors regulating every part of their activities. An older vehicle, with nothing but sparks handed out to the cylinders by a physically rotating distributor, might have shrugged the herf off.

He closed up the umbrella, pulled it back in. Ignacio's footsteps crunched across the gravel. If Ignacio had thought about it before, he would have realized how much more ominous this was than the engine. Just the methodical step of a man in no hurry about killing.

"Stand up," Charis whispered. "Reduces your cross section. And be quiet."

Bernal rolled to his feet, making as little noise as possible. Then, in sudden inspiration, he crept over to the phone on the end table, picked it up, and dialed his own cell phone number.

He heard a few bars of the theme from *The Twilight Zone*. Then he hung up.

"Nice," Charis whispered.

Ignacio would have no way of knowing what Bernal's phone sounded like. Bernal had done his best to make it seem like there was someone else in the yard. Someone who had not remembered to switch off his phone and had fumbled for it, desperately, and managed to switch it off after one ring. Someone else loose in the yard would be much more dangerous than two morons stuck thirty feet up in a sheet-metal trailer.

Ignacio moved quietly across the gravel. Bernal could just see his shadowy shape against the paler ground. How long would it be before he realized that the phone had been one he'd already confiscated? Bernal had no idea where he had stashed the things.

"There have to be motor controls in here somewhere," Bernal whispered. "No way he was going to leave the override somewhere outside, where someone else had ultimate control."

"Good thinkin', Lincoln," Charis said. "But he must know it's hard to find. Coded?"

For a second, Bernal looked back at the phone. Could he activate things by dialing a certain number? Nice idea, but unlikely. But what else—?

"Try the TV remote," Charis said, as Bernal was already moving toward it.

Charis went around the couch. As she passed the fireplace, she brushed against a coffee cup on the mantel. It fell to the floor and broke.

The bullet that came through the wall was shatteringly loud. Pictures sprang off their hangers, and the entire marble mantel clanged. Charis fell forward.

Threw herself forward. She had to have done that. There was no way Ignacio could have gotten the drop on her. It just didn't make any sense. Not sure anymore whether standing up or lying down was better, Bernal compromised and scuttled over to her in a crouch.

She had not thrown herself forward. She was unconscious, and there was blood in her thick hair. He couldn't tell immediately how much.

"Charis!" He'd always made fun of people in movies who yelled at unconscious people, but the knowledge that Ignacio could drop him just as easily was all that kept him from doing it. "Are you okay?"

He felt at her head, half-anticipating that part of it would be blown off, and he would feel the shattered edges of her skull in his fingers.

But it was all there, a solid sphere, and when he prodded one specific spot, she winced and moaned, though she did not regain consciousness. Incautious, now, of Ignacio and his weapon, Bernal ran to the kitchen and yanked a dish towel out of a neat stack of them next to the Garland stove.

Out in the yard, an engine. Had Ignacio managed to restart his truck? No, too quiet. This was another golf cart.

Ignacio fired once, then twice more in quick succession. But not up at the trailer. Bernal heard a ricochet, but the cart kept coming. It smashed into something. From the loud cascade that followed, it had clearly hit some rack of car parts. It backed up, turned, and tore down another aisle. Its sound disappeared, and there was nothing but silence.

Bernal grabbed a glass and filled it with water. He ran back to Charis, put her head in his lap, moistened her lips, and put pressure on her wound. He looked around and saw that the samurai sword had been ripped off its lacquer display rack by Ignacio's last shot. It looked like its hilt had struck her.

Her eyes snapped open.

"You got hit in the head. Not the bullet, something else. Do you want me to quiz you about commonly known facts?"

"I'm not sure you and I know the same commonly known facts, Bernal." Her voice was calm, even a bit sleepy.

"I think something happened to Ignacio."

"What?"

"I don't know."

He helped her to her feet. She was coming back into focus.

"Don't go near the window," she said.

But he didn't listen. He was so sure . . . he peeked out of a corner and there, lying at the base of a parts rack, was a pair of feet.

"I think it's okay," he said.

After a moment's hesitation, she moved to join him. "You may be right."

39

The black shape of the mobile home floated above them, creaking slightly in a night breeze. The truck stood, door open, silent.

Ignacio lay crumpled on the ground, just around a corner. His head was pulpy, the side of his chest was pushed in, and his arm had been forced out of its socket. Charis knelt and checked him over. "Yeah. Dead." She glanced up at Bernal. "What happened?"

"I couldn't see—"

"Best guess."

"A golf cart ran into that rack. Stuff fell off of it, hit him in the head."

They stood there, looking down at him. His gun lay on the concrete near his head. His dead face was smooth and inoffensive.

"Who killed him?" Charis said.

"I don't know."

"No matter what he told you, it looks like it was him

in charge of them the whole time. He screwed up, lost control of one, and got himself killed."

They both listened. The yard was silent. No cart moved.

"It's him," Charis said. "The Bowler. The Easter Bunny. You saw the sword, the cleavers. I'll bet any amount of money that when the lab guys get in here, they'll get matches on vertebrae."

"If it was Ignacio, then there's nothing to worry about," Bernal said. "But if it wasn't . . ."

"Fair enough. You want to go out there and look for Hesketh?"

"No. But if we don't, it might be gone by the time anyone gets here." Bernal looked over to the vehicle parking area. It looked like Patricia's rig was gone. It had been there before. So she had gotten away. He felt a surge of overwhelming relief. Despite his insistence on finding Hesketh, he was almost convinced that Charis was right. Ignacio had been the killer.

Still, he had to be sure. He checked Ignacio's car, but all that was in there were two aromatic bags of takeout from a Brazilian churrascaria in town. They were still warm. Something about this false evidence of life struck Bernal. He leaned his head against the door.

"Don't lose it, Bernal." Charis pulled him by the arm. "I need you functional. Let's go."

The silence in the yard was now unbearable. Nothing moved, nothing was operational, and his own footsteps on the gravel were unpleasantly grinding, as if something was being damaged as he moved.

The aisle he moved down narrowed and ended in a curtain made of dozens of dangling hoses from old gas pumps. As he pushed his way through the rotting rubber, the heavy nozzles clanked and bashed against his ankles.

In a few minutes, the police would be here, and they

would seal off the yard completely and go through it piece by piece. Not because they believed in the existence of Hesketh, but simply to make sure they had all the evidence needed to tie Ignacio Kuepner to the Bowler murders. He just had to make sure that Hesketh did not get away before then.

Had Ignacio forced poor Patricia to make the call that brought Bernal here? Bernal didn't think so. He had probably just given her the space to make it, knowing that she would after he beat her. Charis had told Bernal how psychopaths perceived normal, mentally flabby, purely contingent human beings. It would have been easy for Ignacio to exploit his and Patricia's obvious and pathetic needs to get them to do exactly what he wanted them to.

Beyond was a wide trench filled with what looked like waste oil. Grooved concrete sloped down to it. A rank of cars stood there, their headlights gazing mournfully into the greasy Lethe in the trench. Bernal recognized a Rambler with its Chrysler building–shaped taillights and an MG. Someone had been doing some kind of work here, because a red rolling tool case stood nearby, each of its drawers crowded with hand tools.

He heard a thump. He looked around. Where had it . . . ?

It came again. This time he localized it: a rusty Impala. He walked slowly toward the car.

Something shifted in the trunk.

He remembered the Peugeot by the Black River. He remembered the car in which Aurora Lipsius had died. Ignacio was dead, but there was something here that was still alive.

He felt in his pockets, but they hadn't found where Ignacio had tossed their cell phones, and he was without a way to communicate with Charis. But if he left to find her, Hesketh, or whatever was in there, might find a way to escape and vanish. Or come after them.

A strip of something white hung out of the edge of the closed trunk. Bernal forced himself to go closer to it. It was fabric.

It was the edge of the white jacket Patricia had thrown on after they had made love.

"Patricia? Is that—?"

He was rewarded by an enthusiastic kick from inside.

Once again he had to unlock something stubborn and physical. This time, heedless of damage to himself or the car, he levered up under the lock with a breaker bar, complete with scored grip handle, that he'd found leaned against the tool case. He put all his weight into it, and the lock ripped right out of the trunk's metal.

Patricia lay inside, bound with nylon straps, her mouth closed with duct tape. As gently as he could, he pulled the tape loose.

"Behind you," she said. "In the tool case. Box cutter."

Sure enough, a few moment's investigation brought up an orange box cutter. Working carefully, he cut the nylon between her hands, then between her legs.

He took a packing pad and folded it into a makeshift bed. Then he lifted her out and laid her down. She was shockingly light. Her skin was red and creased where the nylon straps had cut in.

He kissed her forehead, sweat-sticky and plastered with hair. "Don't worry," he said.

She turned her head away from him. "What happened?" Her voice, unlike her body, was strong. "What happened to Ignacio?"

"He tried to shoot us."

She sat up. "Where is he? Did he escape? Is he gone?"

"He's dead. A cart crashed into a stack of parts, and a transaxle fell on his head."

She stared at him for a moment, her pale eyes wide. Then she fell back and started to cry.

40

Charis had proved surprisingly willing to come over to Ungaro's lab to talk things over, but he guessed that it was because she no longer thought any of it mattered.

It was two days after Ignacio's death. Bernal had undergone another round of questioning, but the satisfaction of identifying Ignacio as the killer had led the police to not press that connection too hard.

"I communicated with Muriel," Bernal said. "I know it was Muriel."

"If you say so," Charis said.

"You think it was Ignacio, sitting at a keyboard in his trailer, chuckling to himself as I walked right into his trap."

"I don't know what to think. All I know is you shouldn't be sitting here by yourself."

"I got nowhere else to sit and no one else to sit with." Bernal had not meant it to sound as bitter as it came out.

"I had Muneer to take care of me," Charis said. "He

held on to me and let me cry on him. I'm a slobbery cryer, Bernal, so it's even more of an achievement than it sounds. My sinuses clog right up, snot—"

"I get the picture." Though he really didn't. He imagined her tears as some kind of disastrous natural event, like a hurricane.

"And he cooked for me. He's one of those guests-over show-off type cooks, I pick stuff up for the day-to-day, but he can put out some real food when he needs to. You wouldn't think you could improve a big plate of nachos, but his are definitely the best. It's probably the lard. That's usually the secret. Even his brownies are the best."

"Lard?" Bernal said.

"I don't ask. But there was one thing he didn't make me, and it looks like you could use it."

"What?"

"A pizza."

"A—don't you mean, what *you* need?"

She shrugged. "I've been out of the house all morning, and I am getting hungry. What do you take on it?"

"Mushrooms and green peppers."

"What, you think there's really a healthy version of pizza or something? Pepperoni?"

"If you want."

"I want, Bernal. Believe me, I want." Pizza delivery was on her phone's speed dial.

The light coming through from the loading dock, and the memory of the first time he had met Patricia Foote, reminded him that he hadn't yet seen her. Physically, he knew, she was pretty okay. Having a couple of other people to kill had distracted Ignacio, and he'd done a slapdash job of beating her up. She'd been in much worse shape that first day he met her, when she'd come here to tow Charis's Hummer. He remembered her almost falling out of her tow truck, all bruised up from some earlier discussion with her boss.

Patricia was sequestered somewhere, and Charis either didn't know where or had been instructed not to tell him. He knew Patricia had some small house, out of town. He presumed she was holed up there. At some point he would go and see her.

"They found Aurora Lipsius's head frozen in an operational medical freezer buried under a stack of antique radiators," Charis said. "Bunch of other stuff in that freezer as well, including a slab of sushi-grade hamachi yellowtail. Got to hand it to Ignacio, there wasn't any kind of business he wouldn't get into. But hers was the only head in there. It had been frozen fast. No decay, nothing. ME says it must have gotten chilled within a few minutes of decapitation. Don't get too excited by that."

"By what?"

"By the freezing."

"I'm not excited. There's a hell of a lot of difference between a medical freezer and a cryogenic suspension. It's amazing how Hesketh worked out its way of taking heads. Step by step, establishing the lure, the slicing method, means of preservation . . . and I'll bet a few of those heads were just decoys, regular murders, so no one would get on the scent of a homicidal AI. Which reminds me . . ."

"What?"

"Anyone find that thing I saw in the back of the Ziggy Sigma van? The . . . headtaker, or whatever it was."

"It wasn't in Ignacio's yard. Patricia Foote saw something that resembled it—a welded box with an attached compressor—but then it disappeared, shipped off through some one of Ignacio's channels. No one knows where it went."

To find that Prelate and Vervain were just some kind of junk-recovery service, and worked for Ignacio like everyone else, was a disappointment. He'd hoped to find the headtaker, and examine it, and prove . . . he didn't know what. That Muriel had once been inside it, maybe.

"With Lipsius's head, that means everything's pretty well accounted for, right?" Bernal said. "Except for two things."

"One is Muriel's head. What's the other?"

"Madeline." There was no sign of Madeline Ungaro. There were hints in the lab that she'd been planning a camping trip, so campgrounds and backcountry areas across the country had been scoured, thus far without success. To Bernal, she seemed frictionless. She had slid right out of the situation and vanished.

"You're not worried about Madeline. You're just mentioning her so you don't seem callous."

"Um . . . jeez, Charis. I'm doing my best here."

"They'll find her. One way or another. At any rate, she hasn't been a piece on our board here. But, right, everything else is accounted for. The samurai sword that fell off the mantelpiece and knocked me down was the sword that beheaded Christopher Gambino, the third victim. Still had dried blood cells on it, and the edges matched. And among all that kitchen gear, they found the cleaver that did Damon Fry. Nice carbon steel one, and it was Chinese. Looks like he used it at least one more time, the ME thinks for disjointing a chicken. But it left enough signs to link it up. Ignacio Kuepner was the Bowler. He killed Christopher Gambino, Aurora Lipsius, Warren St Amant, and Damon Fry. And, it looks like, Muriel Inglis."

"What's the evidence that he killed Muriel?"

"Circumstantial, thus far. In popular thought 'circumstantial' means 'lame,' but it's the most common foundation of a case. Muriel clearly had an interest in his place. Part of her own little investigation. She was seen around Ignacio's yard a couple of times. And you told me someone saw him at her house that night."

"I did. It might be hard to get him to testify."

"Not so important. They're not trying to bring a case against Ignacio. He's dead. They're just trying to put all the pieces together."

"And do they fit?"

"Better than you might think. Christopher Gambino, for one. Worked with Hess Tech, like I told you. Responsible for picking up some repurposed parts from Ignacio's Devices & Desires. During the course of that, it seems, from what your gal Patricia says, that he got interested in her. Not too odd, she's pretty cute." She gave him a look which he refused to acknowledge. "He got worried about her, what was going on with her. Natural, when her skin is the kind that shows bruises so well. He started hanging around, trying to get her away, to get her free. Kind of an obsession with him, sounds like. He must have pissed Ignacio off."

Bernal had an odd feeling, following in the footsteps of the earnest Christopher Gambino, who had also tried to help Patricia out of her terrible situation. He too had probably come into the yard late at night. Had he too had sex with her, there in Ignacio's trailer? Maybe Charis was the only thing that had stopped Bernal from becoming another Bowler victim. Bernal tried to keep his mind on what they had to figure out. He could talk this all over with Patricia when he saw her.

Or, perhaps, never ever bring it up.

"And later, when she was investigating what Ungaro had been up to, Muriel must have tracked that back, linking Hesketh to the Bowler." The more Bernal thought about it, the more sense it made. "She probably didn't know about the drugs. I mean, Ignacio *was* smuggling drugs, wasn't he?"

"If that was going to be the only charge, he'd be clear. Not because he wasn't doing it, but because no evidence survived. He had this high-volume emergency shower back there. That, and a little incinerator powered by some kind of arc furnace. They found some empty bags but nothing with enough on it to take to court."

"Let me get this straight. We're heading toward where he has all of his souvenirs, the weapons he had used to kill various people, and he goes to take care of his drugs instead?"

"You just won't give up, will you?"

"You haven't answered my question."

"He took care of the drugs first. Us second. We were in his house, where his souvenirs were. He couldn't just pop in there and dispose of them, not until we were taken care of. And, if you've forgotten, he almost succeeded in doing that. He raised us off the ground, took care of the drugs, and came back for us. It was pretty close to being 'us dead and disposed of, drugs and murder weapons gone.' There will always be things we won't be able to clear up."

There was a beep outside. Bernal followed Charis out into the sunlight. It was a warm day, the first day when the warmth seemed sincere rather than a smile pasted on a lurking winter. Charis collected the pizza from the kid behind the wheel. Fresh growth was starting to conceal the apartment parking lot across the stream, where Bernal had found the traces of Hesketh's path just a little over a week before.

Hesketh, which had been something real that had vanished that day and seemingly had never returned.

"So it's all settled," he said.

"They'll find her." Charis took a big bite of her own piece before pulling one out for Bernal. "Don't worry. One way or another, they'll find her. Here. I know these aren't your kind of thing."

She plucked a couple of pieces of pepperoni from the piece she was about to hand him and placed them on her own. Bernal found himself irritated. He hadn't ordered the pepperoni, but now he was anxious to feel its bite.

"What are you going to do now?" he said.

"You mean now that I have nothing but a busted anti-AI activist organization with only one staff member? I don't know. Why?"

"Well, you helped the police solve a major serial killer case, didn't you? You thinking of going back into police work?"

"Nah." If she hesitated, it was barely noticeable. "Probably use that cred to pick up some regular PI work. I got a buddy, he does a lot of corporate malfeasance stuff. Faked trip reports, employees taking confidential information out on their flash drives, that kind of thing. Boring as hell, but it pays good, and might be a chance for some regular hours and some thinking about what I really want to spend my life doing. I'll give up the lease on my office, sell the Hummer."

Something had been nagging at Bernal, and the discussion of her office brought it to the surface. "What happened to your fence that day, you remember?"

"Hell, yes, I remember. Had endless trouble with the landlord. Had the nerve to complain about the footings we put in. When it was all his fault in the first place."

Bernal's slice was growing cold and floppy in his hand. "How was it his fault?"

"He'd had a contractor in to regrade. Place floods when it rains, he sometimes gets six inches right at the garage. I've complained about it, other renters have complained, he finally decided to do something about it. So he had this guy in, laid drainage pipe, all sorts of shit, seemed to work. Less water this spring, anyway. But some kids got in, looks like. Started up the Bobcat, got right through the security fence. I'd blamed cognitive activists, but it looks like, this time at least, I was unfair."

"They ever find the kids?"

"Nah. When do they ever find the kids? They'll either

get picked up for something worse later, or they'll straighten up and never enter the system. Doesn't really matter. What's your point?"

Without another word, Bernal went over to the control and raised the door to the loading dock. Sun roared in, and he had to blink against it for a moment before he could see anything.

There, that set of parallel scratches through the stains on the concrete floor. He'd taken them for granted, but now they seemed to mean something. Mentally, he superimposed the image of the Hummer the day he had met Charis, the day the thing had stopped working and required a tow. He thought it had been right there, right beyond where the scrapes ended.

He pulled out his phone and flipped through the pictures he had taken that day. The last one was of the loading dock. He'd been focused on the inside of the lab and never checked this one.

He flipped it back and forth and what had changed was immediately obvious. The large cylinder that had been lying there, amid the paint cans and other trash, was gone.

He'd thought it was an automatic transmission or something.

It had been Hesketh.

Bernal pulled the Hummer up on a couple of ramps borrowed from another business in the warehouse. Charis dangled legs on the loading dock and watched him.

"Hey, Bernal. Mind if I finish this last piece?"

She'd already had one more than him, but he didn't feel like making an issue of it.

He pushed himself underneath the vehicle. It only took him a moment to find what he was looking for. Two . . . four . . . six circles, pressed into the crust that covered the underside of any car that had been driven off the showroom floor more than a couple of days ago.

"Charis," he said. "I think you better take a look at this."

She grumbled but eventually got on her back and pushed herself under the vehicle. There was a long moment of silence. "What does this mean?"

"Think back to what happened that day."

"The magic day when you and I met?"

"You pulled into the loading area here. You and I had some back and forth."

"You were a real dick, Bernal. I was quite impressed. It's kind of a pity you turned out to be so undicklike when I got to know you better."

"Thanks. I think. Hesketh had come in from a run. Pushed its way in through the back door. Something was badly wrong. That wasn't its usual way of returning. But there was no trace of any central processing unit for Hesketh when I looked."

"We've been through this. Because there wasn't any real brain to the thing. It was just a fancy go-cart. Stick as close to facts as you can, and let me interpret on my own."

"Okay. *Something* had smashed into the lab. There was mud and stuff scattered all over. I looked around and, right, saw no sign of any kind of AI. You pulled in before I completed my search. When you got into your car, you heard some kind of thunk."

She pulled herself out from under the car, but just sat there, on the ground, leaning back against the fender. "Right."

"And then your car wouldn't start. You got a tow from Patricia. Nothing was wrong with your car. Then, that night, a Bobcat goes crazy in the yard where your car was towed, smashes through a fence, and ends up in the ditch."

"Okay. Pretty straightforward. So what am I looking at under there?"

"Evidence that something attached itself underneath the chassis of your Hummer."

"With what, suction cups?"

"I don't think so. My guess is electromagnets."

"Magnets?" Charis looked around the bay. "People have been machining crap in this space for decades. Seems like you should be able to . . ." She walked over to the wall, scraped along its base with her fingers, and showed Bernal what she had managed to get: a sprinkling of iron filings.

Together, they slid back under the car. While he held the flashlight, she let the slivers of metal sift off her fingers and onto the bottom of the car.

Where they dangled, held up by a residual magnetic charge.

"So you think Hesketh came in here that night, shucked its body, and, like some mutant limbless child from a horror movie, attached itself under my car and . . . and what? Why would it stop me from driving away? You were throwing me out, you might remember. I would have been right out of here."

"It might have been a mistake," Bernal said. "Some electromagnetic field that knocked out some part of your starter. Who knows? It does seem to have the ability to control vehicles."

"Like that Bobcat, you mean? That's a guess. You think it got some control of the damn thing, got dragged along until it smashed through the fence, and then lay there waiting for someone to pick it up. Who?"

"My guess?" Bernal said. "Those Badger space enthusiasts. Enigmatic Ascent."

"Why them?"

"I've thought about what happened that night the decoy almost blew us up. They got a message, which I didn't see. But it led them to think that Hesketh was escaping and needed help. They were tearing off to assist when I saw you."

"Any indication what information they got?" Charis said.

"I didn't see the message. I actually thought it was you, sending them off so you could take care of what you thought was Hesketh."

"Not me," Charis said. "I didn't have enough information on those guys at that point to send them a spoof message. I thought I just got lucky when they took off. Until that decoy almost killed us, of course. But explain one thing to me. Why would your Midwestern buddies be so eager to help out a serial killer?"

"They don't know Hesketh is a killer," Bernal said. "But they do think it wants to escape. Some kind of space probe liberation movement. They could certainly answer a few questions for us, if they're not back in Wisconsin by now."

"They haven't left," Charis said.

"How do you know?"

"Bernal, really. I know who's on my turf. These guys rambling around at night, trying to catch sight of Hesketh, like they're some kind of robot-watchers trying to build up their life lists. I don't care how crazy they are, or how little sense their motivations make to a normal person. I tracked them down after your little encounter with them that night Hesketh tried to blow us up. They found themselves a couple of rooms in the Green Acre, up on Cernan Road. It's always the odd tourists, literary butterfly collectors, fugitives, and the like, who end up there."

"Let's go get them," Bernal said.

41

The bolts and welds on the washer arms indicated several generations of casual repairs. Their aging gears engaged, and they shuddered forward and down, spraying spirals of soapy water onto the SUV being tugged through the car wash. Figures were dimly visible behind the water-coated windows. Bernal could hear music thumping inside the car. The underlying rumble of the machinery shifted to a lower register.

"I got Sally to cut the speed on the conveyor!" Charis shouted above the shriek of unlubricated metal as the arms raised themselves back up. "Gives us a few minutes. Wait for those drying carousels to swing by, then jump for it."

"Wha—"

"Now!"

Sally was the owner of the Squeak 'n Whistle, a grumpy man with a gray ponytail and a bulging belly. He had been less than happy to see Charis but had agreed to her demands and allowed her and Bernal access to the car wash through a maintenance door.

A cylinder of flopping cloth, sodden from a swing across the SUV, rained soapy water on Bernal. At the last possible moment before it returned to ready itself for the next vehicle, he jumped after Charis. His left foot slipped, and his shoe was instantly full of the water that ran down the track into the bubbling recycling sump. He yelped and waddled after Charis, who seemed to know exactly when to dodge, when to duck, and when to ignore the various washing gadgets that gestured obscenely at the passing cars.

Charis found a quiet alcove where spare cylinders of pink liquid detergent stood stacked, ready to be attached to the dispensing nozzles.

"Whee!" Charis waved her thick dark hair with her fingers. "My hairdresser is going to kill me. Industrial detergent is really hell on the highlights."

Bernal wiggled his foot in his shoe. Soaked. The sock had fallen down around his ankle, and it was useless to pull it up.

"Sally used to be into whores as well as auto detailing," she said. "Had a whole operation here. A lot went down, but we could only get evidence for a couple of minor charges. But that was the whole point. What can you observe inside this place? Can't man a stakeout, can't stick a listening device that wouldn't get destroyed in a few minutes. Smart, doing your business inside of a washing machine. And it was screened by the legitimate business. People really did get their cars washed here. After Sally got busted, the place got a bad rep, not so popular anymore. Of course, that's mostly because we make him run it fast, the way a real car wash would be. Used to be, you could sit in here for fifteen minutes, get your business done. The working girls loved that quarter-hour rub and spray. Had a real routine going. Get out at the vacuum cleaners, grab a Coke from the machine on the way to the back, find a customer and take another ride."

"And you guys rained on everyone's parade? How rude."

"Cops're used to pissing people off, enforcing all those stupid laws. Sally's toned things down, but I knew he had access to the governor we slapped on the conveyor. He pretty much hand-built this place. If he behaves himself, he just might get by okay. Hey, here they come. Get across to the other side. Front door if that seat's empty, otherwise back. If Sally's done his job, their doors aren't locked, because they're expecting a pre-cross-country-road-trip vacuum at the end to get the wrappers and flattened french fries out. Wait until that spray's done . . . now!"

Bernal missed most of the dribble of scalding water that came out of the back end of the nozzle when it shut off, but he still ended up with a wet shoulder. The front of the reentry-marked Plymouth Voyager emerged from the first set of sprays.

On their way to brace the Enigmatic Ascent crew at the Green Acre, Charis had spotted their minivan bumping through the water-filled potholes at the entrance to the Squeak 'n Whistle car wash and formulated this plan on the fly. "The weirder and more arbitrary the place you interrogate someone, the more off balance they are," she'd said. "And the less admissible in court, of course. But that's not exactly relevant here, is it?"

Bernal felt that he was the one off balance, but there wasn't time to consider that now. The Voyager was next to him. He could see Oleana's serene helmet of hair, which meant the passenger seat was unoccupied. He heard Charis shout something, so he grabbed the handle, pulled the door open, and tumbled in.

Oleana squeaked, turned, and sprayed him in the face with something that burned his eyes. He fell back against the door, his eyes squeezed against the pain.

"Oh . . . Bernal! I didn't know, I'm sorry . . . what the . . . why are you here? Just to say goodbye?" By the end, the shock was gone from her voice, and she was back to deadpan.

"What was that? Mace?"

"What? No. Smell yourself."

Wary of a trick, he sniffed. He smelled . . . moonlight, spring flowers, the scent he remembered from when they had first met. It was still too foofy for her. "Perfume?"

"All I had. 'Happy,' by Clinique. From my mom, every birthday. No Mace. I wouldn't even know where you buy it. You guys use it a lot out here?"

Someone honked behind them, and male voices howled. She peered into her rearview mirror. "Do they think we can go faster?" Another honk.

In the back, Charis had missed a grip on the back of Oleana's seat as she jumped in and crashed to the floor. Len and Magnusen's faces were ashen and startled in the light of their open laptops. They leaned forward and helped her up.

"Hesketh," Bernal said. "What do you think Hesketh is?"

"I don't think you deserve that information." Oleana rested her fingertips on the steering wheel, not as if driving, but as if ready to do so at any moment. Bernal noticed that she colored her nails orange and then bit them. "Who's your friend?"

"Sorry. Charis Fen, meet Oleana, Len, and Magnusen. You know about them. Charis is a colleague. Someone as interested in figuring out what Hesketh is as I am. I'd think you'd be more curious."

Charis took her time about getting up off the floor.

Then she rolled and sat, massive, between their seats. The two men looked down at her nervously.

"Who originally got in touch with you?" Charis said.

"We never knew," Magnusen said. "Anonymous, but with information about a special planetary probe. We couldn't pass it up. So we started watching, when we could. The track information was good."

"You think it was Hesketh itself," Charis said. "The original information came from it. Right? You were supposed to help it."

"Yes," Oleana said. "It said it needed our help."

"Do you know what Hesketh is?" Bernal said. "Do you know what's actually going on here? The thing's a killer—the Bowler. If you think about it, you'll realize it all fits."

All three were silent. The last soap dispenser squirted foam on the windshield.

"We should tell them," Len said. No one else spoke. He looked around, trying to find support. He didn't find any, but at least he didn't find resistance, either. "We know where it's going, so we should just tell them."

"Oh, Len . . . ," Oleana whispered.

"That's no way to do it!" A less controlled personality than Magnusen would have been shouting. But, in his context, his voice was just as startling. "You can't just guess . . . we know what we've been working for . . . understanding, cooperating, helping, we've been part of something bigger, on a mission, trying to get something achieved. . . ."

"We were gamed, Magnusen," Len said. "Taken advantage of. All of us were."

"It's not a killer. I don't believe it's a killer."

"Okay, fine then. But do you think we need to help it? To assist it in making its escape? Do you think someone's really trying to destroy it for no good reason?"

"Do you really know what it is?" Bernal said.

"Just tell us," Magnusen said. "Don't try to take advantage of our pride or our solidarity or anything to persuade us to an emotional position. Just give us what you think and why we should agree."

Bernal and Charis exchanged a glance. She nodded.

"Hesketh *is* intended and designed for planetary exploration," he said. "But it went wrong. Its substrate is frozen human heads, taken from a cryobank. I don't think it got ahold of an abnormal brain or anything, but in a kind of pragmatic way, it set out to get more processing power by obtaining more heads. Perhaps it didn't have the context for when it was proper to recover a functional head. It found someone to help it out, to do the work of killing in the human world. That person, Ignacio Kuepner, is now dead. Hesketh is trying to escape. We're trying to stop it."

"It fits," Len said. "God knows, Magnusen, it fits."

Magnusen scowled, not as an expression of disagreement but one of deep thought. "Okay. But if it's about to leave the planet for interstellar space, what does it really matter? It's still a magnificent mission."

"Magnificent? The thing's a killer! You may not believe in titanium dickeys, but you know that."

"You didn't hear me deny it, did you? But, I mean, it's not like we're worried about future crime here, are we? There's only one Hesketh. This is a pretty unique situation, and you can't torque your system around to deter unique situations."

"I can't believe I'm hearing this! Are you really going to argue legal theory right now?"

"It's all just theory, until you find yourself on the receiving end."

Len choked in exasperation.

"Magnusen." Oleana's voice was calm. "This is serious. Please let's help catch this thing."

"I . . ." Magnusen worked his mouth as he looked at her. Then he squeezed his eyes tightly shut. "Okay."

"Don't hold anything back," Oleana said.

"I go for it, you know that." He looked at Charis and Bernal. "We've been getting a lot of chatter. All over. Groups like ours, other information . . . I put it together, got—"

Len cleared his throat.

"Len helped . . . Len and I got the information together. Never mind who did what. That's not relevant now, is it? We're a team, we're good at what we do. There's a line, a chain of transfers. Been used a couple of times, become kind of routine.

"An Aeroflot aircraft, usually Tupolev 124 or 154, flies from one of the 'stans to Vladivostok. An irregular run, carrying the kind of thing you carry from corrupt former Soviet Central Asian republics: opium, weaponry, looted archeological finds, specialized gear from defunct labs. Things get transferred to a Korean Air 747 long-distance freighter, which takes the cargo to LA. Then things get variable. Usually, though, it gets massaged into a regular package, something clean, and goes via some bulk shipper to an airport in the northeast, ranging from Chicago to Boston and down to maybe Philadelphia. From there, a small plane, a Cirrus SR-22, flies the package into Cheriton airport."

"That's probably how Ignacio got his stuff in," Charis said.

"Yeah, but what's important is that it works the other way too. Stuff goes out. And something's ready to go out this morning, early. We think it's Hesketh. The Cirrus has filed a flight plan that takes it over to O'Hare by morning. A FedEx Airbus 300 is set up to take it, and it's pretty big, and lot of freight is getting paid. Then, nothing certain, but there's some nice flight matchups, with an Aeroflot Antonov 124 already sitting on the tarmac at Vlad with nothing obvious for it to do. The AN-124 is one of the world's largest freight transport aircraft.

This one belongs to the Russian Space Agency and is usually used for transporting things like rocket boosters. Our guess is that it's heading across Central Asia to Krainiy Airport, which serves the city of Baikonur, Kazakhstan. That's the nearest city to—"

"Tyuratam," Bernal said. "Your old tourist site. Where the big boosters burn."

"We were hoping to go there," Magnusen said. "To see it take off."

"The tickets are a rip-off," Oleana said. "I'd rather go to St. Thomas. I'm getting some good prices."

Both Magnusen and Len stared at her in shock. Switching vacation plans from central Kazakhstan to the Caribbean meant a real change of priorities. Bernal didn't know whether Oleana's decision not to spend her vacation feeling steppe dust between her teeth was what had led to her decision to reveal all, but more arbitrary things had certainly happened.

"I don't know how fussy the Russians are going to be about Hesketh," Len said. "They need the dough."

"They've never been fussy about anything," Charis said. "If they could have kept severed heads alive, they'd still be worshipping Stalin and probably happy as clams about it. Damn it! We're running around Cheriton looking under rocks, and Hesketh's boosted everything to a whole new level."

"Ignacio must have contacts all the way out there," Bernal said.

"And why not? Once the Soviet Union collapsed, they were the biggest source of dangerous junk on the face of the planet. I'm sure Ignacio would have wanted a piece of that."

Bernal looked at the faces of the Enigmatic Ascent crew, expecting to see crushing defeat. Instead, they looked . . . interested. Having fun. Len and Magnusen huddled over a single screen, checking out launch windows from

Tyuratam, while Oleana was on the phone to some fellow enthusiast in Smolensk, who had some information about Russian government plans. They spoke in French.

The van was finally pulled through the last water spray and under the flopping noodles at the exit. They turned the car over to Len for a last vacuum.

Bernal and Len pulled the van over to the automotive interior cleaning area, while the others spread out, like people talking on their phones do, and circled at the far end of the parking lot like moths. Two cylinders, red and yellow, bubbled, promising obsolete scents for their interior. The corrugated hose of a vacuum cleaner dangled from an overhead cable. Its compressor cylinder was decorated like a little robot, with arms ending in metal clamps.

"That night," Len said. "The night we met you. We got a message." He cranked up the vacuum and poked the nozzle under the front seat.

"I remember."

"Hesketh wanted a pickup, over on Cooper Road. It was supposedly just lying out there, injured. Something had happened to it."

"At number 37?" Charis's HQ, just as he had thought.

"Right. But when we got there, there was a fence down, and someone had already picked it up."

"Who?"

"Didn't see. Just a vehicle, a truck. We didn't know that was what had happened until we looked around where it had been pulled out. Saw some big tire tracks. And we found some crap, papers and stuff. Not wet, looked fresh, like it had just fallen out of something."

"What kind of stuff?"

"This was mostly paper crap. Some beer coasters that someone had trimmed into O-rings, like you'd use for attaching an exhaust pipe or something. A template for drilling holes to attach an under-desk keyboard drawer. And someone had used it to drill holes and then kept it. And a fax . . . well, look, here." With a furtive glance over at Magnusen, he pulled a folded piece of paper out of his pocket. "I made a copy. On the sly, kind of. Magnusen wants to seem so smart, like he figured it all out from first principles. He did some decent research, I'll give him that, but without the luck of finding this thing, he'd have nothing."

At the top it said WANT TO IMPROVE YOUR SALES PRODUCTIVITY 330%? It was the same sheet that had come out of the old fax machine in Charis's office. But below, where Muriel's message had been superimposed, was, instead, a FedEx waybill, with a bar code. Hesketh must have spit that out for Ignacio to use in arranging its transportation. Magnusen had used it to figure out Hesketh's planned route.

Hesketh had communicated however it could. Muriel had managed to send a version with her own message superimposed to Charis's machine. The other had gone to Ignacio, who had come out to recover Hesketh.

But there was a bit more. Below the bar code was what looked like a photograph of some stretch of outer space. He could see a piece of nebula, a spray of stars. Part of the image was obscured with something like a bar or a support strut.

"Is this Hesketh's final destination?" Bernal pointed at the nebula.

"Dunno. Maybe it's planning its escape route in complete detail, clear out to the Lesser Magellanic Cloud or something."

All the evidence pointed to Hesketh's attempted departure from the Cheriton Airport. They should all be on that, attempting to intercept, and setting up backstops in case it evaded them, to stop it somewhere else along the line. So Bernal, deliberately and consciously, tried to falsify this hypothesis.

It was a mental process he'd worked out after that package had exploded in his hands. The only way not to see what you expect to see is to change your expectations and see if things still look the same. And, necessarily, the path to falsifying the Tyuratam hypothesis was through Prelate and Vervain, the only people he knew for sure had seen the headtaker up close and personal and who worked for whoever had wanted it recovered. Seeing Prelate and Vervain was something he'd hoped he'd never have to do.

The vacuum nozzle buzzed. Len pulled it out from under the seat and yanked off the hamburger box that was stuck on it.

"Get out of the way, you moron!" someone yelled.

Bernal looked up. A man with a mullet, wearing a vinyl vest that revealed a fleshy arm with a tattoo of a grinning Coyote buggering the Road Runner, glowered from a black Silverado with a silver death's head on its hood. Molten flux had dripped down the grille from the crude welding job.

His passenger, a smaller version of the driver, with bare head poking out through the top of his mullet, grinned at Bernal and flipped him the finger. A Playboy Bunny air freshener dangled from the rearview.

In getting a look at the photograph, Bernal had stepped out into the route cars took out of the wash. "I'm sor—"

"Son of a bitch." Something sprayed across his feet. The pickup backed and roared past so close that Bernal had to jump out of the way. It fishtailed into the street, burned rubber, and was gone.

Bernal looked down. A Coors can rolled against his foot, spilling froth. So he could add littering to their other crimes. He was lucky they hadn't winged it at his head. Len picked it up and dropped it into a half-melted blue plastic trash barrel.

"I miss the Midwest," Len said.

Bernal tucked the copied sheet into a pocket. "Better get your ass back to Baraboo, then."

42

Charis was organizing an interception of Hesketh in cooperation with Enigmatic Ascent. But, instead of being part of that exciting operation, Bernal was chatting over old times with his buddies Prelate and Vervain. He had to find out who they had been working for, and he had to do it alone. No one else could be spared.

"We not know." Prelate was emphatic. "Not know!"

"Bernal, you want some . . . ah, what is this, honey?"

Prelate looked down at the grease-stained white cardboard box held out to her by Vervain. "Pastry. Went to pastry shop, got pastry. You want pastry names? I have no names. I point."

Vervain sighed, then smiled at Bernal. He was impressed with himself. No matter what else happened in his life, he would remember coming here, to the apartment of Quanelle Martin, aka Vervain, and Wanda Grbić, aka Prelate, to find out why the hell the two women had stolen a headtaker and then locked him in a wine cellar.

Vervain wiggled the box in a manner intended to be enticing. "Pick something."

Bernal picked a cylinder with a sail of chocolate sticking out of it. The ladies had been excessively friendly since he had arrived, and they had buzzed him right in. "You were working for Madeline Ungaro?"

"Right!" Prelate nodded. "We know her. She like neighbor, back at the old place, at Long Voyage."

"Did you steal those heads for her in the first place?"

"*We not know about that!*"

"Please, honey." Vervain rubbed her partner's arm. "Let me try to clear this up."

Despite their coziness, Bernal did not get the sense of them as lovers, and, in fact, the electric organ displayed photographs of Prelate with what looked like a husband, taken in a studio back in whatever country she had emigrated from, and Vervain wore an engagement ring with an impressive diamond on it, which she presumably took off when hitting people so that it would not leave a traceable imprint in someone's skin.

"We didn't know anything about Madeline's penetration of Long Voyage," Vervain said. "So, when she gave us a call, we figured it was just because she'd appreciated our work. We do salvage, recovery. We'd talked about it, so she knew. We're always looking for work, and word of mouth is what gets you the referrals."

"Madeline hired you to, what, find a piece of cryogenic gear someone had hidden in an abandoned car?"

"Pretty much. Someone had stolen it from her, she said. And she needed it for a project."

"And then, when I came around to check up on it, you assaulted me and locked me in the basement."

"Poor behavior," Prelate said. "We acknowledge."

"It was all just part of the job." Vervain showed no embarrassment. "She warned us that someone would be coming around after it. There was bonus money in it if we kept it safe. Absolute security is part of our service."

"What did you spend the bonus money on?" Bernal said.

"We got a new dining room table! Jordan's, on sale. A good deal."

"Great," Bernal said. "I'm glad."

There were knickknacks on the shelves of the hutch. A lace tablecloth covered the newly acquired table, with a bowl of blue, green, and red artificial apples directly in the center. On the wall were more family photographs and some nature scenes, at least one of which looked like it had come with the frame. A low bookshelf held books that looked left over from someone's college days, with more than one bearing a yellow USED sticker across the spine.

For all he knew, they genuinely were sorry. All in the way of business, can we just move on here?

"Someone died at that car," Bernal said. "Muriel Inglis was murdered."

"Nothing to do with us." Prelate was stubborn. "We did job, were done. We knew no serial killer man."

"And you delivered the device?"

"We did the job we were paid for," Vervain said. "That's why people hire us."

If they had actually worked for Ignacio Kuepner, there was no way they were going to admit it, not to him, anyway. Madeline Ungaro was their story, and they were sticking to it.

"Where is Madeline Ungaro now?"

"She is gone," Prelate said. "Had special project elsewhere. She met us at Italian restaurant, on Route 2. We had nice pasta dinner, then she took what she paid for. We ask no questions about the rest. Never see her again. Another pastry?" Prelate shoved the box at Bernal so aggressively that the contents almost slid out into his lap.

"No, thank you." Was anything they had told him true? She'd vanished from the scene, but here they were insisting that they had eaten pasta with her somewhere on Route 2, not far from Cheriton. He didn't think they knew a damn thing about Ungaro. The woman was a mirage. Muriel was really dead, and after all his searching, he was no closer to Ungaro than when he had started. "Could I use the bathroom?"

"Sure." Had Vervain hesitated a tiny bit? "It's down the hall, that way."

Perhaps Charis might have made something out of the ranks of toiletries on the window shelf, on the rack in the shower, along the radiator, but the multicolored bottles said nothing to Bernal. Everything was clean, neat, and organized. He found himself checking around the edge of the toilet to make sure he hadn't splashed. He wouldn't want them talking about him after he left.

As he stepped out of the bathroom, he glanced down the hall. Down at the end was a half open door which revealed a bed with a flowered bedspread and a night table with a clock radio on it. Above the bed hung what looked like an out-of-focus picture of a flower taken through a raindrop-spattered window.

Vervain stood at the end of the hall, watching him.

No, not a flower. It was, in fact, a perfectly in-focus astronomical photograph of a brightly colored nebula. What he had thought were drops of water on a pane of glass were the glowing points of nearer stars. They'd been paid, but their employer had decided to throw in a photograph, since he took pictures like that as his hobby.

They hadn't been working for Ignacio Kuepner, and they hadn't been working for Madeline Ungaro. They were working for someone with an even closer connection with Long Voyage, the only person in the whole situation who might have a deep interest in storing and transporting heads and returning them to their proper place.

Norbert Spillvagen. Of course.

He checked his fly, then strolled out into the living room.

Something clamped itself on his arm. Prelate's hand.

"You know how there are all these satellite tournaments to the World Series of Poker, and people buy in, hoping for a shot at the big time?"

"Sure." He tried to turn, as if casually, but was locked in place.

"If something like that comes to your hometown, don't try it. Everybody at the table can take one look at you and know every card you hold in your hand."

43

They silenced him with a strip of duct tape and hauled him out of the apartment, down a back staircase, and into their car, a nondescript sedan, in as many seconds as it had taken them to throw him in the cellar the last time. They were now driving down a dark road, heading out of town. And he'd lost his cell phone again.

He wished he could appreciate their professional service ethic more. They maintained absolute confidentiality. If he hadn't figured out their real client, they would have let him go, no hard feelings, and probably put him on their Christmas list. Now they had another plan.

They hadn't even tied his hands. Wondering if he would be punished, he reached up and ripped the tape from his mouth. Neither of them said anything or even turned around.

Headlights flared behind them. Bernal snuck a glance, hoping for a police car. No such luck. Instead, it was a big pickup, looming over Prelate's smaller car. He was about to forget about it when he saw a glint of silver. A death's head on the hood. It was his impatient friends from the car wash. They'd been honking at him since they were stuck behind the Voyager on a conveyor chain. He slumped back into his seat. His luck, that his last possible human contact turned out to be with assholes.

The great thing about assholes was their consistency. They were always assholes. In sudden inspiration, Bernal held his hand behind his head, where Prelate and Vervain couldn't see it, and gave them the finger. It was something he'd wanted to do back when they'd tried to run over him by the vacuum. The pickup honked. Bernal moved his hand up and down vigorously. The pickup's driver leaned on his horn and pushed up until his bumper was almost against them.

This would all surely attract attention. An accident, a stop for an exchange of insurance company information, and he could get the hell out.

"Who the hell is that jerkoff?" Prelate glanced in the rearview, then accelerated. The pickup kept pace.

Bernal took advantage of her attention to the road to turn around and mouth an obscenity. In high school, he and a friend had spent a long afternoon working out what phrases were most clearly visible when lip read. He now used a few with the highest signal-to-noise ratio, and finished it off with that same friend's favorite tongue-in-cheek and hand-holding-invisible-penis blowjob gesture. He would never have the grace Thad had had with it, but he thought it would work well enough.

It did. The pickup swung out into the opposite lane and accelerated with a roar. They crested a hill. An oncoming car tooted a horn, then, with admirable speed, spun itself out into the drainage ditch by the side of the road. Bernal didn't have a chance to see what happened to it.

The wisest thing would have been to hit the brakes and let the yahoos in the pickup roar on. But no one is wiser in a car than out of it. Prelate accelerated just as the pickup turned back into the right lane.

Their left front fender smacked against the pickup's passenger side just as the pickup slammed on its brakes.

They bounced and spun. Bernal was yanked back and forth, and those distant window lights seared through him like lasers.

They stopped, engine dead and silent. Bernal stared up through the windshield in befuddlement, wondering how anyone could have overlooked this gigantic sycamore while paving the road. Then he knew he had to move.

He thumbed the catch on his shoulder harness, pulled the handle, and was out the door. Cold flooded his feet, and he realized they had landed in the drainage ditch by the road's side. One foot was still wet from the car wash, so it wasn't as bad as it might have been. He clambered up past cans and crumpled cigarette packs to the road.

The death's head pickup stood up there, waiting. Bernal prepared to dive back into the ditch, but all the driver and his buddy did was whoop a rebel yell and tear off down the road. A rebel yell? In Massachusetts? People had really lost touch with their roots. It was all those specialized cable channels and Web sites. Those were people's true homelands now.

With a feeling of floating free, his toes barely grazing the asphalt, Bernal looked down at the car. The driver's side had come to rest against the tree. Prelate struggled with that door as her airbag deflated, then gave Vervain a shove. Tough girl that she was, Vervain had not been wearing her safety harness, and the impact had stunned her.

Bernal ran. First he ran along the road, then, seeing a forest access road, off into the dark woods. His head was clear now.

Within a few minutes, he sensed he had lost them. But he did not slow down.

The road petered out in a couple of hundred yards, so he plunged directly into the trees. He wasn't running now. He couldn't manage it. And now that he wasn't running, the woods seemed harder to penetrate, resisting him with shrubs, leaf-covered streams, slippery rocks.

Bernal could see the connections. Spillvagen had gone through a great deal of trouble to acquire a device for storing cryogenically frozen heads. Where was he planning to get them? Unless he himself was planning a raid on the Long Voyage cryobank, the only other local supply of the things was inside Hesketh.

Did Spillvagen know where Hesketh was? Even if he didn't, it was clear that he had a lot more information than he'd let on. Bernal was wary of Prelate and Vervain, Spillvagen's minions, but it wasn't the paralyzing fear he might once have felt. He was too full of a feeling of a mystery on its way to being solved. Spillvagen just better not stand in the way of solving it.

Ahead, a darkness against the glowing sky: a ridge, a glacier's rock collection, dropped all at once when the fashion for ice ages ended. He climbed carefully. On the other side, a packed dirt trail led down at an angle. Some of the trees had blazes on them, triangles, either metal ones nailed in, or older ones cut into the bark, now almost reabsorbed. That was good. Men had been here, men like himself. Ahead was a parking lot, maybe one with a rustic wood Conservation Land sign and a holder for nature brochures with line drawings of mayapples and deer footprints.

The distant light of a shopping center silvered the trees at the large trailhead parking lot. He looked toward its glow and realized that he was very near where Maura worked.

He desperately did not want to make her useful. But he even more desperately wanted to solve this, to find Hesketh, to find Madeline Ungaro, to find or dispel Muriel.

So he set off down the road. He walked quickly and lightly, feeling like he was finally getting somewhere. He did get a crick in his neck from checking each pair of headlights coming up behind him to make sure it wasn't Prelate and Vervain.

He called Charls from a phone at the Woodland Shopping Center and got her voice mail. She was too busy predicting Hesketh's route to Cheriton Airport and working out a way to prevent it from reaching its flight to answer. He left her a brief message about Norbert Spillvagen and the headtaker, but he wasn't yet ready to claim that he was on the right track to finding Hesketh.

That would come after he confronted Spillvagen.

44

The ceilings of the SuperMax were forty feet high, and the stacks of office supplies almost reached them. Bernal wandered the aisles, momentarily mesmerized by the primary colors of copy paper boxes, file organizers, and highlighters.

He dodged an inventory checker on a Segway and found Maura near the laser printers. She wore a blue uniform with the SuperMax logo, with its row of pens standing on end. It was a hell of a thing to make a grown-up wear, though she must have made some alterations, because hers cut neatly in at the waist.

She turned and looked at him as he came up. She made an arrested movement to check her hair. The wiry curls were untamable, even by the bear-trap clip that held most of the hair behind her head.

"I was in the neighborhood," he said. "Thought I would stop by."

She scanned him, muddy feet up past torn shirt to what, he now realized, must have been a hunted expression. "You're not done, are you? I asked you to stop by when you were done."

She was flushed red, as if embarrassed, but she was serious.

"No, I'm not done. There were two days when I thought I was, but now I know I'm nowhere near done. And I need some help."

"What kind of help?"

"I need a ride. I need to confront someone, and I need to do it soon."

Her pause was long enough that he feared she would throw him out. "I'm about due for a break now anyway. I better be able to eat lunch while I drive you. Is that okay?"

"That's fine."

"Here." She handed him a brown paper bag and backed around a delivery truck. The driver waved to her. "Pull out the sandwich and open it up, will you? Doesn't matter what else I'm doing with my break, but I got to eat lunch or I'll pass out during the rest of my shift. That, or bite the head off a customer."

He opened the neatly rolled top and pulled out an aluminum foil rectangle. The bag was a classic, with a couple of translucent spots that indicated reuse. He uncrimped the foil and handed her the sandwich, which looked like tuna salad on whole wheat.

"I didn't want you to be useful to me," he said. "I really didn't."

"Any reason why? I might surprise you with the things I can do."

"We first overvalue the things that are useful to us, and then undervalue them. I didn't want that."

"That's so sweet."

She was so deadpan he couldn't figure out if she was

making fun of him, or appreciating his thought, or first one and then the other.

She shot out of the shopping center parking lot and merged into the surprisingly heavy traffic heading east.

Maura ate while she drove toward Spillvagen's. Her dark eyes reflected the oncoming headlights. He sensed her annoyance when a larger piece of lettuce pulled out of the sandwich onto her lower lip. She flicked it up with a sharp fingernail and caught it in her mouth.

"Potato chips."

He was starving. But having asked for this, he wasn't going to ask for anything more. He knew she would have gladly given him any of it. But she might feel hungry later in her shift, and he didn't want her thinking about him at that moment. Men were supposed to bring women food, not take it from them. He held the bag open and let her grab handfuls as she drove.

"You have much to do, at this hour?" he said.

"We usually get a late-night crowd, people who need to print their explanation of the universe before the sun comes up and need the neon yellow copy paper so that someone will take them seriously, or who've decided that this is the night they're finally going to get organized, so that they can stop wasting their lives. Most people have a moment or two where it seems that the solution to their problems is hanging folders and a label printer."

"I've made a couple of late-night runs to places like yours myself, in my day."

She didn't say anything. Conventionally, phrases like "why doesn't that surprise me?" seemed so expected that their absence was disorienting.

"There's a granola bar." She put the back of her hand against his. "You can have half. It's blueberry brown sugar jungle nut, or something. They're all pretty much the same."

"Are you sure?"

"Yes. Take it, come on."

He tugged the wrapper open along the seam. He felt the pressure of her fingernails as he put it into her hand, and wanted to just go somewhere else and forget Hesketh, everything. There were other things that were more important.

But Maura had to get back after her break. No sense in getting her in trouble at work. That was important too. He ate his half of the bar in two bites, then folded the packet and put it back in the bag, just as neatly as he knew she would have.

"Just up here." He pointed, and she pulled up to the curb, on the opposite side of the block from Spillvagen's house.

They sat and stared at each other for a few seconds.

"Bernal?"

"Yes?" This was her cue to tell him to be careful.

"Please wait until you're done before you call me again. Seriously. I don't want to be with someone who's always worried about the fate of humanity or something. Makes me feel like I'm in second place."

"You're not in second place, Maura."

She tugged lightly at his sleeve. "I think I know that. But now, go."

He struggled with the shoulder harness for a moment, then got out. She raised her hand and waggled her fingers as she drove away, but did not glance back at him.

45

"Shhh!" someone said.

Bernal looked down. Clay, Spillvagen's young son, crouched behind the pickup truck parked in the driveway.

Bernal crouched down next to him. "What's going on?"

"Dad's going to the Moon!"

The windows of Spillvagen's garage office glowed with light.

"Is he?"

"Yes! He's got the spaceship. I mean, he's going to get the spaceship. It's hidden somewhere. He has to find it."

"It's worse than that, Clay," Honor's voice said from somewhere above them. "Much worse."

She sat cross-legged on the pickup's hood, erect and solemn.

If these kids had been actual dangerous people, Bernal would have been in deep trouble. He hadn't even seen them sitting out here in the dark. No wonder

Charis didn't want him along on any important operations.

"What do you think he's doing?" Bernal said.

"Something crazy, but that doesn't mean I'm going to tell you anything about it." Honor was tart.

"It's important. I need to know."

"Does he really think I need my adolescence to be interesting? Like providing an eccentric dad figure is some kind of benefit to my development?"

"The world is short of interesting people," Bernal said. "Feel glad that you know at least one."

She sighed in exasperation. "My friend Susan wants to be a writer when she grows up. I don't know why. Does she think people are still going to be reading things when we're adults? Whatever. But her parents are super normal. I don't want to be a writer."

"A pity," Bernal said. "What do you want to be?"

"Someone who lives somewhere else."

Something clanked in the garage. It sounded large and metal.

"Can I go in?" Bernal said.

"No!" Clay said in agony. "He said—"

"Go ahead," Honor said. "He needs help. I've been hearing him bumping stuff and swearing for the past hour. Mom won't help him. Says he's crazy. Dad shouldn't try to use his children as some kind of human shields, anyway. Susan would like that aspect of it. Betrayal is an important part of any writer's development, she says. Her parents come to her class presentations, even when it's about, like, agricultural products of Central America. When she's done they even do that 'rock on' thing with their hands that older people like so much." She stuck out her pinkie, forefinger, and thumb and spread them wide, then looked down as if the hand was being shown to her by someone else. "I guess that is kind of embarrassing. Maybe that will be enough to get her there."

"Where is your mother, anyway?"

"In the basement, watching TV. That's not so interesting, is it? Let Susan make that interesting."

"Why don't you go watch with her?"

"Not appropriate for children," Clay said, very serious.

"She watches a lot of shows about teenagers having sex," Honor said.

"It's true." Clay hid his face in embarrassment. "It's true. You can tell by the music."

Honor slid off the hood. "Think of the burden that places on my generation. Come on, Clay. You want to play Yahtzee?"

"Jenga. I want to play Jenga!" Forgetting entirely about his father and his mission, Clay hurtled through the house's side door, leaving it hanging open.

"When you talk to my father . . ." Honor pulled herself to stern attention. "Tell him we fell where we stood."

"You bastard!" The sight of Spillvagen in the "implicitly trustworthy" checked polyester short-sleeved dress shirt and a tie showing saguaro cactuses with Mexicans leaning against them and sleeping under their huge sombreros, enraged Bernal. "They tried to kill me."

Spillvagen sent something skittering away on the concrete when he jumped. "You—the wrench! Did you see where it went?"

"Never mind the wrench!"

"Without it, this thing won't work. You don't want that, do you?"

"I think it went over there." Bernal pointed but did not move.

"Could you help me? I don't have a lot of time."

"I don't know what it looks like." Bernal crossed his arms.

"Oh, for heaven's . . ." Spillvagen dug frantically under the pile of furniture created when he had cleared the garage floor for his new possession. The chair at the very top tilted perilously, and Bernal watched with interest as it wobbled. "You don't know how important this is."

The thing on the makeshift frame of cinder blocks and metal pipe was a garage product, all ropy welds and pop rivets. This had to be the thing hidden under the tarp in the Ziggy Sigma van. Its compressor, flaring cooling fins, whirred quietly. It snaked a power cable to a clunky propane-powered generator, which added its own hum.

He could see the original field device Spillvagen had once described to him, one intended to cool down bodies and heads quickly, readying them for cryogenic preservation under emergency circumstances. Hanging off it was a large insulated blob. It clung to the compressor, looking like a swollen peapod.

That was where Muriel's head had been kept, in between her beheading and her incorporation into Hesketh. It looked like there was room for more than one head in there.

This was what he had seen Spillvagen haul into here the other night, before he and Yolanda tussled in the treehouse. Bernal wondered if she was up there now.

"There," Spillvagen said. "Jesus, it's filthy under here. Melissa's right. I got to clean up more."

"Do you know what this thing has been used for?" Bernal said.

Spillvagen stood up. Something glinted silver in his hand. "Of course I do."

Bernal suddenly realized that he was alone with a man who was desperate to recover three frozen heads. The question was: how desperate?

He turned slowly.

But Spillvagen stumbled past him and sank into his desk chair. He looked like hell. He had graying stubble on his plump cheeks, and his overgrown eyebrows begged for a trim. Spillvagen scratched his head with the box wrench he held in his hand, leaving thinning hair standing. "Bernal. I need help." He finally seemed to think about what Bernal had said. "Who tried to kill you?"

"Who else? Your two recovery agents, Prelate and Vervain. The women you hired to find this thing for you."

"What did they do to you?" Spillvagen seemed idly curious.

"They threw me in a car, drove out to the woods."

Spillvagen shook his head. "They were going to bring you here."

"Here? Why?"

"Because I need your help."

"To do what?"

"Well, my official job tonight is to get the head of Muriel Inglis out of the cryogenic freezer where she's stored. That's what I've been hired to do."

"By who?"

"By something. Someone. I don't know. I've been negotiating. Whoever it is knows that I'm the only one around with the skill and knowledge to get this head out without blowing some gasket or raising the temperature too high. They can't mess around, because they have three other heads that have to be kept at operational temperature."

"Hesketh," Bernal breathed.

"Call it what you want. Getting your buddy Muriel out wouldn't be that big a deal. Sounds like a pretty straightforward job."

"So what's the problem?"

"I want all my heads back. Not just that one, which isn't even one of mine. All three heads stolen from Long Voyage. I suspect there will be problems with that."

"And you want me to help you."

"Well, yes. I didn't know who else I could turn to."

"When are you planning on making the attempt?"

"Tonight."

Spillvagen tried to control his excitement as he drove. "Sounds like that personality boosting thing works better than I ever thought."

"Maybe."

"It's going to be industry standard for cryonic suspension! I mean, that's always been the fear, deep down, that you'd wake up with a functional neural system but no personality to go with it, just balls rolling around on the floor with the juggler gone. Now we can guarantee identity survival. That's a real value add."

"Muriel isn't just a business opportunity for you, Norbert. She needs help."

"And I'm helping her, aren't I? If it wasn't for you, I'd have had her out—" He hit a bump on the road and craned his head out the pickup's back window, trying to see the bed of his pickup. "Hey, is that thing okay back there? It's pretty hacked together. One of those seams gives, liquid nitrogen will shoot out and you'll see quite a show."

"It's fine." They had worked carefully strapping the head storage device down and padding it with chunks of styrofoam from an old stereo. "What do you mean, you'd have had Muriel out already?"

They drove past farms and woods, far out from Cheriton. If you were sufficiently far from a highway exit, the wrinkled geography of central Massachusetts could still feel miles away from anything. Good thing, Bernal thought, he wasn't riding out here with a serial killer who wanted to freeze his head.

He glanced over at Spillvagen, who, hands at ten and two, drove like a determined old lady. Good thing.

"That night at Near Earth Orbit, when you decided to pick a fight with Ignacio. That's why I was there. I'd gotten a message. I have an anonymous message board where clients can leave information for me without being identified, though I usually know who they are. I didn't know who this was, but whoever it was knew a lot about me. About Long Voyage and Yolanda. Offered a deal. If I got that head out, I would have information that would get Yolanda off my back. Evidence that her precious uncle was undisturbed, unaffected, still sleeping the frozen sleep of the just. His head wasn't gone, just mislaid, during all the messing around during Ungaro's violation of our security. I could have had your precious Muriel out that night, in a quick-storage device, not a lot of support, but enough to preserve it."

That fit with what Bernal had seen that night and concluded later. Hesketh had busted out of Charis's yard and gotten Ignacio to pick it up. The Enigmatic Ascent crew had also gotten a pickup message, probably from Muriel, but had gotten there too late. Ignacio had headed to Near Earth Orbit to get Spillvagen to do a little quick surgery and remove the indigestible lump of Muriel's personality. But the volatile Ignacio had picked a fight with Patricia and scared off Spillvagen.

So Hesketh, and Muriel, had been right there that night, probably in the back of Ignacio's SUV, and Bernal had never known.

"It was lying to me," Spillvagen said. "It wasn't giving up Uncle Solly."

"You didn't question where this extra head had come from or anything?"

"I'd have figured it out. Bernal, have you ever been involved with lawyers? You get involved with lawyers, you come back and tell me I should have asked more questions when someone offered me a way out. They stick a proboscis behind your eyeball and suck your brain out. There is nothing, nothing worse."

"Okay, okay," Bernal said. "But now you're after bigger game."

"You got it. Why take one head, when you can get them all?" Spillvagen jerked a thumb back at the headtaker. "And I now have the capability for taking care of them all. Everything back the way it started, and no worries. Frozen heads back in their dewars. I can just get on with my life."

Bernal thought about that. "Hesketh isn't crazy. Well, anyway, not crazy like that. Why would it leave itself defenseless, let you open it right up like that?"

"If Muriel really is disrupting its operations, then it has to get rid of her. Like someone pulling a rotting tooth with a pair of rusty pliers and nothing but a shot of gin as anesthetic. It really doesn't have a choice."

"Because it killed Ignacio," Bernal realized. "Dropped a transaxle on his head. It doesn't have assistance from its acolyte anymore."

That seemed odd now. If Hesketh was desperate to get rid of Muriel's head, why hadn't it waited to succeed at doing that before getting rid of Ignacio? It had left itself open to Spillvagen.

"After Ignacio got killed, I thought about how the Bowler and Hesketh might have gotten together." Spillvagen turned off the dark road onto a narrower and rougher one. Once they were past an old chicken coop, the woods closed in. "I thought about the kind of person who would serve as an accomplice to a homicidal artificial intelligence made out of human heads. Specific personality type, I'd think. Someone as out on the edge as it was. So I kind of looked around, trying to figure out how such a person might have gotten in contact with Hesketh. Now, people online are always making weird connections with each other. One has a boat, the other floats it."

Bernal thought about Ignacio. A sullen, violent man, with a talent for moving complex and illegal gear through various channels, and with a steady supply of parts. Someone with contact with Hess Tech and who seemed to know the story of Long Voyage. It made sense that Hesketh would have sought out someone like him.

"So I checked out the criteria. I shook the data, got a bunch of people who fit. Two came up most often: Ronald Borden, in Klamath Falls, Oregon, and Geoffrey Gregg, in Russellville, Kentucky. Both had been obsessed with beheading animals as kids, and both had an interest in mechanical devices. That was something I figured Hesketh had been looking for when it was recruiting, so I threw it in the mix. Two years ago, Ronald Borden was in an inpatient psych unit in Medford, Oregon, heavily medicated. He hadn't committed an actual crime, but he'd built some strange gizmo out of used car parts that could easily have killed his mother, a prostitute, who decided for unrelated reasons not to come home that night. No one was sure if the thing would have worked, or even exactly what it would have done. Geoffrey Gregg was under observation after having made threats to a young girl in his neighborhood.

"Around that time, two years ago or so, both Borden and Gregg reported getting communications from someone. A rich uncle that was going to get them out and put them into a special room, a government agency that had a specific need for their special skills, a sinister yet NASDAQ-listed organization with an open position. In both cases, the staff saw this as evidence of delusion. Anyway, Borden got his meds changed. Two days later, he escaped from the facility. He was found five days later in central South Dakota, almost frozen to death in a ditch. He was wearing only a light jacket, and it was early December. He had been hitchhiking. Where was he going? He refused to say, but he was on I-90, heading east. Us locals know that as the Massachusetts Turnpike."

"He was coming here," Bernal said.

"Sure looks like it. Borden was returned and placed under constant observation. He's still there. He has never said anything about where he was going or why. Nowadays, apparently, he spends his time looking at old muscle-car magazines from the 1950s and 60s. Quite a collector of the things, actually, with a decent eBay business.

"Gregg was a sadder case. Instead of getting cheered up by the fact that he had a solid job offer, he became obsessed with the idea that all the vehicles he could see from his window were trying to kill him. Late one night he escaped from his room and made it into the ambulance garage of the acute-care hospital that was on the same campus. An EMT found him a few hours later, crushed between the garage wall and the front end of an ambulance. The ambulance door was open and a long length of gauze hung out onto the asphalt.

"That end of the parking garage had a slight slope. Gregg had put the ambulance in neutral, then stood against the back wall and released the parking brake with a gauze pull that looped around the rearview mirror. The ambulance rolled forward and pinned him against the wall. He suffocated slowly, in complete silence. They figured it must have taken him a good hour to die."

"Jesus," Bernal said.

"Interesting thing about both these guys, something I hadn't thought of as a criterion for Hesketh, but which makes sense when you think about it. They both had high native intelligence, *g*, they call it nowadays. But both had sustained some minor but significant brain damage in childhood. When he was three, Borden fell off a porch head first onto a concrete driveway. When he was six,

Gregg got hit in the forehead with an aluminum baseball bat when an overenthusiastic Little League player flung the thing into the stands. Both of them sustained significant damage to the medial prefrontal cortex. That's the part of the brain responsible for aggression control and integrated forethought."

Bernal remembered Ignacio returning to the yard the night he died. He'd supposedly just beaten Patricia senseless. Then he'd come back with two bags of Brazilian takeout. Not like someone trying to make up to his abused partner, just routine, a regular evening event.

Then he'd found his carts running around the yard at night, his love slave cheating on him, and his drug operation in jeopardy. He'd gone berserk.

None of that accorded with what Bernal knew of the Bowler.

Ignacio now seemed like someone with obvious emotions who had been manipulated and maneuvered, and never realized who was the real aggressor and who the real victim. When he'd outlived his usefulness, he'd been discarded by having a transaxle dropped on his head, and had taken the fall for every crime that had been committed.

Bernal remembered the story Patricia Foote, trying to find something to say, had told him about her childhood.

"Something you would get," Bernal said, "if, say, your mother's car rear-ended a truck carrying pipes, and one of them hit your forehead."

"Sure," Spillvagen said. "That would work. Perfect, really. Why?"

"How much farther do we have?"

"About a quarter mile. No, less. See that old sign? Driveway's just past it."

"Stop the car."

"Why? I—"

"Stop!"

The forest was silent in the night. A rough double track ran off to the right, curving through the trees toward a house with a couple of lights on.

"We were wrong," Bernal said. "Ignacio Kuepner wasn't the Bowler. A drug dealer, a smuggler, even a killer. But never the Bowler. He was played, as we all were played, by someone else. And that someone else is up there, waiting for you. You're removing one head. And it's pretty likely that you'll be providing a replacement for it."

"Who? I didn't . . ." Spillvagen swallowed. "My God. What should I do?"

Bernal thought. Prelate and Vervain had taken off with his phone. Charis and the Enigmatic Ascent crew were all down at Cheriton Airport, working on snapping off the transportation end of Hesketh's operations. But they had not anticipated how much Hesketh still had to do before it headed down there. He needed to get Charis here to help him. His every instinct was to move, and move quickly, but he didn't want to go up there with only Spillvagen as an ally.

He stared up the rough road. First he saw it as clearly as if it stood next to him, then he thought he was mistaken, that it was just a shed, or a trailer, or a tractor, and he was imagining what he saw.

But he wasn't.

Charis's Hummer stood parked up there in the darkness by the house. The forest scene on its side made it stand out, rather than camouflaging it. There was some kind of iridescence in the coating.

He didn't know why Charis had come up here or where she was now, but he knew it meant he couldn't rely on her help—and she might be in incredible danger. For now, it was him and Spillvagen.

Bernal opened his door. "Go on up there. Give me a

few minutes, then get to work, just as you were planning. How long do you think it would take you to liberate all the heads?"

"I don't know. Not long. Five minutes, maybe a little more. What are you going to do?"

"Distract Hesketh's guardian, friend. Keep her from coming back there for long enough for you to make sure that Hesketh no longer exists. So work fast. Work as if your life depended on it. And mine too, for that matter."

Bernal swung out of the pickup and set off through the woods before he could reconsider his plan.

46

Sometime in the past, it had been a repair shop or a garage, but there had been no serious traffic up this way in decades. It was a large cinder-block structure shoved up the ass of a small clapboard Cape with dangling decorative shutters and a concrete front step that had settled alarmingly and hung almost a foot off the house.

The woods had straggled their way up to the house. Bernal saw an old birdbath and what looked like the remains of a decorative well, amid the burgeoning saplings.

Where the hell was Charis? He told himself that she'd already taken care of things and would pop up with an apology for not answering her phone. But he could see that the front tire of her Hummer was flat, and she was not trying to repair it.

Patricia was home. Of course she was home. Waiting for Spillvagen, so that she could watch him and make sure that he did to Hesketh only what he was contracted to do. Well, maybe he could distract her. And, if he needed to, take her out.

Hesketh had gone out and found itself an acolyte through a proactive search that would have been the envy of any corporate recruiter. It had found Patricia Foote, a girl damaged in brain and spirit, sitting glumly in a mental health facility, waiting for something to happen. When Hesketh finally contacted her, she must have felt like Cinderella. Under instruction, she had traveled to Cheriton and gotten a job with Ignacio Kuepner, parts supplier to Hess Tech, the company building Hesketh's various bodies. And concealed there, watching Madeline Ungaro but completely invisible to her, Patricia had assisted Hesketh in every step of its plan to become independent and escape. And, meanwhile, had been beaten and abused by Ignacio on a regular basis. That might have been as cover. Or it might just have happened. He remembered what Bob, at NEO, had told him: the contingent is always present. If you try to see everything that happens as planned, you are inevitably deluded.

He didn't think he'd ever untangle the nest of pain and need that had been Ignacio Kuepner and Patricia Foote. But it had finally ended in Muriel's death, Ignacio's death, and probably Madeline Ungaro's death as well.

He walked across the tilting concrete squares of the front walk and knocked firmly on the door. He felt like he should have a bouquet or something. He heard a dull thump from inside, then nothing for a long few seconds.

The door opened, and a pair of startled pale eyes regarded him.

"Patricia!" he said, with all the heartiness of a neglectful lover. "It took me a while to find you. It's great to see you. Can I come in?"

Then he did the hardest thing he had ever done in his life. He put his arms around the woman he now believed to be a serial killer assisting a homicidal artificial intelligence, and kissed her.

For a moment it was like grabbing a manikin, but then she relaxed, fractionally, and at least allowed the kiss.

"How have you been?" he said. "I can't . . . the way you looked, when we found you. I can't imagine what that must have been like. What he did to you. . . ."

"They asked me a lot of questions," she said. "They didn't know . . . why I didn't know."

"About Ignacio?"

"Yeah."

"About what he did?"

"What he did." She pulled away from him. "What did he do?"

"I don't know for sure," Bernal said. "They haven't said."

The place was tiny and dark and hot. There was almost no furniture: just a couch and a tube TV on a chest in the living room and what looked like a kid's bunk bed at an angle to the wall in the bedroom.

He had to keep her distracted. Being incredibly boring was clearly not doing it. By this point, Spillvagen should have gotten into that big garage out back and been working on Hesketh. That is, unless he'd panicked and run. Bernal understood that possibility.

He smiled. "Come on, Patricia. We're alive. Both of us. We made it."

He felt no sexual desire for her whatsoever, but tried to touch her as if he found her irresistible. "Oh, honey . . . it's been so hard. So weird. I don't know how you could have stood it. . . ."

She was as dully unresponsive as any girlfriend who has decided to break up with you but hasn't told you yet.

He tugged her toward the bedroom, first gently, then more forcefully.

A bedside lamp lay on its side on the floor, shooting light at a pile of laundry spilling out of a wide closet with louvered doors. Black metal dumbbells, collars, and weight plates lay in various places on the floor, and a couple of gouges had been taken out of the walls by a poorly controlled bar. The place really was a mess. Another lamp lay broken in the far corner. Patricia made Muriel look like a careful housekeeper.

"Come on," he murmured. "Come on."

She shifted her weight, and they slid past the bedroom door and stumbled into the rear hall. Handmade wooden shelves had been attached on both walls, narrowing the passage to almost nothing.

He felt every bone in Patricia's small body as she moved against him. The acolyte. She was the acolyte, Hesketh's assistant. And she'd done something to Charis. Some piece of information, some loose end, had brought Charis here, to Patricia's house. Where was she? Was she still alive? As far as Bernal could tell, Patricia had no idea he'd seen Charis's car parked behind the house. At least, the way she leaned forward onto him, relaxing her muscles just a tiny bit, just enough for him to feel, just enough to signal some kind of surrender, felt completely natural.

And that was more than Bernal could stand. He could fake lust to conceal Spillvagen's desperate operation in the garage, but knowing that Charis had come here and vanished overwhelmed him.

She looked up at his face, then reached up a finger to touch the corner of his eye. "Why? What's—"

Back in the garage, Spillvagen dropped something. The clink of metal on concrete was as clear as if he stood right next to them.

Patricia jerked her head, listened.

Bernal might have been able to get the jump on her if he'd been just a little farther away, but being up against her made every shift of his muscles obvious.

That was more than enough for her. She was used to reacting like a trapped animal. She raked nails across his face and checked him in the crotch with her hip, then turned and was gone, not having made a sound.

He grabbed at the shelves as he stumbled, and they pulled off the wall, falling on him. The pain seared his face an instant later, and he sucked breath. He pushed himself back to follow her. He looked down the hall into the bedroom. The light from the fallen lamp illuminated the louvered closet door . . . and the thin trickle of blood that came from underneath it.

Charis lay face down in dirty laundry soaked with blood, with shirts and towels thrown over her, and a heavy plate dumbbell on the back of her neck.

"Charis," he whispered. "It's me, Bernal." He picked the weight up off her neck.

Charis rolled over, choking. Her face was crusted with her own blood. He pulled her up until she was sitting, leaning on him.

"You got here just in . . . but . . . Hesketh . . . where . . ."

"In the garage," Bernal said. "But she's in there now. Patricia."

Charis sat up straight, taking her weight off him. "What's your plan?"

Bernal thought for a moment. "I hate to ask this—"

"Just tell me."

"Can you move? Can you do anything?"

"Help me stand up."

"That's not encouraging."

"Just do it, damn it!"

He got her to her feet. She stood, legs spread, and looked at him.

"I was going to go in," he said, "and have you go around. . . ."

She managed a grin. There was blood on her teeth too. It was all he could do to keep looking at her. "Negatory on that. I'm the pro. I'll go in. You go around. Give me five minutes. I should be able to make it to the back door by then. Then give it everything you've got. We'll only get one chance."

Bernal went out the front door and circled the house, moving as quietly as possible. Along its base the house had dead shrubs, stacks of rusted paint cans, the rotted remains of firewood, and castoff pieces of siding, flashing, and roofing. Bernal stood up on an irregular chunk of concrete that had once anchored a clothesline pole and peered through the pollen-streaked glass of the window, trying to scope out the situation before he had to go in there.

Two overhead fluorescents dangling from chains lit the garage. Huge amounts of gear was piled on thick metal shelves. It was as densely packed as Ignacio's itself, and much neater than the personal living space of Patricia's house. The open garage door spilled light onto the sparse gravel of the driveway, but that approach was too obvious.

Five minutes. Was Charis even wearing a watch? What the hell did she think she was going to do? She'd be lucky to live for another five minutes, much less save the day.

Patricia's tow truck stood near the shelves on the opposite wall. Spillvagen's own pickup was pulled up next to it.

Spillvagen squatted in the tow truck's bed, his back

against the retracted boom. Blood dripped down his forehead. Bernal heard him gasp for breath.

"I just got it wrong," Spillvagen said. "I thought the head was on the other end, and I wanted to make sure. . . ."

"Seal them back up." Patricia leaned forward out of the shadows. She held a garden machete in her hand. She'd clearly hit him with it once already, with the blunt side.

"You'll be stuck," Spillvagen said. "You'll still have that head in there."

"Let me worry about that. Get them back in, exactly the way they were."

He wouldn't live more than a few seconds past the completion of his job.

Spillvagen hunched back down. Bernal could just see the curve of his back as he worked desperately at something concealed by the tow truck's side panel.

Bernal knew what he wanted to go for, but he hadn't figured out a particularly good route. He didn't have many choices. He left the window and crept around to the open garage door. He knelt and peered around the edge.

Patricia stood absolutely still, arms crossed in front of her, a machete resting on her shoulder. He would have expected her face to be frozen and expressionless as well, but it wasn't. Instead she wore a look of concern, like a mother watching her child being treated in an emergency room. There were clinks as Spillvagen worked, and the sobbing of his breath.

Behind Patricia, Bernal could see the door to the house. For an instant, he thought it was an illusion, a result of the way his blood was pounding in his head, but no, the knob was really turning, really rotating as Charis turned it from the other side.

Bernal was already running when the door creaked open. Patricia, ready for one last trick from within the house, was whirling toward it, her machete blade catching the light.

Charis jerked the door back, and the machete splintered into its edge. Patricia yanked the blade free, and turned back, toward Bernal. She'd realized that Charis's move had been a decoy.

Charis had gained Bernal a few seconds, but not enough. Patricia's face was expressionless as she faced him with the blade. She gave no sign of knowing who he was, or caring. She seemed to be looking past him to something else, as if she had already disposed of him.

The headtaker hummed on the tailgate of Spillvagen's car. It was on, waiting to receive the heads, but nothing was going into it now. Not even Muriel. Bernal caught a glimpse of Spillvagen in the back of the tow truck, where a dull metal cylinder lay strapped to the ridged bed, surrounded by cables. Hesketh. Hesketh itself.

Bernal grabbed at the heavy welded flange as he went by it. The massive headtaker resisted for a moment, but then slid off the tailgate and onto the concrete floor.

It bounced with an astonishingly loud thunk. Then, as Spillvagen had predicted, a weld popped, liquid nitrogen sprayed out, and frozen mist filled the air. In an instant, nothing was visible but white.

Bernal threw himself at Patricia. She had been expecting him to dodge the machete, like a sensible person, and wasn't ready for a straight attack. His shoulder caught her and smashed her back against the shelves. Oil cans and car parts rang on the floor. The machete's handle jabbed his back. He thought she lost her grip on it, but couldn't hear it hit the floor above everything else.

He tried to push her back again, but she twisted and slipped from his grasp, and he smacked his head on the shelf. He stumbled, then dove through the flaring pain, and threw himself after her.

A miss would have dropped him full-length on the

concrete floor, but he managed to grip fingers onto her belt. She stumbled. He pushed forward with his feet, and they both fell against the truck.

Its engine roared up, deafening in the enclosed space. Taillights and headlights glared through the mist.

The transmission thunked, and the truck backed into the shelving. Bernal and Patricia spun together as the driver's side door slid past them, and he thought the rearview mirror had hit her.

Spillvagen shrieked and clambered over the side panel. The tow truck reversed direction, and Spillvagen toppled behind it.

The tow truck seemed to fill the entire garage. Bernal pulled at Patricia, to get her out of the way, but she twisted, forcing him to switch his grip.

The truck hit and pushed Bernal and Patricia back. He was stunned. Was Patricia the acolyte or just another decoy? The vehicle didn't seem to care whether it killed her, as long as it got him.

Glass shattered as the driver's side headlight hit the corner of the massive workbench. Metal groaned, and the truck stopped. It spun tires for a moment. Bernal and Patricia were pushed together in the corner left between the workbench and the wall. Equipment and supplies cascaded off the workbench. A flicker of something caught Bernal's eye, but it was gone before he could identify it.

The tow truck reversed again and pulled back, hitting Spillvagen's pickup.

Patricia shoved and, before Bernal could react, he found himself in front of the workbench, out of the safe area. The headlights flared in his eyes. The tow truck's engine roared up.

Another rumble came from overhead. For an instant he crazily thought it was an avalanche or the roof coming down on them.

But it was the garage door, coming down to seal them all in.

The tow truck turned its wheels and, instead of cutting Bernal in half against the workbench, shot out of the garage, scraping its cab roof against the descending door.

Patricia pulled herself free, taking advantage of Bernal's moment of distraction. She hit the ground and rolled, just making it under as the door hit the concrete.

"Dammit!" Charis hung from the doorway to the house and thumbed the control. The door rumbled up again, to reveal a silent, empty drive. The last remnants of the mist puffed out into the night.

"She's going to kill them!" Charis slumped in the bed of Spillvagen's truck, a wad of blood-soaked paper towels pressed to her face. "Those guys are sitting at Cheriton Airport expecting some kind of FedEx package, not an active AI accompanied by a killer. We have to save those poor bastards."

No one had a phone, and Patricia's house did not have a landline. They were alone in the woods.

The last time it had backed up, Hesketh had smashed the side of Spillvagen's truck, creasing the wheel and driving a length of fender into the tire. The engine would start but would not continue to run. Spillvagen now sat in the cab, hands on the wheel, staring down the gravel drive.

Outside, Charis's tire was still flat. The spare was also flat. She'd tried to blame Greenpeace for that as well, but Bernal thought there was a limit to what they could be held responsible for. It had been an official Social Protection vehicle for quite some time now. That Social Protection did not actually exist didn't get her off.

Bernal felt panic himself. The image of Oleana and her Wisconsin buddies facing Patricia pulsed in time with the pain in his skull. He searched through the tangle of crap on the smashed workbench, with no idea what he was looking for. There had been a flash of something, during all the excitement, something he had noticed . . . but he now had no idea what.

He took a deliberate breath. "We have to think."

"Think? There's no time. We have to do something."

He found one thing of use in the mess. "Do this, then." He tossed Charis a tube of Super Glue. "Glue your cuts shut. We're out of paper towels, and you're making a mess."

She caught it clumsily, with her left hand. "What, no duct tape? What the hell are you looking for there?"

"Please don't ask me that. That airport thing is a distraction. A decoy. I'm sure of it. But . . . we need to figure out where Hesketh and Patricia are actually headed. How Hesketh really hopes to escape. Talk about something else. Please. Going the wrong way faster doesn't get you to your destination."

Charis ran the glue tube down her cheek and pinched the cut closed with thumb and forefinger.

"You saved my life when you knocked on that door, boy. I haven't thanked you for that yet. So, thanks."

"You're welcome. What the hell were you doing here, though? I had no idea."

Charis made a face, then winced and prodded the shiny line of the drying glue. It seemed to be holding, for now.

"I was just tying up a loose end. And almost got tied up myself. They found Madeline Ungaro's body."

Bernal froze in his search. "Where?"

"Sunk to the bottom of the oil sump at Ignacio's. I hear they almost didn't check there. That's a big toxic-waste disposal problem, huge paperwork, DEP guys, Feds from the EPA, all sorts of people had to get involved. All official Bowler victims were identified. They were really looking for Muriel's head. But there Madeline Ungaro was, weighted down under it all. Dead since the night Muriel disappeared, her head still firmly attached."

All this time, Bernal had half thought, even hoped, Madeline was alive somewhere, that she had slid smoothly out from under as she always had before. "That sounds like a loose end getting tied off."

"I guess it should have been. But here's the thing. Earlier, Patricia had told me that, among other things she had seen shipped off by Ignacio, presumably to Kazakhstan, was a big welded box. She was careful to be a bit vague, but her description matched that of the thing you had seen in the back of the Ziggy Sigma van. I liked that, it matched up with everything else. When you called and left me a message that it hadn't been Ignacio who hired those gals, Prelate and Vervain, to find the headtaker, but, instead, your loony buddy Spillvagen, I felt like erasing it. Who needs alternate explanations when everything is nice and clear?

"But it bugged me. Why had she said she saw the headtaker at Ignacio's when it was clearly somewhere else? What had she actually seen? Had she seen anything at all? So I dropped by. To check up on her, tell her that Madeline's body had been found, just the usual gossip kind of thing, before I headed for the airport to meet our Wisconsin buddies.

"So we chatted, and I brought it up, kind of an 'oh, by the way, I just want to make sure I understood' thing. I didn't have any notion that she was a killer, but I guess she figured I was smarter than I turned out to be or maybe that she just couldn't take the chance that I'd figure it out. So she went to take me out, right then and there. Crazy, huh? I mean, she's a tiny gal. I kind of outweigh her. But she's *muy* fast. I might have ended up dead if you hadn't stopped by. You interrupted her. She shoved me in the closet, dropped that weight on my head, and left me there to choke my life out in her dirty underwear."

She paused. "I must say though, it was almost worth it, to hear your seduction technique. Very smooth."

Despite the gravity of the situation, Bernal found himself blushing. He directed his attention to an old thermal fax machine. Its buttons were surrounded by the gray of sweat and skin cells, and it still bore a handwritten sticker telling people how to remove a paper jam. A wire harness ran from it to a SQUID very much like the one in Ungaro's lab, this one dangling from a welded frame by a tow truck chain.

Hesketh had certainly had a more sophisticated comm setup back at Ignacio's yard. It had had all sorts of connections, been able to control the yard's carts. And those connections had been used by Muriel, too. Then it had been forced to hide out here at Patricia's, and she had been reduced to a high-tech equivalent of mind reading: pulling electrical potentials out of the cryogenically frozen brains and translating them into instructions spit out by a fax machine.

"It was Madeline's work inside that thing." These were Spillvagen's first words, though he did not take his hands off the steering wheel of his useless vehicle or his eyes off the empty driveway. "Had to be. Muriel's head. It was wired in, set up, each frozen nerve tract in its proper position to interface correctly. It wasn't some kind of plug-and-play setup."

"Probably the last thing Madeline did," Charis said. "Before Patricia Foote killed her."

"She must have made that choice." Spillvagen shook his head. "To help her creation survive, even if it meant her death."

"It probably meant her death anyway," Charis said pragmatically. "No matter what she did." She looked at Bernal. "You may want to think about things, but—"

"I think this fax machine is how Hesketh communicated with Patricia while it was in here," Bernal said.

Bernal leafed through the curling thermal sheets scattered on the floor. Sometimes a sheet would have a single instruction, like "Wash the blade in boiling water and replace it in its location." Sometimes there would be tiny scrawled words packed all across the page. Most of them were jumbled nonsense, like "bird beard bard bored," with tiny bits of instruction interspersed, sometimes in separated words and even letters. Patricia had clearly had to piece them together. Sometimes there was a sheet that was fairly clear, like the one the Enigmatic Ascent crew had found after Patricia had recovered Hesketh from the ditch below Charis's yard.

"Did Hesketh say anything of interest?" Charis said.

"It's not what Hesketh said that's interesting. It's what Muriel said, pretending to be Hesketh."

So, all along, Patricia had found ways to receive instructions from her master, her deity. Ever since it had recruited her from Green Valley. She'd done what she was instructed to do, glad, at last, to have a structured life and to be obeying someone who cared about her. When Muriel regained consciousness within Hesketh, she had found ways to piggyback her own instructions, her Satanic Verses, on what Hesketh was telling its acolyte. Those false instructions had seemed to come from Hesketh but really came from a part of its own processing that it had only intermittent control over: Muriel's brain. Patricia had had no way of authenticating these communications. If she had been used to getting commands from Hesketh through a certain channel, and a new command came through that channel, it was something she had to listen to. Muriel had taken advantage of a lack of error checking.

He reached into his pocket and pulled out the fax the Enigmatic Ascent crew had found, the one Len had given him at the car wash. A bar code indicated transshipment to the cosmodrome at Tyuratam, next to a picture of something that looked like a nebula, with something that looked like a bar along one side.

With that as a guide, he found it in the mess of stuff that had fallen to the floor: a metal strut, cracked and slightly bent from impact, amid some hex nut boxes. It had somehow matched his memory of the nebula image. Sometimes, just by chance, you actually saw things clearly.

He held it up. It was clearly the same as the strut that appeared in the picture, partially obscuring the nebula. Presumably something had been wrong with this one. It had already been cracked when the truck hit and bent it. Patricia, with precise requirements, had rejected it and replaced it with another.

He walked over to the car with the fax sheet. "Norbert, can you identify this location in the sky? It may be where Hesketh is heading."

"I don't know if identifying that would help anything," Spillvagen said. "Even if it's heading in this direction, it will be, let's say, quite some time before it gets there."

"Just take a look."

Spillvagen frowned at it. Then his face smoothed. He chuckled. He laughed. That startled him, and he came out of his funk. "The easy answer is, the Horsehead Nebula. But that's just a little joke. Who knew?"

"What?" Bernal was irritated. This was no time for screwing around.

"Who knew that our cowgirl had freckles? Remarkable detail. I've never found out who the artist was. One of the unsung geniuses of our era, really."

With that as a clue, the picture snapped into focus. This wasn't any kind of astronomical photograph. He was looking at a small part of the Near Earth Orbit cowgirl's leg, right at the fringe of her short skirt. The Horsehead Nebula was on her skirt, and the blobs next to it were freckles and fine hairs, right beneath the curve of her butt. The strut was part of some structure just out of the image.

"That *is* where Hesketh is headed," Bernal realized. "Oleana, Magnusen, and Len might be waiting for it at the airport, all set up, ready to trap it, but that's not where it's going."

"Where? The diner? I doubt even a malign artificial intelligence could stomach the food."

"The diner. Near Earth Orbit." Bernal thought about all the work Patricia had done up there in the fake spaceship and the associated machinery. Those damn HVAC units had taken an incredible amount of maintenance. "That has to be how it's planning to escape. We don't have any time. This is where we have to go. To stop Hesketh and save Muriel."

"Bernal." Spillvagen grabbed his wrist. "Don't take for granted that Muriel's still alive in there."

"Why not?"

"I disconnected and reconnected her. Fast and under pressure. That's no joke. And if we do somehow get her out of Hesketh, where will we put her?" He craned his neck and looked behind his pickup. "That headtaker is completely lunched. I have no idea if we can get it operational. It'll take hours, even if we can."

"We'd have been dead if I hadn't done that!" Bernal found himself yelling. "Are you saying it's my fault? That if Muriel—"

Spillvagen released him. "I'm saying you should be ready. Spiritually. Emotionally. However you need to be."

"Are you standing by to assist me?"

"I don't think I'm the best choice."

By this time, Charis had climbed out of the truck's bed and was standing over them, glued and ready for action. "He's just trying to give it to you straight. You don't have to be grateful, but stop yelling at him."

"Sorry, Norbert." Bernal spoke as calmly as he could. "You did everything you could."

He found himself thinking of Naomi Wilkerson. He told himself that it was because that printer might have chattered again, leaving one last message from Muriel. Naomi was the only person who might have more information directly from the source. He knew she was sitting there, waiting.

But even as he thought that, he knew that wasn't why Naomi came to mind. There might certainly be a message from Muriel, and if there was he had to have it, but what he needed from Naomi was something different.

A message from a still-living Muriel was one thing. The last words of someone who was now dead was something else altogether.

"You think that damn rocket on top of the diner is real?" Charis said. "What kind of sense does that make?"

"How much sense does any of it make?" Bernal said.

"Oh, now there's a compelling argument."

"Are you disagreeing with it?"

"No. I just wish you could at least try to make it seem sensible. But you've given us a reasonable proximate goal. I'll buy that the airport is probably the last place we should go. Now, how do we get to Near Earth Orbit?"

Bernal turned to Spillvagen. "Norbert. Go out on the road and wave."

"At who?"

"Who do you think? Someone who's always got you under observation. I only hope she's still sober enough to give us a ride."

47

Bob the waiter stood out behind Near Earth Orbit, on break, smoking a cigarette and squinting into the darkness, trying to discern the plots being hatched out there, when Yolanda drove them all up. She was sober enough, but irritated at acting as a taxi service. And she claimed Bernal had run down her phone battery talking to Naomi.

She slowed her car to a stop an inconvenient distance from the diner, killed the engine, and leaned her seat back, as if ready to take a nap.

Patricia's tow truck stood by the diner's back door, dark and silent. Bernal didn't have time to feel relief at having been right about where she was headed. There was too much else to do.

"That paella made me puke for days," Yolanda said.

"Order the burger!" Bernal and Spillvagen said together.

"Hey," Bob heard them, but did not seem offended. "Bernal. Somebody's waiting for you."

Bernal stared up at the diner roof but couldn't see anyone up there. "Who?"

"Older lady, orange hair. Ordered some french fries, but hasn't eaten many of them. Maybe she's saving them for you."

Naomi wasn't supposed to be here. He had called her as soon as he talked Yolanda out of her cell phone, and Naomi had answered instantly, as if waiting for his call. A one-line message had come in from Muriel.

She had asked him where Muriel was, and he had refused to tell her. He didn't want her anywhere near a killer like Patricia. She would have to do without the spiritual solace of being near Muriel. She hadn't pressed him.

Bernal cautiously strolled over to the diner. He couldn't see anything on the roof, but a ladder stood against the wall.

Naomi stood in the rear doorway. She was heavily made-up, with long curled eyelashes, and her red hair gleamed as if lacquered. On a hanger in her hand, blowing gently in the night breeze, was Muriel's blue summer dress.

"Muriel said, 'Leave it up to me,'" Naomi whispered. "She wasn't about to go into a long explanation, even if she had time. What she understands is no longer what we understand."

"What are you doing here?" Bernal said. "How did you find us?"

Naomi smiled gently. "If you want to hide your destination, avoid having a harpy screaming in the background about 'never getting food poisoning under that damn cowgirl's ass again.'"

Yolanda had been protesting their destination, Bernal realized. He'd filtered her out, intent on Naomi's low, calm voice. But Naomi had paid attention to everything.

"You should leave," he said. "It's dangerous here."

"I'll stay out of the way. But whatever you were planning, however you were going to rescue her . . . leave her. Let her do what she has to do."

"And the dress?" Bernal said. "Did she ask for that?"

"No. This is for us. For you and me and whoever else is watching. I wanted to see her there, one last time. Just as I did when I realized she was not dead. Please don't make fun of me."

"I won't," Bernal said. He remembered the scent she'd brought into Muriel's room. She had a gift for making the dead seem real. He took the hanger with the dress hanging from it.

"Bob," Charis said. "What did Patricia take up with her?" With her wounds stuck together with superglue, her face had an oddly makeshift look, as if Patricia Foote had put it together from spare parts.

Bob looked up at the cowgirl and rocket ship. "She got me my cooljuice! In some weird high-tech cylinder arrangement. Some other gear too. She's always putting gear up there. Between you and me, I think she steals it from work and resells it. But I'm glad I got my Freon. It's really been stressful, thinking about the summer coming up and all."

"I got news for you, Bob," Spillvagen said. "That wasn't contraband Freon Patricia Foote hauled up there."

"Really?" Bob said. "What was it then?"

"An artificial intelligence based on cryogenically frozen human heads, originally intended for planetary exploration but unfortunately turned to serial murder during beta testing."

"Sure," Bob said. "What are you taking up with you to deal with it?"

"Oh, this?" Bernal said. "A blue cotton summer dress."

"Rayon," Naomi said. "It's rayon."

Bob took a puff on his cigarette, but did not seem to have any further questions.

Curved sheets of smooth inner thigh rose above. Now that he looked, Bernal saw how detailed the sculpture was, with tiny gold hairs that started as the curve of muscle moved the front of the thigh. And there was the Horsehead Nebula on the skirt's seam. No one could see these things, not from the highway, not from the parking lot. Only standing here, right next to everything, could you feel like a tiny homunculus confronting the cowgirl's massive femininity.

The lower two-thirds of the decorative rocket that the cowgirl rode had panels removed. Where you would have expected to see supporting struts, and maybe a bird's nest or two, was a dense network of pipes, pumps, compressors, and wiring. The nozzles at the end led to massive combustion chambers.

Beyond a tangle of HVAC equipment both real and fake, lay the cylinder that contained Hesketh, on a sling that looked like an emergency stretcher. A pair of electric motors would reel it up into the rocket's belly and shut the curved panels behind it. In another world, another life, Patricia would have been an engineer or an artist who worked big.

"Careful, dammit," Charis said behind him. "Stop right there. Don't you see that?"

She picked up what looked like an old TV aerial off the gravel roof and reached past him.

There was a snap and a thunk.

"What . . . ?" Then Bernal saw it. Charis had yanked on a black thread stretched across the opening between two pieces of equipment. A tension spring had fired darts through where he would have been. Two of them had bounced off a large AC enclosure and fallen to the roof. They were vicious spikes with fins made from razor blades.

"Got to give it to her," Charis said. "This gal works fast."

Patricia must have picked the technique up from her crossbow-building boyfriend, Merrick.

"Wait here." Charis faded into the darkness, moving with absolute silence.

Bernal tried to absorb everything about his surroundings. Here, leaning against the waste stack vent, was what looked like an electrical panel. On top of that was a transformer box with a small toggle switch on it. The little silver lever was easy to miss. But he was positive that it was the main launch switch. When they made the movie it would be much larger and impressive looking, bright red with an OSHA-approved grip, but here it just had to close a control circuit that didn't carry a lot of amps. He reached for it. It was what Muriel had asked him to do: initiate the launch sequence and let her take care of the rest. He wouldn't have to go any further into whatever nightmare Patricia had created ahead.

But he couldn't. He just couldn't. If there was still a chance to save her, he had to take it. He held Muriel's dress by the hanger, letting it billow out in the predawn breeze. It was like she was with him. It was like she was there.

He turned to call for Charis—and felt a sharp blade bite into his neck. For an instant, he felt as if he were right back in Ignacio's yard.

He didn't move his head and couldn't even swallow. He was afraid his Adam's apple would shred against the blade as it went up and down.

Patricia didn't say anything, though he could feel her hot breath on his cheek and the trembling of her muscles. She had to reach up to do it, but she knew what she was doing. Her only communication was to push the sharp edge until he moved. He stumbled toward Hesketh.

"You don't need to do this, Patricia," Bernal managed. "There's still time to stop."

"Her head has to come out," she whispered. "I was going to put Missy Madeline's in its place, just for fun, but I lost track of it. Yours will have to do."

"But . . . what for?" He felt like an idiot, trying to come up with persuasive reasons for her not to kill him, but he couldn't stop himself. "I won't be frozen, my brain will be completely useless."

"Hesketh doesn't need your brain. No one needs your stupid brain. I just need the weight of your head to make sure the center of gravity stays in the right place."

It was the only remotely funny thing he'd ever heard her say.

"Why Madeline? What did she ever do to you?"

"She had it all," Patricia said. "But she didn't understand anything. She didn't get it. Hesketh needed someone. It found me. She tried to tell me she wanted to be inside it, to please make her part of Hesketh. Instead, I used her to make sure your friend was in there. Stupidest thing I ever did. I need to get her out." She looked up at a sound Bernal could not hear. "Your buddy is good and stuck now. I picked up a crowd-control grenade that came through the yard. I kind of miss Ignaz, you know? He had so much cool stuff. Now, please shut up and let me get done with this."

She turned him, facing into the night and the wind. And, for an instant, she hesitated. Afterward he would remember that hesitation as the tenderest reaction anyone had ever had to him. A cold-blooded serial killer had paused before killing him because he meant something to her.

Context is everything.

He lifted up Muriel's dress and let it slip from the

hanger. The light fabric blew over his shoulder and into Patricia's face.

She raised her hand to pull the fabric away and loosened her grip. He dove forward and pulled himself free.

Patricia moved, instantly, to interpose herself between Bernal and the thing she most wanted to protect, Hesketh. For a moment he stood facing a demon with a head of blue flame, and then she managed to get the dress off. She waited for him to come get Muriel.

But he had learned his lesson. Muriel had told him to leave it up to her, and he was going to.

He turned, dodged around the air conditioners, and jumped for the control.

He flicked the toggle switch.

He had to hand it to Patricia. She could build a functional device. The motors hummed to life. The cylinder of Hesketh rose smoothly off the roof and up into the rocket's belly.

Compressors grumbled as they spun up in the rocket overhead.

"Charis!"

"Over here. Careful, these damn things are sticky. I don't need you stuck here too."

She'd been trapped by something similar to what she had used to capture the Hesketh decoy that night under the powerlines. Adhesive bands had stuck to her jacket and pants, binding her to a rocket-supporting strut.

She'd already shrugged off her shirt and was struggling out of her tight jeans. Bernal reached out a hand to steady her.

"Thanks," she grunted. "But you have to guarantee you won't look. Muneer wouldn't like it. And it might strike you blind."

"I'll take my chances," Bernal said. "Is that a thong?"

"Man, you are really pushing it."

He'd expected Patricia to be right after him. But, with the start of the launch sequence, she had moved to play her role on the ground, to make sure her creation made it.

With a sharp snap, the engines ignited. The flames glowed blue like rangetop burners. For a moment Bernal wondered if they had all been wrong, if the thing really was nothing but an extremely detailed fake, no realer than the cowgirl. Then the sound grew louder.

They sprinted for the ladder.

Spillvagen goggled at Charis as she came down in her underwear.

"Where's Patricia?" Spillvagen said.

"Don't worry about her," Charis said.

Bob stepped out of the kitchen, wiping his hands on a cloth. He craned his neck at the cowgirl. "What the hell?"

"Better run for it, hairnet boy," Charis said. "Your kitchen is getting flambéed."

"Anyone else in there?" Bernal said.

"Nah. I run the kitchen at this hour. But I should make sure—"

"Run!"

They made it to the far end of the field. Bernal turned to scan the roof. An erect figure stood there, flickering in the waves of heat from the exhaust, looking up at the rocket, and Hesketh. Was that a blue dress floating overhead? It was too dark for Bernal to be sure.

The main fuel flow came on. The engines roared, then thundered. The sound rose exponentially. Flames poured out across the roof of the diner. The entire structure shook.

Then the roar became intolerable, and the engines flared. There was an explosion. Flames everywhere, smoke, thunder.

For a moment, Bernal thought the rocket had just detonated on the roof, unable to detach itself from the tangle of gear to which it was connected. Then the nose of the rocket pushed its way out of the mass of flames and, moving faster and faster, tore its way out from between the cowgirl's legs and blazed up into the sky. The thunder of its passing echoed from the hills.

Pieces of cowgirl flew everywhere. Her head came off and bounced once on the parking lot and her shattered visage landed on a car, leaving one complete, untouched baby-blue eye staring up into the sky. A booted leg formed a triumphal arch. Fragments of star-spangled shirt skidded across the asphalt.

For a moment the rocket rose smoothly.

Then, as clearly as if an invisible hand had come down from the sky and grabbed it, the rocket rotated and dove straight for the ground. The fuel tanks detonated, spreading flames across the fields.

Muriel had imposed her will.

Hesketh was gone.

So was she.

Bob stopped, openmouthed, gazing at the flaming remains of what had once been his place of employment.

"Airliners sometimes drop giant chunks of green shit-filled ice from their lavatories," he said, mostly to himself. "They don't like to talk about it and pay off big for those incidents, in exchange for getting it hushed up." But his heart wasn't in it.

Bob sat down on a guardrail, facing away from the huge tower of smoke that rose from the flames, snapped his washcloth, folded it neatly, put it on his knee, and watched the half moon as it slowly sank and vanished in the lightening sky.

48

Oleana, Len, and Magnusen got to Near Earth Orbit just as the rocket lifted off. They had had an argument over what kind of nozzles Foote had recycled, with Magnusen insisting on a Soviet Proton model while Len plumped for a Japanese H2-A. They were as precise and impassioned in their terminology as wine snobs, and with as little actual practical result.

While they yammered, Bernal sat in the front seat of their minivan.

Naomi reached in and handed him a handkerchief.

"At least . . ." Bernal wiped his eyes. "At least she died doing exactly what she wanted to do."

"That doesn't make it a bit easier," Naomi said. "It won't actually help to pretend it does."

"Okay. I won't."

When he was done, he folded her handkerchief up, finally noticing the embroidered monogram. For Naomi, this was probably a kind of business card. He reached it out to her.

"Keep it," she said. "I have plenty."

The parking lot filled with police vehicles, fire trucks, Homeland Security sedans, and gawkers. The fire was out. Police and looters battled vigorously over the remains of the cowgirl.

Yolanda had driven off, with a promise that Spillvagen would be hearing from her lawyer. Bernal would be interested to hear how the case went.

Spillvagen had consoled himself by taking off with a cowgirl fingertip the size of a bowling ball, with a clean, dark-red fingernail, barely damaged.

Had Hesketh really existed? Bernal found himself wondering. He could see a theory where Patricia Foote was someone who communicated with something she interpreted as an artificial intelligence, on whose behalf she acted, but which was actually nothing more than a sophisticated vehicle control with no consciousness or will of its own.

Or that Hesketh had been an innocent AI with no homicidal tendencies until falling in with a bad-actor human being, who had corrupted it. If Madeline had been around, he suspected that would have been her theory.

He would never be sure.

"Muriel was there, wasn't she?" Spillvagen said. "On the roof. I saw her."

"Yes," Bernal said. "She was there."

The sun was rising. It was time to get some breakfast. Despite the fact that he had never liked the food, Bernal was sorry Near Earth Orbit was gone.

Something touched his cheek. He jerked, turned around.

A breeze that had come up with the sun had blown a

scorched shred of the summer dress off the roof and into the rear of the Voyager. As Bernal watched, it too drifted out over the parking lot. It had seemed like a sign, for a moment, but was nothing of the sort.

Life was full of that sort of thing.